DUNGEON LORD

HUGO HUESCA

Edited by
JOSIAH DAVIS

Hugo Huesca © 2017

Cover design by James T. Egan of Bookfly Design.

Www.bookflydesign.com

1

CHAPTER ONE

ARPADEL

Dungeon Lord Kael watched what remained of his legacy as it burned to ashes. His brave monsters lay broken at every passage and corridor, his traps were defeated, his magic was spent and dry.

Only the last line of defense yet stood: Kael himself and his closest lieutenants, and a score of so of his remaining monsters—the ones loyal enough that were ready to die for him, or the ones stupid enough that they hadn't managed to escape from the dungeon that was now a death trap.

Later, the songs would claim that the last Dungeon Lord of the Arpadel dynasty faced his end with a glorious charge against impossible odds. That he met sure death with stoic scorn and a grin; that he jumped at the idea of meeting his ancestors at the gloomy halls of the Dark god Murmur.

The truth was...slightly different.

"Dung-eaters!" Kael bellowed with such force he almost broke his voice. He kicked a nearby treasure chest so hard that the ancient wood splintered against his armored boot and sent coins, gems, and trinkets sprawling like guts all over the floor. "Those dung-eaters! Look what they did to my dungeon!"

What few remained of Kael's followers had the presence of mind to take a step away from the maddened Dungeon Lord, and not one dared to take a coin from the floor. Probably because he was a tower of a man—well over nine feet tall—with giant's blood somewhere on his family tree and well known for his temper. Only Kael's two lieutenants were dear enough to him to be sure his rage wouldn't shift toward them by the crime of proximity, so they stood by his side at his stone throne.

"I would damn my soul again for a chance to rip the entrails away from those...those...*Heroes*," Kael grumbled as his rage slowed.

"Murmur is not in the business of making crappy bargains. He'll have little to pay for a soul that's going to belong to him in just a bit more time, anyway," said Bishop Leopardus, who floated placidly at Kael's right. Leopardus' body resembled a giant puffer-fish and was big enough to swallow a grown man whole if the need arose. His mouth occupied the middle section of his body and was wide enough to handle such a bite. His red hide was spotted with white.

"Don't listen to this fat asshole, he's just pissed he has to meet his death hungry," said Warlock Chasan, the second of Kael's lieutenants. Chasan was an old half-demon—no one was sure what the other half was—who had spent his life serving the surviving members of the Arpadel bloodline. He had seen the rise and fall of Kael's father and grandfather and half a dozen aunts and uncles. He would serve no one after Kael.

"If Master Chasan enjoys putting words into my mouth, perhaps he should put his head into it, too, and see what happens," Leopardus growled, but there was no real animosity behind his threat. Kael knew that the Warlock and the Bishop were friends behind their constant bickering.

"Enough," Kael said. "Who says I intend to die tonight? Unlike my Dungeon, I am still standing, and no one shall say that Kael Arpadel sold his hide cheaply."

He flashed a confident smile at his friends and made damn sure his surviving minions saw how little he cared about the danger of death. He even barked a strident laugh that for a second was loud enough to mask the clamor of battle coming from behind the stone doors of the chamber.

Lord Kael laughed more for the benefit of his people than for himself. Not even the most detestable kaftar deserved to die under the command of a cowardly Dungeon Lord.

The kaftar, the hyena-men, received Kael's boast with a roar of their own, a bark-laugh that sounded like they smelled. The two dozen warriors were all that was left of the once great kaftar clan that had manned Kael's dungeons and raiding parties.

The kaftar chieftain stepped away from his warriors and raised a broken scimitar at the stone doors. "Brave words, my Lord Kael! You made my cackle proud to have fought and died under your command. I ask of you, allow this old kaftar one act of pride and let me lead the charge against the Heroes once they breach the chamber. Let the battlefield be primed with my blood and, gods willing, with the blood of your enemies."

While the kaftar warriors barked their approval, Kael examined their chieftain with his Evil Eye. The green eldritch light set his eyes aflame for a moment. It was clear that the chieftain was hurt. Kael could see the drops of blood—red so dark it was almost tar—streaking from a dozen cuts and wounds and spotting the gray fur of the kaftar. It was clear the chieftain would not survive the battle, and Kael knew the chieftain was aware of the fact.

"Very well," said Kael. "You've been a loyal, honorable warrior. I admit now that the distrust I held against your kin when I was young was unfounded. It will be my honor to fight with you...my friend."

The chieftain guffawed deeply, a prideful warrior choking back tears. He turned to his cackle, who waited expectantly for his command with their little, yellow eyes, and raised his scimitar. "For Kael!"

"For Kael!" they barked as one. The few surviving monsters next to the kaftars joined the yelling, raising tentacles, spikes, and other appendages. "For the Dungeon! Death to the Light!"

The Dungeon Lord nodded grimly at the display. Once, a long time ago, before age and hunger had taken their toll on his Attributes, two hundred minions would've joined that display. Perhaps the man he once had been would have crushed the people that now strode across his Dungeon's passages, killing and pillaging wantonly.

Perhaps.

But right now, Kael smiled genuinely. The few survivors may not be much...but they were *his* people.

Lord Kael went to battle with his pride intact.

In fact, a somber royalty seemed to take hold of his posture— a grim visage that returned most of the handsomeness of his youth.

The doors of the chamber shook. Clouds of dust exploded toward the kaftars. Outside, the sound of battle stopped. It was time.

"Send the apprentices away," Kael whispered to Warlock Chasan while the kaftar had their backs turned. "Send them through those spider tunnels and tell them to fuck off. They'll be useless in battle, and there's no sense in them dying tonight."

The old warlock glanced at his friend. "You've grown, my Lord. Your family is proud of you, wherever they are."

"You know damn well where the fuck they are, my friend."

"Indeed, my Lord. I'll be back in time for the main event." The warlock scurried to the corner of the chamber where the group of apprentices huddled together like a litter of freezing puppies.

The Dungeon Lord watched Chasan go. Seconds later, he saw the stone doors crack and break like clay under the assault of rending magic from the other side.

The noise of the doors as they fell was deafening, like the roar of some ancient abomination from the Wetlands. One huge slab of rock flew atop an unlucky kaftar and unceremoniously crushed him. The survivors pulled back.

A cloud of dust rose all over the chamber. From the opening left by the doors, five humanoid figures stepped in.

"For the Dungeon!" Kael unslung a huge claymore from his back and immediately activated all the auras and enchantments he knew. He felt the wave of heat burst from his body like a physical entity, and his vision blurred at the intensity of it. But his step didn't waver. Soon, power flooded through his muscles.

He leaped to meet the advancing adventurers while his monsters encircled them, ready to give their lives to give him a chance to land a *Crushing Blow* or perhaps a *Devastating Cleave*.

There was a lull in movement as both sides waited for the dust to settle. Soon enough, Kael caught a glimpse of the beings who had devastated his last Dungeon.

These are no men, he thought with a fury that drowned the pangs of fear he felt.

They had the faces of men and women alright; they had the features of Ivalis' people.

But they are no men.

Their eyes were glassed, crystal, like mirrors decorating a Royal Hall. Nonliving.

And yet they could see. Their necks jerked with unnatural movements here and there, while their bodies faced forward, their gazes flayed wildly about like they were trying to see every corner of the place at once.

Much to his chagrin, goosebumps traveled through Kael's back. Under his helmet, drops of sweat threatened to fall over his eyes.

Still, whatever these... *Heroes* were, Kael knew there were protocols to follow. He welcomed the visitors like a Dungeon Lord should:

"You never should have come here, slaves of the Light! Know that you'll meet your demise in this most noble hall of Arpadel Lair, under the blade of Dungeon Lord Kael and the brave men and monsters who follow him! For I am the last member of a proud and noble bloodline who still remember the time when the Lordship was great and feared and—"

EDWARD WRIGHT SIGHED over his mic when he heard the elven assassin mutter something like, "Screw this monologuing, I want to fight this Boss already!"

"Calm down, Ryan, he may give us some clue for our quests," Edward suggested without any real hope of being listened to. He had little doubt of what was about to happen next.

His old computer monitor showed in barely 39 frames-per-second how Rylan Silverblade, Ryan's character, interrupted the Boss-guy's speech by leaping toward him with his dual-wielded daggers raised high.

"Ah, there he goes again," groaned Lisa in the Discord chat. "I really hope we didn't miss something important."

The battle had begun. Rylan's daggers reached the Boss—Kael, according to his health bar—and slipped through the cracks in the armor plate, scoring a critical hit. Cartoonish blood splattered from the Boss along with a -253hp notice. It was enough to one-shot any minion they had encountered so far in the dungeon.

But this was the Boss, and he had 3000hp to throw around. Kael roared in rage and surprise, but reacted by instinct with a brutal swipe from his claymore, which was so thick it may as well have been a tree branch. It missed Ryan, thanks only to the assassin's daily power *shadowstep*.

The elf disappeared from the claymore's range in a flutter of black leaves and reappeared ten feet away. Right in the middle of the mob of kaftars...Which proceeded to go to town on him, barking that hideous laugh of theirs all the while.

The assassin wasn't built for tanking, nor for dealing with more than one opponent at a time. He leaked hp like a faucet.

"What the fuck?" Ryan instantly started, over the Discord chat. "Where is my healing? Lisa? Healing? What do you think you're here for?"

"I'm trying!" Lisa said. "You jumped too far away, I can't reach you!"

"That's because you suck!"

The giant red balloon with the teeth had floated into the fray and was throwing debuff magic onto Mark's tank character so fast that the stout dwarf was left immobile, while half the kaftars swarmed him and rained hits on his armor with their scimitars.

Ed clenched his teeth. Mark's job was to establish a safe battle-line for the casters—Ed and Lisa—to work while Ryan flanked the elite minions. Hell, with Ryan in the middle of the battle, Ed couldn't even *fireball* the bunched-up cluster of mobs as he had planned.

Now, Lisa was frantically trying to reach Ryan, taking constant damage from suicidal monsters all the while. Sure, thanks to her holy buffs they only did -10; -20hp damage at most, but those added up quickly, and her mana potions weren't infinite.

It was up to Ed to make a decision. He saw the lead kaftar—a chieftain, proclaimed the game screen—jump toward his character with a howl of rage. Ed distractedly clicked on him and saw his character's auto-attack roast the hyena-guy to cinders before he was halfway through his leap.

"Pull back, Lisa, you need to cleanse Mark's debuffs," Ed said. At the same time, he pulled his character out of range of the kaftars and cast a *freezing beam* at the red balloon to take the aggro away from Mark.

Ed was better equipped to deal with debuffs than the dwarf. The ideal target would've been Lisa's Cleric, of course, since she had stacked the Spirit attribute, but Lisa had trouble of her own. Ed had to improvise.

"Ryan's gonna be pissed!" Mark warned them while Lisa countered the curses away from his character, though the dwarf was then able to cleave three kaftars with his battle-axe.

"He'll be more pissed if we get wiped at the very end of the raid," Ed pointed out. It was true. Even though their situation was Ryan's fault, he wouldn't see it that way.

"Cleric, you fucking suck," Ryan exclaimed. "Where are you going?! I'm running out of potions here!"

Ed's Wizard and the red balloon were busy exchanging magical devastation, but his screen reached the center of the battle where Rylan Silverblade was getting his roguey ass handed to him by the Boss, the remaining kaftars, and the other elite mob —the ugly Warlock.

It was clear Ryan wouldn't last much longer. He was already using the potion hotkey more than his combat ones. Never a good sign.

"Use your *acrobatic leap*," Ed advised him. "Get safely back behind Mark until Lisa's done with him."

"Who do you think you're talking to?" Ed was sure he heard Ryan spit at the mic. "Rylan Silverblade doesn't retreat from rabble like this! Now, do as I say, ignore the dumb minions, and get over here to help *me*!"

Ed muted his mic before swearing furiously in his cramped room. It wouldn't be the first time they wiped because of Ryan, even if he would never accept it.

The game, Ivalis Online, was an old rogue-like with a permadeath mechanic. So if their characters got killed during the Boss fight, not only would they have wasted an entire evening but entire months of leveling the characters from scratch.

Ed didn't have that kind of time anymore. And they were so close to ending the raid...

His fingers acted on his decision before he realized any had been made. He cast his daily offensive spell, a lance of ice that did piercing damage and ignored 30% armor. It worked like a charm on the angry balloon—the lance pierced its tough hide like a hot nail through rubber. Its remaining health vaporized under the critical hit, and Ed's Wizard received a chunk of delicious EXP for his trouble.

The game was old, several years outdated by anyone's standards, but the developers' attention to detail was impressive. While the torn flabs of red skin floated everywhere around the battlefield, the Boss roared at the sight and launched a massive combo of claymore swings against Ryan's Rogue.

Normally, the Rogue would've been able to dodge most of the attacks, but he was still surrounded by a few remaining kaftars. That meant a penalty to the Agility attribute...and that Rylan Silverblade's health was suddenly down to its last 100hp—it rose fast thanks to a potion. Not fast enough, though.

The Warlock chose that exact moment to launch a lance of his own as if inspired by Ed's attack of choice. The *shadow strike* pierced Rylan straight through his leather chest plate while tendrils of darkness climbed through the inside of the Rogue's body like coils of electricity. As the Rogue's corpse fell to the ground, Ed saw that the tentacles were coming out of the eyes, mouth, and ears.

Charming.

The Boss stepped over the corpse with his claymore raised high, letting the three or four remaining mobs regain some of their low morale. Then Kael rushed Lisa.

Unfortunately for him, Lisa had already finished cleansing Mark. The dwarf calmly stepped into the way of the Boss' charge and stopped it cold with a defensive talent of his tower shield. Chips of stone flew away from under the dwarf's heels and he took a massive 200hp hit for his trouble. But taking those kinds of hits was his job.

The Boss recoiled from the impact and staggered. Ed chose

that moment to *fireball* the area right behind him. Flames erupted as—

"What?!" Ryan's high-pitched voice was all over the chat. "Fucking bullshit! That's fucking bullshit, it's not fair that the Boss can combo with his minions! Fuck you, Eddie, this is all your fault! Thanks for wasting my fucking time!"

Then he disconnected.

"He's going to remember that in the morning," Mark commented while Lisa healed him. "Maybe you should have let us wipe, Ed."

The Boss and the dwarf exchanged furious blows strong enough to break the bones out of lesser warriors even if blocked.

While they fought, Ed and the Warlock—the only remaining minion—exchanged spells as fast as their Mind attribute would let them. For a mere elite mob, the monster managed to survive a lot of abuse. For a second or two, that is.

"Maybe I'm tired of putting up with him. Perhaps he'll calm down when we give him his share of the loot," Ed said. They could load Ryan's new character—probably Rylan Silverblade the Fourth—with the old one's loot and whatever items they got from raiding the dungeon.

"That would be very reasonable of him." Lisa sighed. As soon as the Warlock died, she switched from healing Mark to debuffing the Boss, making him do less damage, move slower, and be more vulnerable to Ed's spells.

To Ed, the battle's results had been decided the second after the Rogue had fallen. There was still mop-up to be done, though.

There was no surrender mechanic in Ivalis Online.

As if thinking the same thing, the Boss suddenly switched aggro away from Mark—which netted Kael even more penalizations—and leapt straight at Ed's Wizard.

The claymore rose over Kael's head, covered in the red aura of the berserker-type talents. Ed's fingers flew over the keyboard and pressed the *teleport* hotkey. His Wizard reappeared behind Mark and away from Kael, just in time to see how the Boss' sword cracked the floor as it came down.

When the Boss turned to them, Ed swore he could see something akin to disappointment in his eyes.

Nah. The game isn't that detailed.

Mark charged the Boss, but it was Ed's Wizard who got the last hit. Kael died to a particularly mean *stalagmite* spell that went through his helmet like it was made of butter. Clear, pure ice pierced through, but it was dark red after its tip reappeared at the helmet's end.

Ed felt a rush of tired satisfaction when his screen was showered with EXP, a level-up, and a bunch of magical items that would look very, very good on his character.

Also, away from the demands of the Boss battle, he started thinking immediately about what he had done.

Ryan was not going to be reasonable about it.

"Tomorrow is going to be a bitch," Lisa said while her Cleric stepped over Kael's corpse on her way to looting the chamber. "I hope we don't get fired for this."

"Oh, shit. I guess it will," Ed said. He took out the earplugs and rested his back against his chair. His room was lit only by the screen of the computer.

2
___

CHAPTER TWO

KATABASIS

The next morning, just as Ed arrived at the Lasershark store, he was called to the manager's office. As expected. He left his backpack at the lockers, greeted Lisa and Mark, passed a hand over some wrinkles on his purple-and-pink uniform, and went to face the music.

The office was closed, so he had to wait until the manager deemed fit to press the button to release the electronic lock. Ed waited for almost five minutes before the electronics buzzed and the fake-wood door opened with a smug, "Come on in, Eddy," from inside.

Ed took a deep breath and tried to bury the cold anger deep in the back of his mind. Anger would not help pay rent. Anger would mean letting the other guy win.

You're going to hear his bullshit and you're going to let him vent and you'll be back at work in no time, he reminded himself. *No mouthing off. Just take it, Ed.*

He stepped inside and closed the door behind him before flashing his best retail smile. "You called, boss?"

Ryan was half seated, half sprawled on his leather chair with his moccasins over the mahogany desk. He matched Ed's smile with one of his own that made him look like a saint with his golden locks of hair and his cherubic cheeks.

He looked little like his characters in Ivalis Online. Instead of a rugged assassin or rogue, he was thin and handsome in a "boy band" kind of way, and he dressed to impress. Blue silk shirt and trousers for him, none of that Lasershark uniform for the owner's son, no.

By contrast, Ed had forgotten to shave this morning. He was tall and gaunt, with unruly black hair that was almost blue. To the employees watching from the ample window of the office— Ryan loved a good show—it probably was like seeing a down-on-his-luck hobo being sentenced by a golden archangel.

The two of them may have each been twenty-five-years-old, but were very different.

"Eddy, Eddy, *Eddy*," Ryan sang without dropping his smile. He sat straight and pawed lazily at a stack of papers on his desk. "What am I going to do with you?"

"What do you mean, boss? Did I do something wrong?" Ed asked with enough saccharine in his voice to bake a cake.

Ryan pretended he hadn't heard him. Instead, he read the papers like it was the first time he had seen them. He frowned and looked at Ed for a second before returning to the papers. He did that a couple of times before he started to make *tut-tut* noises with his tongue.

Ed said nothing. He wasn't going to give the asshole the satisfaction.

He could feel the gaze of the dozen Lasershark employees behind the window, all the way back from the first floor. He entertained the idea of reaching to the drapes and closing them to take Ryan away from his spectacle, but he discarded it.

Just wait it out and he'll get bored, Ed told himself.

Finally, Ryan set the papers down. "Eddy, these numbers of yours look terrible this month. Your performance evaluation has a terrible score, you know? I can't help but wonder if your commitment to the Lasershark team is as strong as it was when you started working here."

You're the one who makes the evaluations. "Is there anything *specific* about what I did wrong?"

"Watch your tone, you're talking to your superior." Ryan said it so fast and so naturally that Ed didn't have time to say anything before Ryan went on. "The review says you are terrible at following orders. Which paints a poor picture of you, since following orders is all you're here for."

Ed knew Ryan was goading him.

No, you want us here, the little minions of your kingdom.

"Following orders? Funny, never had a problem with that, boss. This surely isn't about you getting yourself killed in game last night, is it?"

Ryan raised a golden eyebrow in a perfect imitation of incredulity. "Surely you can't be so immature, Eddy? What does that game have to do with your job?"

Ed deeply regretted the day that Ryan had overheard his chat with Lisa and Mark about their Ivalis Online escapades. Ryan had butted into the conversation and invited himself to the group. Being their boss, there was no way they could refuse. It didn't take Ryan long to proclaim himself the leader of their adventuring band.

Which meant that all the good drops went to him, all the mistakes were the fault of Ed and the others, and all the successes were thanks to his guidance.

Ed's smile dropped an inch. He could feel his heart pounding in his chest, and he hated himself for letting a pampered prick like Ryan get so far under his skin.

Just let him vent, just let him vent, just let him vent. He had managed to survive five months at Lasershark so far and jobs weren't so easy to find in the current economy.

"See, that's the problem with you, Eddy. You try to look too deep into things. I don't pay you to *think*. If you were good at that you would be sitting in the manager's chair. And that's *my* chair, Eddy. Which means I'm the one qualified to think. Which means I'm the one *giving* the orders. For example, when I say you should stay late and clean, you don't ask for overtime. You follow orders. And when I say, let Lisa ignore the stupid fucking minions and go back to heal me while I deal with the Boss, you do that, you *idiot*."

"I see." A dark, primal part of his mind demanded that Ed lunge at Ryan across his expensive desk, that he swipe away the laptop and the papers and smash Ryan's cherubic face against the mahogany over and over—

He took a deep breath. He recalled the advice he had heard in high school. Don't fight back against bullies, because then they win...That sounded even more stupid now than it had back then.

When he got his Computer Science degree, Ed had believed it was the kind of situation he wouldn't have to deal with ever again. After all, there were no bullies in computer-related fields, right?

We're all nerds anyway, right?

Well, retail is a different beast, and after a mean economic crisis and a downsize from his cozy, corporate IT position, retail at Lasershark was the best Ed could get.

So, he would just smile and nod until he climbed the corporate ladder again. Until he was high enough that he wouldn't have to deal with people like Ryan.

"I should fire you on the spot," Ryan said after a pause. "But I am a fair man and I think you deserve a second chance. After all, you've learned your place, haven't you?"

"Yes."

Ryan nodded, satisfied that Ed was playing along. "Okay, I'll give you another chance. But on one condition. You must show me that you've compromised with Lasershark, that you're ready to follow orders."

"Fine," Ed said. He didn't like where Ryan was going.

"So, here's an order, Eddy. I want you to delete your Ivalis character."

"What?" the request had come so far out of left field that it took Ed by surprise. "What for?"

"To prove you can follow orders," Ryan said. He wiggled his eyebrows smugly. "You can see it as a test of character, too. Actions have consequences, and you shouldn't get to keep playing your high-level Wizard while I have to start over for your mistakes."

That's bullshit, and you know it.

"Or maybe you prefer to quit?" Ryan went on. "Your call, Eddy."

Ed's hands closed into frustrated fists. What kind of parent spawned a douchebag like Ryan?

You can just level up another one, the part of him that insisted on being rational and mature reminded him.

It was not exactly true. Lasershark left him each day with less and less free time. Mark and Lisa were getting online less and less to do raids. In a way, he knew the group would not last much longer—Ryan had already put the final nails into the coffin of their adventures.

The raid on the Dungeon Lord Kael was the last time they were going to raid together in such a scale, Ed was sure of it. That was why he had insisted on winning instead of letting the team die saving Ryan. He had wanted the last time to *matter*.

It was a dumb way to feel about an outdated videogame, but lately Ed felt that little he did in his life mattered. He was probably kidding himself thinking he'd rise on the corporate ladder, with people like Ryan being the gatekeepers.

So, he had to find small meanings where he could.

He sighed. The cold anger that had been simmering in his chest was nowhere to be found. "Fine, Ryan. You win. I'll delete the character tonight. Are you happy?"

Little meanings don't pay rent.

Ryan smiled beatifically. "I'm sure this will be an important life lesson for you, Eddy. Now get back to work—you'll have to stay after closing to make up for the lost time."

Ed sighed again, this time with relief. At least it was over. He turned his back to Ryan and went to the door feeling like a red balloon deflated by a *stalagmite* spell.

"Oh, and one more thing," Ryan said. "Go tell Lisa that she's fired."

Ed stopped cold in his tracks. He faced Ryan again.

"What?"

"She's useless," Ryan explained. "And worse than useless, she listened to *you* when I gave her an order. I'm her boss, not you."

"She works harder than any of us," Ed said slowly. He couldn't believe what he was hearing. Surely no one could be this much of an asshole. "Really, Ryan? Over a *game*? She only healed Mark because I asked her to."

"I don't give a fuck, Eddy." Ryan grinned. "This is my father's store. Lisa is fired."

Ed stood there, mouth agape. He was sure he looked like an idiot, but he was too stunned to react.

"What are you waiting for, dumbass?" Then Ryan did something he had never done before. He snapped his fingers. Once.

"Out of here!" He snapped them again. Twice. "Chop, chop!"

To Ed, the sound was as loud as a pair of gunshots next to his ears. They drowned all noise, leaving only buzzing silence.

He closed his mouth and turned to the door.

"That's right," Ryan said behind him. His voice barely registered.

Ed reached for the door handle and manually locked the electronic mechanism.

"What the fuck do you think you're doing?" Ryan asked him.

Ed slowly, calmly, walked back to the desk.

"Ryan, Ryan, Ryan," he said. "What am I going to do with you?"

Ryan started to stand up. He reached for the plastic phone at one side of the desk, the one used to call security. Ed's arms, as if they were acting of their own accord, lunged for the neck of Ryan's shirt and caught him mid-movement. Ryan tried to push himself free, but Ed was already pulling him down with all his strength.

Papers fluttered away when Ryan smacked hard against the mahogany. His laptop broke and flew out of sight. The manager's legs flailed in every direction trying to get some leverage to free himself from Ed's grip. It was useless. Ed was grabbing him so tightly his knuckles were white.

With one hand, Ed smacked away the remaining papers and the phone. With the other one, he grabbed a handful of Ryan's golden curls, pulled his head up, and yanked down hard against the desk before the guy could react.

There was a muffled scream and Ryan's limbs went flailing all over like they were made of rubber.

Ed heard the crack behind the hit, but couldn't be sure if it was the wood or Ryan's nose.

So, he smashed Ryan's face again.

This time, flecks of blood spattered Ed's purple-and-pink uniform, as well as the desk. Ryan's scream switched from surprise and pain into pure agony. Ed let go of the manager's hair and watched as Ryan slid down the desk and fell to the floor with a gargled, bloody whimper.

The expensive silk shirt was ruined with blood staining the chest, and Ryan's angelic nose was smashed to a bloody, broken pulp, same as his lips. He raised one trembling hand to his face and whimpered loudly when he saw his blood-stained fingers. With the other hand, he tried to push himself off of the floor, but to no avail.

Behind Ed's back, he could hear people banging on the doors.

Security, probably. He paid them no mind. Instead, he calmly walked over to the crumpled form of Ryan and towered over him until the guy looked at him with scared, confused eyes.

"I quit, asshole. Consider that my notice. Also, you're a terrible Rogue."

CHAPTER THREE

ENTER THE BOATMAN

Time passed afterward like it does in a dream. Someone had called the police. Hands were dragging him toward a police patrol while the faces of the Lasershark employees passed around his field of vision like apparitions. The reflection of the red and blue sirens gave their faces a ghostly blur and made him get the beginnings of a nasty headache.

He must've been walking because the scenario shifted periodically until he was inside the car, which smelled of synthetic leather and sweat. A police officer banged the door closed, and the noise startled Ed back into reality.

The man left with bored, casual strides to meet with Ryan, who was lying against the wall of the storefront, with a wet rag streaked with pink covering half his face. They talked for a while with Ryan shooting hateful glances at Ed occasionally.

Ed looked away. Now that the cold anger had left him, he didn't care much about Ryan or what he did anymore.

A small crowd had formed around the storefront, with people trying to crane their necks to listen to the policeman and others whispering among themselves. More glances in Ed's direction. Disapproving stares, scandalized hands covering their mouths. A construction worker with a Subway bag listened to a Lasershark employee's version of the events and then made a circular gesture with his index finger around his ear while vaguely nodding in Ed's direction. The employee shrugged and nodded and looked away, like Ed's madness was contagious.

Guess public opinion is already decided on this one, Ed thought.

He recalled Lisa's words when she had rushed to him as the police (or had it been the store's security?) dragged him out. "Oh, my God, Ed! What have you done?"

On the other hand, Mark had walked to him with a smile from ear to ear and had lifted his phone high so Ed could see it clearly. "Dude, that was fucking amazing! You went on a rampage, just like in the movies! I have it all recorded, you went Terminator on his ass! The look on his face was priceless!"

Ed shifted to a more comfortable position in the patrol car's seat and smiled to himself.

He was as surprised with his reaction as Ryan had been. Ed had never thought he was capable of such...violence.

It had won him nothing. Hell, he was in more trouble now than ever before in his life. He sure as hell didn't have enough money for a lawyer, and Ryan was going to press charges without question.

For the first time in a long, long while, Ed felt like his life was moving. Things were happening, and it was thanks to his own actions.

He looked at Ryan, still talking to the police officer, until the manager felt his gaze and looked back. Yeah, that was a hateful look. He wasn't so cherubic anymore. Ed maintained eye contact and then winked at him. Ryan looked away.

Perhaps he'll forget about firing Lisa, Ed thought. He decided to consider that another win.

A second police officer opened the driver's door and went inside the car. The smell of his cologne flooded the enclosed space and intensified Ed's growing headache.

What the hell do you use, Eau-de-morgue?

The officer grunted to himself as he fidgeted with his keychain. He stumbled around the car dashboard with enough clumsiness that Ed started to suspect the man was drunk. Finally, he managed to get the car going.

"Uh, aren't you going to wait for your partner?" he asked the man. Behind him, Ryan and the first officer were still talking, and the crowd was dispersing now that the show was wrapping up.

"He came in his own car," the policeman told him. His voice sounded ragged and hoarse, like someone who had been washing his throat with tequila since he was a baby.

The Lasershark store soon disappeared from Ed's view. He was surprised how little he cared about what was going to happen to him now.

"He's going to press charges, you know," the officer finally said. "He'll probably want to milk you dry after this. Not only did you kick his ass, you humiliated him in front of his underlings."

"Eh," Ed shrugged. "What's he going to take away, my ramen?"

"How about your freedom? A good lawyer can easily trump-up what just happened back there. Have you locked up on attempted homicide. Or worse."

"That's bullshit," Ed said. "If I had wanted to kill him, I would've."

The policeman cranked his neck to stare at Ed's face. He didn't stop driving as he did. The man's face was covered by the shadows of the patrol car and the steel net separating them, but his smile was white and perhaps a little too big for his face. It could be a trick of the light, of course.

Ed wished he could crank a window open. The cologne was getting under his nostrils now. It was both sweet and sour in an entirely disgusting way that he could not place.

Uncle Jonah, he decided, but he discarded the idea with a mental sneer.

"It won't matter one bit. You know that, Edward. Ryan has the power to make your life hell, and you lack the power to defend yourself against him. Sure, you may not care *now*, but will the memory of having broken his nose be enough to sustain you while you spend the next couple decades rotting away in jail?"

Ed rested one cold hand against his forehead which was now pulsating like a live thing.

"Who are you?" he asked. Uncle Jonah? No, no way. He hadn't seen his uncle since he was a kid. It was hard to remember *why*, with that cursed migraine...

The man hadn't looked at the road for a while now, but they were straight in the middle of it, even though it was suddenly the dead of the night.

"Why, I'm a talent-hunter of sorts, Edward. I'm interested in you, and I have a proposal I think you'd like to hear."

"So, you aren't a police officer? *Agh*, my head..."

The smell—and the pain—was so intense now that tears streaked down Ed's cheeks. Wafts of warm odor hit him every time the man spoke. Through the daze of the migraine, Ed realized why. It wasn't a cologne. It was the man's breath.

He recalled Uncle Jonah now—he had died in a car crash when Ed was nine. The entire family had gone to the funeral. Given the severity of his wounds, the body was still inside the funerary clinic. Nine-year-old Ed had let go of his father's hand and had wandered off on his own through the corridors of the place, letting his curiosity roam free. He had gone beyond the modest chapels and beyond the clerk's desk, beyond the heated furnaces of the crematorium, until he had reached a place with an AC unit spewing a current of cold air. He recalled the metal tables and the men in clinical attire working on the mangled body of his uncle—an amorphous black and pink blob in the mist of Ed's memory—with rows and rows of tools and chemicals strewn around them in shelves and containers of all sizes. Little Ed had started screaming by then, which had scared the living hell out of the adults there. An elbow had pushed one container and it had shattered against the floor—which was strewn with drains for the corpses' fluids—and the smell had been overpowering. It had made little Ed's nose hurt and burn and it had smelled

Just like this. Just like his breath.

"Ah, little Edward. No, I'm not a policeman. I'm only the Boatman. Haven't you looked out of the window yet? Does this place look like your Earth to you?"

No, thought Ed while his gaze tried to make sense of the dark world outside his window. *No, it does not.*

Ed opened his eyes again. He must've fainted at some point. His head felt better now, so he dared to look around.

He was still in the backseat of the police car. The man was still looking at him, his face still covered in shadows, his smile still impossibly white and just a bit too wide.

At least the smell wasn't as overpowering now.

That's because you have it all over you.

"The transition can be rough the first time," said the man, giving him a friendly nod.

Huh. Necks aren't supposed to rotate that far behind someone's back, an alarmed part of his brain thought.

Know what? Let's take one thing at a time, the rest of him suggested.

"Who are you? What's going on?" That was a good start.

"I'm the Boatman," the man reminded him. "You can call me Kharon if you need a name to go along with the face. As I said, I'm a talent-hunter. I've been watching you for a bit, you see, and the idea of seeing you waste your potential in a jail cell for the rest of your life was too much for me to take. So here you are."

"Kharon," Ed repeated the name like it was some kind of anchor to keep him from madness. "Kharon, either I have gone

mad, or you need to be clearer. We're driving in the middle of...
well, it looks like Hell...and your neck should be broken with the
way you're looking at me. Did I die at some point and haven't realized it until now?"

"This is not Hell, Edward. This is a space of transition. A
buffer between worlds, if you may. And please, now that we're far
along into the trip, don't look at the inhabitants closely. They
can't harm you while you're with me, but viewing them has nasty
effects upon the mortal mind."

Of course, Ed looked out before he could stop himself. He
saw towering, impossible shapes bloating the apocalyptic horizon. Living shapes that dwarfed mountains. Shapes that moved—
no, they were hunting each other.

Ed felt his mind start to unravel and he looked away while
goosebumps traveled down his back. "Oh, shit."

Kharon barked a laugh. "I swear, every time I say, 'don't do it,'
you people go and take a look. Like clockwork! Here, I'll take that
memory away. Otherwise, you'll have terrible dreams at first and
then go barking mad before you turn thirty."

The shapes left Ed's mind like an unwanted guest.

"Thanks," he said. Kharon laughed again.

"Have you gotten your bearings straight yet? My job will be
much easier if you aren't having a histrionic fit while I try to
recruit you."

While having a nervous breakdown seemed like a perfectly
acceptable thing to do given the circumstances, Ed had never
been the kind to have those anyway.

"Just say things straight," Ed said. "Don't keep the vague and
mysterious act going if you want me to hear you out."

"Negotiating already, before you even know what's going on?
Good boy. That's a useful habit to make. It will either make you
live longer, or will get you killed while you're still starting out.
Both will ensure I don't waste my time."

"Mysterious and vague," sighed Ed while he massaged his temples. "Remember?"

"My apologies, Edward. It's the force of habit. You see, the world where I come from takes these rituals very seriously...But I'll give your way a go, to show you I mean business. The 'job vacancy' as you'd call it, has been recently created. Last night, I mean. By your very own hand, in fact—"

"What?" Last night he had been playing Ivalis Online. Kharon was implying Ed had killed someone...He started to get a very nasty suspicion, only to have it immediately confirmed by Kharon's next words.

"Edward Wright, in name of the Dark God Murmur, I extend you the offer to become a Dungeon Lord of the world of Ivalis."

CHAPTER FOUR

MURMUR'S GAMBIT

E d blinked without saying anything. *Ivalis.*

Kharon stared at him with a smug smile, like he had made the revelation of a century.

It was too much for Ed. He *had* to clarify. "*Ivalis Online*? Like in the videogame? You want me to become a videogame's Boss?"

"That's one way of—"

"Ah, great. I should have known," Ed sighed. All the signs were there. "I've gone insane, haven't I? I'm being kept at some asylum right now, frothing at the mouth, and I'm hallucinating this whole thing."

He shot a glance at the corner of the car—while carefully avoiding the windows—as if he expected to catch some intern taking notes by a corner.

"Trust me, Edward, your imagination isn't that good," Kharon told him. "How about you hear me out, see if what I have to say makes sense, and then you decide for yourself?"

Ed couldn't shake away the idea that Kharon was enjoying his distress a bit too much, even if his words were concerned. "Can you at least fix your neck?"

Kharon's body made a full turn while his head remained static. "Better?"

"...Yes."

"Good. Now, as I was saying. Ivalis. Ah, you're going to love it there! An old world with a young civilization, filled with possibility. So much a determined young man can do over there—there are no limits to what he could achieve!"

"You're talking about a videogame. It doesn't have particularly good graphics, and don't take it as an offense, but the storyline was a bit disjointed. It was mostly an excuse to kill shit and level up."

Nothing wrong with that, of course.

Kharon's tongue licked the inside of his teeth. At least, Ed hoped it was his tongue. It was black and slimy. "I know all about the game. That's the reason you got into my sights in the first place, Edward. Let me assure you, Ivalis—a real world, mind you —came first. How long have you played Ivalis Online?"

"About a year," Ed said. "It was made by some indie company, I think. They haven't made anything else." He could vaguely recall the name of the developers, *Pantheon*. The name appeared when you first loaded the game, along with a Sun with eight flames that looked like arrowheads.

"That company doesn't exist." Kharon dismissed Ed's train of thought. "Their offices are empty—I've checked. But what's really interesting is that about a year ago, so-called *Heroes* appeared everywhere across Ivalis. They are merciless creations that look human yet aren't, unyielding machines of war that never stop until they are dead. And they are *hard* to kill, Edward."

A tickling, cold sensation passed down Ed's back. *Is he saying what I think he's saying?*

"They murder and plunder wantonly. Most of their victims are monsters and other Dark-aligned beings, but their preferred targets are the Dungeon Lords."

Oh, shit.

Kharon went on, "These *Heroes* chose a bleak time to cull the Lordship ranks, Edward. The bloodlines that once prepared the Lordship for the most noble mission of opposing Alita's chosen are not what they once were. And with the Heroes around, I fear the Lordship is at risk of being vanquished from Ivalis and its kingdoms."

The number of questions flaring inside Ed's mind fought with each other to be the first to come out. The one that won wasn't the most demanding or the most logical, but it was the strongest. "Isn't that a good thing? Aren't the Dungeon Lords the bad guys?"

Kharon shrugged at him. "Not from the Dark's perspective. No one likes to be slaughtered by a nasty Hero that kills you because they want your boots."

Ed had to resist the urge to whistle and play innocent.

"Last night, a group of Heroes ravaged the last holding of the noble and ancient House of Arpadel and killed its last living heir, the Lord Kael," said Kharon. Although he spoke without a hint of accusation in his voice, Ed had no doubts the strange man knew *who* had been behind that. "They did so mercilessly—which isn't that bad—*but* without adhering to Ivalis' ancient rituals...indeed, they killed him without letting him even finish his last monologue."

Ed was suddenly very aware that he was at the mercy of this strange, probably undead, being. What would happen if the man stopped the car and asked Ed to step out? Just leave him there in Cthulhu countryside and let the *things* there do as they wished.

Ed's nervous smile gained a notch of the manic tint in Kharon's own.

"So, his Dark Majesty Murmur has found himself in a bad position. Whoever is behind these Heroes is willing to break rules that *everyone* has respected for generations. Alita's Church claims to have no involvement, of course, but their Empire expands happily through the ravaged territory the Dungeon Lords leave behind."

Which may not be a bad thing, Ed reminded himself. Ivalis Online's storyline may have been disjointed, but he clearly recalled seeing the torture chamber in some of the minor dungeons his character had gone through.

"We need new blood to fill the ranks, strong people with new ideas. Young men and women who have that...*knack*...for leadership. People who can use their Lordship status to its fullest capabilities. Sadly, with its reputation for being a short-lived career, there's almost no one worthy in Ivalis to take up the mantle for themselves."

"That's not doing much to convince me," said Ed. "And I fear you may have gotten your guy wrong. Why me? I mean, I guess I could do a decent enough job. But why not a soldier? Hell, an African warlord sounds more up your alley."

"Who says we won't recruit those when the time comes? You're the first—you won't be the last. There's no Chosen One in the choir of Murmur, Edward, there are only men who desire power and are willing to take it for themselves. And the Hungry One knows you. He Who Comes in the Space Between Heartbeats...asked for *you.* What is left for us poor mortals but to answer his commands?"

"He sounds charming, Kharon," said Ed, "but take no offense, this seems like I'll end up being the minion of an evil god, and I've worked in retail before, so I know it's not all it's supposed to be. I really don't feel like sacrificing innocent people to your Hungry One. Or like sacrificing anyone at all. If your 'power' transforms me into someone I'm not, that would be exchanging one kind of slavery for another."

Kharon mulled over Ed's words for a bit before saying, "So you fear the mantle of Lordship will change the core of who you are."

"As I said, no offense."

"I've offered the mantle to many people, Edward. Very few ever concerned themselves with the fine print."

"And how did that work for them?"

Kharon barked another laugh. "A cautious Dungeon Lord is one whose dungeons may last a while. Don't worry, Edward, the mantle won't force you to become someone you're not."

Awkwardly, Ed realized he had no way of knowing if Kharon was telling the truth, but he didn't miss the emphasis the man had added to "force."

Like he could read Ed's thoughts, Kharon added, "I won't lie to you, I have no need. If you decline my offer, I'll simply take you back to the real vehicle I stole you from. See, Murmur *could* make you hear mysterious, dark voices to corrupt and influence you once you accepted the mantle. But that's not how he operates. He's not the kind of Dark god who is content doing cruel deeds at random, he's the kind of god who *philosophizes*. He likes to make a point during his deals with mortals."

"Go on," Ed told him, intrigued, despite the fact he felt like the guy in horror movies who gets sweet-talked by the devil.

"Have you ever seen the play *Faust*? It's from your world."

"Sorry, no. I've heard it's about a guy who makes a deal with the devil."

"Faust is a doctor who thinks he has seen all there is to know," explained Kharon, "so he offers the devil, Mephistopheles, a contract for power. The doctor thinks he can resist the devil's influence and use the power to do great good that would otherwise be impossible.

"Mephistopheles agrees. He thinks that having great power is enough of a corruptible force in itself for Faust to succumb, so he decides to let the doctor roam the world and act as he pleases, betting that in the end his acts would advance the cause of the Dark. In those terms is the deal forged, and the screenplay itself becomes a treatise of morality. Is a man capable of resisting the influence of great power in order to achieve great deeds? Or will having power be enough to align him to the cause of the Dark?"

"I see," said Edward. His mouth was dry and he could feel his pulse accelerating. For all he knew, Kharon was making up the story of Faust; Ed had no way of knowing. But the meaning behind the words was clear. "Murmur is betting that just by being a Dungeon Lord I'll become evil. And I'm betting my intentions are better than that."

How long had he wished that he could show people like Ryan the world didn't need them? That one could both have authority over others, and be a decent human being?

That one could have power and not abuse it, that one could grow and advance his own life without becoming a raging asshole.

Kharon extended his arms in quite the dramatic fashion. "Thus," he said, "the term 'Faustian gambit.' Which is exactly what the Dark One himself does with the Lordship. Just a gambit."

"How does the play end? Who wins?"

"Will that really change your mind, Edward?" Kharon shrugged. "There are many versions of *Faust*, and the end usually satisfies the morals of the audience. If it's a cautionary tale, Faust's sins are too great, and he's dragged to hell. If it's a tale of redemption—something trite, like the love of a woman, redeems him and he goes to heaven after he dies."

For a while now, Ed had known that his life was stagnating. That no matter how hard he tried to move forward, he was stuck thanks to forces—to people—outside his control.

The teachers that demanded he solve a problem their way, even if he knew another, fastest one. Or the ones who favored the students that sucked up to them.

His boss at his former IT job who got promoted instead of better-suited options because he was golf-buddies with an executive.

Ryan, who enjoyed the benefits of his parents' business and used it to make the lives of others miserable.

I'm trapped, Ed realized, with his hands curled into fists. If he said no to Murmur's Gambit, it would be like admitting he, Ed, could become *just* like the people he despised if he were to be in their shoes.

It would mean turning his back on everything he believed in.

Kharon would return him to a jail cell where not only would he lose his freedom, but he would spend the rest of his life knowing he had failed himself.

And Kharon knew it.

When Ed met his gaze, the man's smile gained new shades of meaning that escaped Ed.

"So, no dark, mind-corrupting magic?" Ed asked.

"None. If there's any, the deal will be broken in your favor."

"Your god won't try to stop me when I do whatever I want with these powers, even if it means joining the Light?"

"Not even Murmur himself will be able to take the mantle away from you once the Pact is made, only death can do that. But —" he said, "—I suggest you wait before you go and try to join the Light. Just until you familiarize yourself with Ivalis, is all. After all, you're going into a world with different customs and traditions than your own."

Ed nodded. It sounded reasonable enough.

"Very well," said Kharon. The car lurched to a stop and the door to the side of Ed unlocked itself. "Since it's decided, please step out of the vehicle. There's not enough space in here to do the deed."

Ed exited the car slowly, trying to ignore the cramping in his legs and trying not to think of the giant creature-things in the edges of his vision. He also took care to leave the door open just in case Kharon was about to leave him stranded.

Outside, the landscape hadn't changed—it was still the apocalyptic world without sun, enveloped in a reddish light that looked like some invisible titan had made the clouds bleed. Ed realized the paved road—some kind of dark marble—was surrounded by tall walls of reinforced, polished stone. He had missed them while trying very hard not to lose his sanity gazing into the abyss—or whatever it was they called something so ugly it made you go insane if you looked at it.

The walls reminded him of a labyrinth, though they had the added function of hiding the horizon from his field of view.

"Very well," said Kharon as he stepped out of the vehicle. "Let us begin."

Ed realized that Kharon was taller—much taller—than he first had expected. His legs unfolded as he left the car and just kept going up and up until it was clear Ed was seeing something impossible. Kharon was so tall his knees were at Ed's face-level, and so thin it looked like a small wind might send him flying.

The policeman uniform shifted and changed shape and colors, extending until it transformed into a black, old, and dirty cloth that covered the man's body. It reminded Ed of the shroud people used to cover Death when they drew her.

Ed gulped loudly. Kharon's appearance was decidedly non-human, and it was a strong reminder of the magnitude of the deal Ed was about to make; that there would be no chance of turning back.

So, Ed clenched his jaw and stood firmly with closed fists, hoping he wouldn't lose his nerve.

"Good, that's the spirit," said Kharon. His knees folded in ways that implied many hidden joints where none should be, and his back bent and bent until he was face to face with Ed, who saw the man's face for the first time. Besides the smile and two tiny black eyes that would've been more at home in a spider's head, there were no distinctive features. No ears, no nose, no lines of age on his forehead. Only a chalk-white skin the texture of wax.

"Don't let what's about to happen scare you, Edward. It's all part of the procedure," Kharon warned him. Their closeness brought back his dizzying breath in tufts that made Ed's head spin.

With that, Kharon stepped back a couple steps and bent unto

himself. His long, rail-thin arms hugged the dirty cloth around his torso and he pushed. And he *heaved.*

"UAGHHH!"

"Uh," Ed's voice died in his throat as he saw Kharon's throat go through severe, terrible, *slimy* heaves that made his entire inhuman body tremble and shake with the effort. "Are you...are you okay?"

"UAGHHH!"

Was the man *dying?* From what Ed managed to see, Kharon's face was contorted with effort and pain—still smiling—and *something* started to bulge inside his white neck.

Feeling like he may vomit himself, Ed stepped back as the bulge rose up and up.

What the hell is that? It should have torn Kharon's throat apart.

"UAGHHH!"

The bulge reached the back of his mouth. Ed's eyes widened as he saw something black and pulsating and covered in goo start to pry Kharon's jaw open. More and more—"

It was an organ. Ed could see veins over the black mass. Long tendrils of brown saliva fell to the floor, and the rocks sizzled as if exposed to acid.

It was half-way out now. Kharon used his hands to help the rest of the organ emerge. It came still connected to arteries inside the man's body, long chords that looked like tendons. The organ pumped, and the arteries engorged rhythmically...

It was a heart. That black organ was a heart.

With his chin and cloak covered in saliva and lines of blood, Kharon chomped down on the arteries.

Ed looked away, but not fast enough to avoid seeing the black, tar-like substance erupt out of the severed veins.

"Fuck!" Ed felt like all the blood in his body had turned to ice. He grabbed the door of the car to stop himself from falling to the floor, and he may have run away if he had somewhere to run to.

"Aaaahhhh," Kharon's moan came from somewhere far away,

and it sounded satisfied like someone who had just managed to get rid of a particularly painful ingrown toenail. "Ah, that was a hard one."

Then came wet noises. Ed turned—despite very much not wanting to—to see Kharon cleaning the black tar-blood off his face with the edges of his cloak.

The other hand held the heart with long, pale fingers. The organ still pulsated as strongly as if it were still connected to a body.

Ed tried to speak, but no words came out.

Still clutching the heart, Kharon's smile was now directed at Ed. The smile wasn't white now, but covered in streaks of tar. "The hard part is over. Now, Edward, be very still. I'm going to tear out your heart and replace it with this one."

And he crept toward Ed fast as a nightmare, so fast Ed didn't have time to scream.

ED GROANED. Kharon's wax-like face was right in front of him and his tiny, spider-like eyes were focused on Ed's chest with a hunger that added a malicious glint to them.

"Stay back!" Ed gasped. He tried to push the monster away, but Kharon had Ed's arms pinned under his own, and they were surprisingly strong.

Kharon's gaze shifted to him. His smile was still marred with the tar of his own blood. "Oh? Awake so soon? You're a sturdy one, Edward."

A terrible suspicion arose in Ed. He realized he wasn't standing anymore, but lying on the cold marble floor. Behind Kharon, Ed could see the charred sky. "What—"

He looked down, to his own chest, and discovered with dismay that the operation had already begun.

Huh, he thought with dubious calm while his mind recoiled

in horror, *so that's what my heart looks like. A bit underwhelming, I'd say. I thought it was bigger.*

He tried to say something, but his throat had closed and was refusing to listen to his commands.

"Sorry you saw that," Kharon replied while he pried Ed's exposed ribcage open with a smaller pair of arms that had been so far hidden inside his cloak. "I took away your memory of the last few minutes so you wouldn't be traumatized for life. You shouldn't be awake, Edward."

A cold, tiny hand caressed Ed's beating heart.

Ed trembled and, using an overwhelming amount of willpower, he fought back the horror. "Can you put me under again?"

"But of course," Kharon replied. "Who do you think we are, savages?"

Relief flooded Ed just as a pale hand passed over his eyes, and then it was whiteness.

THE TOWERING MONSTROSITY hungered and laughed as it caressed the pink, beating rock in its hands. Ed's gaze shot up and up across a body bigger than any man-made building, that rivaled a world in its vastness. A great vault supported by charred bones that were like pillars and corridors and chambers and passages. Across them, tar-like blood flowed freely and without spilling, following alien laws of physics that no life-supporting universe could fathom.

Ed's splintering headache had returned with a vengeance; but now, in this realm where silence was absolute, he could distinguish that the needle-like pain was, in truth, millions of soft, whispering voices screaming at him, over and over again, but in such a low intensity—or from so far away—that his own heartbeat had been enough to drown them.

But he had no such problem now. What were they saying?

The being's face was shrouded by darkness. But across its forehead shone a white crown made of silver and its eyes were two malicious stars, forever burning in place.

The hands rose and rose across impossible distances, still carrying the tiny—yet perfectly visible—pulsating rock with its humble, pink, warm light. Soon it reached the being's mouth—or at least the place where the mouth should be—and Ed could see the leviathan tremble with pleasure and expectation as the pink light fell down a throat made of shadows. It must have taken years for the fall to end, but time didn't matter here.

The God trembled with orgasmic pleasure when the stone reached its stomach. It was so small, so insignificant, yet it provided it with such satisfaction...Ed saw how the blood carried the stone in its currents through chambers and passages and falls and bones and guts and muscle, all embedded with uncountable rocks like Ed's own, pulsating with their own pink light, so many that he soon lost track of his own. The rocks formed the foundation of the being's body, of this God-Dungeon that spanned time and space.

Ed could hear the voices. They were singing. "It's only him, it's always him, he's the only Lord that matters, the one who comes in the silence between heartbeats, all the dungeons belong to him, all the dark spaces belong to him, he's the dungeon that matters, he's the dungeon, he's the dungeon, he's the dungeon—"

The God's eyes gazed upon Ed, and it was suddenly aware of the young man's presence. Ed screamed as the vast head shot at him like a meteor; he screamed as the darkness parted to reveal a wide, white smile...

CHAPTER FIVE

NEW BLOOD

"Are you okay, Edward?" asked Kharon. His tiny eyes glinted with concern. There was no divine monstrosity in sight, only the Boatman. "You should have no memories of the procedure, and you have a new heart which is as good as the old one, if not better. The Pact is forged, young Dungeon Lord. Arise."

Ed jerked up with a scream, and he shoved Kharon aside as Ed's hands frantically passed all over his own chest. His work shirt was gone, and he was naked from the waist up, but the skin and the muscles of his torso were intact like nothing had happened. No exposed ribs, no beating heart, not even a scar. His chest looked perfectly normal, but the face of the god that had devoured his heart—his former one—was still fresh in Ed's mind and his body trembled in horror...

He stumbled on his knees, shaking so hard he was in danger of falling on his face. He looked up, straight at Kharon, and suddenly all the fear and horror had been replaced by raw fury. The world was bathed in a green, eldritch tint and Ed's eyes felt feverishly hot.

The young Lord willed his body to stop trembling. He leapt

up and grabbed Kharon's thin neck with enough force to make the hunched figure try to straighten.

"What have you done to me?" Ed demanded through clenched teeth. He was face to face with Kharon and close enough they could've kissed.

Ed's veins weren't filled with blood, they were filled with fire. He could barely think straight, and the impulse to push on that frail neck until it broke like a twig was almost overbearing.

"What," he repeated, "have you done to me? You said you wouldn't mess with my head—"

Kharon raised his arms in surrender, although he didn't seem particularly concerned for his life. "And I haven't, my Lord. If I had, the deal would've been broken in your favor. What you feel is your own body's doing—as a response to your new heart. Everyone's body reacts differently. It seems yours is overflowing with a mix of hormones. Adrenaline and testosterone are natural parts of mortals' functions and you'll soon regain control. Try, in the meantime, not to snap my neck. It would annoy me if you did."

Letting his hands slowly open was almost painful with all that primal, burning fury hammering his temples and the veins of his neck, but Ed managed it after a deep breath. Kharon fell like a rag-doll before regaining his composure and doing the same multi-jointed trick to remain at Ed's height.

"See? You are already doing better. Just be careful of your temper over the following weeks and you'll be dandy. I can tell that the Hungry One was right about you. Most people would be trembling with fear by now, not up on their feet and threatening me with death."

Ed shot him a sarcastic grin. "Your god *is* mistaken, asshole. After what I've seen of him, what he's about, I'll never do *anything* to help him. I'm going to take whatever power I have and use it to thwart him at every chance I have—"

Kharon's arms went up in surrender once again. "As I said

before, what you do with your mantle is up to you, my Lord Edward."

"What happens now?" asked Ed.

"Now," Kharon said, "we set you on your way, my Lord."

The Boatman reached one of the black marble walls that hid the horizon from Ed's view. "This will do," Kharon said. He patted the stone twice as if he were admiring the masonry.

"I can't help you much now," the man told Ed, "lest the Light be made aware of our interference. I suspect that remaining in the shadows will be your best bet to avoid the visit of a group of Heroes not unlike the ones that killed Kael. That, of course, is your choice."

Ed nodded without committing himself to any course of action.

"Still, you'll need smart minions who can help you acclimate to Ivalis. And a safe base to grow your strength. You *could* get both once you step outside this portal, if you're fast enough. That's the gift Kharon, the Boatman, offers to celebrate the birth of Dungeon Lord Edward Wright."

Before Ed could ask Kharon what portal was he talking about, the man muttered under his breath a set of snapping words designed for mandibles and not for human mouths.

The black masonry in front of Kharon pooled and seemed to become liquid. It began to glow a ruby red while it slowly acquired the consistency of molten rock, only without the heat. The portal acquired the shape of a flat oval with lines of fire around its edges, and Ed had the overwhelming impression he was looking at a doorway.

He glanced in Kharon's direction, unsure whether or not to trust the man. Kharon hadn't lied to him yet—that he knew of— but he had also never given Ed much time to consider his options. And the thing with the new heart was definitely crossing a line, no matter how the Boatman chose to interpret it.

"Before you go to make your fortune," said Kharon, unaware

of—or ignoring—Ed's doubts, "you should know a few things. First, are you aware of a certain heat coming out of your eyes? That the world looks...say, a certain shade of green? Good. Now, look at your hands."

Ed did. He saw the eldritch light reflected over the lines of his open palm and realized it was coming from his eyes. Then the light changed, and it concentrated through the air like blazing lines of vapor which formed letters and numbers.

Ed found himself staring at the following:

Edward Wright

Species: Human
> **Total Exp:** 100
> **Unused Exp:** 0
> **Claims:** Lordship over: 0 dungeons.

ATTRIBUTES
> Brawn: 8
> Agility: 10
> Endurance: 9
> Mind: 11
> Spirit: 11(+1 Dungeon Lord Mantle bonus) =12
> Charm: 11(+1 Dungeon Lord Mantle bonus)=12

SKILLS

ATHLETICS: Basic (III) The owner has trained his body to perform continuous physical activity without penalties to their Endurance. For a while.

-Basic rank allows them to perform mild energy-consuming tasks (non-combat) such as running or swimming without tiring. Unlocks stamina-related talents.

TALENTS

EVIL EYE: Allows the Dungeon Lord to see the Objectivity of any creature or item. If the target of his gaze possesses a strong Spirit (or related Attribute or Skill) they may hide their information if the Lord's own Spirit is not strong enough.

Energy Drain: Active. Very Low.

DUNGEON LORD MANTLE: The mantle is the heart of the Dungeon Lord and represents the dark pact made in exchange for power.

-It allows the Dungeon Lord access to the Dungeon Lord status and powers, as defined by the Dungeon Screen.

-It allows the Dungeon Lord to create and control dungeons, as per the limitations of his Dungeon Screen.

Energy Drain: None.

"THIS IS A CHARACTER'S SHEET," Ed muttered. "You're sure this isn't a videogame, Kharon? I've used one just like this for my Ivalis Online playthrough. Except this one looks...mediocre. Where is the spell list? Where are my health points and my damage-per-second? My item list?"

"As I've said, Ivalis is a very real place," Kharon said. "You're looking at the physical manifestation of its own magic. There are no 'health points' in Ivalis, although there *are* experience points. You'll find that your videogame follows the laws of magic of our world and not the other way around, which is probably the reason the game's creators chose your world for their plans."

Kharon nodded to himself as he went on, "Ivalis' magic system is called Objectivity, and is well known among all of its inhabitants. They can't access it as easily as you can with your gaze, which is known as 'the Evil Eye.' You can turn it on and off as you will."

"*Evil Eye?*"

"Well, we weren't the ones who named it." Kharon shrugged. "The reason your status seems empty is that you know of no spells and hold no possessions or claims. If you want more in-depth descriptions of what your skills and talents do, simply focus on them. I'd advise you to leave such inquiries for later on, since your future minions are already in dire straits as it is. If you manage to save at least one of them, they'll be glad to explain the intricacies of Objectivity to you."

Ed took his gaze away from his hands and the status screen disappeared. "My highest attribute is a boosted 11, so a 12. Is that number high?"

He needed to know this if he was going to jump straight into unknown danger.

On a whim, he tried to access Kharon's stats for comparison, but all he got for his troubles were a bunch of "?????" lines.

"Humans average a 10 across all their attributes," Kharon said with a condescending gesture. "Are you ready to traverse the portal?"

Once again, Kharon was making sure that Ed had little time to think things over. The young Lord considered refusing for a moment, just to spite the Boatman. Then he discarded the idea. From what he understood, people's lives were at risk, and he could do something about it. To refuse just to anger someone would be something that Ryan would do. A random use of authority without any of the responsibility. It would mean failing on the path he had proposed for himself before having started.

Ed stepped forward. "Do I just walk into it?"

"Indeed. Good fortune, Dungeon Lord. May your nights be exciting and pleasing to the Dark."

Ed took a deep breath and walked out of the world of nightmares and into Ivalis.

CHAPTER SIX

THE WITCH

C olors changed in an instant. His cheap work shoes were suddenly out of place in the uneven terrain of a dilapidated cave. Sunlight filtered through a tunnel's entrance not far away from him. He took in his surroundings.

He had appeared in front of a crude stone altar covered with a dirty, red rag as a tablecloth. It was decorated with violet flowers of a kind he had never seen before, and a tin medallion of a crude craftsmanship sat by the center. It was made to resemble an open eye partially eaten by a headless mouth.

The rest of the cave was empty. There had been a recent cave-in, from what Ed could gather. Parts of the ceiling had fallen and the entrances of other tunnels were covered by boulders bigger than a man. The floor was cracked and dusty, but it had been of human make, once. Small oil lamps were strewn between the altar and the last tunnel exit like crude guiding lights and gave the cave an eerie atmosphere with the dancing fire. Ed saw two crude, empty sleeping rolls at opposite ends of the cave, and a pelt bag.

The cave was cold, enough to make Ed shiver and wish he still had his shirt. And it was empty, not counting himself.

Ed shrugged and took a step toward the sunlight at the end of the tunnel.

"Wait," Kharon's voice called from behind the altar.

Ed jumped with surprise, but hurried to turn back to find Kharon's upper body floating in midair with his lower half nowhere to be seen.

"It's dangerous to go alone," the Boatman told him with a mocking grin. His arm appeared into reality carrying a wooden stick that he extended to Ed. "Take this."

Ed grabbed the stick. It appeared to have been roughly worked on by a blunt knife.

"This," Kharon added, "is Alder's walking stick. May it serve you better than it did him."

"Thanks, I guess," said Ed. The wood felt rough and real in his grip, and along with the cold and the sharp edges of the rocks beneath his feet, it erased any doubts remaining about the reality of his situation.

Kharon nodded without an ounce of shame and disappeared.

Outside, a woman screamed.

ADRENALINE SHOT through Ed's veins and made his heart race and his body tense with excitement. He was in an unknown world, facing unknown danger, with a stick as his only weapon and dressed only in his work pants.

The woman screamed again.

Ed ran to the tunnel's exit and climbed across the rubble. As he left the tunnel he could hear more sounds, and the sunlight became brighter and made the cold diminish slightly.

It was the sound of a fight, with several people cursing, yelling, and struggling. Ed hurried his half-rush, half-climb until he exited the tunnel, then had to cover his eyes when the sunlight became piercing.

"Stay away from me, you disgusting pigs!" That was the

woman screaming again. Her accent reminded Ed of Count Dracula's exaggerated accent in movies.

"Give us shiny things or die, human!" That voice was hoarse and nasal. It was followed by a chorus of other voices that agreed with the sentiment. "You are surrounded!"

"Alita's tits! Lavy, just give them the stupid trinket!" A male's voice.

"I won't lower myself to the demands of *batblins*," said the woman, Lavy. "If they desire my arcane symbol, they can pry it from my cold, dead hands!"

Ed forced his eyes open and blinked furiously while they got used to the light. The tunnel had led him to a rise in a rock formation with the action happening a few feet below him, at the formation's skirt. He saw two human shapes with their backs against the trunk of a tree and a dozen smaller figures surrounding them.

"You heard the lady, bros!" said the batblin. "Get at 'em!"

"Dunghill!" exclaimed the young man.

There was movement as the first batblins advanced. They seemed to be armed with sticks—no, with farming equipment.

Lavy exclaimed, *"Blazing whip!"*

A line of fire surged from the woman's hand and she cracked it against the batblins nearest to her. The batblins cursed and pulled back. The acrid smell of burnt fur reached Ed's nostrils.

His eyesight had cleared by then, and Ed took in the scene unfolding in front of him. The batblins were small humanoids of mismatched proportions, protruding bellies, and hanging flaps of skin. They were covered with gray fur and their heads looked like those of a bat. Pointy ears almost as tall as their faces, leaf noses at the tip of triangle-shaped snouts, glinting, mouse-like black eyes, and parted lips that pulled back to reveal blunt fangs covered with saliva.

Ed had seen them before—while playing IO. They were low-level encounters, almost exclusively found in open territory and rarely inside an occupied dungeon. Scavengers, opportunists, nasty little critters.

Of course, the dated graphics of the game barely matched reality. All the game's batblins were based on the same model, while the rabble members he was seeing here were very different from each other. They had angry scars streaking their bodies, bald patches, burn-marks, and rags and straps that served as clothing and makeshift armor. Some of their bellies were bloated like balloons. Other batblins were skinny and malnourished. They were all covered in dirt and grime in varying degrees of nastiness.

Even at this distance, Ed could smell the lot of them. It wasn't pleasant.

Their leader, a portly batblin with a wide snout, tried to brush aside Lavy's whip with his makeshift spear. That earned him a burn to his shoulder.

"Agh!" he exclaimed while his fur simmered. "What are you waiting for, fools? Rush her down, she can't smack us all!"

The batblins behind him didn't move. No one wanted to be first.

Lavy smiled in satisfaction. She was a young woman dressed in a knee-length woolen dress and trousers. She was somewhat younger than Ed, or so she seemed. Her long, frizzy black hair was tied behind her back, and her pale skin was splotched prawn-red. It was the type of skin that burned under the sun, while failing to tan. Her eyes were of a dark purple, almost black, and shone maliciously while covered in shadows and runny mascara.

"That's right, we're mages!" said the young man behind her. "Run away or suffer the destruction of our arcane wrath!"

He was dressed in the same woolen outfit as Lavy and was sitting—or lying?—with his back against the tree's trunk. His bowl-shaped hair was an almost orange blond, and all of his features seemed to consist of pointy ends and clumsy gestures of his long limbs. His eyes were a washed-out blue, and they were wide with badly concealed fear.

"Shut up," Lavy mouthed at him. Just when Ed started to think she had the situation under control, the whip vanished from her hand with a puff of smoke.

The batblin leader took a step toward her, slowly, fearfully. His shoulder still smoked.

"Away, scum!" Lavy gestured at him, but no new whip was produced.

What are you doing? Ed thought. *Cast it again.*

Her spell had been a simple one, low-leveled. Ivalis Online used a cooldown system; the weaker the spell's strength the faster it could be used again.

Yet, she didn't cast the spell again.

Ed examined the batblin.

- *Batblin Cloudmaster. Exp: 50. Brawn: 7, Agility, Spirit, and Endurance: 6, Mind and Charm: 5. Skills: Brawling: Basic V, Knowledge (Hoia Forest): Basic IV, Survival: Basic VII. Talents: Cloud Swarm, Cloud Morale.*

Ed skimmed the green words without delving too deeply into their meaning, since the batblin was already gaining confidence that no new magic attack was coming. He took a step forward, then another, ignoring Lavy's constant threats.

Seeing as their leader wasn't getting roasted, the remaining batblins advanced close behind him. Their lips curved upward in slimy smiles.

"It would be a fine time for you to stand up and defend my honor, you useless child," Lavy told the blond man.

"My ankle is sprained, I think," he grimaced, holding his leg. "Toss them the trinket? Please?"

"No trinket!" exclaimed the batblin leader. "You harmed me! You'll pay, humans!"

Lavy backtracked until she was against the tree, next to the other human.

The batblins closed in, and Ed jumped from the tunnel's entrance while roaring as loudly as he could.

The batblins and the humans barely had time to react in surprise at his sudden rush when he was already skittering across the dirt—barely keeping his footing—and reaching the fray with the rage and grace of a moderately big boulder.

"More humans!" one of the batblins announced. "It's a trap!"

Ed brandished Alder's walking stick high over his head before anyone—batblin or human—had time to react and heaved it with both his arms like a baseball bat against the leader of the group. The batblin barely had time to whimper before the hit struck hard against his temple with a dull thud. The batblin's feet left the ground for an instant, and then the walking stick broke in two.

The batblin cloudmaster screamed in pain and fell to the ground stunned and clutching at his head, moaning in a pitiful way. He was bleeding from a gash under his ear, but not profusely. The blood was the color and consistency of used motor oil.

"Sneaky humans!" the batblin groaned. "Get 'em, boys!"

The other batblins advanced with their hoes, sickles, and blunt kitchen knives pointed in Ed's direction. Ed's eyes sensed the danger and delineated a confusion of stats and numbers in such a manner that he had to blink and will the numbers to become smaller and less intrusive. Because of that, he only glanced vaguely at the information of the Evil Eye. The cloud-master had been the strongest one.

Ed was stronger than all the batblins, but they were more numerous and they were angry, and he suspected that, stronger or not, a foot of rusty farm equipment through his guts would ruin his day all the same.

It was clear he'd need to apply an out-of-the-box tactic.

He pressed the jagged end of his half-stick against the cloud-master's neck. "Stay back! I swear I'll kill your boss if you take another step!"

"Gah! Wait, you fools!" added the cloudmaster. "Let me go, human!"

Ed heard the young, blond man mutter something behind him like, "Oh, that's my walking stick, isn't it? I was wondering where I'd left it..."

The batblins looked at each other, at their boss, at Ed. They stopped in their tracks, but they didn't lower their weapons.

"I'll kill him," Ed swore.

For a moment, Ed thought he had them. Then, the batblin at the front of the rabble shrugged. "I never liked Drusb—he's an asshole. Unk thinks Unk should be new cloudmaster!"

"You go, Unk!" one of the other batblins said.

Another one: "No, I should be new cloudmaster!"

"Whoever kills the human first is new cloudmaster!"

"Yes!"

Oh, shit. He deeply regretted not having read up on Ivalis Online lore books regarding batblins, but Ryan's constant nagging for the group to level up as fast as possible without paying any attention to the lore had left Ed with little time.

"You giant piles of dung!" Drusb yelled at his group. "I'll kick your asses for this!"

"You shut up—no one talks like that to Cloudmaster Unk!" said Unk. He leveled his sickle in Ed's direction.

"Wait!" Lavy appeared next to Ed while holding the other half of Alder's walking stick. She had her gaze focused on the line of batblins. "Wait one second, Unk. There's two of us. If you come at us first, I swear upon Hogbus that we will gut you like a pig. In fact, even if you overrun us, we'll certainly kill whoever attacks first."

Unk stopped and considered this turn of events. "Silly wench, you ain't smarter than Unk. Vogkord, you go first!"

Vogkord, next to Unk, looked at his new cloudmaster with alarm. His bat ears trembled. "Like hell I will! Those humans are strong, Unk."

"This is an order of your cloudmaster," Unk said.

"They'll kill me! How about we send someone no one likes first?"

Unk passed one dirty, hairy hand with unkempt, black nails over his double-chin. "Smart Vogkord. I name you my new advisor. Klek, you go first!"

The batblins *laughed* like they were at a party and someone had made a particularly clever quip. The former cloudmaster at Ed's feet groaned in shame. "I'm so dead."

"Yes, come here, Klek!"

"Klek, you useless rat, you go first!"

A batblin about a head smaller than the others, at the back of the group, tried to turn and run, but the others grabbed hold of him and pushed and kicked the poor batblin to the front. Ed realized Klek wasn't even armed with a sling; he only had a small rock in each of his hands. A pair of fearful, black and brown eyes looked at him while the batblin trembled.

He looks like a puppy. Do I really have to kill a puppy to get out of this?

"Idiots," the batblin was whispering non-stop. "Idiots, idiots, idiots. Can't you see? Can't you see his eyes?"

"Shut up, Klek." Unk pushed him forward. "No one cares about a pair of shiny human eyes."

"Eeeek!" Klek fell forward while his rocks fell forgotten to the ground. Out of the corner of his vision, Ed saw Lavy turn to him with wide eyes. She started to whisper something.

The rest of the batblins seemed to judge Klek's fall a good enough distraction because he ran toward Ed and Lavy.

Drusb started squealing like a pig and covering his face in terror. Ed ignored him and jumped over Klek's head, his half-stick raised high above his head and the pointy end aimed at Unk's ugly mug.

I hope there's no scoreboard here, because getting killed by low-level critters in the first five minutes is going to make me look very silly, Ed thought. That's a mouthful for someone's last thoughts.

Whenever Ed had played Ivalis Online, he had realized that the most frequent parting words were, in fact, something like, *Ah, fuck.* Or the always popular, *Whoops!* Even, *I'm sure we can take them.*

Ed pushed a hoe away with a smack of his hand and stabbed Unk's collarbone instead of his eyes. The batblin screeched like he had received a mortal wound and fell backward into the other batblins...And then Ed was surrounded.

I'm sure I can take them, Ed cheered himself while a lot of rusty, pointy ends were hoisted in his direction.

"He's a Dungeon Lord!" yelled Klek, mud-faced, still lying behind Ed. "He'll kill us all!"

Like a charm, the batblin circle took a collective step away from Ed. Arms faltered and ears flared up in alarm. They all started to chatter at once.

"A Dungeon Lord?"

"Impossible!"

"His eyes!"

"No Dungeon Lords in Starevos!"

"Look at his eyes!"

"Must be a trick!" declared Unk. He tried to push more of his batblins towards Ed, but this time they all had firmly planted their feet in the ground.

"It's not a trick," said Lavy. "That's the Evil Eye you're seeing."

"He looks like a wraith!"

"Fools!" she went on. "You really don't know how close you were to annihilation! Do you even understand the terrible eldritch powers this Dungeon Lord was about to unleash upon your stupid hides?"

Everyone, human and batblin alike, turned to stare at Ed. He lowered his weapon and stared back.

"Um, my Lord," Lavy whispered at him with a hand covering her mouth so the batblins couldn't see her lips. "This would be an excellent time to unleash a bit of your eldritch powers. Maybe fry a batblin or two? It would help underscore my point."

Ed covered his mouth the same way Lavy did. "I'm kinda new at this. The Evil Eye and this stick are my entire arsenal."

"Alita's tits," she groaned. "Are you telling the truth? Fine, listen up...I'll handle it if you offer me a pact, under the condition that you aren't lying. That you really are a new Dungeon Lord, and that you don't have ill intentions towards me, or my underling."

The batblins looked at them expectantly, more like an audience waiting to see some fireworks and less like an angry mob.

"Fine by me. Now—" Ed felt like that one time he had shown up at a surprise quiz back in college without having studied. "—how do I make a pact with you? Do I just ask or—?"

"I accept," declared Lavy. She flashed a triumphant smile like she had just won the lottery.

Black and purple mist surrounded Ed out of nowhere and filled his limbs with a tingling sensation as if his skin were crawling with fireflies. His heart fluttered.

The batblins *ooh'ed* and *aah'ed* as the mist gracefully extended itself as tendrils crossed the air until they reached Lavy's chest, then passed through the wool of her dress as well as her skin.

Ed's Evil Eye suddenly was keenly aware of her stats, without an effort on his part, and in a much clearer way than the batblin's had been.

Lavina Odessa Trevil of Devon

Species: Human
    Total Exp: 250

Unused Exp: 0
Claims: None

ATTRIBUTES
Brawn: 6
Agility: 9
Endurance: 7
Mind: 12
Spirit: 12(+1 Minion of Dungeon Lord Edward Wright)=13
Charm: 11(+1 Minion of Dungeon Lord Edward Wright)=12

SKILLS

COMBAT CASTING: *Basic (II)* - Pertains to the speed and efficiency of spells cast during combat or life-threatening situations.
-Basic status allows the caster to use spells every 20 seconds - 1 second per extra rank. The caster must say their names aloud and perform the appropriate hand gestures.

KNOWLEDGE (WITCHCRAFT): *Improved (I)* - Pertains to the owner's knowledge of a specialized, secret topic. This skill allows access to the Hex subdomain's spells.

TALENTS

SPELLCASTING: *Basic (I)* - Domains: Rend(Hex), Sight.
Forbidden: Healing - Represents the owner's magical ability.

-Basic status allows the caster to use and learn all basic related spells of their domain. Extra ranks improve each individual spell's characteristics, such as range or damage.

-Allowed spells: 1 basic per day + 1 basic spell due to Dungeon Allegiance.

Energy Drain: Active. Varies per Spell.

RESIST SICKNESS: Basic - Allows its owner to resist disease and sickness.

-Basic status grants resistance to non-magical sickness as if the owner had Endurance of 15 in optimal conditions (clean, well-fed, rested)

Energy Drain: Constant. Very low

DUNGEON MINION - The owner is a Minion under the command of a Dungeon Lord. The Minion receives bonuses according to the Lord's power and is recognized by all the Lord's dungeons as an allowed entity (unless otherwise specified).

SPELL LIST

BLAZING WHIP - RENDING(HEX). Creates a whip made of arcane fire.

Duration: 5 seconds per spellcraft rank.

Range: 5 feet + 1 feet per spellcraft rank to a max of 20.

WITCH SPRAY - Targeted spheres that curse their target with

minor burning damage and cause hallucinations (resisted by Endurance or Spirit).

Duration of sickness: 1 minute.

Spheres: 3 + 1 per spellcraft rank to a max of 15.

CROW FAMILIAR - The user creates a number of magical crows from a drop of the user's blood. The crow has the intellect of a non-magical crow and follows the user's instructions to the best of its ability, with little sense of self-preservation.

Duration: 1 minute per basic skill rank.

Number of crows: 1 per skill rank, to a maximum of 20.

"EXCELLENT," Lavy said. "What a great day to be a witch!"

She pointed a bony finger at Unk. The batblin's grin turned to fear when he realized his rabble had taken a step away from him. "Dungeon Lord Wright has shared his power with me...He's far too powerful to bother unleashing magical doom upon the likes of you, so I'll do it for him! Behold! W*itch spray!*"

The air trembled for half a second around Lavy's finger, and then a string of violet fireflies blazed out of her fingertip and darted toward a terrified Unk.

At that point, the batblins turned tail and ran, screaming for their lives, while Lavy cackled madly.

The fireflies reached Unk as he turned his back to Ed and tried to evade the magic attack. Half a dozen violet sparks erupted against his fur as the fireflies reached him and exploded, leaving small, smoking patches of burnt hair. The batblin fell-face first to the ground, smacked his head against a rock, and started convulsing and frothing at the mouth.

Ed saw how Drusb, the former batblin cloudmaster, ran at full speed in his cloud's direction, and how he stopped for a second to kick Unk in the belly and kept running.

Unk didn't convulse for long. He managed to crawl his way in the direction of the other batblins, still foaming at the mouth, groaning and crying all the while.

The screams of the batblins could be heard long after they were out of sight, but soon the forest was silent.

"Cowardly little creatures," Lavy said, "that *witch spray* was the only extra spell I got from the pact. If they had called our bluff, we would've been in trouble."

"That was your last spell?" Ed asked her.

"Indeed."

Ed sighed and threw his broken stick to the ground.

A part of himself had hoped he'd arrive at Ivalis already a powerful being, capable of making short work of critters like the batblins. It seemed that the so-called customs of this world involved making him start from the very beginning. He would have to grind his way into relevance while trying to survive all the dangers this place had to offer.

All of it in only one life. There was no respawning in the real world, if Ivalis could be called that.

CHAPTER SEVEN

THE BARD AND THE BATBLIN

The blond guy got up and strutted over to them with a friendly smile. Ed couldn't fail to notice that his supposedly sprained ankle gave the guy no signs of pain.

"Well done, you two. I would've helped, of course, but my ankle was too bruised."

"I can see that," Ed told him sarcastically.

"Maybe I wouldn't have sprained my ankle if you hadn't stolen my stick," the guy said, more in jest than in reproach. "By the way, your entrance had excellent heroic timing. Reminds me of when the hero, Dasius, arrived in the nick of time to break the siege of Castle Aptera. In other words, it's nice to meet you, my Lord. My name is Alder the Bard, at your service."

He extended Ed an open palm that Ed shook more out of instinct than anything else. There was something about Alder's careless expression that made it hard to dislike him, even if the Bard had left both Ed and Lavy to fend for themselves.

"Same, Alder. I'm Edward," said Ed. Having his heart replaced and being transported to Ivalis gave him, in his mind, no excuse to forget his manners. "I don't know who Dasius is, but I'm glad I arrived in time."

"You should have him flayed for his insolence." Apparently Lavy was immune to the Bard's charisma. She told Alder, "How do you dare imply a Dungeon Lord can be heroic? And to compare him to *Dasius*, the Scourge of Lotia!"

"Ah, don't be like that. In Heiliges, it's a compliment."

Okay, thought Ed, *those are a lot of new names and places I don't know anything about.* Things were moving too fast. He needed time to process it all.

"That's the problem!" Lavy said. "Lord Wright, if you desire, I'll end my association with this Heiligian...roaming minstrel at once."

Alder's smile became a bit strained. "Trust me, Lavy, sometimes it's hard to stand you. If you weren't busy sucking up to the new Dungeon Lord, you would've realized that he came from the ruin's tunnels. The tunnels where all other entrances are caved in. You know what that means?"

The young woman's eyebrows shot up. "The Portal? But we couldn't get it to open...did the Dark hear my summons?"

The last question was directed at Ed. He raised his hands and sighed. "I really don't have enough information to answer that question, Lavy. A man...thing—he called himself the Boatman— transplanted me from another world, called Earth, and dropped me here not even an hour ago. This is all quite new for me. He said that if I saved you, I'd be able to win my first minions."

"You met Kharon?" asked Alder. "Awesome. I've always wanted to see what he looks like. It would make my poems more realistic."

"Another world," Lavy muttered. She scratched her temple. "So, they sent you to save us? But you only have a hundred experience points...I asked for someone powerful. Someone capable of avenging my Lord Kael."

At hearing the name of the Dungeon Lord he had killed, Ed started coughing. Was it suddenly getting hotter in the forest?

"It's another of the Dark's skewed deals, I bet," offered Alder. "See, whichever Dark entity answered your pleas, Lavy, they did bring a Dungeon Lord capable of saving us...even if he needed a bit of help."

"I hate it when you are right," Lavy said. "And the price of the deal is that we get to cast our lot with an inexperienced Lord. One who will probably get himself killed, soon enough. No offense."

"We'll see about that," said Ed. He wasn't sure if he agreed with Lavy's assessment of his chances, but he hadn't come to another world to complain about having to risk death. That part had been very clear in the deal he had made with Kharon. "I plan on doing my best, if that's any consolation."

Alder placed his open palm upon his own chest. "It's enough for me. A deal is a deal, my Lord. I offer you my services, for whatever they're worth, on the conditions that what you're saying be true, that you are who you say you are, and that you do not harbor any ill intentions towards me or my associate."

Ed made a mental note to ask them about pact-making, since both of them had made similar demands. Then he nodded and said, "That's fine."

"Then I accept your offer," Alder said, although Ed wasn't actually sure he had extended one. In any case, the tendrils of mist soon appeared and connected the Bard to him.

Alder Loom

Species: Human
    Total Exp: 200
    Unused Exp: 0
    Claims: Bardic School of Elaitra - Journeyman.

ATTRIBUTES
   Brawn: 7
   Agility: 9
   Endurance: 8
   Mind: 10
   Spirit: 9(+1 Minion of Dungeon Lord Edward Wright)=10
   Charm: 12 (+1 Minion of Dungeon Lord Edward Wright)=13

SKILLS

KNOWLEDGE (BARDSHIP): *Improved (I)* - Pertains to the owner's knowledge of a specialized, secret topic. This skill allows access to the Bardic subdomain's utterances.

BARDIC PERFORMANCE: *Basic (IX)* - Represents the Bard's capacity for performing under the pressure of an audience without penalization to the Bard's magic.
   -Basic status allows the Bard to suffer no penalty to performing an utterance in the presence of a crowd if there's no danger involved.
   -If danger is involved, each extra rank of Basic allows the Bard faster utterance casting and to maintain the casting better if they suffer damage or are attacked.

SURVIVAL: *Basic (VII)* - Represents the owner's capability to survive when far from civilization. Basic ranks imply they can survive in a non-lethal environment and situations. They can build a standard campsite, know that some berries are dangerous, how to start a fire, and how to hunt small prey.

TALENTS

BARDIC UTTERANCES: Basic (III) - Allows the Bard to use utterances, the magical variant of the Illusion and Control hybrid subdomain: Bardic.

-Basic ranks allow the Bard to perform any basic utterance that they know.

-Allowed utterances: 3 basic per day + 1 basic utterance due to Dungeon Allegiance.

Energy Drain: Active. Varies per utterance.

EMPATHY: Basic - Allows the owner to sense emotions in humanoid creatures familiar to the owner.

-Basic status lets the owner sense strong emotions that their targets are not actively trying to hide.

Energy Drain: Active. Low.

DUNGEON MINION - The owner is a Minion under the command of a Dungeon Lord. The Minion receives bonuses according to the Lord's power and is recognized by all the Lord's dungeons as an allowed entity (unless otherwise specified).

UTTERANCE LIST

NIMBLE FEET - CREATES an area of effect around the Bard that allows them and their friends to retreat as if they possessed an Agility of 15. This effect ends if the users enter combat.

Duration: 5 minutes.

ED HAD ALREADY RECRUITED his first two minions. Not too shabby, he guessed, for a first day at work.

I really need to stop and take a good look at all these new mechanics, he thought. For the most part, they worked more or less like they did in Ivalis Online, only without Health Points and other specific details. For example, damage was only implied and never specifically stated. Skills and talents like the Bard-related ones that Alder had, Ed had never seen before.

He discovered that by focusing on a certain aspect of someone's character sheet—he knew no other way to think of the information—he could get an expanded look at what it did. That would come in handy.

"Ah," Alder sighed with satisfaction once the mist had disappeared. "The bonus to my Charm will come in handy later."

Ed nodded wisely. He didn't need to be an Ivalis expert to guess that **Charm** and Bards were naturally tied together.

"Well done, Lord Edward," said Lavy with a courteous smile. "You've secured yourself the services of the powerful Witch Lavina as your first minion. As you surely have noticed, I specialize in both Spirit and Mind attributes, which makes me an exceptional advisor as well as spellcaster. My suggestion is that you keep me out of harm's way, in a position where I can rain magical ruin upon your enemies. I can also handle the boring aspects of dungeon management when you are away or otherwise indisposed. Finally, as you surely have already noticed, I'm an attractive young woman. I'm sure you don't need suggestions regarding *that.*"

She batted her eyelids at Ed while Alder groaned audibly.

Almost everyone who has dated a crazy ex at some point in

their lives has an internal radar about said craziness. Ed's own radar issued him a formal warning, declared a red alert, and set itself at DEFCON 2.

"Ahem," he said noncommittally.

"Before we start dispensing nobility titles," said Alder, "shouldn't we take care of our short-term survival? My Lord, you should get started on your dungeon before nightfall, otherwise we may get stuck with Hoia's more...nasty inhabitants."

"Good idea," said Ed, grateful for Alder's assistance. "What kind of monsters are we talking about?"

"Spiders and snakes," Lavy shuddered. "A lady's worst nightmare."

"That doesn't sound too bad," Ed said. "Giant spiders and snakes are low-level critters even weaker than batblins, aren't they?" When playing Ivalis Online, he sometimes didn't even bother auto-attacking the spiders while crossing a forest. They couldn't get through his Wizard's armor.

"Well, then you can deal with them," said Lavy; then she remembered her manners, "—my Lord."

"The altar should be a good place to start a dungeon," said Alder. He gestured back at the rock's rise that hid the entrance to the tunnels. "Shall we go?"

Ed nodded, and the three of them turned to leave. A whimpering sound behind them startled them.

Ed saw a small figure still sprawled in the mud, too terrified to run like his cloudmates had. The batblin was looking at him with scared, pleading mouse-eyes.

"Um," said Klek, "could I become your minion? My cloud is a bunch of assholes."

THE BATBLIN LOOKED VERY small and pathetic, covered in mud and shivering in fear. Ed's Evil Eye had little trouble prying a statline from Klek, and it wasn't very impressive.

- Klek, batblin. Exp: 10. Brawn: 4, Agility and Spirit: 6, Endurance, Mind, and Charm: 5. Skills: Brawling: Basic II, Knowledge(Hoia Forest): Improved II, Survival: Basic IV. Talents: Cloud Swarm.

"A stinky batblin?" asked Lavy during the couple of seconds that Ed was busy reading the stats. "No way I'm letting a batblin sully the reputation of my—I mean, Lord Wright's dungeon. Best to put it out of its misery."

She grabbed a rock with both hands and made her way towards the batblin, who started to plead for his life in too quick a voice to be understood.

"Wait," Ed told her. Lavy didn't hear him, or pretended not to. She reached the batblin and raised her rock. Klek covered his face with his twig-like hands.

"I said, *stop.*" This time it was an order, and it was as if his voice was frosted with ice. A flash of black-and-purple mist passed through both his and Lavy's bodies for an instant before disappearing again.

Lavy stopped, the rock still high above her head. She looked back at Ed. "What?"

Ed remembered what the batblins had said about Klek. *"Let's send first someone we don't like!" "Yes, let's send Klek!"*

"Klek, you useless rat, come here!"

Ed walked to the trembling figure. "You can join me, Klek, but I have to warn you...I'm new at this, and I'm kinda winging it. I do promise no harm will come to you from me, or my people." He shot a warning glance at Lavy while he said that last part.

"But, he's useless," the young Witch complained.

"I accept," said Klek immediately, like he expected Ed to change his mind at any time. The batblin made no conditions. "I accept...My Lord."

Ed nodded while the tendrils of mist did their shtick. Klek's expanded statline was identical to the short version Ed had already seen. No secret talents for the batblin.

"Now, stand up," Ed said. "And stop trembling, please."

The batblin stood, but he still shook sporadically. There was a happy, almost maniacal glint in his eyes, like he couldn't believe he was still alive. "Klek promises he'll be useful. You won't regret this."

"I already regret it," whispered Lavy in Ed's ear. "If I knew you planned to open a *charity*, instead of a proper dungeon, I may have thought better about my own pact." Ed noticed this time she took care not to let the batblin hear her.

"So, saving him is charity, but saving you wasn't?"

"Saving a fair lady is never charity," she said, but there was a glint of anger in her eyes. "Less when you do a half-hearted job and need *her* to help *you* save yourself. You remember that, or you'll spend many nights in a cold bed...my Lord."

"And you are not talking to a nervous tween desperate for a lay," Ed snapped, feeling his blood boil. "*You* remember that, next time you try to make my decisions for me. If you don't like it, you can fuck right off."

He walked away from her, still fuming, ignoring Lavy's indignation. He heard her say something like, "—don't know what a 'tween' is—" before leaving her behind.

With Klek jogging next to his legs, not unlike a lapdog, Ed reached Alder the Bard, who was already halfway up his climb to the tunnel's entrance. As he did so, Ed made an effort of will to turn off his Evil Eye, because his flaring temper, the green tint, and the heat flowing out from his eyes were giving him a slight headache.

"So, you've met Lavy," Alder said when he saw Ed's approach. "Let me say, after two night's camping with her alone in the woods, I would've been eager to join *anyone* who approached. Hell, a batblin Dungeon Lord would've done it for me."

"I bet," said Ed.

The two men and Klek reached the tunnel's entrance, while Lavy strutted toward them angrily, still at the rocks' skirt.

"Since we're already immersed in the age-old Bardic tradition of talking about women," Alder went on as they backtracked through Ed's approach into the tunnels, "let me take the liberty of sharing some advice with you, my Lord—"

"Please, call me Edward. Or Ed." In his current mood, if people kept referring to him as "my Lord," it would get to his head *fast.*

"Lord Edward," nodded Alder. "You say you're from another world, right? I reckon that you may be unfamiliar with our customs. Perhaps you're as naïve as Numerios the Pure was when he first adventured out of Chourmondeley Keep at age fifteen—"

"I don't know who Numerios is—"

"Klek—I mean—I don't, either—"

"As I was saying, my warning is this. Your position as Dungeon Lord comes with many advantages that almost make up for the fact you'll suffer an early, painful death at the hands of some Heiligian adventurers. One of such advantages is, you'll attract the attentions of a certain kind of lady—or gentleman. While this may sound like a perfect situation to the inexperienced, naïve young man—"

"I'm not nai—"

"—you should be aware that they are not attracted to the person, but the title. We call them dungeon-diggers where I come from. Lotia calls them something far nastier, but don't ask me to say what, since I'm a Bard and all Bards are sworn to never foul their mouth with such romance-sullying words—"

"You talk a lot," Klek pointed out. They were almost upon the altar cave by now.

"Ahem. Well, anyway, Lavy is a dungeon-digger. She became

the apprentice of Warlock Chasan with the obvious—obvious to the entire dungeon, I mean, though *she* probably didn't realize it —intention of seducing our Lord Kael and charming him into placing her in a position of authority otherwise undeserved."

"Did it work?" asked Ed. He wished he hadn't broken Alder's stick during the fight with the batblins; it would've come in handy with all the rocks lying around.

"Not even one bit. Kael was well into his fifties, a widower, with his children dead by different circumstances. He saw Lavy as the pampered, probably psychotic apprentice of his Warlock and barely gave her a second glance. This didn't sit well with her, but you didn't go around second-guessing Kael's decisions if you wanted to keep your hide."

"Charming," said Ed.

"Ah, Kael was one of a kind," said Alder with a nostalgic shrug. "In any case, you've been warned, Lord Edward. Whatever you do next is up to you."

"Please keep rock-lady away from me," pleaded Klek.

Ed decided to let the matter rest. "Thanks, Alder."

They had arrived at the altar's cave. Now that he had more context, Ed realized the two sleeping bags at opposite ends belonged to Alder and Lavy. The tin symbol in the middle of the altar must've been Lavy's trinket.

"We'll have to return to town soon, for more provisions," Alder said when he caught Ed's gaze. "But this place should do as a temporary base of operations. It used to be one of Kael's advanced outposts, a long time ago, before Lavy or I joined his service. He lost it to adventurers, as it happens. Starevos is far away from both Lotia and Heiliges, so he retreated here after his defeat inside the Arpadel Fortress. He was meaning to reconnect with this dungeon when the Heroes invaded his base and killed him."

"What happened to his last dungeon?" asked Ed.

Alder shook his head. "It collapsed shortly after his death.

You see, dungeons are built to outlast even their Lord's demise. But something about these Heroes...they cause the dungeons they conquer to lose integrity shortly after their rampage. It's very strange—a kind of magic I'd never heard of before."

Alder's expression made Ed feel a pang of guilt.

Remember, these people are not the good guys, he told himself. He may have read very little on Ivalis Online lore, but it was clear the Dungeon Lords had earned their bad reputation. They raided, blackmailed, stole, raped, and murdered to their black hearts' desire. The villagers or soldiers that gave his Wizard character the quests were always eager to get rid of the dungeons' infestation. Dungeon Lords drained the life out of human and non-human holdings by stealing their crops and killing the farmers and soldiers, leaving the hold undefended against the monsters of the land.

Ed may be a Dungeon Lord, but he had little intention of acting like one. Alder and Lavy were...peculiar, but they didn't strike him as *evil.* He would give them the benefit of the doubt. But in the fight between Light and Dark he held little doubt as to his loyalties.

However, he would have to distance himself a bit. Gain more information. *Alder mentioned a town,* he thought. *That would be a good place to start fixing this mess.*

CHAPTER EIGHT

DUNGEON BUILDING 101

The Witch joined them shortly afterward. "If you have finished whispering among yourselves, perhaps we should get the dungeon started? Daylight won't last forever, and we're running out of oil."

"That's because you spent it all on your ritual." Alder nodded in the direction of the road of tin lamps toward the altar. "But you're right. Lord Edward...well, how new are you to the Lordship? I'd love to explain the dungeon-building process to you, but I don't know much about it. As you can guess, Lord Kael kept his secrets close to heart."

"That he did," said Lavy.

Ed shook his head. "Kharon left me no indications about... anything, really. But wait. Let me see what I can do."

Now that he was away from combat and not drugged-up with adrenaline, his mind found it easier to think. He felt more like himself. He wasn't a fighter like Kael had been; he was a strategist.

"How do people become Dungeon Lords, usually?" he asked after a while.

"By performing a dark, complicated ritual," said Lavy. "If they make a single mistake, their soul gets snatched by some abomination from the Wetlands."

"Or they are approached by a dark entity at the service of the Hungry One in a time of great personal need," added Alder. "There's no ritual required in that case."

Ed nodded. So there were at least two ways of becoming a Dungeon Lord, and there might have been even more. "Have you ever known of a Dungeon Lord who didn't know how to create a dungeon?"

"Now that you mention it, no," said Alder.

"I see where you're going, but it isn't useful," said Lavy. "Perhaps there *can* be Lords who lack the knowledge to make a dungeon. We wouldn't know it, if they die before becoming famous."

"Let's hope that isn't the case," said Ed, "or we are in trouble."

Since having secret, specialized knowledge didn't appear to be a prerequisite to becoming a Dungeon Lord, he decided to assume the process was somewhat instinctive.

He directed his attention inward, to his new heart, trying to goad it into unleashing, like Lavy had called it, eldritch might...or something like it.

Nothing happened. As far as he was concerned, his new heart functioned exactly like the old one had.

Instead of feeling frustrated, Ed focused more and more at the problem at hand. He thrived when he had a clear problem to solve. If necessary, he was prepared to spend an entire day and night figuring it out.

Since his heart wasn't providing him with an answer, he tried the only power he was aware he had. With a push of will, he activated the Evil Eye. The sensation of heat flowing out of his eyes resumed, and the world gained a greenish tint. He was vaguely aware that Lavy was blushing, and that Klek had jumped away at the sudden outburst of eldritch light.

"Sorry, should have told you I was going to do that," he

muttered. His attention was elsewhere. He looked at his hands and summoned his stats.

There was something new.

- You have gained 21 experience (3x7 batblin, non-lethal encounter). Your unused experience is 21 and your total experience is 121.
- There are new talent advancement options for you:

Resist sickness (15 experience) - Allows its owner to resist disease and sickness.

-Basic status allows the owner to resist non-magical sickness as if they had Endurance of 15 and were in optimal conditions (clean, well-fed, rested)

Energy Drain: Constant. Negligible.

RESIST POISON *(25 experience)* - Allows its owner to resist poison. Higher levels include a resistance to venom.

-Basic status allows the owner to resist non-magical poison as if they had Endurance of 15 and were in optimal conditions (clean, well-fed, rested)

Energy Drain: Constant. Very low.

RESIST ENVIRONMENT *(20 experience)* - Allows its owner to perform and survive in threatening environments for prolonged periods of time.

-Basic status allows the owner to survive in extreme environments such as tundra or a desert, even if they lack proper protections.

-The owner will last 1 extra day in a moderate environment, 1 extra hour in a dangerous environment, and 1 extra minute in a lethal environment such as freezing waters.

Energy Drain: Constant. Very low.

SPELLCASTING *(40 experience)* - Represents the owner's magical ability.

-Basic status allows the caster to use and learn all basic related spells of their domain. Extra ranks improve each individual spell's characteristics, such as range or damage.

-Allowed spells: 1 basic per day + 1 basic spell due to Dungeon Lordship.

Energy Drain: Activated. Varies per Spell.

IMPROVED *reflexes (50 experience)* - Allows the owner to experience increased reaction time for a small burst of time.

-Basic status elevates his reaction speed to a degree dictated by the owner's Agility, for a duration of 3 seconds per use.

Energy Drain: Activated. High.

PERCEPTION *(20 EXPERIENCE)* - Allows the owner to experience an improvement to their attention to detail and memory. They can see things that would normally pass undetected.

-Basic status lets them see as if they had a Mind of 15 and a Spirit of 13, as if they were focused, clear of mind, and well rested and fed.

Energy Drain: Activated. Moderate.

"INTERESTING," Ed said. "I gained a bunch of experience for the batblin encounter. Almost enough to buy my first *spellcasting* talent."

The prospect of gaining tangible, honest-to-God magical

powers excited him. He almost skipped reading the other talents' notes, but he would've made for a lousy gamer if he missed details like that.

Advanced reflexes promised to make him into Neo...for three seconds. It was the most expensive talent, though, and it was activated, with an elevated energy cost per each use.

He still salivated at the thought of going around dodging bullets—arrows, he guessed—like a stone-cold badass.

Besides p*erception*, the others weren't as interesting, but they promised to keep him alive longer. To be able to resist poison would be very useful if someone tried to spike his drink. A resistance to the elements and to disease would make him live longer than the average medieval peasant.

But none of those talents were as attractive as magic. The choice was clear. First, he would hold on to the unused experience, then he would figure how earning experience worked, and then he would work for his magic. He would probably go for the reflexes after that.

We can figure my progression later, he told himself. *Don't get sidetracked. You have to prove to your minions that you are a Dungeon Lord.*

"Gee, you already can buy *spellcasting*," Lavy said bitterly. "Must be nice not to have to study for years just to earn the chance to buy the first rank, along with the opportunity to cast one meager spell per day."

"That's why people are still entering the Lordship even with the high risk of painful, slow, agonizing death," Alder told Ed, as if to explain Lavy's bitterness. "Dungeon Lords can learn magic without the years of studying it usually takes, among other things. I can see that you have mostly common talent options, besides reflexes and magic. That should improve once you earn more skills and raise your attributes."

"And how do I do that?" asked Ed. Ivalis Online had a point

system. You gained a couple skill points every time you leveled, along with increased health. It seemed the real Ivalis worked in an entirely different way. There were no levels anywhere on his character sheet. He would have to learn to measure power the hard way.

"You have to work for them, of course," said Lavy. "You can't expect to get *everything* for free."

"To be honest," Ed flashed her a grin, "I prefer it this way. It wouldn't be the same to gain a power that I haven't earned. It wouldn't feel like it's mine that way."

He had given his own heart in exchange for his Dungeon Lord title. No, not only that. He had given up his own world, along with everyone he knew in there. He'd never see Mark and Lisa again, nor what little remaining family he had left.

Ed would fight anyone who said he hadn't earned his mantle.

Lavy didn't debate the point.

In any case, he was still lacking a clear way to use his powers. He returned to the task at hand.

Ed had one dungeon-related talent in his character screen. The *Dungeon Lord mantle* said he could access a Dungeon Screen.

He directed his Evil Eye toward the cave's surface, hoping to activate said Screen. Instead, he found something different. When he focused, the rock gained a certain ethereal quality. Faint lines of energy formed at his feet and extended under the altar, behind the wall of rock, then disappeared in every direction almost like a spider-web.

Ed focused on the lines and, as if responding to his will, they became more clear, easier to follow. A tingling sensation similar to the one caused by the mist that had recruited his minions began to spread all across his body, itching to come out.

Klek ran to one corner of the cave as Ed extended his arm and pushed two tendrils of mist into existence. Acting by their own accord, the tendrils slithered to the floor and coalesced into two small figures, gained solidity, and transformed into living, breathing creatures.

His mist-creations looked at Ed with big, insect-like eyes that occupied almost half their heads. They were ugly beings, clearly magical. A gigantic mouth occupied the lower half of their head, while their eyes seemed to fill all the remaining upper space. Their jaws were muscled, like one of those abyssal fishes that were more teeth and mouth than anything else. Their hide was rough and leathery, of a muddy-brown that made them difficult to distinguish from the cave. In fact, their skin had rocky protrusions imitating the stones of the cave, as a sort of natural camouflage.

They were about half of Klek's height, so they barely passed Ed's knees. Both of them were dressed only in a purple-and-pink sash that looked vaguely familiar to Ed, with an even more familiar insignia stamped in the middle. They had no visible genitalia or any other distinguishing features. They were identical to one another, but moved independently.

The first thing they did was smile maliciously at Ed—he saw three rows of shark-like teeth—and give him a deep, deferential bow.

"Huh," Ed said. "I didn't expect that to happen."

"Those are your drones," said Alder with a smile. "You must be making progress—drones are an integral part of any dungeon. They are like tiny construction workers. Kael had a veritable fleet of them running around his holdings at any time."

"Is that the insignia you had in that other world of yours?" asked Lavy. She lined in closer to the drones to examine their sash, clearly without any fear of the monsters' teeth. "I've never seen a creature such as the one on your coat-of-arms. Maybe I was wrong about you, Lord Edward. You might be stronger than you look if you have a bloodline such as that. What's that thing it carries on its back?"

Ed sighed. The little drones were displaying their purple-and-pink sashes at Lavy with almost vulgar abandon, chattering and laughing in some nonsensical language.

"That," he explained, "is a laser. The 'monster' you're seeing is called a shark. A lasershark, I guess. It's a...sea creature."

"Impressive," said Alder. "Is that what we should call you? Lord of the Lasershark?"

"Absolutely not. Not ever. Not even as a joke."

His two minions looked at each other and shrugged. "As you wish."

Ed looked at the spot behind the altar where he had arrived in Ivalis. *Is this your doing, Kharon, you dick?*

The young Lord made a vow to figure out how to change his drones' vestments as soon as he could.

THE TWO DRONES seemed to possess wills of their own. They were about as nasty as a hyperactive three-year-old, and when left of their own accord they went straight to terrorizing Klek.

Ed ordered them to stay away from the batblin—who had started to whimper—and he discovered they listened to his commands pretty much instantly. If he asked them to dance, they did so. If he asked them to jump, they jumped. They weren't robots, though, and they performed said actions in their own way. Which mostly meant they acted annoyed as hell.

"What are you doing?" asked Lavy after a couple rounds of experimenting.

"I'm figuring out what I can do with them," Ed said. One drone was standing on the shoulders of the other, and both were trying their best to imitate a coordinated dance. The one on top made eye-contact with Ed and flashed him an obscene gesture with his tiny finger while they pirouetted. "Their stats are very low, they have no skills, and their only talent simply says *drone*."

"They're drones," Alder pointed out.

"That may mean more to you than it does to me," said Ed. "The first part of gaining a new ability is to learn its limits and its rules. You said before they were some kind of construction workers? No offense, but they don't look very useful for that."

The drones heard him and showed Ed their long, forked tongues.

"They're diggers," said Lavy. "Kael's looked—and acted—different from yours, but the size was the same. They are not useful for fighting, though. They disappear easily, but Kael acted like it was trivial to replace them."

That earned Lavy another obscene gesture from the drones. She responded in kind.

Ed ignored them all and scratched his chin.

Creating the drones in the first place had been somewhat instinctive. Using the Evil Eye to focus on the underground lines had seemed to trigger it. It was fair to assume both were related.

"Fine. Listen up, you two," he told the drones. "I want to create a dungeon here. I have no idea how to go about that. I want you to either do it for me or show me how. That's an order."

Another deep, sardonic curtsy, then the drones ran to the altar. Ed followed each movement. His life could depend on knowing how his powers worked.

Scratch that. He held little doubt his life *did* depend on figuring out his powers.

The drones studied the altar, sniffed it, circled it. They seemed to be admiring the workmanship.

Lavy started to get nervous once the first drone licked the white stone. "I don't like where this is going."

Before anyone could react, the drone unhinged his jaws and its mouth widened, like that of a snake, far beyond what a human being could manage. Three rows of sharp, tiny teeth glistened in the lamplight for a second...and then closed around the altar's rock in a single, fluid motion.

There was a loud crunching noise that sounded like a small explosion in the confined cave. All that Ed knew about life told him that the drone had just broken all its teeth against the stone of the altar. Instead, the critter threw its head back—its eyes shiny with glee—to reveal a mouth-sized chunk of stone missing out of the altar.

The other one, at the other side, took a bite of his own with the same result.

"I really hope," said Lavy, who had suddenly gone pale, "that you have the favor of whichever Dark entity is looking at this, because that's their altar you're eating."

Ed recalled the vision he'd had back in Kharon's realm, of the monstrous thing that lurked there and fed on hearts. He shivered. Perhaps he should recall his drones…

But they were working too fast, and in a matter of seconds the altar had been reduced to half its size. The drones gave no signs of having trouble eating all that rock, even if it was several times their bodyweight. It didn't even slow them down.

In fact, they were shaping the stone of the former altar. Ed half-turned away in disgust when the drones started *spitting* on the white surface and pawing at it with their bare hands. They molded the stone as if they were kids working with clay.

Biting and spitting, biting and spitting, over and over, working the stone faster than any human could. In minutes, a project that should have taken days was finished, and the drones retreated with satisfaction.

The altar had been converted into a small, rough throne of sharp edges and graceless contours. The spit of the drones evaporated in seconds and gave the throne a polished look, almost like a statue.

"That's kinda cool," Ed conceded. With his Evil Eye, he saw that the throne was built upon a spot where the energy lines converged. In fact, it was as if the throne itself was pulling them closer to it, connecting to them.

Under the glow of the Evil Eye, the throne shone slightly with its own light. It pulsated rhythmically, like a heart.

"That's the dungeon's Seat," said Alder. He walked slowly

toward the throne. "The heart of any dungeon."

"It's not very safe to have it so close to the surface," added Lavy. "But it should do for tonight. Have your drones build me an appropriate suite. And don't think you'll get to share it with me—you lost that chance thanks to your impolite attitude."

"*My* attitude, you say—" said Ed, before dismissing her with an impatient gesture. He examined the throne. He could *feel* something similar to the sensation he'd had when pulling up his own character sheet. He reached for it, drew it to the surface...

Caves

Dungeon Lord Edward Wright.
 Drones 2
 Dominant Material Cave Rock

THREAT 0 - REPRESENTS how aware the outside world is of the dungeon and how willing / able / ready they are to do something about it. A 100 indicates imminent destruction.

OFFENSE 300 - A representation of the strength a dungeon's forces can muster during an attack (raid or invasion) outside the dungeon itself. It indicates the experience they would award as a group, if they were defeated.

DEFENSE 300 - It represents the defensive capacity of the dungeon, the experience the population of a dungeon would award if they were to be defeated during the defense of said dungeon. It's multiplied by a percentage given by the dungeon's upgrades and defenses.

MAGIC GENERATED 1 - Measures the magic created by the Sacred Grounds that can be put to use in different endeavors or to power dungeon upgrades.

MAGIC CONSUMED 0 - Measures how much magic is consumed.

POPULATION
    3 adult humans.
    1 young batblin.

AREAS
    Living Zones:
    0

MILITARY FACILITIES:
    0

RESEARCH INSTALLATIONS:
    0

SACRED GROUNDS:

    • The Seat.

PRODUCTION:

0

DEFENSE:

0

DUNGEON UPGRADES

None.

"SEEMS AWFULLY EMPTY," sighed Ed after reading the sheet. He missed having a tutorial to guide him. But he *was* making progress.

The drones were construction workers. And the concepts in the dungeon sheet gave him some ideas as to what he could do.

First of all, we need a refuge. The Seat seemed to claim an area by itself, so he ordered the drones to clear one of the tunnels previously covered by the cave-ins.

The two critters went to work gleefully, eating at the giant boulders like they were enjoying a delicious banquet.

"I need you to make an effort, now," he said, turning to his two human minions. "You served under another Dungeon Lord. How did Kael go about building all the rooms and chambers of his dungeons? The drones work well with rock, but what about wood, and metal, and other construction materials?"

Back on Earth, while playing Ivalis Online, he had paid little attention to the dungeons he had raided because Ryan gave them no time to enjoy the lore or the scenery. It had seemed to him that all the spaces the team moved through had some kind of function. Barracks with beds in all shapes and forms, kitchens... torture chambers, prisons—

"Well," said Alder. "You're right that they don't work well with anything other than rock and dirt. For any complex materials, Kael had big, well-guarded storage facility and treasure chambers."

Those I remember, Ed thought. *We called them the loot rooms. They were at the end of the dungeon, and we always reached them after killing the Dungeon Lord.*

"When Kael wanted to build, say, a training facility near the barracks, he had the drones go to the storage silos and get all they needed from there. Wood, iron, steel, straw, you know. He got those in the first place by having the drones mine the dungeon's whereabouts, or by raiding nearby towns and villages. The drones can use the raw material to build more complex structures, but nothing more difficult than what a mediocre craftsman could do."

"And the treasure chamber?" asked Ed. His drones were deep into the tunnel by now. He and Alder had to yell to be heard with all the constant *crunch, crunch, crunch.* The drones made enough noise for an entire construction crew back on Earth. "What's that for?"

"Besides the obvious, you mean?" Lavy laughed. "I'm better suited to tell you that, as it is an arcane matter. You see, Lord Edward, the rules of Objectivity are quite clear. Not even the gods are exempt. You can bend the rules, perhaps, but you can never, ever, break them. The first one is, 'the numbers will never lie.' You can hide your stats if your **Spirit** is high enough, but you won't ever be able to change the numbers themselves to something they are not. If you want to change a stat, you can only achieve that by transforming the piece of reality that the numbers represent."

Lavy obviously found keen pleasure in explaining the basic workings of Objectivity to her Dungeon Lord. Ed had no problem with that. He was anxious to learn more about his situation and how the world worked.

"Go on," he said.

"Next rule, and perhaps the most important, is 'power comes at a price.' Every creature, god and mortal alike, who rises beyond their natural lot in life, does so at a cost proportional to the power they acquired. Now, the Bards and the—*ugh*—philosophers enjoy the metaphysical assertions of this rule, but anyone who is actually useful recognizes a simpler meaning. As in, you can *literally* pay for your power. If there's any material you lack, you can trade gold or gems—anything of value, really—in exchange for it."

She flicked her hair, satisfied, as she finished her explanation.

Ed clenched his jaw. There was something she had said, no, the way she had said it...that had made him shiver. He recalled the torture chambers and the prisons of almost all the dungeons he had seen in Ivalis Online.

Dungeon Lords liked to raid villages and keep people as slaves...but according to what he had learned, they had no need for human labor if their drones did all the heavy lifting.

Which meant...

"You mentioned other valuables," he told Lavy. "Like what?"

Her smile became cold. "You're a perceptive one, Lord Edward. There's value in many things, not only in gold and treasure. Experience points are valuable, for example, and there are two ways to earn them. The first is to survive and learn from an event where your life is at risk. The second is to kill a living being and take their experience for yourself. You know what that means?"

It meant that people could use the experience points of others as payment for magical power.

Ed's blood turned to ice. He was very tired, and he felt very, very far away from home.

"You can sacrifice intelligent beings in exchange for your dungeon's resources. It is, in fact, the fastest way," Lavy went on. "It has an excellent rate of conversion. For example, that batblin you took under your wing would be enough to make an elegant, comfortable bed."

CHAPTER NINE

CULTURE SHOCK

I t took Ed a great effort of will not to scream at the Witch or to attack her. He had to remind himself that, as far as he knew, she hadn't actually sacrificed anyone.

As far as you know, he remarked. *What if she has? What if they both have? What will you do then?*

It wasn't something he could postpone until later, a decision he could make after a good night's sleep. It was something he had to deal with *right now.* He had believed Alder and Lavy weren't evil; they looked too normal, too *human,* in a world where he had seen monsters like Kharon and the ancient deity he served.

He had forgotten evil doesn't need a monstrous appearance to blossom. A young Witch and a Bard could be enough.

Ed had sworn he would never become the evil underling that Murmur wanted.

If he allowed things like human sacrifice to slide, Ed had little doubt he would fall into that path sooner rather than later.

I'll just ask them. If they say they have, I'll break the minion pact.

Before he could change his mind, before he had a chance to think it further, he committed himself to that course of action.

With a grim smile on his face, he asked Lavy, "Have you sacrificed anyone?"

Something in his tone of voice made Alder look up from the stone Seat which he had been examining. The Bard's gaze fell on Ed's expression and Alder turned, alarmed, to Lavy. "Lavy—"

"Why," Lavy was already answering, and her smile was sharp, tinted with something close to savageness under the Evil Eye's light, "are you looking for advice, as to how to begin? It's not that hard, or so I've heard. You need an altar. You need holding cells, made with stone and iron if you're feeling fancy—"

"*Lavy*," Ed said, "have you sacrificed anyone, yes or no?"

"Since you are so desperate to know, no, I haven't. I'm a lowly apprentice—I barely stepped out of the Warlock's library during my time with Chasan."

Ed nodded. He felt a pang of relief, but he forced it down. He wasn't done, yet.

"Alder?" Ed asked.

"I'm just a Bard," Alder said simply. "My only goal is to live an interesting life, and to witness *history* as it's made. I've never killed anyone in my life, human or not. I want to see history, not create it. That's a job for a Dungeon Lord."

"What about Kael? Did he sacrifice people?" In a way, Kael was his predecessor. Ed felt somewhat connected to the man he had only known through combat.

"Oh, yes." Lavy's smile appeared bitter. "Kael sacrificed many. Humans, kaftars, elves...he sacrificed Dark-aligned and Light-aligned without distinction. That, he did. But he never sacrificed an innocent. Not even once."

THAT'S GOING to have to be enough, Ed told himself. Why did he care, anyway, about what kind of person Kael had been?

"Why do *you* care?" Lavy asked.

"There won't be any sacrifices with me," Ed added.

Perhaps the smart move would've been to hide his intentions, to pretend he was on the same page as all the other Dungeon Lords the Bard and the Witch were accustomed to.

But how was he supposed to maintain a lie such as that? He didn't know those Dungeon Lords. He didn't know where Lotia was, or Heiliges, only that the two were enemies. He'd had no idea the Dungeon Lords had a reason to pillage and raid other than "because they're evil."

No, my only chance is to make things clear with them.

"That's fine with us," said Alder. Whatever he had seen in Ed's expression must've disappeared by now, because the Bard relaxed. "Not *all* Dungeon Lords go around performing human sacrifices to Dark gods. Some of them come from more civilized places than Lotia's countryside."

"And they live very little thanks to their sensitivities, Alder," Lavy said. "Their dungeons are smaller and weaker than their counterparts, and the other Dungeon Lords don't take to their presence kindly."

Ed raised his hands, though whether it was in surrender or to end the conversation, he was not sure. "That's a risk for later. Right now, I need time to process all this. It has been one hell of a day."

A waft of cold air breezed around him and made him shiver. His drones were done clearing the tunnel. Apparently, cleaning the debris had taken them a bit more effort than the altar's rock, but in the end it wasn't a challenge for whatever magic powered them. Ed could hear them skittering around whatever new location they had uncovered.

He chased the clacking of the drones, then realized he was going blind into pitch-black darkness, returned for an oil lamp, and retraced his steps. Alder and Lavy, even Klek, followed him after a while.

Their talk of sacrifices seemed to have put a damper on every-one's mood, and they spoke little after that, but curiosity is a powerful social glue.

"Supply storage," Alder whispered when his own lamp added strength to Ed's.

Ed nodded. It was a small room, made even smaller by a partial cave-in that had eaten up half the space. It was strewn with a bunch of rotten and broken matter that in another life had been grains, cloth, torches, and other things he could not identify.

The smell of rot was almost overpowering to him, to the point he had to avoid taking any deep breaths. But his companions seemed unaffected. Perhaps he was more used to city life than he had anticipated.

"Can the drones use this—" he gestured at the broken remains of the storage "—to build living quarters?"

"Dung and rot don't have much market value," Lavy pointed out. "Try asking for three straw beds; that should be easy enough to transmute."

Ed nodded, but instead of putting both drones to the task he sent only one. He looked away when he realized the little crea-ture ate the rot and the debris with the same glee it ate dirt. The other drone went helpfully to his side.

"I noticed you didn't have a fire outside," said Ed. He spoke to Alder, since he recalled it was the Bard who had a wilderness-related skill. "I don't know much about the wilderness, but a campfire is a must have in my world. Are Ivalis' monsters attracted to fire, or is there some other reason not to have one?"

Alder's features weren't helped by the lamp light. He looked gaunt and ghoulish, the lively glint of his eyes seeming to depend very much on sunlight. Perhaps he was just tired. "I was about to make one when the batblins attacked us. Some creatures are indeed attracted to fire, but *usually* they live deeper inside Hoia

Forest. And many more creatures won't go near a fire. In general, it is smart to have one."

"Then, I'm going to send this drone to build it for us. Lavy, you said they can gather resources, right? I assume that includes firewood."

To Ed, this was a crucial experiment, even if it didn't look like it. If the drones—and by extension, his power—knew how to create things he did not, that would be a huge advantage. When his companions made no objections, his drone went barking out of view in the direction of the forest.

Without its partner to help, the remaining drone worked much slower at cleaning the room, but it still made faster progress than a human could have. Once it had finished eating about a third of the debris and the trash, it stopped, fixated its gaze to the floor, and began dancing.

"What's it doing?" asked Ed.

"Transmutation," said Lavy. She had her back against a wall opposite Ed and Alder, and looked bored. "A terribly complex spell that even Master spellcasters have trouble with. To a drone, it's like breathing. I have no idea where all the dung it eats goes, but right now it's being converted into straw."

She was right. A loose pack of straw grew all at once, like a flower, in the spot where the drone was dancing. There were no fireworks, nor any special magic symbols, just a bunch of matter being created out of nowhere.

Once it was done, the drone admired its handiwork for a moment, nodded in satisfaction, and went back to clearing the room.

The bed didn't look particularly appealing. Ed walked over to it and inspected it. It was straw, alright, but it smelled of sulfur.

I'm going to need a blanket, he realized. *And a coat.* He had never expected Ivalis to be so cold. His character never complained when he walked through miles of snow dressed only in a silk robe.

But right now, Ed was very anxious for his drone to finish making that fire. Caves, as it turned out, were very cold.

What remained of the day went by like a blur. When the campfire was done, Ed, Lavy, and Alder ate what remained of their provisions next to the blaze. It was around that time that Ed discovered his drones sucked at making both blankets and shirts, but the itchy, sulfur-smelling, ill-fitted, ugly cloth was better than going around naked from the waist up.

Night arrived early, although he had no way of telling time except by the sun's position. Without anyone being in the mood to talk, Ed finally was able to catch a rest.

The sheer magnitude of what had happened started to dawn when stars that he never had seen in his entire life blanketed the night well beyond what his sight could reach. Ivalis' moon appeared bigger than Earth's, although it was only half-full. If he squinted, he could see its surface scratched by craters. It seemed to him like the face of some ancient, scarred god looking down on him.

For all he knew, the moon could be exactly that. There was much he didn't understand. For example, if said moon was really closer to Ivalis than to Earth, what did that do to the tides?

What did the ocean look like in this strange world?

He had been kidnapped by forces beyond his understanding and thrown into a world that wasn't his own.

Alder and Lavy had told him they didn't expect him to live long, even with the powers of a Dungeon Lord. He had much going against him. The forest that his campfire couldn't reach was bathed in impenetrable darkness, and it was silent in the way a lurking beast is silent. If Ed closed his eyes and went beyond the crackle of the fire, he could hear insects and the occasional screech of a bird. And very far away, he picked up the faint howl of a lone wolf.

It was him against Ivalis. Perhaps, he'd have the help of a Witch, a Bard, and a batblin, but that was it. He owed allegiance to no one—there was no one above him to drag him down. Whatever happened next would be only because of the decisions he had made.

A faint smile crept on his face. For the first time in his life, he felt free.

CHAPTER TEN

NIGHT CRAWLERS

I oan hated the night. As a Ranger, he knew all too well that most creatures hungry for human flesh went out of their holes after the sunset, looking for prey.

The need to be safe against the night's children had forced humanity to gather together in huts, then villages, then cities and kingdoms, to push back against the lurking monstrosities of the Vast Wetlands. Civilization developed of the constant struggle that humans fought against extinction.

He looked at the flimsy walls of Burrova, and shivered. What amounted to a big wooden fence could do little to save the village against the horrors of Starevos. As far as he was concerned, civilization was a lost cause. Mankind's cities would only last until a big enough monster awoke from its slumber and made its way from the Wetlands into the world of man...and started feeding.

Luckily enough for him, he was a Ranger. He could survive on his own.

"Do you see anything?" asked his watch-partner, Gallio, a gaunt man of thirty with a tired gait. "The torches destroy my eyesight."

"They're here," Ioan said, simply. He couldn't see them, even with his *Night Vision* talent, but he was skilled in the way of the predator. All the signs were there, if you knew what to look for.

At the skirts of the forest, a branch broke. A bush trembled without breeze. The silence was too deep, too absolute.

"They are here, and they're watching us," he added laconically.

"Do you reckon they might try and climb the walls tonight?" Gallio's breathing was heavy. He had always struck Ioan as a man used to pretending he wasn't scared.

Ioan held little love for the broken man, even if Gallio was an integral part of Burrova's survival—and thus, Ioan's own, for the time being.

"They're only scouts," he told Gallio. "Babies. But they are many. Testing our defenses, no doubt. Looking for a breach. If they find it, they'll strike."

"Disgusting," Gallio muttered. "Using their young as scouts and cannon-fodder...I've never seen a region so foul and so inclined to the Dark as Starevos."

"Nothing to do with the Dark." Ioan held little love for the Heiligian's moralizing. The Ranger was a Starevos native. "The Queen culls her spiderlings of the weak by using them in this way. If she didn't, her cluster would grow too big for Hoia to feed, and it would eat itself during the winter. This is nature, Sheriff, it has little to do with your Light and Dark."

The outskirts of Hoia Forest were silent and immobile to the untrained eye. But they were watching the two men as they stood atop the walls of Burrova. Ioan had no doubts about it. The scouts—the spiderlings—would go back to their Queen and report about what they had seen.

"So you say, Ioan," said Gallio. Ioan saw how the fingertips of the Sheriff caressed the old mace's hilt at his waist, a tick he had when he was nervous. "But my homeland doesn't have spiders as big as a grown man. You only find beings such as these the farther away we get from Alita's blessed temples. I'm of half-a-mind to summon the watch, gather our torches, and burn these monsters out right now. Let them report *that* to their Queen."

Ioan's own hand closed in a fist. If they moved now, instead of tomorrow, it would be disastrous. He had to drown out the impulse to backhand Gallio and shove him out of the crude parapet, out of the wall's safety and into the forest below. Depending on the way he fell, Gallio probably wouldn't even have time to scream.

Cowardly little man!

Ioan took a deep breath, then another, until he calmed down. This wasn't the wilderness, where it was every man for himself. This was civilization, while it lasted. He was not a savage.

"They are nightly creatures, these spiders," he explained. He relaxed his fist and patted the Sheriff on the back in a friendly manner. "I know how you feel, Gallio, but it's going to be safer for everyone to wait until the morrow. We'll cull their numbers then, while they're slow with sleep and their bellies are full."

Gallio nodded. "You're the expert, Ioan. Thank the Light Burrova can count on you. I can barely justify the bread I eat, as it is."

That was too much. Too much! Ioan broke the deep silence of the forest with a clear, joyful, belly-laugh. He patted the Sheriff— Burrova's broken Inquisitor—happily, and this time he meant it. "Come, Gallio, no sense in wasting away our energy staring at the enemy. Let's enjoy a mug of Andreena's brew before parting ways for the night. We'll have trouble enough at sunrise."

With that, both men left the palisade, Gallio just behind Ioan. The Sheriff glanced in the forest's direction one last time before reaching for the wooden steps.

Hoia was silent. And it was watching.

KLEK'S SCREAM saved their lives.

Ed was pulled apart from deep sleep by the terrified screech, and before he had any idea what was going on, he jumped up from his straw bunk with a small yell of his own. "What? What's going on?"

It was dark. Too dark. The city had never been so dark, the billboards, the street-posts, the malls that never closed made sure the night that filtered from his small window was never too deep.

This was different. The only light he had was the trembling, yellowish shine of an oil lamp almost empty. Besides the faint circle of light, he could see nothing. Klek's scream echoed back at him, and it carried with it scratching noises, constant, hollow. They came from inside the walls.

Ed's memory threw the events of the last day back at him. Ryan. Kharon. The pact. Ivalis. The campfire. Going to sleep feeling more tired than at any other point in his life.

Klek screamed again. "They're coming!"

"Klek!" Ed yelled at the batblin. Where was he? Somewhere far from the lamplight circle. "Who is coming?"

Opposite of Ed's bunk, Alder tried to jump up, missed his footing, slipped, and fell face-first into the ground. "Ouch! What's going on?"

Ed could hear Lavy cursing the gods as she stumbled to her feet.

The scratching noise was closer now. As Ed's eyes acclimated to the little light, he could see movement at the farthest wall of the cave. Tiny slivers of rock came loose and fell. Soon, cracks appeared on the surface. Small ones, but they were getting bigger by the second.

A tiny, hairy leg appeared in one of the cracks, casting an unnatural shadow in the yellow lamplight. It was followed by more legs—and a body the size of Ed's fist. It was covered in coarse black hair, with a pointy horn atop dozens of tiny eyes, and a pair of moist mandibles that clicked at the air.

The spider didn't come alone. Many more followed. Too many cracks to count, too many legs to count. Mandibles clicked here and there, the legs skittering around the walls in the dark far beyond Ed's reach.

"Spiders!" Lavy helpfully pointed out. The young Witch rushed at the tunnel that connected their improvised quarters with the Seat chamber. "Don't let them bite you!"

Ed could see the spiders dropping to the floor, *click click click,* rushing at the light. Alder screamed and ran, following Lavy's footsteps.

Klek screamed again.

"Klek!" Ed yelled. The batblin's voice came from somewhere at his right, away from the light. "Get out of here!"

Without thinking, Ed ran to the lamp in the middle of the room, just a few steps away from the nearest spiders, and tossed it into the upcoming cluster. The glass broke, and the oil spread, but failed to catch fire. A spider *screamed* in clear rage and pain. The blackness was absolute.

Could the spiders see in the dark?

Ed turned and ran back in a straight line at the tunnel's entrance while calling to his drones with a desperate mental command—

"Klek!" he said aloud. "I'll collapse the tunnel, get out!"

Something hard and hairy hit him as he ran, and Ed flew at the ground with a scared grunt. The spiders! They were going to surround him. He imagined the wet mandibles pinching his skin, *feeding*—

He had no idea where the tunnel's entrance was. Alder and Lavy were screaming at him, but he could not focus.

A small hand closed around his ankle. Ed instinctively kicked at it, and struck at something. The hand went away, there was a whimper, and the hand returned.

"Sir!" It was Klek's voice. "This way!"

Ed jumped up and fumbled around in the dark, but not for long. The batblin's hand grabbed his and pulled him in a random direction. Ed followed, while he heard the *click click click* come closer and closer.

The screams of Alder and Lavy became clearer, and he could see the faint reflection of Alder's lamp in the tunnel. Above Ed's head, his drones were biting furiously at the tunnel's roof.

Ed and Klek reached the Seat chamber followed by a wave of black creatures. The young Dungeon Lord caught a glimpse of Lavy looking for a weapon and Alder standing near the cave's exit, gesturing at them wildly to follow him.

I can't let them spread out of the tunnel, Ed thought with desperation. If he did so, they would just follow his group into the forest, and he wasn't sure they could outrun the spiderlings in the dead of night.

"Keep going, Klek!" Ed shouted as he shook away the batblin's hand and stood with his feet firmly planted right at the end of the tunnel. He turned toward the approaching spiders in time to see a boulder twice his size fall down near the middle of the tunnel and cover half of the available space.

The boulder crushed the closest spiders, and Ed was sure he imagined the dozens of little *crunches* more than he really heard them under the deafening boom of the rock as it fell. He had the faintest sensation of loss and was aware he was missing one of his drones.

He had just earned a bunch of experience.

- You have gained 35 experience (spiderling swarm, lethal encounter). Your unused experience is 56 and your total experience is 156.

The remaining spiders started climbing over the boulder and across the walls, undeterred.

Work faster! Ed thought. He activated his Evil Eye, and the green light gave the fist-sized spiders a ghost-like aura.

- Horned Spiderling. Exp: 1. Brawn: 1, Agility: 3, Spirit: 2, Endurance: 1, Mind and Charm: 1. Skills: Web-slinging: Basic (I), Pack Tactics: Improved (I)... Talents: Venom (Basic), Web (Basic), Spiderling.

The information blotted out Ed's entire field of vision. He pushed it away with a grunt and fought down panic, trying to recall the feeling he'd had when summoning the drones. The underground lines were right there at his feet...

"Edward, they're poisonous!" Alder warned him all the way from his position at the entrance of the tunnel. "Get away from them!"

I can't do that. It would be stupid. Their only shot was to stop them *now*.

"Sir!" Klek called somewhere behind him.

The spiders were almost upon him.

Ed used the only power he knew so far and threw a newly minted drone straight into their ranks. The drone came to life with a bark of glee, then realized his situation, turned to stare at Ed with betrayed eyes, and the spiders started to devour it.

Ed created a third drone next to the one at the ceiling. *Bring it down! Now!*

Working together, the drones freed another boulder. This one came down like the cave itself was collapsing. A tremor threatened to throw Ed off balance, into the feeding, frenzied spiderlings. He vaguely realized the critters were using their horns as much as their mandibles to break through the drone's skin.

The boulder fell away from the first one, smacked against it, and bounced into a bunch of spiders at Ed's side, making the half-eaten drone explode in mist in the process. A rain of smaller stones and dirt fell down on the tunnel, raising a cloud of dust that engulfed the surviving spiders, and Ed.

"Oh, shit," Ed coughed. He stumbled backward, fell on his ass, scrambled back up. He was vaguely aware that he was not done fighting. But he was weaponless. He was unarmed. His drones were useless except as a distraction—

He jumped away from the tunnel. He had done all he could. The dust began to settle. He realized only a small number of spiders were left on his side of the cave-in. He could see their black shapes as they *screamed* with their little voices, jumping and shaking off the dust as it fell on their eyes. They were blind and stunned.

Ed turned to Alder. "Get here! Bring the lamp, quick!"

The Bard stared as if Ed had gone mad, but Ed's frenzied gesturing made him react at last.

Lavy had found a big rock—her only weapon—and was rushing to Ed's side.

"No!" he told her. "Stay back!"

The spiders started to get their act together, to push forward through the dust.

I really hope I'm not about to blow us all up, Ed thought.

Alder reached his side, began to say something, but Ed caught the Bard's lamp and pushed him back. "Now get the hell away from the cave!"

"What?"

"You insane dung-eater!" Lavy exclaimed as her eyes widened when she saw the way Ed was holding the lamp. "Alder, run!"

With a speed born of desperation, Ed used his Evil Eye to bring up the familiar window of his talent options.

This one, he thought, focusing all his will into a single option. *This one!*

His body felt different, although he had little time to identify in what way.

Time was running out.

With his free hand, Ed caught Klek, raised him over his head, then passed the batblin over to Alder like a sack of potatoes. Then Ed ran the same way as his companions, away from the cloud of dust. The spiders followed.

They are so fast!

Alder and Lavy reached the exit and kept running. Ed stopped and looked over his shoulder at the cloud of dust he had left well behind, then saw the black shapes cackling madly while they ran after him.

The dust didn't extend much farther than the tunnel's mouth, and he was as far away from it as he dared. But he had absolutely no idea if that would be enough—

He threw the lamp with all his strength toward the dust. The tin lamp traced an arc through the air, almost in slow motion. No, *really* in slow motion. The lamp had stopped at the highest point of its path toward the dust.

A wave of heat *exploded* out of Ed's entire body, every muscle in his body roaring to life as if overdosed with medical-grade adrenaline.

His newly acquired *Improved Reflexes* had bought him three seconds.

He ran faster than he had ever run. He felt like his legs, his entire body, was already on fire, as if he carried the explosion inside himself.

It was very painful.

Three seconds.

Alder and Lavy were still running, halfway into the tunnel's entrance. It was, though, as if they were wading through water. Klek, who was slung over Alder's shoulders, was pointing at Ed, big eyes wide with astonishment.

Two seconds.

Ed crossed the distance to the tunnel's exit, screaming without realizing it, "—*shiiiiiiiiii*—"

One second.

Ed reached his companions, still screaming. His legs felt like they could snap at any moment, just break like twigs. Even the muscles in his arms and torso felt red-hot, right at his very limit.

He started to pass them just as time resumed its normal course.

A burst of heat and force hit him square at his back, enveloped him, passed him by. Ed felt the skin of his back sear. Air rushed out of his lungs, and he lost his footing.

He was vaguely aware he was rolling through the ground, hitting every part of his body with hard and sharp surfaces. He screamed, tried to grab a hold of *anything,* failed, started to roll downhill—

He came to a stunned stop in a damp patch of grass, his mind overwhelmed with pain and confusion.

How badly was he hurt? He had no way to know.

You're alive, he told himself. He groaned in pain. *At least you know that.*

He groaned again and clutched at his head with trembling hands. His forehead pulsated painfully and the world was spinning even with his eyes closed. His ears wouldn't stop ringing.

Opening his eyes revealed the starry sky mocking him far above. He was sick with nausea and heat—the heat! His legs were on fire, he had no doubt about it—but looking down revealed that apparently they weren't.

With an effort, he managed to sit down. His minions—his companions—were lying in the grass in similar states as his own. Alder was sprawled in the grass, complaining pitifully, with Klek lying on the Bard's head. The batblin's fur was simmering and smoked a bit, and he was just coming to his senses.

Lavy was already up, though her movements were erratic, similar to those of a drunk. She caught Ed's stunned gaze, shook her head, tried to speak, coughed, tried again:

"You insane dung-eater," she told him, her voice a bit too high. "If the dust had been just a *bit* more tightly packed, we would have been history!"

Ed answered her with a groan. He shook his head to clear it, patted at his ears, trying to get the ringing to die down.

Too hot! He turned off his Evil Eye—it was making him feel feverish—but not before reading the newest status screen.

- You have gained 15 experience (what remained of the spider swarm. Lethal encounter). Your unused experience is 21 and your total experience is 172.

He finally found the strength to speak, "Are you kidding me? Crushing them with a big rock earns me thirty points, but killing them with a goddamn explosion only gives me half of that? That is just not fair!"

CHAPTER ELEVEN

BURROVA

The morning found the four members of Ed's group licking their wounds at the simmering circle of the campfire. No one dared venture again into the cave, so Ed had a drone go and make sure it was safe, and that no spiderling reinforcements were coming.

Like Lavy had said, it was a miracle they were relatively unharmed. Ed's back had suffered some minor burns, and his new shirt had been reduced to rags, but the only other consequences of his crazy stunt had been some scraps and a lot of bruises.

His fever dissipated quickly once he turned down his Evil Eye, thanks to the cold air of Starevos. For a while, he didn't even shiver. He was content to catch his breath and let his body rest for a bit.

So, that's what it means for a talent to have a high energy drain. He wasn't feeling like using *improved reflexes* anytime soon.

Lavy had managed to escape the tunnel unharmed, though her hair was a mess of twigs, dirt, and smoke. For his part, Alder was as bruised as Ed, but most of the damage he had tactically absorbed by falling on his face.

Klek was covered in the shitty blankets Ed had ordered his two remaining drones—he could do three now, without any additional effort—to begin crafting non-stop out of transmuting twigs, fallen logs, and other forest-matter. The batblin had fallen asleep again without trouble and was even snoring a bit.

As far as Ed was concerned, the little guy deserved the rest. Klek had gained fifteen experience points yesterday when his cloud had betrayed him and left him at the mercy of the humans. Back at the cave, when Ed had been lost in the darkness and about to be surrounded by spiders, the batblin had used those fifteen points to buy the talent *echolocation*, which he had used to find Ed and lead him to the tunnel.

The Bard nursed his swollen nose and shivered. "You said you were a new Dungeon Lord? I hardly believe it—*fireball* is at least an improved-level spell."

"That wasn't a spell," Lavy said. "Wherever this Earth is, it seems people are smart enough to know dust is flammable, but not smart enough to know not to make an explosion in front of their faces."

Ed sighed. According to his stats, he was almost twice as experienced as he had been a day ago. That didn't feel right.

"Ah, to be fair," said Alder. "I kinda miss the explosion now. I can barely feel my toes. How are the blankets coming along, drone friends? You think you can hurry a little?"

The two drones hissed at him and spat on the blanket they were working on.

"That's some attitude," Alder complained. "The fabric they make barely holds together. I would think they at least should show some humility."

"They're useful only for making dungeon-related constructions," said Lavy. "Small pieces aren't their forte, much less mundane things like blankets or clothes. Of course they don't like it."

"Everyone's a critic," said Ed. He was feeling much better now, but he was hungry and thirsty. And he had recently discovered one of the less-frequently mentioned disadvantages of living in a medieval-ish world like Ivalis. Having to relieve himself in some damp forest with only dry leaves as a method for hygiene had soured his mood instantly.

First chance I get, he thought, *I'm going to figure out how to build a serviceable bathroom.*

But he had more urgent matters to attend to.

"We need to leave," he told his companions. "Sooner, I think, rather than later."

"Do we?" asked Lavy. She didn't seem to be in the mood for walking.

"We don't know if there's more spiders where those came from," said Ed. "More could come back."

"They were spiders," said Alder. "They were hunting. There's no need to overthink it. They're dead now, and I have fifteen new experience points to show for it."

That didn't sit right with Ed. "I know I'm new to Ivalis, and it may work in ways I'm not even aware of," he said. "But...That many spiders? There were hundreds of them, and their status said they were only babies. Spiderlings. Where the hell are you going to find food to feed a swarm like that? Is Hoia Forest really that big? What I am trying to say is...their behavior doesn't strike me as normal. What do you think?"

"Hoia is huge," said Alder, extending his arms over his head. "Really huge. I think hundreds of fully grown horned spiders could easily find food here."

Ed nodded. The Bard had *survival* as a skill, and he didn't, so that was the end of the discussion.

"You're wrong," said Klek under his fort of blankets. "Spiders get to grow very big. As big as a human. Some as big as a horse. Thousands of them could strip the forest bare."

"Ah, yeah? What do you know, anyway?" Alder said.

"Sometimes they eat batblin." Klek shrugged. "Adults hunt in groups of two to...four. Not hundreds. They like to chase us around, toy with us. Pick a fat batblin, pierce him with their horns, paralyze him with venom, cover him in webs, then they bring it back to their lair to feed on his insides. The spiderlings are disposable, they are not hunters. This was not normal."

Alder looked at the batblin, then at Ed. He made a gesture as if he was gagging. "Well, I don't know, then. I've never seen an adult spider. I hope I never have to after tonight."

Ed glanced at the forest, mulling over Klek's words.

Would I even see them coming?

One of his companions had said there was a village nearby, he recalled. The group's provisions had been lost during the explosion, in any case, and none of them were equipped to hunt.

The idea of going back to civilization both scared and excited Ed. The Witch, the Bard, and the batblin were, so far, his only links to the world of Ivalis—not counting the things that wanted to eat him. Although the idea of staying hidden in the scorched cave had some primal appeal, it wasn't a hard decision.

He stood up. "We'll go to that village you mentioned. At the very least, we can come back with weapons, though we don't have to come back at all. There ought to be a place in Starevos that's not infested with spiders, right?"

Lavy grunted and jerked up. One of the pants of her trousers was slightly torn at the side, revealing pale, almost blue-ish skin. "I would drown a baby in exchange for a hot breakfast. What are you waiting for, Bard? Let's go!"

THE CAVE'S entrance had been hidden at the edges of a cliff southwest of Burrova, close to the wilder parts of Hoia Forest, but not deep enough that its most lethal inhabitants would take an interest in the dungeon. In theory.

While Ed and his companions strutted through the forest,

Alder and Lavy gave him all the background information he'd need to pass himself as a normal human.

"First of all, unless you go around using your Evil Eye, people won't have a way to tell you're a Dungeon Lord. There *are* spells that could identify you—more now that you don't have ways of countering them. But Burrova's far enough from Heiliges that there isn't any Inquisitor or Cleric powerful enough to cast them," said Lavy. She was covered head to toe in the crappy, drone-made blankets, same as Alder and Ed.

If someone met them on the road, Ed's procession would've been a ridiculous sight. But Ed was *warm* with his blankets, and that was all he cared about.

"This region is called Starevos," Lavy went on, gesturing to the surrounding space. "It's a mountainous region with Lotia to the south-east and the Vast Wetlands far, far to the south. It's a tough, cold place where farming is hard and monsters have not yet learned to fear humans' settlements, so there are frequent attacks. Most of those monsters are venomous."

"And they like to eat batblin," added Klek, who was walking next to Ed. The small batblin spoke little, instead being content with staring deeply at the three humans, like he was studying them or trying to figure them out. While the batblin didn't appear to be affected by the cold, he was still enveloped in the blankets. Ed guessed that Klek may simply enjoy having clothes besides his dirty loincloth.

"Why would anyone want to live here?" asked Ed. He glanced at the shed leaves, branches, and bark that formed the detritus of the forest's soil.

"For the adventure!" declared Alder. "A wild region, with lots of *possibility!* A place where history is made, where there are still Dungeon Lords other than the Lotians, where men from another worlds are transported so they can find their fortune! Oh, Starevos—the wild frontier where death and love live in harmony!"

He looked at Ed and Lavy expectantly. When neither reacted, he grimaced and said, "That was a quote from Archbard Estanislao—"

"Sorry, I'm not from around here, remember?" Ed told him.

"Don't listen to him. Alder's here more for the women than for the *wild frontier*," Lavy said with a mocking grin.

"Well, there are different kind of wild frontiers," Alder said. "Different kinds of men are required for each. My kind of frontier involves exotic women with skin of bronze, dark hair, and deep eyes where a man can either find redemption, or lose himself—"

"Yeah, save the speech for them," Lavy said with a laugh. "Perhaps there's still a woman in Burrova that hasn't heard it, yet."

Ed laughed, too, though he had little idea about his companions' activities other than that they used to be Kael's minions. He realized he knew little to nothing about them.

There was something in the cold air of the forest that made it very different from the air he was used to in Earth. Hoia's breeze carried with it so many aromas—Ed couldn't recognize them all. He smelled leaves and other vegetation slowly decomposing, humidity, mud, and the smell of trees whose names he couldn't pinpoint.

Are there trees like these back in my world? He wondered.

"In short," Lavy resumed their conversation, "Burrova is one of many Heiligian outposts in Starevos. Right now, they have little strategic value, but the Militant Church hopes that they will manage to tame Alder's *wild frontier* after enough years. If they succeed, they'll gain a stronghold to threaten Lotia by ground, instead of having to rely on the Heiligian Navy."

I could use a map, thought Ed. But he was beginning to get an idea about the politics of this new world. At least he wasn't as clueless as he had been yesterday. Now, he recognized some names.

"Burrova's population is mostly Heiligian and natives of the region, so you'll need a good cover if you don't want people to suspect you," Lavy went on. "What do you think, Alder, could we pass Lord Edward for a Lotian?"

"The hair color is right, but his eyes are too dark. He won't pass for Heiligian, either, though; he lacks the mannerisms, the grace, the education, and the sensitivity. He wouldn't fool anyone for a second."

"Well, fuck you too," Ed muttered.

"I agree, Alder," said Lavy. "How about we say he's from Constantina? That shouldn't get him many questions. No one likes Constantina."

"Undercity, huh?" said Alder. "Well, that can work. He lacks the fishy smell."

"He doesn't have to be a harbor worker."

"That's not what I meant," said Alder. "As the saying goes, 'Never sleep with your purse and neck bared in Undercity, unless you want both cut before morning.' "

Lavy laughed again. Then, both she and Alder looked at Ed, who was staring at them with a completely clueless expression. They laughed harder at that.

"We'll have to do something about these references, Alder," groaned Ed. "You keep forgetting I can't understand them."

"Eh," said Alder. "Explaining them would kill the joke."

REACHING Burrova took them much longer than it should have, because they decided on a long detour through the forest so they could arrive at the village from the east, instead of the south.

When they were close to the east road, Alder and Lavy explained their covers to Ed. She pretended to be Alder's wife, which helped her avoid suspicion because of her obvious Lotian heritage. Since Kael's last stand, which had happened three days ago, they had visited Burrova for provisions at least once, pretending to be travelers from neighboring towns.

"We didn't stay for long, though," said Alder. "A bunch of

survivors from the Kael raid, mostly apprentices like us, tried to get past outposts like Burrova with the intention of reaching Undercity and scrambling away through Stormbreaker Harbor. Of course, they got captured by the militia within minutes, and the lot of them got shipped to the galleys, or the gallows. We only managed to trick them because I'm obviously a Heiligian citizen, and even then it was close. We'll need a very good story to justify why we're still here, though. Don't worry about that. As a Bard, coming up with good stories is my job."

Ed nodded, then asked, "Why try to go to Undercity? That's to the north, right? Why not go the other way, to Lotia?"

"By the way," Lavy chimed in, "don't ask questions like that when we reach Burrova. It will mark you without a doubt as a stranger from another world, and those are usually brought here by Dark magic."

"Duly noted. Thanks for the heads-up."

"The reason," added Alder, "is that the south is no-man's land. Too close to the Vast Wetlands. You'd need an army to get through. A bunch of apprentices, without provisions or adequate clothing? I don't think they'd manage to get past Hoia Forest, much less reach the mountains. No, the only realistic way to reach Lotia is through the east, and that's a trip of many, many months through kaftar territories. Hell, even *elvenlands,* and those may be as dangerous as the Wetlands, according to some. It's still an impossible venture for a bunch of apprentices.

After Alder was done with his explanation, Ed realized that all the Bard had said was true for the three of them, too. It seemed that Kharon had chosen to drop Ed right in the middle of the action.

Kharon had said that Starevos was a good place for a young Dungeon Lord to grow. To Ed, it seemed that such strength came heavy with risk. It wouldn't be easy to leave Starevos. He was, essentially, trapped.

Power came with a cost.

Not like I have somewhere else to be, he thought. If he wanted to survive in Ivalis, he must start by surviving Starevos and all its dangers.

Soon, the road to Burrova was visible through the tree-line. As far as Ed knew, they had been walking for hours, but the day still hadn't lost the sleepy air of a cold morning. His legs and arms still pulsated painfully, and he was sure he'd suffer from cramps tomorrow. Still, the sight of the road reinvigorated him.

"We'll have to drop the blankets here," said Lavy. "They're clearly not man-made. If anyone asks why you're shirtless, tell them you lost yours while taking a bath in the river. They'll think you're an idiot, but that's better than raising suspicion."

They braced themselves for the bite of the cold to return to their bodies. It wasn't as brutal as it had been in the morning, but Ed's bruised chest still turned an unhealthy shade of blue.

"What about Klek?" he asked. "Will he be safe?"

"Say he's your slave," said Lavy. "He's a batblin, so people won't care. And you're from Undercity, they'll expect you to be quirky—such as using a batblin as a guide."

Ed neatly placed the knowledge that there was slavery in Ivalis in a mental box of "things to worry about later."

"I'll do it," said Klek. "Should help avoid me getting shot on sight."

And that was that.

They reached Burrova not long afterward. Ed had been expecting the standard fantasy village of movies and videogames —including Ivalis Online—so in a way, he found both what he did and didn't anticipate.

Burrova appeared small to his eyes, which were accustomed to the sprawling metropolises of Earth. It was small, and isolated from the outside world by a big wooden fence as tall as five or six men.

Palisade, his brain offered the adequate word. *That's a palisade.*

The idea of using wood as a defense had never appealed to

him before. It sounded like a flimsy, cheaper alternative to stone walls, but seeing the real thing made him adjust his opinion a bit.

Burrova's palisade didn't look flimsy. It had *depth* to it, and enough space for two or three men to walk comfortably shoulder to shoulder at the top of it. Two men were standing in such way over the entrance, which was used partly as a bridge that could be raised, if need arose, by pulling on thick ropes that connected it to the palisade.

When Ed and his companions got close enough to Burrova that Ed could see the white in the sentinels' eyes, they reached other people using the dirt road, or secondary ones connected to it. They were farmers, by the looks of it, with strong hands and backs bent by years of heavy work. Their skin was bronze, as Alder had described. They carried baskets filled with vegetables, tied to their backs and shoulders by straps. Some baskets looked as heavy as Ed himself, and the farmers carrying them were often old ladies who seemed to have little trouble with the weight.

The clothing was made of wool, like Alder and Lavy's simple dresses, but everyone else wore many more layers over the tunics. Brown capes, turned almost white by the sun, thick overalls that covered shoulders and arms. Old people wore several of them, one over the other. A few wore pelts, from animals Ed didn't recognize, over the attire.

It looked, to Ed, very uncomfortable and itchy. It also looked warm. He wished he had a pair of those overalls. Even a shirt would've been nice. He was so cold he could've used his nipples to cut glass.

While he walked alongside the farmers, he garnered as much curious looks as Klek, who was almost hugging Ed's leg and staring closely at the ground. Some farmers scowled at them, but no one said anything.

"Everyone is too busy with their own shit to bother us, and we don't seem like a threat," explained Alder with a whisper. "Bothering us is the sentinel's job."

Once the four of them reached the wooden bridge, the sentinels standing over the palisade gestured at them to stop, while letting the farmers close to them go into the village.

All the villagers who carried goods with them were then stopped by a third sentinel, this one guarding the entrance. Most of the villagers grunted and complained loudly at this third man, and some even went red in the face, but all of them tossed small, green rings or what looked like scraps of metal, into a box the sentinel carried with him. The sentinel then handed them a small parchment from a pile next to the box, and the farmers finally entered the market.

"Halt!" said one of the sentinels atop the palisade. He was wearing a dirty leather coat and a dented over-sized helmet the shape of a bowl. He was younger than Ed by several years, and malnourished in a way the Earthling couldn't exactly relate to. The sentinel was missing several teeth and the others were clearly rotten. His face was scarred with pockmarks and exuded such a rank of acrid booze that Ed could smell him without trouble. "You came to buy, or to sell?"

"I've seen you two before," said the other sentinel. He was a bit older, with more meat to his bones. He had a nasty scar that crossed his mouth and made him look like he was scowling constantly. His demeanor wasn't aggressive, though. Just curious. "Yesterday, I reckon. You said you came from Prolav, didn't you? What are you still doing here, and who is this shirtless mongrel you have with you? And, by Alita, is that a batblin he has with him?"

Alder greeted both guards with a wave. "Hi there, friends! The mongrel is an Undercity fellow, Edward, who we found lost. We brought him here so he didn't get killed by kaftars or the spiders. As you can see, he has had such bad luck that he even managed to lose his shirt. The batblin's name is Klek, and he was supposed to be our friend's guide through the wilderness. I'm sure you can guess how that went. The smelly critter was also born and raised in Undercity and has never set foot into Starevos' wilderness. Edward bought him for half a vyfara."

As if on cue, Klek took a few steps away from Ed and did a crude curtsy at the sentinels. "Klek wants to be useful!"

A small part of Ed erupted in cold anger, and he had to remind himself it was all an act.

The sentinels laughed. The same one from before said, "An Undercity dimwit, then! Why have you ventured here, friend Edward? Surely our humble village is a sad substitute for Stormbreaker's whorehouses."

Ed lacked Alder's talent for improvisation. He stared at the sentinel with his mouth open for a second, and then he started, "Uh, greetings, ah, good...sir—"

He heard Lavy groan under her breath.

"I came all the way here to do business. You see, I am—" Ed went on. One second too late, he realized he had absolutely no idea what *business* could mean in this world. He could *assume* Burrova and Undercity were the standard fantasy settlements, but he had assumed as such before, and he had been wrong. The guards would expect an answer that made sense, and if he said something strange, they would be very suspicious.

He and Lavy exchanged panicking glances while Alder stared at the sentinels with a shiny smile.

Ed activated his *improved reflexes*. Instead of moving, he stood frozen in place and *thought* for a very long second.

He frantically looked back at all the information he had gathered from his companions' descriptions and chitchat, and to the precious little lore he had found by playing Ivalis Online.

In a way, in gaming terms, this was a lore test. Some games liked to reward players that listened to the NPC dialogue by having small tests that only a player who had paid attention could solve. The sentinels, to Ed, were a timed test with more dire consequences than usual—because real life had no respawns, and no savepoints.

I'm a farmer? No, I don't look like one. Undercity is a port, anyway—

A sailor? No idea what I'm doing here, then—

Even though he wasn't moving, all the muscles in his body were taut and tense and exuding so much heat it was overwhelming. Thinking, using the *reflexes*, required a constant effort.

A second had already passed. He watched the sentinel's expressions change in slow motion.

Merchant? I have no goods. Perhaps I lost them? To what?

Thinking of merchants getting assaulted made him think of monsters, and merchants and monsters made him think of...

"I am an adventurer," he proclaimed triumphantly, his voice firm and sure. "I'm here in search of worthy work—if the pay is good."

He saw the tension leave Lavy's body. The sentinels' smiles returned to their faces.

"Ah, an Undercity cutthroat fancying himself a great hero," said the first sentinel, the one with the pockmarks. "Let me guess, you owe money to some unsavory character and you're no longer welcome in the city? Don't even think about starting trouble here, *adventurer.*"

Ed shrugged, which the sentinels took as confirmation. They talked with each other for a brief moment, and then the second one nodded at Ed and his companions and gestured for them to cross the bridge.

"This may be your lucky day, friend Edward," the second sentinel told him. "There's work to be had this side of the drawbridge, if you're up for it. Talk to Ranger Ioan, or to the woman, Kes. They'll go spider-hunting in only a few hours. Someone as —*ahem*—tough as you surely won't have any problems with that?"

The young Dungeon Lord had to make an effort not to burst out laughing. He could get paid for spider-hunting?

Hell, I would've done it for free!

"Thanks for the tip," he said. "As it turns out, I've a score to settle with some spiders. See you around, friends."

He crossed the drawbridge, leading the way. Alder caught up with him, still smiling placidly, but there was panic in his eyes.

The Bard managed to whisper to Ed from the corner of his mouth, "Uh, surely, you aren't thinking on taking that offer, right?"

Ed grinned widely and winked at him. "Haven't you heard? I'm an adventurer now. Killing monsters is what adventurers do."

If someone had poured a bucket of ice-cold water on Alder's head, his expression would've been the same as in that instant. "Alita, have mercy on my pour soul."

Lavy caught up with them and clung to the arm of her "husband" with a dreamy expression. Her eyes, though, glinted maliciously.

"If you want her mercy, perhaps you should stop swearing on your goddess' tits every time things don't go your way, my dear," she said.

CHAPTER TWELVE

ADVENTURERS

The first impression Ed had of Burrova was that it didn't justify the palisade built around it. The ground was completely covered by a thick crust of mud, and the dirt road that was the main avenue was kept free of the filth only by the constant passing of hundreds of feet.

The buildings were sparse, and instead of the small huts that Ed was expecting to see, they were all built of planks, a clay-like mixture, and stone. They were mostly stores, as evidenced by the small, carved signs next to their fronts.

"Not what you imagined?" asked Lavy while they waded through a small sea of farmers, vendors, and other characters.

"I try not to expect anything," said Ed, shrugging. "But where are the homes?"

He was certain that the entirety of Burrova could fit within a single block of the city he had lived in all his life.

It wasn't *empty,* though. On the contrary, the flow of people was constant, and so was their *smell.* Ed had to dodge and push his way among a crowd of farmers that were possessed by a happy frenzy of activity. They recognized each other in the crowd, shouted greetings or traded insults, made bartering deals for later.

Klek clutched at Ed's leg. The young Dungeon Lord glanced at the batblin and realized that, to Klek, this was the biggest gathering of people he had ever seen in his entire life. The batblin looked everywhere, like he expected to be drawn and quartered at any second. Ed placed a protective hand on the batblin's coarse shoulder and made sure to keep the guy away from kicks and shoves.

"Not many live behind the palisade," Lavy said, still hugging Alder's forearm like she was a newlywed. "Technically, this is Burrova's heart, not the village itself. Almost everyone you see around here lives in farms north of here, away from the forest and the roaming kaftar bands."

Something like a market, he thought. Then he corrected himself. This was the *marketplace,* the one upon which all modern versions were based. It was the heart of civilization.

Not everyone carried food, Ed realized. Some carried other materials: cloth, leather, tools, and sacks of what looked like heavy, colored dust that had to be transported in crude cartwheels.

I think that's carbon, he guessed. The man who pushed that cartwheel cursed and elbowed his way through the crowd and went straight to one of the buildings, a low, open-fronted shed with a furnace right in the middle of it. Ed counted five apprentices bent over different tools, a blacksmith overseeing them. He was a huge man covered in carbon-grime.

"Come," said Alder. "We need food, and clothes for you."

"You have money?" asked Ed.

"What little we could scavenge from Kael's dungeon before it collapsed," Alder said. "Just a few vyfaras. It should be enough for today."

Another reason to find work, thought Ed.

The crowd wasn't walking aimlessly, but with a purpose. The

dirt avenue led them straight to the heart of Burrova, a wide circle with only one building near its center. The ground there had been stripped bare of grass or vegetation by the steps of a multitude of people, day after day.

The smell of people was more pungent there, and the air was filled with acrid sweat, spilled alcohol, and other disgusting substances. The shock of switching from the pure forest air to this almost made Ed dizzy. He shook his head to clear it and dove into the crowd with a confidence he didn't feel.

He was a city guy. He knew, to the very core of his being, that the trick to surviving huge gatherings of people was to pretend he had somewhere to go, and then act accordingly.

So, he followed Alder and Lavy looking like he was in his element, while on the inside he was doing his best to get used to the heat and the smell of the crowd.

Some people set their goods straight on the ground over rugged pieces of cloth. Others carried a series of planks and leather strips on their backs that they used to create store stands in minutes. The market, right in front of Ed's eyes, slowly took shape.

It was like watching a plant grow in fast-forward. Stands sprouted here and there, the crowd shifted and divided to give space to the vendors on the ground. The smell of people was slowly fought back by others more pleasant.

"This is like magic," said Klek. "So much food..."

Apple pies, charred veggies, fresh loaves of bread, wheels of cheese the size of a child, and milk so thick it may as well be cream. There were cauldrons as big as a man—Ed couldn't fathom how they were carried—filled to the brim with soups whose vapor filled the air with meaty promises.

"Oh, God," Ed muttered. "I'm so hungry."

Alder patted him on the back, "Let's go fill our stomachs, then —courtesy of Kael's coffers. Perhaps, once your belly is full, your good judgment will return and you'll rethink your...adventuring ideas."

"Buy a tunic first," said Lavy. "And remember, you're supposed to pay *us,* not the other way around. Don't get used to this, my Lor —ahem—friend Edward."

"Duly noted," said Ed, who at this point was willing to sell a kingdom for one of those sensual meat pies a couple stands to his left.

Alder followed his gaze. "Sorry, that's a bit out of our budget. It's pottage for us, my brave leader. Don't worry, it's quite good. I know a gal who has been refilling the same cauldron for years without stopping, and the flavor is quite the delicacy."

The same cauldron for years, Ed thought. He sighed, closed his eyes so no one would see the flash of green, and bought *resist disease* right then and there. He was left with only six free points of experience, setting him even farther away from his goal of getting *spellcasting.*

But risking an early death due to dysentery—or whatever sickness was surely fostering around Burrova—would be an extremely dumb way to end his adventuring. He was from another world, and for all he knew, he was missing centuries of immunological responses the surrounding people already had.

I just hope my presence here isn't going to kill them by giving them the flu.

That would *definitely* count as cheating on the side of Murmur and Kharon, if that was how they planned to come ahead on their gamble.

After that, Alder got him a tunic exactly like his and Lavy's, and the four of them devoured the stew a kind old lady served them in exchange for a few green rings from Alder's purse.

The stew was dense with fat, sprinkled with vegetables and the occasional chunk of tendon or meat-related product— without actually being meat. It didn't *look* palatable, or even all that healthy, but the taste was passable.

Ed ate until he was full. He was *raving* hungry, even if he hadn't gone all that long without eating. Using his *improved reflexes* twice in a day had its cost, it seemed.

The only one who really seemed to enjoy the stew was Klek. The batblin ate and ate and ate until there was a noticeable bump in his belly. Granted, he was smaller than the humans, so he only needed two full portions to be satisfied. The batblin burped with a drowsy, dreamy expression and used his furry hand to wipe away the remains of stew from his snout-like mouth.

"Thanks for the food," Ed told his two friends and the old lady. Now that his stomach was full, his mood was greatly improved. "Ma'am, could you point us in the direction of Ranger Ioan? I heard he was in need of adventurers."

Alder groaned. "Here we go. Not even time for a healthy digestion."

The lady pointed them to the single building near the center of the marketplace and said it was the town hall. Ed thanked her and they went on their way.

"Are you sure about this, Edward?" asked Lavy while they waded through the crowd. It was nearing midday, and the market crowd was in full swing, a storm of activity unlike anything Ed had ever seen before. "Neither of us are fighters; I'm not sure the Ranger will even take us."

"Oh, I hope he won't," said Alder.

"We need money, don't we?" Ed said. "But that's not all. I've been thinking, this adventuring business may be the answer we're looking for."

"What do you mean?" Lavy asked.

"Well, I'm not planning on living hidden in a cave my entire life," Ed said. "That's not why I'm here. But we can't leave Starevos unless we reach Undercity, right?"

"Yes," said Alder. "Although, I'm not sure how 'let's get killed by a horned spider' will help us with that."

"Simple. People trust adventurers, don't they? We stay around for a while, we get paid, we help people out, and earn experience points while we do so," said Ed. "Eventually, I just tell people I'm going to return to Constantina and you're coming with me. When we make the trip, we're stronger, we're well known, and we have some coin. What's not to like?"

"I feel like you aren't listening to the 'getting eaten by spiders' part of my argument."

That wasn't Ed's only reason. He believed the spider attack wasn't just a random occurrence, like Alder had insisted. If Burrova was getting ready to attack the monsters, it meant something had gone down the night before.

Ed couldn't just ignore it. An attack like that, the same night that he had been transported to Ivalis?

It couldn't be a coincidence.

"You don't have to come if you don't want," said Ed. "Just return to the cave, or stay here. I'll find you."

"Without us, you'll get killed," Lavy pointed out. "And I don't believe we're getting a replacement Dungeon Lo—*ahem*, a replacement—anytime soon. So, I'm going with you, but I'll stay far from the action, and remember, I'm only worth two spells. After those, I'm going to run away, and you'll be on your own."

Alder sighed. "Rushing headlong into danger is part of the Bardic way of life. I just wish it didn't have to be spiders. I'm deathly allergic to having hundreds of eggs injected into my guts."

THE TOWN HALL was wider than it was tall, built out of wooden planks without varnish or other treatment, giving Ed the impression it had been hastily built and Burrova had sort of sprouted around it. The hall was a good fit for the rest of the place. The only building constructed out of stone was a small church next to the western wall of Burrova.

There was an elderly clerk sitting at a crude bench next to the entrance to the hall. He was dressed in the fashion and demeanor of bureaucrats everywhere, and he barely gave Ed a second glance when the young Dungeon Lord approached him.

"We're looking for Ranger Ioan," Ed said. "For the spider business."

"Hum," the clerk said. "He's at the back, I guess."

That was all he said. He went back to grazing, or whatever he was doing.

Ed forced away the urge to choke the man and went in the direction implied.

The inside of the hall was bursting with a different kind of activity than the market. Around eight or so villagers were lazily sitting or standing in front of a desk to the right of the entrance. Behind the desk, a portly man dressed in a more expensive version of the villagers' tunic was frowning at one angry woman while taking notes on a parchment.

"That's Governor Brett," Lavy whispered at Ed. "The hall doubles as his manor. He was appointed by Heiliges to run Burrova as some kind of punishment. No idea as to what. Probably whore-related, if you ask me."

Judging from Brett's expression, the punishment had been effective. From what Ed managed to put together from their conversation, he and the woman were arguing about chickens.

"All devoured," the woman exclaimed, "and nothing left but entrails and feathers. Someone has to pay for this!"

"If you catch the fox," Governor Brett said tiredly, "I'm sure you will punish it effectively."

"No fox," said the woman. "Someone opened the corral's door, I know it—"

"Your husband is a drunkard, Marya. Perhaps the culprit is within your own home."

"Don't try to shift the blame on my dung-brained husband,

Brett. You and I know Nicolai spent the night with the shoemaker—"

Lavy nudged Ed along, and he realized he had stopped to eavesdrop, "Let's go, oh mighty adventurer. I fear if you keep listening, we may end up involved in a most noble chicken-related quest."

Ed lost the trail of the conversation, mostly due to Alder's snickering, and along with Klek they reached the back of the hall.

They arrived at a fenced garden, which doubled as storage for the hall. Ed saw rusting farming equipment, such as harnesses and plows, next to moss-covered sacks of grain and clay pots filled with stagnant water.

A small group was gathered at the other end of the garden, inside the shade offered by an oak that was either malnourished or still young.

This group consisted of about five people, three men and two women. They were standing in a circle, and there was a rack of weapons in the middle of the gathering. When the group saw Ed and his companions approach, the conversation died down.

"Oy," said Alder, "good-day, friends. We're looking for Ranger Ioan. We heard he's in the need for adventurers."

That earned them a bunch of looks and expressions, none of them positive. Five pairs of eyes passed over Ed, and he had the clear sensation that what they found wasn't all that positive.

"Here's Ioan," said one of the men, a sun-bitten man with an unkempt, auburn beard of several days. He smelled strongly of mint and wine. "I am, indeed, in search of adventurers, though I don't see any around here."

Ed almost blushed. The difference between his group and Ioan's was clear. The Ranger wasn't wearing the plain, cheap tunic of the market—he was dressed in black, curated leather armor damaged by time and, perhaps, battle. Over it, he wore a dark green cape with a cowl pulled down, of an almost fluid material that seemed to flow heroically in the breeze. At the

Ranger's hips, half-hidden by the cape, were the hilts of at least two swords, tough and efficient, and strapped across his chest were four black knives. On his back, he carried a quiver and a carved short-bow.

The woman closest to him shared his tanned skin, had short hair tied in braids, and was dressed almost exactly like him, down to the cape.

The other three weren't Rangers, but they were armed and armored, and, in short, they all looked like adventurers should.

I wonder how many experience points they have, Ed thought. His eyes itched with the desire to activate his Evil Eye and see for himself. He wished he knew how Lavy or Alder, who didn't have his power, managed to see stats themselves.

"Perhaps the batblin is the hero, and the others are his servants," said another man, standing the end of the group. He could've been Ioan's cousin or brother, since they shared similar features; but he was wearing the guard uniform: cheap leather at the chest, leather braces, a wooden mace hanging by a strap at the hip, and a cheap red tunic over it all.

"Hilarious," Lavy muttered, rolling her eyes. "Can't we leave them to become spider-food, now?"

"Mind your manners, Vasil," said the third man. He was the shortest of them all and had long, pale blond hair that was almost white, cut sleek. He was tanned, strong, and had a powerful chin that would've earned him an acting job back on Earth. His back was tense, and he was armored like Vasil, only he was wearing a hardened leather ensemble and his mace was steel, and engraved with fine runes that Ed couldn't decipher. Instead of a red tunic, his was purple, and had more in common with silk than with wool. It was clear, though, that it had seen better days, and the fabric was patched and sewed all over.

"*We* are the adventurers," said Ed. He decided not to let the taunting get to his head. For all he knew, this was how warriors talked to each other. Yeah, that sounded right. They were sizing him up. "You want help hunting spiders, we want to get paid. Are we doing this, or what? I don't have all day to waste, I could be getting drunk right now."

Alder whispered at him, "You almost sounded like an Under-city cutthroat, Edward. Nice try."

I've had lots of practice, Ed thought. Granted, those were fictional games, and the people standing in front of him didn't look fictional at all. So, he decided to take the macho bullshit up a notch, to be sure.

"And, pray tell," said Ioan, "how do you intend to hunt spiders if you're not carrying any weapons?"

"I see there's enough weapons in that rack over there." Ed pointed to the middle of the circle. "More than enough for me and my companions, unless you're planning on carrying that lance inside your ass. In which case, you should have told the guard this was a pleasure stroll, and not business."

The Ranger's eyes widened at hearing that, and for a moment Ed feared he had overdone it. He held no doubts about what the results of a fight with the Ranger would be.

But instead, Ioan scowled and turned to the man in the purple robe. "You know something, Gallio? I've seen spawns of the Vast Wetlands that would curl the blood of a grown man, but there's nothing as foul and disgusting as the kind of men Under-city breeds."

Gallio smirked, "At least he's here looking for work and not for trouble, Ioan. I say we give them a chance. The Light is not one to deny honest work for anyone who asks for it. And these three look old enough to decide if they want to risk their lives or not."

Ioan shrugged and said, "I defer to the wisdom of your gods, then. I hope the Light will assume responsibility when they're killed."

Ed opened his mouth to speak, but Ioan cut him off by turning sharply to him. "I'll assume you're ready to go. Daylight is our ally against the horned spiders, so wasting it is not an option. I'll also assume you know what you're getting yourself into, friend adventurer. Your stats don't seem all that impressive to me, and judging from your *endurance*, you aren't able to use those *improved reflexes* more than a couple times. Know that we won't slow down for you, and if we leave you behind, the spiders aren't likely to give you a quick, painless end."

Ed almost turned pale at the mention of his stats. But neither Alder nor Lavy reacted with anything more than disinterested looks at the weapons rack, so Ed assumed that Ioan couldn't see the *Dungeon Lord mantle* talent, or anything of the sort.

"Noted. What about the pay?" he asked.

"If you live, our Sheriff here will pay you an entire quarter-Aureus for your team to divide," said Ioan, nodding in Gallio's direction.

Ed turned to Alder, "What do you think?"

"That'll do," the Bard said simply, keeping up his bored, professional facade.

"Deal," said Ed. He made a mental note to figure out later what the hell a quarter-Aureus was and what you could buy with it.

"Good," said Ioan. He motioned at Gallio, Vasil, and the second Ranger. "We still have one last preparation to make, so meet us at the southern gate in half an hour."

He glanced at the last woman, who so far had limited herself to watching the exchange with growing impatience. "Kes, do you mind helping our adventurers outfit themselves for the hunt?"

Kes was the first person Ed had seen who was not entirely human. The closest word to describe her was "elf," given her pointy ears, white hair cropped short, and hazelnut eyes, but she wasn't attractive like the elves he had seen in movies or videogames. She looked like a bird of prey, with pointy, elongated bones and rough skin burnt by the sun. Her nose was hawkish and her lips were a thin, severe line. Her body was built for fighting, with no curves except for those of her legs, which were so muscled and powerful it was almost grotesque. She was armed with a long lance and a short sword similar to a Roman gladius.

"I'll take care our cannon-fodder is well-equipped," she said with barely a glance at Ed and company. "We wouldn't want to make a poor impression on Amphiris, now, would we?"

"Amphiris?" Ed whispered to Lavy and Alder while everyone but Kes left the backyard in a hurry.

"No idea," said Alder. Lavy shrugged.

"She's the horned spider Queen," said Kes, who had shifted closer to them and was sporting a wide, predatory smile full of sharp teeth. "Bigger than a horse, with mandibles capable of tearing a man in twain in a single bite. Her venom is so dense it kills instead of paralyzing, and her web is as strong as steel. We're going to hunt her today, and you're going to be in the front lines... friend adventurer."

There was something in the way Kes smiled that was more disturbing than any of Ioan's taunts.

CHAPTER THIRTEEN

THE HUNTERS

L ittle Ilena went out while her mother was away. She wanted to see the brave group that was headed to hunt the horned spiders. She almost squealed with excitement at the idea. All the kids in Burrova were talking about it, and many had decided to meet near the South Gate to watch the heroes go.

A good daughter would have stayed with her brothers by their market stall, waiting patiently for their father to return, but that would mean she wouldn't get to see the adventurers leave.

The older kids had laughed at her fantasies of heroes setting off on a brave quest, like in the Bards' tales of old.

"It's only Ranger Ioan, Sheriff Gallio, their helpers, and three thieves from Undercity," they had told her when they passed by her family stall in the marketplace. "No heroes here. No hero cares enough about Starevos, much less about Burrova, to come all the way here."

But Ilena knew better. Surely the Sheriff, the mercenary, and the two Rangers weren't incredibly interesting, as far as heroes went, but what about the three strangers? She had always dreamed of a tall, dark, handsome foreigner that would appear one day to carry her away from the farm and her brothers' constant bullying. Maybe she was old enough now to earn such attention? Maybe one of those Undercity thieves was actually a lost prince in disguise. Ilena had heard the story of the Assassin Prince of Undercity who had been executed years before she was born. Perhaps he had faked his death, in secret, and was here now?

The possibilities were endless. She had to know.

Since Father's hangover could make him sleep until well past midday, and all her brothers were older than Ilena—more interested in their games or in hollering at the farmer-girls their age—surely they wouldn't miss her for an hour or two?

It was easy to slip past them using the movement of the crowd, almost dancing around a sea of legs and dresses that only last summer would've been a death sentence for her. Nowadays, people seemed to move as if treading water, allowing Ilena to squirrel her way through the crowd like a rabbit darting into its burrow.

She went past the market, hollered a greeting at the lady who was curdling milk at the edge of it, and made her way into a mud-covered alley between a communal house and Heorghe's forge. The mud and the grime made a mess of her warm, fur boots and splattered her wool skirt, but she barely paid any attention to it. She could see the South Gate and the black forest sprawling beyond it.

The garrison was stronger here than at any other point of the palisade, with frequent guard patrols across the balustrade, each with longbows whose quivers included the few enchanted arrows that Heorghe had managed to forge.

The guards would've seen Ilena drawing near, for sure, had their attention not been focused on the party of nine that was about to leave the safety of the palisade.

The little girl reached a group of rotten barrels half an arrow-flight away from the gate, which made for an excellent spying position. Other kids had apparently thought the same, because she could see their silhouettes hunching among the shadows of the dead tree next to the barrels. She nodded a curt greeting to them, and the dirt-covered faces did the same. Ilena felt a twinge of pride, like she was a member of the Thieves Guild and this was a mission.

She could see the two Rangers—Ioan and Alvedhra—leading the group. Ioan looked anxious to leave while Alvedhra kept her usual mousy expression.

There was something about Ioan that Ilena found comforting, even attractive, like she had known him for far longer than even her own father. Every once in a while, the Ranger stopped by her farm after returning from his travels to Constantina and shared exotic candies with her and her brothers.

Am I in love with him? She asked herself, trying to tie her feelings to the way the wandering Bards talked about love in their tales. Maybe he felt the same. A couple days ago, after his latest trip, he'd offered a special candy, only for her, and she had sworn to keep the secret, so her brothers wouldn't demand their part.

After Ioan and Alvedhra were Sheriff Gallio and his aide Vasil. The patrols of the palisade looked at Gallio with respect and deference, but Ilena barely gave him a second glance. He was short, and grim, and his white-blond hair was always caked with sweat to his forehead. He lacked the dignity with which heroes generally carried themselves.

He's a poor sonofabitch exiled from his homeland, her father had said once. *An Inquisitor who lost the Divine Bitch's favor because he was a coward. We're stuck with him as our Sheriff because Heiliges doesn't want to risk losing anyone useful.*

Ilena agreed with her dad. Gallio's mace looked too big for him.

Along with the Sheriff and his aide was the mercenary, the woman from gods-knew-where that was sharing a shed with

Alvedhra, according to her mother, who would squint in disgust every time she mentioned it.

She wasn't interesting. All skin and bones, and a face that was definitely non-human. Ilena wondered for a second what someone like Alvedhra saw in her, and then her attention drifted to the last four members of the party.

There was a young woman about Alvedhra's age, with the pale skin and purple eyes that marked her as a Lotian. Could she be a Witch? She was aware that not all Lotians were Witches or Warlocks, but what else could this one be? She moved as if she had a personal vendetta against dirt and mud, and armed with a sad little dagger, and had ill-fitting leather braces as her only armor. The only way Ioan or Gallio would have let her go with them was if she had magic to bring to the table.

Next to her was a tall Heiligian armed with a sword that looked heavier than he could lift. He carried a long, wooden lute in his hands...that Ilena recognized as belonging to Governor Brett. So, he was a Bard? One who had to borrow an instrument, at that, so he couldn't have been a very good Bard.

The last one...the last one was looking straight at her.

Ilena jumped a bit when their eyes made contact, and she felt a pang of surprise and panic at being discovered, even though she wasn't technically doing anything wrong.

The man looked away, disinterested. He examined the dead tree where the other kids were hiding, squinted—perhaps he saw them too—and then looked away.

Ilena couldn't place the man's features. His skin tone could be Heiliges, perhaps mixed with Starevos...but he was shaped differently from both of them. That left Undercity. Perhaps Ioan had met him there, during one of his frequent trips?

Ilena was aware that Ivalis was bigger than Lotia, Starevos, and Heiliges, but it was a vague awareness. As far as she was concerned, her family's farm was at the center of the world, Burrova at the outskirt, and Hoia Forest at the very edge.

Anything else was part of a Bard's tale, and Bards, nowadays, sang solely about Lotia and Heiliges and the war that was brewing.

Perhaps the man was a warrior from any of those far-away places, or an assassin. It was hard to see, though, because warriors like Ioan and Gallio were shaped differently than he. They had strong, lithe muscles, and powerful forearms that looked as if made of steel. This man wasn't fat, but he lacked the definition of a fighter. He couldn't be a noble, because then he wouldn't be an adventurer.

Who was he, then? Another Wizard? Still made little sense. He was armed with a spear, a short sword, and had a couple knives strapped to a leather armor that barely covered his chest— said armor belonged to Burrova's guards, Ilena reckoned. She just couldn't place him.

That's my stranger, Ilena decided. The man met all her requirements. He was mysterious, he was tall-ish, he could be handsome if he did something about that dirt-covered hair. And there was an element of danger to him, something unnerving about the way his eyes glinted in the sunlight, something that made her heart race and her head pulsate painfully...

Scratch scratch.

Ilena clutched her forehead and willed the migraine to go away. That couldn't have been the man, since the pain had come and gone at random, a week ago at most. Since she had gone playing in the woods, perhaps, although the memory was faint in her mind.

She flashed her dark stranger a smile and hoped he would look back at her before leaving.

Notice me, she hoped. When he turned his back to her and stepped forward to the first line of the formation, in front of Ioan and Alvedhra, Ilena fought down disappointment with the usual nonchalance of a farmer's daughter.

Come back alive, she thought, instead, as the eight adventurers

—and the batblin—left the safety of Burrova's walls and disappeared into the woods.

The village seemed smaller now without them. Ilena sighed and wondered if she should head back to the family stall. The migraine was making her hungry, but she knew her brothers would refuse to feed her until Mom came back. And lately she hadn't been able to stomach the soup. The vegetables just weren't cutting it for her. Was this how it felt to grow up?

Scratch scratch.

She was so hungry, and her head hurt so badly...Mom was still angry about the chicken, but no one suspected Little Ilena. It was a long way back to the farm, but the girl knew there were a lot of stray cats and dogs roaming around the alleys of Burrova.

To think of vegetables and porridge made her stomach churn with nausea, but the memory of the bloody, tender, warm, and delicious chicken meat—oh, still twitching!—she had eaten the night before made her ravenous with desire.

Strays would have to do. Ilena was growing up. She needed meat.

Scratch scratch.

THE WAY to the heart of Hoia Forest took the group close to Ed's cave, but not close enough to make him fear discovery. Along the way, their formation had changed, since combat was approaching and they needed the Rangers' knowledge of the terrain to lead them.

Ioan walked next to Ed, easily navigating the roots and rocks that were, to Ed, invisible obstacles that made him lose his footing every other step.

"Have you fought spiders before?" Ioan asked Ed and his three companions.

"Only the smaller ones," Ed answered truthfully. "The spiderlings."

Ioan nodded. "Those can be as dangerous as the spider-warriors if you're not ready for them. The cluster we're up against is a newer one, forced into proximity to Burrova by the other clusters, away from Hoia's middle. Alvedhra and I estimate they have about a dozen fully grown warriors, two princesses, and Amphiris, the queen. The spiderlings are the bulk of the coven, as usual, with half-a-thousand active across all the cluster's territory."

"That's a lot of spiders," said Alder, just a couple steps behind Ed. The Bard looked up at the trees and the bushes while clutching at the hilt of his crude, iron sword.

"Usually, they aren't clumped up," said Alvedhra, who had fallen behind to chat with Kes. "And the queens won't send *all* their spiderlings into combat, since that would be wasteful even for them. I'd say we'll face two hundred, at most, before we have to deal with the warriors and the Queen."

Lucky us, we have already thinned their numbers, thought Ed.

"If *Lady* Lavina here does her job, the spiderlings won't be anything to worry about," said Kes. The sarcasm of her voice was apparent, since Lavy was having more trouble with the unmarked road than Ed. He saw how Lavy struggled against a root that caught her feet, cursed at Kes and some gods whose names Ed hadn't heard before, spat on the ground, and rushed back into the middle of the group, her pale face red with anger and covered in dirt and sweat.

"You saw her stats," Gallio said from the back. "She has *combat casting,* which is better suited for the *fireball* rune than your own talents, Kes."

Just before the group had left for the forest, Ioan and Gallio had returned with a small, metallic chest rusted along its edges. It was one of Burrova's emergency defenses, Gallio had told them, sent from Heiliges by caravan each year along with other supplies. This chest contained a small bag with white rocks on them, engraved with silver filigrees.

"These are *fireball* runes," Gallio had explained as he selected a group of stones and handed them over to Lavy and Ioan. "They were crafted by a powerful Wizard from the Church. We won't take all of them, since that would risk leaving Burrova defenseless, but four of them should be more than enough. Your friend, Lavina, will carry one, Ioan another, and I'll carry the rest."

The plan was to use one or two *fireballs* to get rid of the attacking spiderlings. With the firepower of the remaining ones, and the expertise of the Rangers, dealing with the adult members of the spider-cluster should be easy as pie.

Keyword here being *should.*

Ed wasn't so sure. The Rangers and the Sheriff were banking on the idea that the spider Queen would sent the spiderlings as a group, followed by the warriors, and she herself would remain away from combat, protected by the pair of princesses.

That...wasn't how Ed would do it, had he been in Amphiris' place.

He looked up, the same way Alder was looking.

Had he been in her stead, he would fill the trees with spiderlings and rain them down over the group. Their bite was paralyzing, right? Even if it was a weak effect, surely ten bites would slow even Ioan down, and it would negate the use of the runes due to friendly fire.

Then, while the spiderlings were still raining down, he would send the warriors rushing in from all directions. The forest was deep and dark—it would be easy to surround the group without being seen.

After that, once he was sure the adventurers didn't have an ace up their sleeve, he would rush in himself, guarded by the two princesses, to take down the strongest member of the group—that would be Ioan. The battle would end then, with everyone surrounded by warriors and weakened by the bites of the spiderlings.

Capture the survivors, paralyze them, cover them in webs, and use them to replenish my lost spiderlings, he finished. That's what he would do, in place of Amphiris. He had fought against hundreds, perhaps even thousands, of bosses across different games and settings. It wasn't that hard to put himself in their shoes.

But Ioan didn't look worried. He wasn't even glancing at the trees, and the man had fought spiders before.

That's the problem with me, Ed thought. *There's too much I don't know. Information is more valuable than a thousand experience points.*

The spiders, perhaps, weren't as smart as he thought. Perhaps they lacked organization, or were limited in other ways. Perhaps Ioan and Alvedhra had hidden powers that Ed hadn't taken into account. He couldn't see their stats without his Evil Eye, after all.

A signal of Ioan brought him back to reality. The Ranger was still moving at the same brisk pace as earlier, but now his gaze was fixed upon a distant spot that looked as dense with foliage as anywhere else.

"They know we're here," said Ioan.

Ed's pulse accelerated while he tried to see whatever had triggered the Ranger's alarm, but he caught nothing other than the movement of the wind and the singing of distant birds.

"What do we do?" he asked the Ranger.

"Keep moving, act normal," Ioan said. "Lavina, Gallio, be at the ready with those runes. It won't be long now."

The group was deep into the forest, well beyond the distance that Ed and his companions had covered to reach Burrova. The trees were close together, and their crowns covered the forest in shadows. Now and then, Alvedhra stopped to glance at a dead branch, or to examine the foliage-covered soil.

"Some batblins were killed here," she said at one point while passing a gloved hand through the shrubbery. "Wolves, I think."

Ed saw Klek tremble at the mention of wolves.

"Yes," whispered the batblin, too low for anyone but Ed to hear. "Wolves. Hungry, nasty wolves. Worse than spiders, sometimes."

Ed clutched his spear and took a deep breath. It would be no use to lose his nerve now.

Ioan led them to a small glade where the terrain was more or less flat, and they could see decently across the understory.

This is where we wait for them, Ed thought, and Ioan confirmed it when they reached the center.

"Get ready," the Ranger said. "They're coming."

Ioan and Alvedhra grabbed a handful of arrows from their quivers and stabbed them into the grass. Kes sighed grimly and drew a crude, nicked longsword made of iron. Ed and Lavy exchanged glances while Alder clasped at his lute with both hands. Gallio whispered a soft prayer that Ed couldn't hear, and Vasil spat on the ground and drew his sword.

"Stay in the center," Ed told Klek. "If things look grim, run away."

"Sure," answered Alder, instead, "that's what I was going to do, anyway."

Lavy sighed and said, "Just get this over with already."

She didn't need to wait long. At the edge of the glade, opposite from where they had come, the foliage started to tremble.

THE SPIDERLINGS FLOWED out of the vegetation like wine from a barrel. Under daylight, they seemed even worse than they had in the cover of the darkness where Ed had first met them, since now he knew what they looked like.

Each was the size of a fist, black and hairy with chattering mandibles and glinting black eyes. Ed's ears were full of their snapping, and the sight of those saliva-covered mandibles made his body twitch with anticipation and fear barely kept at bay.

"You are going to burn!" Lavy exclaimed, stepping forward, her arm raised with the white rune held high.

"Not yet!" exclaimed Ioan. He caught the Witch's forearm and pushed it down. Ed, for an instant, thought they were about to die from a friendly *fireball*, but Lavy clasped her jaw and looked at Ioan with wild eyes while the spiders closed the distance to them.

"They're not clumped up enough!" Alvedhra explained.

Ed immediately caught her meaning. If they used a rune on each of the three clusters of spiderlings, they'd have only one left for Amphiris later on, not even counting the warriors and the princesses.

But if they push us back into the woods, we'll get ambushed for sure, he thought.

There was a simple solution. Without stopping to think, he rushed to meet the three waves of spiderlings, his spear at the ready, a scream frozen in his throat.

"Edward!" Lavy screamed. "What are you doing?"

"Let him!" Gallio yelled behind Ed. "He's got the right idea!"

That's encouraging, thought Ed as his spear got in range of the first spider of the middle wave. He stabbed at it, and the iron tip pinned the critter to the ground and crushed it into a pale blue mess with a gluey *crunch.*

He felt a vague, metaphysical awareness that he had just gained a single experience point. Perhaps he would live to earn a couple more.

The spiderlings were fast, but they weren't agile, and they couldn't avoid even his clumsy, untrained attacks. It would've been a winning maneuver if there had been two spiderlings instead of a couple hundred.

Ed retreated without turning his back on the spiders, stabbing all the while, missing more than he hit, stealing glances to his sides, trying to remain a step farther ahead than the advancing tides at his flanks without letting himself get surrounded.

Don't think about what they do to prisoners, don't think about what they do to prisoners...

He needed them to bunch up. If the monsters had even an

ounce of strategic thinking, they would simply scatter around him without breaking their formation.

From what Ed could see, they were doing exactly that.

"Ed!" Alder called out in warning.

Ed's gaze returned to the front just in time to see a spiderling jump at his face with its eight legs spread out like a hairy, venom-filled hand. It *screamed* at him as it surged through the air—

Ed's blood turned to ice as terror drowned whatever reason he still had. He let go of his spear with one hand and swatted at the spider-projectile without stopping his backward run.

The spiderling went flying sideways with a dull *thud* and its scream died mid-flight, but Ed's hand erupted in scorching pain as if it was on fire. Ed screamed and almost stumbled on his own feet, only catching himself in time to see three more spiderlings jump his way—

He ducked, turned back to his companions, and ran. A small weight hit his back while he took his first step, and he felt tiny, hairy feet try to find a hold on his body—then a piercing, stabbing pain near his right shoulder-blade.

The young Dungeon Lord shook himself while he ran, and the spiderling lost its footing, stumbling away from him.

Ed realized he was screaming a brave battle-cry. It sounded like, "Oh, shiiiiii—"

The rest of the team was yelling something at him, but he barely paid them any mind. Numbness was starting to spread over his back and his hand...

You have to clump them up, he reminded himself. Risking a glance to his left and right, he realized the other two waves weren't chasing him, but more like running along with him—straight at the other adventurers.

One-handed, he reached with his spear and swatted at the wave of spiderlings to his left. Blue blood splattered on the green grass...And caught the attention of the spiderlings around their pierced companions. Spiderlings broke formation to reach Ed, and that caught the attention of others, in such a way that the wave was soon flooding at him instead of with him—

"Edward," Lavy wasn't screaming anymore—she was calmly walking toward him, just a few yards away, side by side with Kes and Ioan. "Move away."

Then she raised her rune. Next to her, Ioan did the same, while Kes rushed straight at Ed with her sword drawn—

Ed jumped—or finally lost his footing—and propelled himself through the air just as a nasty number of legs crawled all over his back and his legs.

The rune in Lavy's hands glowed a neon blue, so close to Ed that he could see the strange symbol engraved in the stone flash with arcane energy, shift, and turn in the air like it was liquid light—

The *fireball* boomed past Ed's head with a deafening roar, and all the bones in his body shook as it passed. There was no heat, though. Only an explosion of force half-a-second afterward, somewhere behind him. The impact caught Ed, drew the air out of his lungs like an NFL linebacker tackling a baby, and pushed the Dungeon Lord to the ground, sending him rolling in a stunned heap.

Ed bit his tongue as he rolled over, and his mind blanked for a second. He was vaguely aware there was a second explosion following the first one, and that smoking pieces of *meat* were raining all around him.

He tried to stand up, on instinct, and he felt the stabbing pain of another spiderling bite on his back. He rolled on his back, shook away the critter, and opened his eyes in time to see a bunch of surviving spiderlings, some of them still smoking, rush straight at his face.

Before he had time to even think of using his *improved reflexes*, someone jumped over his head, sword at the ready. It was Kes. The mercenary's face was frowning with focus, and she didn't appear to fear the spiderlings at all. Just as the first of them jumped at her, she screamed:

"*Cleave!*"

And her sword shot through the air like a living projectile, neatly slicing the spider in two and then switching directions mid-air in a way that defied physics, arcing back and down the path where it had come from, reaching another spiderling who was just barely leaving the ground, slicing it in an arc of blue goo, and then yet another slice at a third critter.

Ed could *feel* the air around Kes' body rise in temperature, like the mercenary was surrounded by a mirage. He had the faintest idea that the amount of energy she had expended would've been enough to floor him.

Instead, she didn't even wince. She followed her first attack with another two *cleaves*, killing six spiderlings and breaking the momentum of their charge. This time, her jaw clenched with the effort, and a pearl of sweat danced down her forehead.

Ed stood up, groaning, helped by someone's arms. He realized it was Alder, whose eyes were glued to the scarred ground where the two *fireballs* had destroyed the spiderlings.

"You're insane," the Bard whispered at Ed. The both of them watched as Kes and Alvedhra stepped forward, with Ioan and Lavy retreating back near Ed, Alder, and the others.

The two women made short work of the remaining spiders, so fast it wasn't even a battle, but more of an execution. Alvedhra's scimitar wasn't the best weapon to deal with the small critters, but she moved in short, precise bursts that anticipated the spider's movements perfectly.

She knows them well, Ed realized. She had clearly fought them before, just like Ioan.

A few seconds later, only a couple dozen spiderlings survived, and they retreated back to the tree-line, still screaming in that unnerving way of theirs.

Ed, Lavy, and Alder watched them go, the three of them panting and trying to regain their breaths.

"How many did we kill?" asked Ed. A few steps in front of them, Kes and Alvedhra were chasing down the stragglers and eliminating those that were left.

"How many did *I* kill, you mean," Lavy said. "I have no idea, but only ten experience points for all that is a scam!"

Alder looked at her like she had gone insane, but Gallio cut him off before the Bard could speak:

"You still earn experience for killing spiderlings? Well, if you survive the warriors you'll earn a lot more than that."

"What—?" started Lavy, but then the three of them turned to see that Gallio was nodding toward their backs.

While they were focused on the spiderlings, the spider warriors had approached them from the path the adventurers had taken in the first place.

Ed counted two groups of three black, hunched shapes the size of a San Bernardo, heads covered with many eyes and crowned by a horn sharp like a short sword, and clicking mandibles oozing yellowish saliva. They approached the adventurers without the hurry of their smaller versions, with the countenance of a pack of wolves about to surround their prey. The sight of them sent shivers down Ed's back. There was no way, no *way* he could take that many—

Someone tugged at Ed's trousers. He looked down to see Klek's grim expression staring back at him. The batblin was carrying Ed's spear, and Klek offered the weapon to him with an encouraging gesture.

"You can do it, my Lord," Klek whispered. "You can do anything."

The sight of the batblin's child-like faith in him was so unexpected that Ed almost laughed. Instead, he caught himself in time, nodded vigorously at Klek, grabbed the spear that was being offered to him, and said:

"It's gonna be a piece of cake, Klek. You'll see."

The batblin's ears rose at the weird expression, but Ed had no time to explain. He had to put on a good show for the batblin.

He charged at the nearest group of spider warriors, Gallio and Vasil at his sides, roaring madly at the monsters like he knew what he was doing.

CHAPTER FOURTEEN

THE HUNTED

Gallio was the first to reach the spider warriors. His mace gave him little distance between himself and the powerful mandibles of the monsters, but he swung it with such force the spider had to jump back on pure instinct to avoid having its face crushed to a pulp.

Vasil reached his side an instant later and his spear scratched the mandibles of the second spider, leaving a long, pale blue gash on its side. The spider roared and tried to charge the man, but Gallio jumped at it, using Vasil's back as leverage for a half-roll. The Sheriff stepped on the monster's head before it could react, and the mace swung down in a blur of steel that ended with a direct hit to the spider's forehead.

There was a meaty crunch. The spider's horn broke, sending chitin flying everywhere, and the exoskeleton of the creature caved just under the horn's stump, ruining half of its eyes and spewing blue goo everywhere.

The spider screeched in agony and collapsed, throwing Gallio in front of the other two spider warriors. The creatures tried to pounce on the man, but Ed and Vasil were already upon them, driving their spears into the soft flesh of the spiders' mandibles and eyes, forcing them back. Gallio recovered and rolled back into a standing position.

"Excellent hit, boss," Vasil said while taking out an eye from his spider warrior.

Ed saw out of the corner of his eye how the other group of three spiders were engaged by Alder, Lavy, and all the others. There was a violet, arcane flash followed by one of Lavy's taunts.

All good over there, he hoped. *Let's focus on dealing with these.*

His spear hits lacked the strength or the technique to pierce the chitin of the spiders, which was as thick as armor, but he followed Vasil's methods and aimed his strikes at the faces of the monsters while trying to secure Gallio an opening to deliver a killing blow.

The spider warrior in front of him screeched when Ed's strikes got too greedy, and its mandibles crushed the wooden shaft of his spear in the blink of an eye.

Ed stared at the splinters of his weapon as they fell, and at the charging monster—at those mandibles aimed at his belly—and he jumped back. Gallio immediately sprang forward, his mace covered in spider blood, forcing the monster back.

"Sword," the Sheriff suggested.

Ed nodded and clumsily drew the iron weapon. His next thought was, *How the hell do I use this?*

The two spiders had changed tactics and circled the three men, trying to find an opening in their formation. They didn't know that Ed's sword was as effective as a stick on his hands, which bought him time to think.

He risked a quick look at the other group and saw how Alvedhra and Ioan were using their scimitars to swipe at the spider's legs. Their three monsters were still alive, but all were already lacking one or two legs, replaced by blue stumps.

Good enough, Ed thought. He stepped forward and swiped at the legs of the spider closest to him. The monster jumped back, dodging the iron, and bent its midsection mid-jump, aiming its back at Ed's face.

Oh, shit, he thought as a string of white goo flew at him, fast, too fast for him to react—

A hand pushed him away, and he barely managed to stop himself from falling. He swatted at the second spider who had approached the opening, and his sword managed to strike a solid hit on the monster's right foreleg. The leg came off neatly at the middle, and the spider toppled down over Ed, its weight hitting him like a sack of bricks. They both stumbled to the ground in a heap, snapping mandibles too close to his face, hairy legs trying to pin him down, blue goo and web spraying all over his body...

Ed screamed in panic as a line of hot, gluey web fell on his face, and his eyes widened when the mandibles finally found him in the confusion and shot toward his neck—he barely had time to activate his *improved reflexes.*

Time came to a standstill as the mandibles stopped in their path, now slowly threading the air like it was honey. Ed realized he was still screaming, but the sound of his voice was slowed. The spider's midsection was pinning him down to the ground, stopping him from rolling away, but his sword arm was still free.

He pushed against the ground with his other shoulder, gathered all his strength, and shot his sword point-first into the mouth of the spider, right in the middle of its mandibles. He felt resistance when the iron found flesh, and then his wrist registered the sickening movement of the sword when said flesh gave way. Spider blood sprayed in blue droplets while Ed's sword kept going and going, deeper into the spider's mouth, whose eyes were just now widening with surprise, though not yet registering the pain of being pierced.

Time resumed its normal flow just as the spider's entire body shook wildly, tearing the sword away from Ed's grip with such force that it sent a jolt of pain through his entire arm. The mandibles of the creature hit the ground next to his neck, and its entire body collapsed in a convulsion of death and agony, with most of the weight pushing Ed into the ground and pinning him there.

Ed fought for breath, looked away from the convulsing, smoking creature, and saw how the remaining warrior charged straight at him. Vasil tried to pierce the spider, but the strike merely scratched its torso's chitin, and the creature ignored the guard in favor of the defenseless Ed.

"Agh!" Ed said bravely while trying—and failing—to push the dying spider away from his body. The other one reached him in a single second, its horn aimed down, straight at Ed's torso, where it couldn't possibly miss.

An arrow, suddenly, was sticking out of the spider's head, eliminating one of its eyes. The shaft was glowing with pulsating red energy, and it exploded in a miniature explosion of the *fireball* spell, a stream of force driving down into the spider's flesh, tearing chitin and muscle apart like they were paper, taking out a chunk out of the spider's head. Ed saw how the life left the charging monster's remaining eyes as it toppled to the ground, momentum making its corpse slide mere feet away from his own face.

In the end, Ed was left staring face-to-face at several rows of dead eyes.

"Fuck you, Murmur," he whispered. Soon, Vasil was by his side, helping him push the weight of the first spider away from his torso. Ed took a deep breath when the weight on his lungs was alleviated, and he stood up.

"Quick, help me free him," Vasil told him while he rushed to Gallio's side. It had been the Sheriff who had pushed Ed away from the web attack, and for his troubles the man was now glued to the glass, covered head to toe in the white strands. He was trying without much success to break free, and Ed could see Gallio was only succeeding in gluing himself further.

Behind Gallio, the others had managed to fell one of their

spiders, and the surviving two were covered in blue cuts and missing several limbs. The monsters hissed at Kes and Alvedhra while the two warriors threatened them with their swords, forcing them back. Alder and Lavy were right behind them while keeping their distance as not to interfere.

Ioan was a few feet back and was nocking a new arrow to his bow. He nodded in Ed's direction before shooting at the surviving warriors.

"We actually won," muttered Ed while he and Vasil worked as fast as they could to cut away Gallio's webbing using their daggers. Klek soon joined them when the batblin sensed the clearing was safe enough for him. Ed handed him another dagger and the three of them were half-way done freeing the Sheriff when the two remaining spider warriors disappeared back into the tree-line. Four spider warrior's corpses littered the clearing, along with the broken remains of countless spiderlings. "We made them retreat."

Next to him, Alder groaned at Ed's words.

More figures entered the clearing, moving so silently their approach had to be pointed out by Gallio's frantic, web-covered muffling. Ed turned in the direction the man was pointing at with his only free hand and discovered that Amphiris had joined the battle, followed by her two daughters, four fresh spider warriors—plus the two that had retreated—and all her remaining spiderlings, which flowed around their mother's legs like a living tide.

"We must run away," said Klek, his former confidence all but forgotten. "We must run away *now*."

Then Amphiris spoke with a guttural, inhuman voice that sounded, to Ed, as if thousands of invisible spiders were crawling into his ears. She said:

"Well, well, well. The prey saves us the trouble of hunting for it and even brings my children a worthy feast. Tell me, oh meal, which one is the Dungeon Lord that hides among you? The smell of Sephar's Bane has marred the entire forest for weeks, but you're carrying it with you."

THE SIGHT of the spider Queen and her overwhelming forces had as much an effect on the seasoned adventurers as she had on Klek.

Kes turned to Ioan and told him, "You said she would never attack with her entire cluster!"

The Ranger ignored her. He was drawing another arrow while chanting two quick words that added a red, pulsating energy to the shaft.

"She shouldn't," Alvedhra answered the elf without drawing her gaze away from the spiders. "This is not how they hunt."

Ed resisted the desire to *scream* at them. To base their entire battle-plan on a *she shouldn't* was idiocy!

She could speak! She was intelligent, not a wild beast like her children appeared to be, and so she was capable of acting in ways other than her *normal.*

And now she had them surrounded, and she knew there was a Dungeon Lord among them.

It was Gallio who spoke first, as soon as Vasil managed to free the Sheriff's mouth from the splash of web that covered it.

"There's no Dungeon Lord here, monster. Haven't you heard? Kael Arpadel is dead. You'll find no new master in Starevos."

"Please, don't provoke her," Alder suggested. He and Lavy had been slowly drawing near to Ed and Klek, no doubt getting ready to turn tail and run.

"A new master!" Amphiris half-roared, half-laughed in that hair-splitting voice of hers. "What need should a queen have with a master? No, Inquisitor, my cluster is not looking for ownership. It's looking for revenge."

"That's why you have been attacking Burrova's farmstead?" asked Kes. "For vengeance? You're in need of a history lesson,

Amphiris. Sephar's Bane happened a long time ago. Maybe you're just afraid of the dark."

At the mention of Sephar's Bane, the spiders grew restless, their clicking gained a furious note, and some of their warriors had to contain themselves from rushing at the mercenary.

"Please, don't provoke her," Alder said again.

"Puny mammal," Amphiris said with a dismissive click of her mandibles. "You understand nothing of ancestral memory. You have to rely on Bards' songs to remember the past. You may think you understand spiderkin, but you're merely a snack to me. Of course I remember the smell of the Bane that killed my mother and her mother before her...and it's smeared across everyone here."

At that, Ed saw how almost everyone recoiled in horror: Alder and Lavy, Klek, even Kes and Alvedhra.

"You lie," said Alvedhra.

"You won't live long enough to find out," said Amphiris. Then, she nodded to one of the two princesses by her side. If the Queen was the size of a war horse, towering well above Ed, the princesses were at a point in between the Queen and a warrior, with horns sharp as short swords and chitin marred by old scars.

One of them took a couple steps forward and her horn pointed at Ed. "That's the Dungeon Lord, Mother. As sure as you are our Queen. He's the one who killed your brood in that cave—he has the smell of kin-death all over him."

"I see, Laurel," said Amphiris. "Excellent."

"Edward?" asked Gallio, half-turning in the restraints of his web prison. "What is she talking about?"

Ed tried to shrug at him, but the gesture came without heart.

"No way," he heard Ioan say. "He doesn't even have two hundred points of experience. Is the Dark One really so desperate that he's willing to recruit weaklings?"

Just ignore him, Ed's brain suggested. The Queen was approaching, followed by her court.

They were almost clumped enough for the remaining two *fireballs*. Why was Gallio not using them?

Ed realized why when his gaze fell on the Sheriff. He had indeed tried to grab them, but the web tugging at his arms had caused the two stones to slip out of his grasp. They had fallen a couple feet away from him, and his struggle had glued him in a position from which they were unreachable.

"Dungeon Lord," called Amphiris, like a dignitary from one kingdom crossing the field to meet another. "You have unleashed Sephar's Bane on my domain. For this abomination, you *will* die, after your body is used to feed my brood. But let it be known that Amphiris, Mother of Spiderkin, respects the ancient traditions! You have a right to a last speech. Waste it with tricks, though, and it will be gone."

Ed looked carefully into the eyes of everyone there. They were clearly out-gunned by the spiders, but if only he could reach the runes, that could change...

He raised his hands, as if in surrender, and stepped forward, away from Gallio and closer to Amphiris' brood, but also closer to the two runes.

"I have no idea what you're talking about," he said.

"Ed, don't get any closer," Alder said. "I have this Bardic utterance that's handy in retreat. I'm going to use it so we can run away."

Not yet, Ed thought. They would be leaving Gallio to be devoured, or worse. And the man had saved Ed's life. He had taken the shot that was meant for him.

So, he shook his head at Alder and whispered, "Wait."

The Spider Queen ignored the exchange. She was busy hissing with anger. "You deny your Lordship? Is your goal to trick these humans? If that's the case, we have nothing else to say to each other."

"No, wait!" Ed hurried to say, realizing the Queen was about to attack him. "I *am* a Dungeon Lord, as your daughter said. But I have no idea what you all mean by Sephar's Bane. That's not my doing...I just arrived here."

"Dunghill," said Lavy.

"Shit," agreed Alder.

"What?" whispered Gallio, his eyes widening in surprise and fear. "No way. You can't be—you are lying! Arpadel is dead. The Heroes destroyed all he had left. There's no reason for a new Dungeon Lord to come to Starevos. This place lacks the resources to create a powerful dungeon."

You tell that to Kharon.

Ioan turned to aim his bow at Ed. "A reason? There is one if Amphiris is telling the truth—if he wants to release Sephar's Bane among the outposts."

The arrow shaft glowed an angry red. Ed recalled what that same magic had done to a spider warrior's head, and his mouth went dry.

"Listen to me! I don't know what you're talking about!"

Ed inched closer to the runes. Could he manage to use *improved reflexes* again? He could feel a tingling numbness spreading across his back and hand where the spiderlings had bitten him, and his body still burned from the effort of killing the spider warrior. This time, however, the fever was not abating.

He wanted to see whatever new experience he had gained, try to buy a new talent like he had done in the cave, but he was sure that Ioan would shoot him the instant he activated his Evil Eye.

"So you say, Dungeon Lord," said Amphiris. "But even the puny humans know that your kinship is built on lies and deceit. You say you just arrived in my forest? Maybe after making a trip to the Wetlands?"

Ed wanted to scream in frustration. He didn't even know what the Wetlands *were!* Now even Alvedhra was pointing her bow at him. Her face was contorted by sheer, raw hatred. And Kes had shifted her stance as if ready to fight across two fronts; the spiders, and Ed.

"Edward," whispered Lavy. "In a fight, everyone kills the Dungeon Lord first, unless they're idiots. *We need to leave.*"

Not yet, Ed thought desperately. Vasil wasn't done freeing Gallio yet. And even if he turned and ran, he had little doubt that Ioan would kill him instantly. Even *if* he managed to dodge the arrow, the spiders would give chase. He needed to wait, ready himself for an opportunity.

If it didn't appear, he would have to create it. But could he really risk using the reflexes again?

"I have no idea what the Wetlands are," Ed said. "If Sephar's Bane is the reason you attacked me last night, you're looking in the wrong direction. Let me help you find it, Amphiris. Stay away from Burrova, and we'll look for it together."

"You *are* a Dungeon Lord," muttered Alvedhra in astonishment. "And now you're asking the Queen to become your minion?"

"That's what he wanted all along," said Ioan, a grim expression on his face. "He must be part of Kael's surviving apprentices. He evaded capture, struck a Lordship pact, and has been trying to build a power-base to leave Starevos. Perhaps what Amphiris is saying is true. Kael must've had a mindbrood's egg hidden somewhere, and then this guy retrieved it. It makes sense."

"Edward," said Gallio, as Vasil finally managed to undo the last of his restraints and the Sheriff stood up, still wielding his mace. "Release your entire stat-line to me. I know what the Lordship talent looks like, I'll speak on your behalf if you're innocent."

Ed flashed him a sad smile and stepped away from the Sheriff.

"Shoot him, Ioan," said Kes.

Amphiris laughed. "Ah, to see my food play with itself fills me with pleasure! I must reject your offer, oh mighty Dungeon Lord. Nothing I saw during your fight with my warriors indicated you may have power worth following. Besides...I've grown to enjoy the taste of farmer's flesh."

"Klek, the runes, please. Don't let them notice you," whispered Ed. Without looking to see if the batblin did as asked, the young Dungeon Lord turned to face Ioan and the rest of the adventurers and activated his Evil Eye.

Waves of heat poured out of his gaze while the world gained an eldritch taint. He saw how the adventurers gasped in surprise, anger, and fear. Before Ed could speak, Ioan let his arrow loose.

There was a flutter of purple-and-pink robes and the arrow exploded mid-flight, releasing a cloud of sulfurous smoke.

Gallio rushed at him, his mace held high, but he stumbled when a very surprised drone appeared in another cloud of smoke, right between the Sheriff's legs. As Gallio fell, he brought Vasil down with him.

Then, the spiders charged at everyone, their horns aimed low, their eyes glinting with hate.

"Runes!" Klek called, and Ed's palm shot toward the small hand that clasped the two stones. He grabbed them just as he began running, followed by the batblin.

"Retreat!" Ed called at Alder and Lavy. "Fucking run!"

"*Nimble feet!*" Alder said, also sprinting, holding his wooden lute high. The air seemed to dance around him, to glitter, and Ed could hear a frantic musical beat right under his ears.

His legs, his entire body, were suddenly well rested and itching to go for a run. Even the numbness in his back seemed to recede. He moved faster, as if he was in his best physical condition, and Lavy, Alder, and Klek seemed to be caught by the same effect as well.

They were outrunning the coming spiders, they were outrunning the adventurers, they were moving faster than any other creature in the forest.

A woman screamed just as Ed reached the treeline that his friends had already reached.

Cursing under his breath, he turned back. Alvedhra had fallen under the charge of a now dead spider warrior, and she was completely covered by spiderlings that bit mercilessly. Next to her, Kes was desperately trying to free her, but she clearly didn't dare use *cleave* and risk hitting the Ranger.

Vasil, Ioan, and Gallio weren't running anymore, but they were fighting against the remaining warriors, clearly overwhelmed, while spiderlings surrounded them all and Amphiris and her daughters circled them from afar, their backs ready to spew web at them the second their guards lowered.

Ed stopped for half a second to calmly consider his options. He looked back at the edge of the clearing and felt the effects of *nimble feet* slowly recede as the distance to Alder grew.

He rushed back into the fray. He tossed his spear aside, grabbed a rune in both hands, and aimed it straight at the spider warriors.

"*Fireball!*" he roared, and arcane destruction erupted from his hands.

CHAPTER FIFTEEN

THE MERCENARY

The twin explosions sent tumbling monster and men alike, and the impact made Ed's bones shake inside his body. Torn spider legs and charred chitin rained and peppered his shoulders and head.

He didn't stop to see if he had killed the spider cluster; instead he rushed at Alvedhra, who was still half-covered with spiderlings.

With a roar that was half a battlecry and half a scared whimper, he kicked at the spiderlings, trying his best to keep them away from the Ranger and to make them stop biting her.

Kes had fallen near her, and she wasn't moving. The mercenary had hit her head on a rock, and red blood was marring the surrounding grass.

"C'mon, Alvedhra!" Ed urged her as he grabbed a furious spiderling and crushed it between his hands, ignoring the sickening crunch and the even more sickening splash of blue gore that followed. "Move!"

The woman's head was red and bloated and covered in tiny bites like chickenpox. There was yellowish foam frothing from her lips, and her eyes were misty and distant.

Ed looked back and saw that the spiders were the first to recover. Amphiris was alive and unharmed, along with her daughters. The runes had killed half the spider warriors and a score of spiderlings. Thanks to Ed's rune, the adventurers were still alive, since aiming for the Queen would've allowed the other spiders to finish the party off.

But Vasil wasn't moving, and Ioan and Gallio were just coming to. The Sheriff stumbled blindly across the grass, looking for his mace.

Piercing pain shot through Ed's neck. He roared and caught the spiderling that had managed to clutch at his leather jerkin.

He had never been more angry and scared in his entire life. He held the critter by its mandibles and tore it in half.

All of Ed's body was *pleading* for him to run away. The other spiders were already stumbling back up, and their rage made his look like a temper tantrum.

He clenched his jaw and summoned six drones out of thin air. The forest was filled with ley lines, but he didn't care about that. He commanded four of them to help him free Alvedhra of the remaining spiderlings, then sent the other two to distract the spiders away from the other adventurers.

The drones weren't useful as fighters, but the extra pairs of hands were incredibly helpful, and a couple times the spiderlings went after them instead of Ed or Alvedhra. When that happened, the drones disappeared in puffs of smoke, as even a weak attack was enough to destroy them. But Ed simply summoned them back, fighting against exertion, sweat dropping off his forehead.

After what could've been seconds or minutes, the Ranger was reasonably free of spiderlings, and Ed's arms and legs were covered in blue gore.

"Good. Now carry her," he ordered the drones. "You know where our dungeon is? Get her there, I'll follow you."

His other two drones had been destroyed. He summoned

them again, dropping one of them by a spider warrior's legs and the other one near Gallio. "Hand him his mace!"

Ioan was back up and was filling the warriors with arrows, but his quiver was running empty.

They needed to start running. As did Ed.

He stumbled toward Kes' body, fighting against the paralyzing agent coursing through his veins. He wanted to buy the *resist poison* talent, but he was aware that poison and venom weren't the same thing, and the stupid-fucking-talent clearly said that only higher levels of it had *resist venom* as an option.

"Kes! I can't carry you and run, you need to wake up," he urged the woman. He shook her as hard as he dared.

The mercenary's eyes opened and focused on Ed's. She scowled. "Get those drones away from her!"

Her hands searched her hips for her dagger, so Ed jumped away. "I can't do that. We need to get away, now!"

As if to punctuate his words, Vasil, Gallio, and Ioan were already pulling back. Ed's two drones near them had been destroyed again. Gallio was screaming something at Kes, gesturing furiously at her to get up and come with them, while the spider warriors tried to surround them despite their wounds, and the spiderlings began again to pool across their big sisters' feet. Amphiris and her daughters marched in Ed's direction.

It was too much. Ioan and Vasil ran for their lives, and after one last, desperate look, Gallio did the same.

"You want to infect her," Kes spat bloody saliva at Ed's boots. "Don't you? That's why you came with us."

"For fuck's sake," Ed said. "Shut up with that!"

What can I do to make her believe me? Anything he said, Kes would believe was a lie. He had no time to reason with her, no time to prove to her that whatever conceptions she had about Dungeon Lords didn't apply to him.

So, he didn't. He extended a hand to Kes as black mist spread across the space between their bodies. "I am not lying. I won't harm Alvedhra, or you. I offer you a pact as proof; accept it and come with us, or die here and leave her in my hands."

Kes eyes widened. She shook her head, jumped back on her feet, looked at the coming spiders and then at Alvedhra's figure as Ed's drones carried her out of the clearing.

"A pact! Now? You truly are a monster—" she said. Ed sighed and turned to leave.

"Wait!" Kes called. "I—I can make a condition, right? Promise she won't set foot in any of your dungeons. Only then will I become your minion—"

"Sure, sure, now fucking move!" Ed growled. His gaze was fixated on Amphiris. She wasn't charging him, but strolling leisurely his way. Why?

She fears I still have runes left. Smart. She *would* charge when he ran.

The pact with Kes was struck, and the mist united her and Ed, who barely noticed it. He was sure that, in any other situation, he would've been deeply touched by the mercenary's concern—hell, she thought she was sacrificing herself—for Alvedhra, but right now—

Both the mercenary and the Dungeon Lord ran for their lives, with the giant, horned spider and her daughters following behind.

"Dungeon Lord!" called Amphiris from somewhere behind Ed and Kes, "Come back! It's not polite to leave a Queen hungry!"

The mercenary and Ed reached the edge of the trees, with the four drones that carried Alvedhra still moving through the foliage. Ed stopped for half a second, looked back at the spider Queen, and told her:

"We'll meet again, Amphiris. You can bet your life on it." He flashed her a nasty smile.

Then, without an ounce of dignity, he followed after Kes.

"That would've been threatening if you weren't running for your life," the mercenary told him when he reached her side.

"I'm just getting the hang of this 'ancient traditions' deal."

They had the advantage in the forest, at least against the huge Queen, who would have a hard time charging at them in the reduced space between the trees. The princesses, on the other hand...

"You know where we're going, right?" asked Kes when they reached the four drones.

The drones were dragging Alvedhra rather than carrying her, and the unconscious Ranger had her hair covered by broken branches, her face marred by cuts and swelling, and enough mud to double as camouflage.

"No," Ed admitted. "The drones...know the way."

I hope.

Neither of them dared to waste time looking back to see if they were being followed. They were getting away from spider territory, and that had to be enough. Ed had no time to worry about his friends, or about Kes' party; he had only time to push his legs forward another step, and another, his lungs burning with every breath of cold air.

The venom and the exertion of using his *improved reflexes* repeatedly were taking a toll on him, making him barely able to run on par with even the stunted walk of his drones. It was clear that Kes could've left them behind, had she wanted to. But the woman's gaze was focused on Alvedhra, and Ed had little doubt she was willing to make a last stand defending the fallen Ranger if it came to it.

"Hurry up," Kes told him. "Make them run faster!"

The drones hissed at her and gestured obscenely.

That's pretty much all they can do, thought Ed, who had no breath left to talk with the mercenary.

Behind them, the sound of crunching branches and chitin

brushing against bark reached them clearly. How close? A mile, or a foot?

Ed's legs felt as if they were made of lead. He willed himself to keep moving.

He had only one dagger left, the other lost in the clearing along with his spear and his sword. If it came to a fight, he'd have to do with chucking drones at the three spiders.

It would have to be enough. He hadn't come all the way to Ivalis to die to a goddamned trash mob.

He had killed his fair share of horned spiders in IO! To his character, they had been barely more threatening than a batblin cloud; a way to farm experience between towns or dungeons.

No, it would not do to let them kill him.

But how long could he keep this pace? How much had he run already?

His heart was beating madly inside his chest, spreading fire through his veins and lungs, but he had little doubt his limits were approaching. Yesterday, he had been a retail employee, his only physical activity being the rare morning run.

Jogging through a city was a different experience than running for his life in a dark, humid forest while being chased by monsters.

A branch scratched his face, leaving thin lines of pain across his cheek. Ed grunted a curse and flicked the sweat away from his eyes.

Next to him, one drone fumbled its grip on Alvedhra and fell to the floor, where it disappeared in a small cloud of smoke. Kes saw it and, cursing loudly herself, reached for the Ranger's shoulder, then with a grunt and a pull, hefted her onto her back. Alvedhra whimpered pitifully.

"Hold on," Kes told her, "we're almost there."

You don't know that, thought Ed, but the mercenary might not have been lying. The trees weren't as clumped together now, and the branches and roots weren't attacking his face and feet as much. Light filtered easily through the leaves, and the sounds behind him were, perhaps, growing quiet.

Then, Kes screamed, and she disappeared from Ed's view, the Ranger leaving with her.

The scenery changed all of a sudden, and the ground disappeared from under Ed's feet. He plummeted down in a heap of arms and legs, flailing frantically, falling, sliding on hard soil with sharp rocks meeting his skin all the way down.

And then, the sliding stopped. Ed was lying flat on his back against the trunk of a tree, his head spinning madly. He groaned, hugged his knees, and fell against the ground. He dug his fingers into the soil and tried to drag himself. He had to keep moving. The spiders, they were coming, they—

"Alita's tits, Ed's alive!"

Ed heard a familiar voice growing close to him. Was it Mark? Hell, he would be happy to open his eyes to find Ryan. Anyone without mandibles.

The young Dungeon Lord shook his head to clear it and opened his eyes. His gaze took a second to adjust to the extra light, and he turned his Evil Eye by instinct. He recognized this part of the forest. It was rockier, and the terrain was scarred and peppered by hills that extended toward the horizon.

Alder stood in front of him, his forehead covered in sweat and his cheap tunic torn to rags, but very much alive, and relatively unhurt.

"I thought we had lost you," the Bard told Ed while extending him a hand to help him up. "But Lavy insisted that competent Dungeon Lords are harder to kill than that."

"She thinks I'm competent?" asked Ed. He accepted Alder's hand and propped himself up.

"Not exactly. She said either you're a competent Dungeon Lord and you would survive, or you would die and we would be rid of a weak Lord."

"Charming." Ed glanced at his surroundings. He and Alder

couldn't have been more than a mile away from the cave. Ed had lost his footing when he and Kes reached the top of a rugged rise in the terrain. He could see the path he had left while sliding on the ground.

Seems like the drones brought us back in a straight line, not taking terrain into account, he thought tiredly. In that case, using the creatures as guides wasn't the best idea. If they had reached a precipice instead of a hill...

He caught a glimpse of Kes' legs protruding from a nearby bush. She seemed to be just coming back to herself, and she was cursing like a sailor. Ed could guess why. The bush was very thorny.

"Where is Lavy now?" Ed asked. Klek was missing as well.

"Ah, well, she and Klek are headed back to the cave," Alder said. "To deal with Klek's former batblin cloud, you see. We ran into them not even five minutes ago. I stayed here in case you made it back."

"Ah, all right, then," Ed said, and sighed. "The batblin cloud. More mobs. That's exactly what I wanted to do right now, deal with more mobs."

He glanced nervously at the hilltop. There was nothing stopping Amphiris and her kin from rushing down and attacking him here, in open space.

Ed hurried to help Kes up, anxious to reach the relative safety of his dungeon.

"Mob? Spiders aren't *that* organized," Alder said.

CHAPTER SIXTEEN

SEPHAR'S BANE

E d ordered his four remaining drones to carry Alvedhra again, since Kes looked as exhausted as he felt. The mercenary didn't complain, though. Instead, she marched next to the Ranger's body, giving Ed and Alder gloomy glances every now and again. Since she was now his minion, and he was thirsty for information about the world, he flashed his Evil Eye at her when she wasn't looking and took a fast glance at her stats, without actually reading the descriptions.

Kessih of Greene

Species: Half Avian
    Total Exp: 432
    Unused Exp: 22
    Claims: Peregrine of the Cardinal Command Army (Revoked), Citizen of the Volantis Enclave (Former).

ATTRIBUTES
    Brawn: 15

Agility: 14
Endurance: 14
Mind: 11
Spirit: 9(+1 Minion of Dungeon Lord Edward Wright)=10
Charm: 8 (+1 Minion of Dungeon Lord Edward Wright)=9

SKILLS

Melee: Improved (IV)
Swordsmanship Focus: Improved (IX)
Survival: Improved (V)
Military Discipline
Knowledge (Volantis Enclave): Basic (VI)
Flight: Advanced (VI)
Drill Instructor: Improved (III)
Hunting: Basic (IX)
Tactics: Basic (VII)

TALENTS

Cleave: Improved
Power Strike: Improved
Shield-Master: Basic
Improved Sight
Regeneration: Basic
Improved Metabolism
Resist Disease: Basic
Resist Environment: Basic
Avian Bone Density
Dungeon Minion - The owner is a Minion under the command of a Dungeon Lord. The Minion receives bonuses according to the Lord's power and is recognized by all the Lord's dungeon as an allowed entity (unless otherwise specified).

THAT'S a lot more skills and talents than what Alder or Lavy have. Or what I have, for that matter. Still, there's something strange about her. From what I've seen about the cost of talents, since she has four hundred experience points she should have quite a few more talents. And what's up with those claims of hers?

He would have to take a closer look at her stats later on, to see if he could figure it out. One of those skills was different from the others, he was sure of it. But, before he could look again, he was interrupted.

"What's the deal with her attitude?" asked Alder.

Ed explained how the mercenary wouldn't trust him with Alvedhra, and how they had ended up forging a pact.

"I can see why she didn't like it," said Alder. "Besides, you know, pledging her life to the living embodiment of the Dark and all that. From her perspective, it looks like you took advantage of her feelings for Alvedhra to recruit her."

"I can just break the pact, right?" asked Ed. He shrugged. "I'm not forcing anyone to remain by my side, much less if they don't want to be."

Alder winced in a way that didn't forebode anything good. "I mean...yeah, you can end the pact at any time, as long as you don't end it because you're planning to break the conditions of it. You would have to wait awhile in that case, let your minion have a heads-up. But..."

"But, what?"

No, Ed really didn't like the way Alder coughed and refused to answer. Instead, the Bard said, "Well, it's complicated..."

"We have all day."

"I'll tell you why it's complicated," said Kes, loudly, without moving from her spot by Alvedhra's side. "I'll even assume you don't know this already and aren't simply feigning ignorance."

Ed looked at her expectantly.

"Sephar's Bane," she said. "That's why—whatever happens—I will never be able to return to Heiligian lands, or see Alvedhra again. That's the price you asked of me, Dungeon Lord, and I won't easily forget it. This pact of ours won't allow me to lie to you, so here's my truth. Once I know what your dark designs are, I will oppose them at every turn, as little or as much as my status as your minion lets me, even if it ends up costing me my life, even against the threat of torture—"

"Fine." Ed waved his hand dismissively. He was tired of trying to explain himself to the mercenary. "Sure, you do that. But tell me, first, what *is* Sephar's Bane and why was its *smell* enough to make Amphiris angry enough to risk her own life against us. You can do all those other things afterward."

Kes scowled at the way Ed ignored her oath, but after a moment's hesitation, she said, "Mindbrood. That was—is— Sephar's Bane."

"I'm listening," said Ed. "Before you keep going, you should know I'm not from Ivalis, but from a different world called Earth. We have no magic—no Objectivity—there. I don't know your culture, or your customs, geography, or monsters. Imagine you're talking to a five-year-old...just don't be too condescending."

"I see," said Kes, dubiously.

"I can vouch for him," Alder told her. "My own pact involved him not lying to me."

"So you say, Bard," she said. "Don't think I've not noticed you're a Heiligian man in service of a Dungeon Lord. A traitor once can be a traitor again. And I'm not one to trust the word of a Bard."

Alder shrugged. If Kes' words had been an insult, he had either hidden his reaction well or he truly didn't care.

"The mindbrood is one of the most terrible creatures to crawl out of the Wetlands," said Kes. She made a gesture with her index finger and her thumb, to indicate a size no bigger than a slug's. "It starts life being quite small, and will spend days crawling around, starving, looking for a host. A giant spider is a favorite prey of theirs, but humans do nicely, too. When they find an unsuspecting host, they crawl through an ear, or their mouth, or their nose. Really, any orifice will do. They travel through the host's body until they reach the skull, and then they feed on their brains. Slowly."

Goosebumps traveled down Ed's back, and that had little to do with the cold. He could picture a slime-covered slug, inching toward a sleeping man's ear, closer and closer...

And yet, Earth had brain parasites. They were nasty, yes, but hardly warranting such a reaction from the spiders and Ed's companions.

"Then what happens?" he asked aloud.

"It's hard to explain, since I'm not a medic," Kes said. "During this part of its life, the mindbrood's body is...like a hard, sticky jelly. As it feeds on the host's brain, it grows, and it molds itself to fit the empty space it just cleared."

Alder distractedly covered his ear with one hand, like he was protecting it from unseen parasites.

"But that's not all it does," Kes went on. "As it molds, it also replaces the parts of the brain that it just ate, bit by tiny bit. That's what the jelly of its body is built to do, understand? According to the Church's Clerics and doctors, the brain contains a person's memories and thoughts. Those should be gone after the mindbrood eats them, but they aren't. Instead, they are copied by its body, and the victim never suspects a thing. They can still think, they lose no memories...they never realize they're slowly being replaced, that each passing moment they become less and less, until they just *wink out*. Leave a mindbrood to feed, and in a couple weeks all that'll be left is a body controlled by a slug hiding in the skull, thinking it's still the person it just ate."

"That's insane," Ed whispered. He remembered how Kharon had spit a black heart out of his body, how Ed had the alien thing beating right now in his chest. Would he even notice if his brain was being eaten right now?

Fuck you, Murmur, he thought grimly.

"And that's not all," said Kes. "That's just part of the mind-brood's life-cycle. You see, the monster thinks it is its own victim, but all the original instincts are still there. Inside the skull, the slug matures and loses its jelly-like quality; then it hardens. Becomes a cocoon. When the time is right, when enough food is nearby, it hatches. It feeds on its former body, and on anyone or anything close enough. It grows strong, becomes a creature capable of making even Inquisitors fear for their life. And then it lays eggs, somewhere with lots of living animals, and the cycle stars anew..."

Hundreds of tiny slugs crawling in a dark night, slowly bridging the distance into an unsuspecting village, through open windows, through straw beds, sliding wetly through an open mouth...perhaps a child's mouth, who just an hour ago was playing with their brothers and sisters, and now would wake up with something slowly replacing them, slowly eating their conscience *and they would never know...*

Ed placed a hand over his mouth and tried to push back nausea.

"I can see why the spiders went insane, if they thought I had brought one of those with me," he said.

Then he went pale. He *had* an unknown entity functioning as a heart. Sure, it didn't fit Kes' description, but maybe...?

Murmur said there wasn't a hidden part to our deal. Only our bet, he reassured himself, though with little success. A 'he said' wasn't a convincing enough reason for Ed to assume he wasn't infected.

And if he was, he would never know until it was too late.

"Tell him about Sephar," said Alder, whose expression was as ashen as Ed's.

"He was a Dungeon Lord," the mercenary said. "A long time ago, before my mother was born. Not a powerful one, like Dantal or Zailos were in their time, but he was cunning, and he was cruel. He built his dungeons close to human cities and raided the cities frequently. He liked to take hostages—women and children

—to force the city to pay tribute to him to ensure their safety. He did this for many years until Heiliges had had enough. The Inquisitors reunited a contingent of heroes and adventurers and struck all of Sephar's dungeons at once. They imprisoned the Dungeon Lord, and they released the captives and reunited them with their families. Sephar had lived *too* close to Heiliges cities; he had nowhere he could hide, no secret base where he could retreat. People thought that was the end of it."

Oh, no...

"Except, during his youth, before he became a Dungeon Lord, Sephar had been a Ranger. An explorer once hired him to lead a team to approach the Vast Wetlands—there are still people stupid enough to try to get close to the unending swamps, but they almost never return. This one was no different. They all died...except for Sephar, who returned to civilization with a Lordship mantle, and a single mindbrood's egg doused in sleeping potions to keep it from hatching."

"The hostages," Ed muttered. Women and children, Kes had said. Sephar liked to take women and children hostage.

"Indeed. Investigations later on suggested that it was part of the contract between Sephar and the Dark entity that had granted him his mantle. Every single hostage was infected with a mindbrood, Edward. Down to the last little girl. A slug eating at their brains, tiny bite by tiny bite. When the Inquisitors found the hostages, they were all drugged by sleeping potions. No one suspected a thing. They thought Sephar just wanted them drugged so they wouldn't cause any trouble. Instead, once the potion wore off, the mindbroods kept eating, and they hatched by the hundreds in the unsuspecting population of three different cities, and a dozen villages."

"What happened then? Could the Inquisitors stop them?" Ed asked.

"Even a single mindbrood is enough to cause a terrible outbreak," Kes said. "The magic required to identify a person infected by one is rare in Heiliges. The creature *thinks* it's the real person, at least until it's too late, so it can naturally fool the Light's detection. After all, a parasite is not Dark-aligned, not even this one. It's but an animal, acting by instinct. In short...it was a massacre. The monsters waited in the shadows at every corner, hiding everywhere. Sewers, abandoned houses, mansions, castles, basements, wells...you name it. Laying their eggs, bringing victims to their nests. Every time the Inquisition thought the outbreak had been contained, entire families hatched again."

Alder flicked a bead of sweat away from his forehead and added, "It was worse than that. At first, no one knew what was going on. Sometimes, even today, monsters manage to slip past a city's defenses and attack the populace. Back then, people simply left the city until the guard or some handy heroes had killed all the monsters and it was safe to return. A werewolf or two can't do damage if they can't find anyone to bite, after all. When the mind-broods started hatching, many townsfolk went to hide in nearby villages or in the countryside. And then the monsters among them hatched..."

Kes nodded grimly, and said, "The entire tragedy lasted almost two months. News about the bloodbath reached even the Volantis Enclave, and it shook my people to the core. It was feared, back then, that the entire kingdom of Heiliges risked extinction. It didn't help that other Dungeon Lords used the confusion to make their own power-moves. The only way the Inquisitors could stop the brood was to kill every suspect, infected or not, and burn their bodies. I'm talking entire cities, Edward. Whole villages, put to the sword, and set aflame afterward. Men, women, children, the elderly. Everyone. Not even the nobles or the rich were spared. The Inquisitors killed even the settlements where no mindbroods had been discovered, just because they were close to a single outbreak. Only this brutality allowed Heiliges to survive, and it hasn't been the same ever since."

"The Culling, we call it," said Alder. "We don't like to talk about it, even if almost all who lived it are dead today. The fear is still there—that even by speaking about it we may end up rekindling it. It's not probable, though. Safety measures are different, nowadays. Better. There are protocols that every peasant child is required to learn as soon as they are able to walk. The Inquisition has better tools, more knowledge, new spells. And less mercy. If necessary, it will quarantine an entire city, close the gates, keep anyone from wandering off."

"And kill them all again, if it comes to it," added Kes.

"More would die if we didn't."

The mercenary shrugged. "I'm not saying I wouldn't do the same in Heiliges' place. I just want our *Lord* here to know what he got himself into. Edward, as you can imagine, Heiliges wasn't happy with the Dungeon Lord. Sephar was subjected to the worst tortures imaginable, drawn out for as long as the best healers in the kingdom could manage. And when his mind was so broken that torture wasn't effective anymore, they tossed him into a brood-filled pit. They feasted on his brain at will, and days later the pit was set on fire. In the end, his own monsters destroyed him, see? That's why the mindbroods are called Sephar's Bane."

"Yes, I can see that," said Ed. He glanced at the mercenary's ashen face. "Is this why you can't return to Heiliges? There's no mindbrood here that I'm aware of. Amphiris had the wrong person, unless Murmur is known to lie during his pacts. Kharon assured me my mind would be left intact, and the creature you describe definitely doesn't."

"They don't lie, even if they like to stretch the truth a bit," explained Alder. "If they did, only fools would accept the mantle."

"It doesn't matter," said Kes. "Don't you understand? It's not enough that entire cities are quarantined under threat of mind-brood, it's the way people think of Dungeon Lords! They're dangerous maniacs, willing to perform the worst brutalities to please their gods! Heiliges doesn't rescue hostages anymore; they have seen what a Dungeon Lord can do by abusing mercy and compassion. Anyone captured by a Dungeon Lord is presumed dead, and if encountered, will for *sure* be dead. The Inquisition won't take risks anymore. This not only applies to hostages, but to *minions*, as well. Anyone who pacts with a Dungeon Lord will share their fate, no mercy allowed. Even after the pact breaks, the crime is never forgotten. If your Bard or I ever stumble into a Heiligian's path, it will be their duty to send the Inquisition our way! Hell, it should be Alder's duty to put an end to his own life, just because of the taint of his association with you. *That*, is Sephar's Bane. And you're tainted, Dungeon Lord, no matter where you come from, whether you want it or not. The mantle is crime enough to have you and yours executed, and nothing you ever do will be able to change that!"

Kes' words lingered for a long time while the three of them kept walking, only Ed's drones making any sound at all in the ensuing silence.

Ed had no idea what his gloomy companions were thinking, but he was barely aware of them. He was only aware that there were ways to make a deal with the devil, and lose, without the devil ever telling you a lie.

This is Murmur's gambit, Ed thought. *There's no need for the mantle to transform me to evil if the entire world is not willing to give me the benefit of the doubt.*

Somewhere distant, far away from the realms of humanity, Ed could sense that a Dark and cruel being, unfathomably hungry and unfathomably vast, was laughing at him.

CHAPTER SEVENTEEN

EXTENDED MEMBERSHIP

They reached the part of the forest that hid Ed's cave not long after, and the conversation had still not resumed. Kes was focused on the unconscious Alvedhra, who had now taken to whimpering and shaking in the grip of the drones. The Ranger's skin had turned a sickly yellow in addition to her bloating, and Ed had little doubt she was suffering a terrible fever.

We need to get her to a doctor, he thought. He now understood the terms of Kes' pact with him. By keeping the Ranger away from his dungeon, maybe she would escape the *taint* of being a Dungeon Lord's hostage—and its consequences.

Unlike Kes, who was already doomed.

Unlike himself, and Alder, and Lavy, who had been doomed from the start. He just hadn't known it. He had boasted to Kharon how he intended to join the Light's efforts against the Dark god as soon as he was able.

The boatman hadn't been concerned back then, and now Ed knew the reason.

Ed bit his lip and closed his eyes. For a moment, he felt very alone, very small in a world that wasn't his, a world he had

naively thought he could tame by an effort of will. He had
believed he could outsmart a god—that he could become
someone who *mattered.*

He trembled, feeling like he was a little kid again, like he was
standing in front of his uncle's dead body, with all the morgue's
employees looking at him with cold eyes and faces hidden by
masks. He wished his parents were still alive; that he could run
back to them and hide.

Then, the moment passed. He clenched his hand into a fist.
He remembered the dream he had had, of Murmur's gigantic
body, how the Dark one already thought he had won.

Fuck you, asshole, Ed thought. *I don't need anyone's support to
screw you over. I can do that by myself. I can tell right from wrong,
and I don't need no Inquisitor to tell me which one is which!*

Murmur had summoned him to Starevos for a reason. It was
clear the reason was related to Sephar's Bane.

Perhaps the spiders' fears were right. Perhaps there was a
mindbrood nearby. In that case, Ed would find it, and he would
destroy it before it could damage anyone. He would ruin
Murmur's plans.

The forest was cold, but Ed wasn't shaking anymore. By the
cave's entrance, at its edge, waited the cloud of batblins that he
had faced on his first day in Starevos. It seemed like yesterday
had been a long while ago.

THE BATBLIN CLOUD looked very different than the confident
bunch that Ed had first encountered. There were slightly more
than a dozen, about fifteen or sixteen of them, but Ed could've
sworn last time there had been more. He could more or less
recognize some faces, although they were marred by fresh
scratches and superficial wounds.

Lavy and Klek faced them all from atop the hill, guarding the entrance to the cave. They didn't look worried, but Lavy's face was as ashen as Kes' and Alder's.

She's also worried about the mindbrood, guessed Ed.

He reached the cloud and looked their leader in the eye. It seemed that the portly Drusb was back in command. Unk was nowhere to be seen.

"Back already?" Ed asked them, focusing on Drusb. "Last time I went easy on you all; I hope you aren't about to test my patience further."

The batblin cloudmaster played nervously with his fingers while the rest of the cloud took a few steps back.

"We don't want any trouble," Drusb said. "We got enough trouble already! No, we want to serve Dungeon Lord Edward. We wish to join you!"

"This day keeps getting better and better," muttered Kes. "Before you open diplomatic channels with the forest vermin, have your drones leave Alvedhra here. I'll go find her medicinal herbs—just remember your part of the deal. No harm can come to her, Edward."

"You can trust me," Ed said, while ordering the drones to do as asked.

Kes gave him a distrustful glance, and she went on her way back into the forest, this time in Burrova's direction.

"You'll just let her leave?" asked Lavy, quite loudly, from her place atop the rise. "She could bring Gallio and the entire guard with her!"

"She's a minion now," Ed said. Besides, he believed that Kes wouldn't do anything that could place Alvedhra at risk. For the moment, he could trust the mercenary to behave.

"What?" asked Lavy. "You were out of our sight for less than ten minutes! It's a miracle enough that you're alive, how did you manage to recruit Kessih of Greene while being chased by the spider Queen herself?"

"Klek—I mean, I—told you Lord Edward can do *anything*,"

Klek said proudly, causing Lavy to roll her eyes. "You see, Drusb? Lord Edward can protect the cloud! We just killed half of Amphiris' cluster and no one died, thanks to him! And I've earned so much experience, I'm very strong now!"

He was *definitely* overstating the truth. Ed had no idea if Klek actually felt that way about him, or if the batblin was merely playing the others.

But whatever Klek was doing, Drusb ended up looking to Ed with big, desperate eyes.

"Please," the cloudmaster said. "We are sorry for attacking you. We can be useful to you, you know? We were telling your Witch all about it, but she wouldn't listen. We can forage for you, raid for you, we can find weapons and armor for you. And we know the forest like no one else."

The farm equipment that the cloud was carrying with it left Ed with little doubt about what Drusb meant by "finding weapons and armor." Still, he *did* need those. He had no money and only a dagger as a weapon, and his companions were similarly equipped.

On the other hand, there was something more urgent than thinking of loot.

"What changed?" Ed asked the batblin. "Yesterday, your cloud was happy to attack me, and now you're begging to become my minions?"

Drusb recoiled in horror, raising his hands to protect his face, "Please, don't take revenge on Drusb! We were only playing, we meant no harm!"

"Like hell you were," said Lavy. Then, to Ed, "Want me to fry them?"

He motioned at the Witch to hold on and then tried to calm the batblin. "What has you so scared, Drusb?"

"It's the hyena-men," said Drusb after glancing nervously about. "There's this cackle of hyena-men that makes camp near the forest, when winter comes. They arrived early this year, and they're angry. They've been coming into Hoia, attacking my cloud for no reason. They have no mercy, and there's a lot of them. Between the horned spiders and the kaftar, there won't be any batblin left by winter!"

Spiders, batblins, and now kaftar, thought Ed, grimacing to himself. Low-level mobs in Ivalis Online were proving to be a lot of trouble in the real world. *What else? A marauding army of gelatinous cubes?*

"I see," he told the batblin. "What else do you know about the kaftar? How numerous are they? What do they want? Who leads them?"

Drusb's gestures became more frantic. "Drusb doesn't know! Many? More than my cloud, and they want to kill us! They're hunting batblins, attacking the spider clusters of the deep forest, listening to no one."

An ugly suspicion nested in Ed's mind. Kes had just told him about the Inquisitors' way of dealing with Sephar's Bane—how they had had to purge entire populations just to be sure the infestation was over.

Amphiris had said that she could smell the mindbrood in her forest. That, by itself, was strange enough. If the mindbrood could be simply *smelled,* it made little sense that they were so hard to detect. Just buy a sense-enhancing talent. Ed made a mental note to ask about this, later on.

The kaftar wanted to kill all the batblins and all the spiders in the forest. Both were intelligent creatures, and with big enough brains for a mindbrood to feed on. Perhaps, the kaftar knew about the mindbrood and were preventively trying to deal with the infection by denying it of sustenance.

It stood to reason that the entire cloud in front of him could be infected. A time bomb, ready to go off.

Ed imagined a slime-covered slug inching its way into his own ear while he slept. He shivered and shook his head.

"It seems that I have a lot do to," he muttered. The battle with the spiders had left him exhausted, and anxious to jump into a bed. But he wouldn't sleep well until he knew he was safe, and right now, he and his companions were very low on the food-chain of Hoia.

First things, first.

He examined the batblins, scratched his chin, and told Drusb, "Are these all the members of your cloud?"

"Eh..." The batblin's mistrust was evident. It seemed that the Dungeon Lords' reputation preceded them.

"No," said Klek, instead. "The women and children don't join our hunting clouds. They are hidden, waiting for Lord Edward's response."

Drusb looked at Klek like he was the worst of the traitors, but Klek just shrugged, and added:

"Drusb will have to trust the Dungeon Lord if you want him to trust you."

"It's fine," said Ed. "I was mostly thinking aloud. See, Drusb, there's this...sickness...that may have taken root in the forest. A very dangerous one, and I'm wary of catching it. Before I let your cloud become my minions, I must make sure you're healthy."

Alder, who had mostly watched the exchange with polite interest, inched near to Ed at hearing that and whispered to him, "You don't have any scrying magic, Edward. How do you plan to do that? Open their skulls and look inside?"

"Nothing so violent, I hope," Ed answered back. "I was thinking of Kes' pact, and yours, by the way. Do you remember them?"

"They're the common terms of any minionship contract. What about it?"

"Perhaps this won't work," Ed said, "but I don't think there's any risk in trying it. You have lived with Dungeon Lord Kael before, haven't you, Alder? Could you stand by me as I try something and tell me if it's a good idea?"

The Bard nodded, and smiled tentatively. "People trying new

ideas with magic always make for the best stories later on. Either they blow themselves up, or they make someone else explode."

"I'm glad you're having fun," Ed said. He turned to the cloudmaster.

"Here's my pact," he said, activating his Evil Eye and summoning the mist that surrounded him during the pact-making process. "You'll become my minion on the condition that you're truly—and only—Drusb Cloudmaster, batblin, and not someone or something else either pretending or believing they are Drusb Cloudmaster, or part of him. This is not an offer that I extend to Drusb Cloudmaster, mindbrood, for that matter. As for my other conditions, listen to my orders and be loyal, as long as it's reasonable to do so. Also, don't be an asshole."

At hearing his words, both Alder and Lavy cursed loudly in surprise, and the Witch made her way down the slope.

Drusb appeared confused for a moment while he ruminated on Ed's words, perhaps looking for a trap in them. He ended up shrugging and accepted the offer, making a stipulation that sounded very close to what Lavy and Alder had asked earlier: he accepted on the condition that Ed spoke the truth, and that he held no ill-intentions to Drusb or his cloud.

Ed held his breath, trying hard not to think about what would mean if the mist failed to create the pact. Would he have to strike the batblin down on the spot?

But in a blink, the mist had connected them. Ed let out a satisfied sigh, and Drusb smiled in triumph. The batblin turned to his cloud and announced, "Our cloud has found a Dungeon Lord! We are going to be rich, boys! Rich and powerful!"

The fifteen other batblins cheered loudly, shaking their ragged weaponry about. Ed recalled the hundreds of batblin mobs he had mowed down while playing Ivalis Online and smiled nervously.

Either rich, or very, very short-lived.

"Edward!" said Lavy when she reached him. "What the hell

was that? Pact magic is supposed to be a protection layer between a Lord and his followers, not—not to be used as a divination tool!"

"It was unexpected," agreed Alder. "But—"

"But, nothing!" she went on. "The Objectivity is not a toy! Abuse it and you'll have bigger problems than the Dark or Light coming for you. Magic regulates itself, and it regulates itself *explosively.*"

Ed raised his hands, trying to get the Witch to calm down. "Wait, Lavy. First of all, isn't the Objectivity supposed to be unbreakable? That's its first rule, isn't it? So, if I wasn't supposed to be able to use the pact conditions in that way, nothing would have happened in the first place. Second, I'm not divining anything, I'm using a pact to protect myself and my minions. That's what it is for, right? If I wasn't supposed to make strange demands like this one, the pact would just be the same every time, with no room for nuance."

To her credit, Lavy actually paused to think Ed's words over. She calmed down, but not completely.

"You can't break the rules of Objectivity, but you can bend them," she said. "Abusing the wording of your talents and spells, things like that. It's the first thing you'd learn not to do, had you studied magic like all spellcasters must. Bend a rule too much, and it will snap back against you, Edward. If we're close to you when that happens, we'll get caught in the blast."

"You'll have to teach me, then," Ed said with a sharp smile, "about these things I must know about magic. But later. I'll have to put my foot down on this. I don't *feel* like I'm abusing the pact, and it is a great way to use it. Aren't you happy? It means you *probably* aren't infected with a mindbrood, either, since I made a pact with Lavy, human Witch, not with a parasite standing in as her."

"Oh, now you really *don't* want to go there," said Alder. "Trust me, Edward, the Objectivity really doesn't like it when you try to *retroactively* change the interpretation of past spells."

Lavy nodded her agreement. The way the Witch looked at the sky, like she was waiting for a lightning bolt to smite Ed where he stood, did more to convince the young Dungeon Lord to drop this line of thinking, than anything she had said.

Mental note, he thought. *Wait until at least you have a couple ranks in a* spellcasting *skill before trying to revolutionize the way people use magic.*

"Noted," he said aloud. "In that case, we'll have to keep an eye on each other. See if anyone starts behaving strangely. I don't think we're infected, but I could bet those were the last words of many actual infected."

"You're already strange," Lavy said, which Ed found ironic, coming from her. "So, if you start acting like a normal, rational human being, I'll start to worry."

Ed flashed her a smile and returned to his most recent minion and the cloud.

"I extend the same pact to all of you," he told the ragtag bunch of batblins. "I accept the same conditions your cloud-master already extended, so unless you have something new to add, just say 'I accept.' "

Fifteen or so calls of "I accept!" followed, and as many tendrils shot forth in the blink of an eye. When it was said and done, Ed had added an entire cloud of minions to his follower list.

"Great," he said in satisfaction. He dusted his hands on his trousers, which were just as dirty themselves. "Now that that's done, how about we make a real dungeon out of that cave? I feel the sudden urge to create a lair, build myself a real big stone throne, and start brooding until a bunch of heroes show up looking for trouble."

He was joking, of course, but Lavy nodded in an approving way, then said with her best formal voice, "Well spoken. That's the proper way. I may yet make a decent Dungeon Lord out of you, Lord Wright."

He left the bulk of his minions by the slope of the cave's entrance and brought Lavy and Alder with him to the Seat room, followed by Klek, who didn't feel comfortable being alone with his former cloud. Since the two humans had been Kael's minions before, they would be more helpful than the batblins in pointing out what elements made up a good dungeon.

Besides, he had ordered the cloud to stand watch over Alvedhra, who was still delirious with fever. He hoped Kes would return soon, and that she would know what to do about the Ranger, since Ed had little knowledge about first aid and didn't even have fresh water to offer the pair.

"We need a hideout," said Ed while he eyed the Seat room. "Somewhere we can muster our strength, plan ahead, recover from our wounds, gather intelligence. A base of operations is what I have in mind. What do you think?"

"You need to build epic fortresses, brimming with secrets and treasure," said Alder. "That will make people talk about you, go mad with curiosity, and your fame will grow. You'll attract more powerful followers that way, as well as the attention of gods and spirits. Songs will be written about you, and you'll shape the face of history."

"Build a laboratory," said Lavy, "where spellcasters can study the secrets of Objectivity and share them with you. You'll become a powerful Lord this way, and people will fear you and respect you, and pay tribute to you."

"I would like a hiding spot where Klek—I—don't have to fear getting eaten by monsters every night. Somewhere safe, filled with traps, and perhaps food. Maybe it can be warm," Klek said, his eyes glinting with hope.

Ed looked at his three minions and scratched his head.

"One day, I hope we can build dungeons that fit all those descriptions," he told them, and he meant it. He liked the idea of treasure and fortresses, and the chance to have a magical laboratory made his eyes wide with desire. "But for today, I think Klek's got the best idea. We cannot grow in power if we're dead, and last night we almost got murdered by spiderlings. I say we make sure our foundations are solid before trying anything too flashy."

"Spoken by the man who, an hour ago, used a drone in the middle of a fight to block an exploding arrow," Alder muttered.

Lavy sighed and said, "Women don't like men who play it safe. But suit yourself. I'll live a happy life if I never have to see a horned spider again."

"I agree with the angry lady," Klek said.

"That's settled, then. Let's start by talking about experience points," Ed said. He turned on his Evil Eye and carefully read the slew of notices that he had accumulated since the fight with the spider cluster.

- You have gained 35 experience (0x hundreds of spiderlings, 25x spider warrior, 10x surviving the encounter with the spider Queen). Your unused experience is 41 and your total experience is 207.
- Your attributes have increased. Spirit +1. Endurance and Brawn +1, conditional on two good nights' rest.
- Your skills have increased. Athletics +2. You learned Untrained Combat +2, Dungeon Engineering +1.
- There are new talent advancement options for you:

Resist poison (25 experience) - Allows its owner to resist poison. Higher levels include a resistance to venom.

-Basic status allows the owner to resist non-magical poison as if they had Endurance of 15 in optimal conditions (clean, well-fed, rested)

Energy Drain: Constant. Very low.

RESIST ENVIRONMENT (20 experience) - Allows its owner to perform and survive in threatening environments for prolonged periods of time.

-Basic status allows the owner to survive in extreme environments such as tundra or a desert, even lacking proper protections.

-The owner will last 1 extra day in a moderate environment, 1 extra hour in a dangerous environment, 1 extra minute in a lethal environment such as freezing waters.

Energy Drain: Constant. Very low.

SPELLCASTING (40 experience) - Represents the owner's magical ability.

-Basic status allows the caster to use and learn all basic related spells of their domain. Extra ranks improve each individual spell's characteristics, such as range or damage.

-Allowed spells: 1 basic per day + 1 basic spell due to Dungeon Lordship.

Energy Drain: Active. Varies per Spell.

PERCEPTION (20 EXPERIENCE) - Allows the owner to experience an improvement in attention to detail and memory. They can see things that would normally pass undetected.

-Basic status lets them see as if they had a Mind of 15 and a Spirit of 13 and they were focused, clear of mind, and well rested and fed.

Energy Drain: Active. Moderate.

ALERT *(30 EXPERIENCE)* - Allows the owner to perceive incoming danger with an almost supernatural sense.

If there are any signs or clue in the environment that the owner could've seen by paying careful attention, he will notice even if he's distracted.

Energy Drain: Constant. Very Low.

"INTERESTING," said Ed after he finished reading, "how I'm worth twice as much experience after two days in Ivalis, while it took me more than two decades to earn the first hundred experience points."

"Did you ever kill a spider your own size, back on Earth?" asked Lavy.

"No."

"Well, there's your answer."

It wasn't just the experience. Even the skill increases were hard to understand—not that he was complaining. Increasing his athletic capacity was a matter of exercise applied constantly over a long time—it shouldn't be enough to run for his life a couple times to increase his *athletics* skill, much less his *endurance* attribute.

When he voiced his doubts, Lavy explained:

"Skills aren't always the direct representation of your capabilities. Especially during the Basic stage, they can also represent your knowledge. In any case, they are important in unlocking talent options and spells, and to be allowed to use certain magic items. Your attributes, on the other hand...those *are* a direct representation of your capabilities. You're raising them fast because they were undeveloped at first, and you're smoothing over deficiencies from your life in your world. Anyway, if you desire to become a spellcaster, you should focus on Mind, Spirit, or Charm. Let your brutes and your mercenaries get their hands dirty."

"That's a fantastic way to get killed by a stray arrow," Alder pointed out.

"Powerful mages have little to fear from pointy bits of wood," said Lavy.

"I can name a hundred mages, including Dungeon Lords, who died by way of pointy bits of wood."

Ed gestured at his companions to stop bickering and focused his Evil Eye on his list of new talents. *Alert* seemed quite attractive in keeping him alive, and it was a constant talent, not activated—which would defeat the whole purpose of it. But he had *just* enough experience points to buy *spellcasting*...

He would have to be extra cautious until he gained enough experience for *alert*. At the rate he was earning his points, though, that probably meant waiting an hour or two.

His free points vanished, and he was the happy owner of new, mighty arcane powers.

A new sensation overpowered his tired senses almost instantly.

Ed felt his body tingle as something akin to static electricity surged through it, delved deep inside his skin and muscles, caressed his bones, then went even deeper, and his consciousness followed along for the ride.

He wasn't standing inside the cavern next to the two bickering humans, he was floating in a warm, vast eternity, with atoms as big as stars occasionally shining in the distance.

He was a gazelle in a sea of yellow grass, grazing peacefully while the Sun warmed his fur.

He was the lion jumping over the gazelle and tearing its throat out.

He was an alien scholar, spending nights unending with his many eyes focused on the pages of his books, trying to learn the secrets of the universe.

He was the eldritch abomination hiding in the folds of reality next to the scholar's seat, waiting for the fool to whisper the incantation that would unleash him upon the unsuspecting world.

The visions gained speed and rushed so fast in front of Ed's mind that he was barely aware of them as they passed him by. He saw pyramids, robed figures, chants and star-maps, unknown plants, and warring tribes.

They all made sense. They were all connected by a simple fact. They could all be explained by numbers. Numbers would never lie to him. Atoms weren't the building block of reality, numbers were. To understand them was to gain the power of a god, and it was all within Ed's reach. He extended his hand to the Objectivity, to the blinding light of knowledge—and just like that, he was back in his body, which was lying in the ground of the cavern, shaking softly, with the faces of Alder, Lavy, and Klek looming above him.

His mind was so confused that he mistook them for alien beings before he recalled that *that* was what humans were supposed to look like. He whimpered softly.

"So," said Lavy, "you just went ahead and bought *spellcasting*, didn't you?"

Ed nodded weakly, still shaking.

"We would have warned you, but it's common knowledge that Objectivity can be an...interesting experience. You saw the numbers?"

He nodded again.

"The first rank is only just a taste," Lavy went on with a smug look, but not without sympathy. "You get to see more with each new rank. It's said it can be an addictive experience, but also an enlightening one. Archmages are quite the eccentric fellows."

Ed mustered the strength to stand up, and Alder helped him along.

"When I bought mine," the Bard said, "I saw the millions of ways you could make music by mixing two chords. Bards think what you see is an experience deeply related to your own soul. If you don't mind me asking, Edward, what did you see?"

"Agh..." Ed said. He coughed to clear his throat and tried again. "I was a lion eating a gazelle. I was also the gazelle."

"Uh," said Alder, after a pause in which everyone just stared at each other. "Ominous."

CHAPTER EIGHTEEN

ADVANCED DUNGEON BUILDING

fter Ed had recovered from the purchase of his new talent, he paid attention to the new screens that his Evil Eye pointed to him.

- You have learned the basic rank of Spellcasting, skipping the normal requirements thanks to your Dungeon Lord Mantle. Your affinities are: Enchantment and Control. The Healing affinity is forbidden to you, due to your association with the Dark.
- Your Mantle allows you to learn two spells. You will know them automatically. You can choose from:

Arcane Bolt - Rend. The caster unleashes a bolt of kinetic energy, strong enough to incapacitate or kill at higher Spellcasting ranks.

Ghostly Visage - Illusion. The caster creates a ghostly image that only a single target can see. The image is simple, and no bigger than a normal human being. It will disappear if the target's Spirit or Mind is strong enough to resist it, or if others interact with it.

Duration: 10 seconds per Spellcraft rank.

ELDRITCH EDGE - ENCHANTMENT. The caster adds a magical flame to the edge of a weapon. This flame makes the weapon magical for the duration, allowing it to bypass weak magical defenses and mundane ones.

Duration: 1 minute per Spellcraft rank.

MINOR ORDER - COMMAND. The caster forces a target creature to follow a simple order, as long as said order is not immediately against the creature's moral code and does not present a threat to its life.

The creature can resist the spell with the Spirit attribute opposing the caster's own Spirit.

Duration: 5 seconds.

"I LIKE HAVING MAGIC ALREADY," he muttered. After the shock of his vision had passed, he had decided he had quite enjoyed it. Numbers *did* make sense; he had always thought so. It was part of the reason he had gone into Computer Science during college, and why dealing with people like Ryan had been so hard on him.

It was also the reason why he enjoyed choosing spells and talents so much.

"I like *arcane bolt*," Lavy suggested, when he explained his choices to his companions. "A magic user shouldn't have to enter close-quarters combat. Besides that one, I'd take *minor order*."

"You can do a lot of fun things with *ghostly visage*," said Alder.

"But it's very limited—only a single target can see it. Bards like to use it to impress people at taverns, though you could also make a black screen appear in front of someone's eyes during combat. I would choose that one, and *minor order*. Both should let you move enemies around, keep them away from you."

"I like *minor order* as well. But *ghostly visage* is more up your alley, Alder," said Ed. "I won't take *arcane bolt*, though. The description says it's non-lethal until I gain more *spellcasting* ranks, and besides, I only have two spells per day. That limits me to two targets at most. I prefer *eldritch edge*. It lasts an entire minute instead of a single attack, so I can do more with it."

"It will also force you to get into close combat," said Lavy. "Be careful. Heiliges specializes in martial prowess, and a mercenary like Kessih would make mincemeat out of any of us in a second. More so because you don't have any defensive spells."

Ed nodded, but he didn't change his mind. A warrior could simply dodge the bolt and then close in for the kill, and he would be more defenseless than with the meager protection of a sword or knife.

He chose *minor order* and *eldritch edge* for his spells, and he enjoyed the tingling sensation that followed, similar to the one before his vision, but without the hallucinations. Instead, he was suddenly aware of the appropriate ways to cast his new spells, their limitations, and their basic uses. The new knowledge simply appeared in the back of his brain, like it had always been there and he had merely forgotten about it for a while.

Ed extended his hand, steaming with curiosity, aware that his body was charged with enough magic to cast the spell he wanted right there. He itched to use *eldritch edge* on his knife, see what he could do with it, but he had to resist the urge. With only two spells per day, he had to avoid being wasteful.

Instead, he summoned all the drones he could muster. They appeared at the same time with dry puffs of mist, eight of them, counting the ones he already had created before.

"Let's get this started. First of all, we need to dig deeper," he said. "Right now, anyone can walk right in and kill us. So we're going to move the Seat farther in, and we're going to hide the dungeon's entrance."

He gave the drones the mental commands and sent most of them to dig a tunnel deeper into the rock. The ley lines that he could see with his Evil Eye gave him a natural idea of where to dig and where not to, almost like studying a topographical map with all the relevant information; so he selected a place that wouldn't cause the cave to collapse on his head.

"You two," he told the remaining drones, "go outside and gather resources. We need wood, and lots of it. Don't take down a tree close to the cave or that'll signal to everyone that we are here. Gather branches or something, you're the experts."

He left the remaining one to be his personal advisor, in the same way he had used the drones to guide him to his dungeon and to teach him how to create it in the first place.

"Lavy, you mentioned a while back that we could transmute one type of resource into another," he said while the drones set about their tasks. "What about rock?"

"Nice try, but it has no value," said Lavy. "Find marble, and you could use it. Wood may work, but you won't like the exchange rate."

Ed nodded. His drones came with a natural understanding of minerals. They could tell the difference between rock and carbon, for example, just as he could tell what places he could dig and where he couldn't. So, he would order them to mine when they weren't working, to try to find useful minerals, mainly iron.

In the meantime, he thought of traps.

Focusing on the ley lines while thinking of rooms and traps allowed him to see faint designs, like a drawing from a not-very-talented medieval monk. Pits with spikes at the bottom, collapsible ceilings, even pressure plates. And the rooms were simple ones, too: living spaces, a training room, a small holding cell, and spaces to store and prepare food. Some of those rooms included equipment, and they came with a natural understanding of what resources he needed to create them.

I couldn't see them before, Ed recalled as he studied the designs. *Is this the* dungeon engineering *skill at work? I wonder if I can extend it by using my own ideas for designs.*

Maybe he should have been an architect, or an engineer.

He went to the collapsed tunnel where he had crushed the spiderlings the night before.

"Reinforce this, turn it into a wall," he told his drone advisor. "In fact, we'll reinforce all the rock, first order of business. I don't want any more surprises crawling out of the walls."

The other drones worked fast, but digging a tunnel with the dimensions he had in mind took a while, and he and his companions started to get hungry.

"The cloud will hunt for you," Klek assured him. "But...ask them to get you something fresh."

Since Alder or Lavy didn't have a better idea, Ed followed Klek's advice and set Drusb and the remaining batblins to hunt for rabbits or gather berries. They had some *survival* ranks, so he was fairly sure they wouldn't pick anything too dangerous.

While Ed was out of the cave, Kes returned.

The mercenary was covered in sweat and was carrying a backpack made of pelts with her. She passed by Ed without acknowledging him and went straight to Alvedhra, parting the group of batblins that was protecting the fallen Ranger.

Kes examined the other woman, grunted approvingly, and muttered about the venom already losing its strength. "They were newborns. Barely enough venom between the lot of them to kill a batblin. Had they been just a few weeks older..."

Ed glanced at the bite he had on his left hand. It merely itched uncomfortably now, and his fingers were a bit numb, which could've been either the cold or the venom's leftovers. His back ached painfully, but that had nothing to do with his bites there.

"What will you do?" he asked Kes, while she took out a clay pot from the backpack.

The mercenary put two fingers inside the pot, and they came out covered in a greenish concoction made of ground leaves and other things Ed couldn't place. Perhaps insect hides? Kes spread the paste on Alvedhra's face, starting at her throat, focusing on the spots marred by the tiny spider bites.

"This will deal with the bloating and clear her airways" she said. "The herbalist told me this many bites may have triggered an allergic reaction in her. She could have died, but she is a Ranger. She has a good deal of toughness and resistance-related talents, along with *minor regeneration*. So, it's only a matter of getting her back into Burrova without Gallio or Ioan suspecting that a Dungeon Lord helped her."

"Doesn't sound like an easy task."

Kes finished her spread and took out another clay pot, this one covered by a lid of the same material. She took away the top, revealing a dirty-looking tea, still steaming, which she slowly, drop by drop, made Alvedhra drink. The Ranger stirred from her dreams and scowled.

"It tastes like a sweaty rag," Kes told her, "but it will make you better. Go on, drink."

Ed felt awkward all of a sudden, but when he turned to leave, Kes gestured at him to come closer.

"Help me carry her to the side of the road," she told him. "The herbalist is going to send her apprentice to 'find her' collapsed there, so they can take care of her without making Gallio suspect a Dungeon Lord was involved."

"Won't he suspect, anyway?" asked Ed. "He must've seen us carry her away, after all. And it's not like he would forget that you care about her."

"I doubt he saw anything more than the dust of his boots,"

Kes said. "He was busy running for his life, which was very smart of him. Remember that, by the way, if you hope to survive in Ivalis. The warrior that lives to old age is not the strongest, but the one that knows when to run."

"I have no problem with that," Ed said.

Together, they carried Alvedhra into the forest, with Kes leading the way and saving Ed all the stumbling onto roots he would've suffered otherwise. The mercenary carried most of the Ranger's weight, but she did so without complaining. Her Endurance and Brawn were higher than Ed's, and she had *improved metabolism*, which added to her stamina.

All in all, they reached the side of the road in a couple hours, after stopping several times to catch their breath. Ed suggested a couple times that he summon a pair of drones to help them, but Kes refused, on the argument that it would give them away as Dark-aligned to any onlooker they came across.

"She'll be safe here?" asked Ed after they had placed Alvedhra atop a tangled bush.

"Yes. We'll wait by the treeline until the apprentice comes."

Ed left the mercenary to give her goodbyes. He hoped Kes' fears wouldn't have to be as real as she thought; that the she and the Ranger could reunite once again.

Kes was back by his side soon enough, and they waited in silence until the Sun was well past midday and Ed's stomach was roaring with hunger.

The apprentice appeared past a curve of the road. She was a portly woman who was whistling some happy tune—quite loudly —as she strolled by, stopping here and there to examine herbs and roots along her way.

"Let's go," said Kes.

They didn't speak on their way back.

THEY RETURNED TO HAPPY NEWS. The batblins had managed to

hunt a pair of horned rabbits while they were out, and the drones had finished the tunnel and three small chambers and were awaiting new orders, while half of them reinforced the cave's structure and the others gathered wood.

The sight of the dead rabbits, which had been mauled by some blunt object, made Ed's mouth water. Still, it seemed like too little food for everyone.

"We saved some for us," Drusb revealed when Ed asked him. "The best stuff, humans don't like, so we...forgot to mention it."

The best stuff was a bucket-load of living insects, shaped like fat beetles crossbred with mantises. These, too, Ed noted, had tiny little horns. The insects were sprinkled with juicy pieces of an acidic-smelling fruit that had spent way too much time in the sun.

It didn't look edible at all, but the batblins stared at them with greedy expressions, so Ed was all too happy to keep the rabbits for the humans.

"I'll cook," said Kes who, besides her gloomy mood, appeared as hungry as anyone else. "No offense, but you look like you've never skinned anything in your life."

Ed nodded and had a drone bring Res a pile of wood to start a fire, then ordered the drone to use another pile to transmute into wooden utensils. When Lavy realized he intended to use the mystical powers of the Lordship for cooking, she started cursing in Lotian and went to keep an eye on the food—she didn't trust the batblins to keep their hands to themselves.

Ed left them to go check on his drones' progress on the new chambers. They were smaller than the current Seat chamber, but he was going for practicality, not luxury.

The only problem was, the new tunnel led well underground, past the hill's height and below the forest's ground. It was dark, and damp, and very cold, and the ley lines indicated he had only a few rock formations to work with. A wrong dig and he would hit dirt, which would make securing the base even harder.

"This will have to do," he said, while using his Evil Eye to survey the building options he had.

The first chamber, the one connected to the tunnel, would become the new Seat room, so he left it alone. The second one, he divided into different living quarters, using his drones to add rock and dirt to improvise thin walls.

Doing this, he discovered a new aspect of his Dungeon Lord's powers. He didn't need to use his drones to create the quarters— he merely needed the appropriate materials. The drones had gathered a pile of branches nearby, and that was more than enough.

The wood was consumed by tendrils of mist that floated out of the walls and floor, but felt to Ed as if they were an extension of himself. The tendrils followed the layout of his Evil Eye's design and manipulated dirt and rock as they passed, changing the shape of the quarters, adding details, crude furniture, even small oil lamps that allowed Ed not to have to rely on his Evil Eye for illumination.

Five different quarters were left, each so small that they were barely more than protrusions in the walls fitted with a wooden bed and a straw mattress. They had hemp curtains for privacy, because the walls were too flimsy for doors.

His small apartment on Earth was a mansion by comparison, but he eyed his hole in the wall with appreciation. This one was *his;* he wasn't renting it. And if he really wanted to, he could build a bigger one at any time.

He was vaguely aware that the living quarters weren't finished. He needed to add air shafts, baths, and latrines, and the last two had to be separate constructions, since he lacked the designs to create water pipes. He thought it over for a second, decided that having latrines inside an enclosed space would be a stupid idea, and chose to build them outside.

That left him with the last free chamber, which he used as storage for the wood and the small pile—a mere fistful—of useful minerals his drones had found. He wasn't afraid that anyone would steal his half-rotten pile of wood, but having the materials close at hand would make constructing things on the fly easier. For example, he added a rough door to the chamber, with a hemp cord to keep it closed. Once again, his Lordship powers created it through the dungeon's misty tendrils; Ed only had to will for it to come to life.

This time, he had to stop to contemplate the possibilities of this magic.

Did Ivalis have masonry guilds? He could put entire cities out of business by producing furniture! He was his own assembly line. He could make a fortune, and not by raiding anyone, but by out-producing everyone else. He could be the IKEA of this world. Were all the other Dungeon Lords insane? Screw Murmur and his plans, he could build entire cities using this power, if he was patient enough, and if he had enough gold.

Which didn't seem like a hard thing to do. From what little of Ivalis he had seen, Ed was sure it was medieval-like in technology and society. No stock market, yet, no banking, *no industrial revolution.*

And here he was, with the perfect set of powers to abuse it all.

He felt the overwhelming need to burst out laughing, and an urge just as strong to proclaim that no one would be able to stop him now. He resisted both, but was left smiling like a maniac in the solitude of his tiny, miserable dungeon, cold and damp and badly lit, and *oh how he loved it already.*

HE DEALT with the air shaft issue by summoning a drone outside the dungeon and having it dig a tiny tunnel into the new Seat chamber. He made the hole even smaller by using the drone's powers to fill it with rock until he was reasonably sure that not even spiderlings would fit through it. Once that was done, he walked back out of the tunnel and into the old chamber.

He ordered the other drones to move the Seat down, which they did by eating it and waddling their way into the new chamber with their bellies and cheeks full of rock. The laser-shark on their tunics looked like a fat dolphin with their belly bulges pushing him forward.

Ed had no idea why he had to use drones for the Seat, but not for anything else, though he discovered that he could not build anything by himself until the drones had finished replacing the Seat. This took longer than he expected, since the drones needed several trips. Once they were done, the ley lines of the cave shifted slightly, relaxing their focus on the former chamber and concentrating more down below.

By that point, the rabbits' smoke filled the air, and made his stomach rumble while he worked. Since the room was exposed to the outside world, he wanted to heavily trap it, but he also wanted to avoid having any of his creatures activate the devices by accident.

He decided that concealment was even better than a strong defense, since it would save him the need to defend in the first place. He had the drones go outside and work on the face of the cave. He had them use the same spit they had used to polish the Seat and reinforce the cave walls to sculpt the exterior.

He added a fake rock face that covered the entrance and left only a thin aperture, disguised by an extra couple of inches of rock protruding to the side that was in the direction people would face if they came from Burrova's road.

This way, the entrance would be invisible except to someone coming from the right direction.

And probably the spiders. So, the next order of business was having his drones create long, sharp spikes of wood. He would've loved to create a pit with them at the bottom, but he was hesitant to create them inside his cave, where his own minions would live, and he was hesitant to trap the exterior, since being so close to Burrova would risk harming an innocent villager.

Instead, he set the spikes along the tunnel's entrance, tied to the walls with hemp rope. They would become makeshift spears, and in the case of an attack it would be easy to use spears to defend the entrance from enemies, since the enclosed space would force them to file into a single line.

He spent a couple lumps of iron—and his own knife—and had his drones transmute a small bell. He simply hung it a couple feet after the entrance, at head-level, and tied a thin hemp strip to it, leaving it dangling in the middle of the tunnel. It was almost impossible to see in the low light, and it would hopefully make enough noise to let his minions know if someone was coming.

Finally, as a way to deal with spiderlings, he used a lot of hemp rope—consuming half of his meager wood and foliage transmuting it—to secure several lumps of rock dust, which he set at the ceiling of the former Seat chamber—now serving as the cave's entrance hall. In the case of a spiderling invasion, he would summon a drone to the ceiling, bring the dust down, and use a lamp to ignite it. He employed a lot less dust than last time, to avoid roasting his own people by accident.

After that, he was finished. The statline of his cave reflected the improvements in real time.

Cave System

Dungeon Lord Edward Wright.
  Drones 9
  Dominant Material Cave Rock

THREAT 45 - LOCAL - Represents how aware the outside world is of the dungeon and how willing / able / ready they are to do something about it. A 100 indicates imminent destruction.

OFFENSE 850 - A representation of the strength a dungeon's forces can muster during an attack (raid or invasion) outside the dungeon itself. It represents the experience they would award, as a group, if they were defeated (but not absorbed).

DEFENSE 1100 - It represents the defensive capacity of the dungeon. The experience the population of a dungeon would award if they were to be defeated during the defense of said dungeon. It's multiplied by a percentage given by the dungeon's upgrades and defenses.

MAGIC GENERATED 1 - Measures the magic created by the Sacred Grounds that can be put to use in different endeavors or to power dungeon upgrades.

MAGIC CONSUMED 0 - Measures how much magic is consumed.

POPULATION
  4 adult humans.
  17 batblin combatants.

AREAS
  Living Zones:
  1 Living Quarters
  1 Storage

MILITARY FACILITIES:

1 Batblin camp - hidden.

RESEARCH INSTALLATIONS:
    0

SACRED GROUNDS:

    • The Seat.

PRODUCTION:
    0

DEFENSE:
    Small dust trap.
    Low-quality defensive spears.
    Batblin sentries.

DUNGEON UPGRADES
    None.

THE HIGH THREAT WAS WORRISOME, but at least the defensive and offensive ratings had shot up, probably in big relation to Kes joining the team.

Ed eyed his handiwork—or his drones', to be exact—with satisfaction, then hurried outside to eat. The sun was setting by now, and the sky was tinting in shades of red and traces of purple.

Ed realized that he could already see the stars, which he didn't recognize, and the moon's outline—except this wasn't his moon, but it was easy to forget—painted near the horizon. It was bigger than Earth's, fuller, and he could see the gigantic craters that peppered its surface.

"You finished playing with your toy blocks?" Kes asked him while he approached the fire. She had skinned the rabbits, leaving the pelts extended close to the fire, while the meat itself roasted on spits atop the flames, charring slowly while she rotated them now and then.

As an answer, Ed gave commands to the drones to build the bath and the latrines far away from each other and out of sight of the cave, but not far enough that they would be overly vulnerable to an ambush.

"Yes," said Ed. "I'm finished playing. Hopefully, I played well enough that we won't get killed in our sleep for a couple nights. How about some food?"

"By all means, grab a seat," Kes said, not bothering to hide the sarcasm in her voice while she pointed at the ground, "I wouldn't want my new Dungeon Lord to go hungry, now, would I?"

Ed was in too good a mood to let the mercenary's misery get to him. He flashed his Evil Eye to take notice of a small update, and sat next to Alder and Lavy to eat while he watched the night approaching.

- Your skills have increased: Dungeon Engineering +2.

Not bad for a couple hours' work.

There was something deeply satisfying about this life. He could live like this for a long time, building things, foraging for food, away from the rest of the world, only he and his minions and his magical powers. It was something he had never experienced back in the city—the chance to make something for himself. He grabbed a handful of steaming rabbit and ate under the stars, with the fire's caress feeling like a lullaby to his tired body.

Yes, Ed thought, watching how the sun slowly disappeared and how the moon rose in its place, *not bad for a couple hour's work.*

CHAPTER NINETEEN

NIGHT DWELLINGS

The meat was dry and lacked seasoning, but it was fresh and hot, and Kes wasn't untalented. To Ed's roaring stomach, it tasted like Alita herself had floated down from Heaven—or wherever the hell the Light goddess lived—and started feeding him grapes with her perfect fingers.

From Alder and Lavy's expression, they were feeling the same thing. A few feet away from them, but still close to the fire, the batblin cloud devoured their bucket of insects, and even shared some with Klek without insulting him—thanks, Ed suspected, to Klek's higher status in Ed's minionship.

Water presented an issue. The batblins had brought a few hornfuls of it from a nearby stream, but it was dirty, and Ed had watched enough nature documentaries to know he wasn't supposed to just drink it in its current state.

"So," he asked, his throat thick with rabbit-fat, "Lavy, what would you say if I had the drones transmute this water into a clean, drinkable version?"

"Clean water is too far removed from a dungeon-building tool or resource," she shrugged. "So you shouldn't be able to, in the first place. Perhaps if you had advanced ranks in Dungeon Engi-

neering and a slew of related talents, you could present your case
to the Objectivity that you wanted to use it to make ice blocks,
like some Dungeon Lords have in the past. But the 'clean' part,
definitely not. Sounds like Healing magic, to me, and we can't
use it."

"See? I'm learning already," he said. "Just keep the knowledge
coming my way, will you? Now, how about having the drones
craft a filtering device? I bet a few glass containers would do
the trick."

"Glass? Those imps of yours?" She actually mulled it over.
Unlike Kes, Lavy's full stomach had left the Witch in good humor.
"Grind for more Engineering ranks. Your drones are too brutish
for glass-making."

"Hum," said Ed. His next idea involved transmuting paper to
use as a filter, but Kes sighed loudly and said:

"By the Light's sweet mercy, do you always overthink things so
much? *Just boil the water!*"

"Oh," muttered Ed. "Yeah. That'll work."

He and Lavy exchanged ashamed glances, then the Witch
scoffed at Kes and went back to her rabbit skewer.

"You should have let them keep going," Alder told Kes after
laughing loudly and almost choking on his rabbit leg. "At the rate
they were going, they were *this* close to starting their own water-
filtering empire. The Lord of Clean Water, people would call our
brave leader."

"How do people do it in Heiliges?" asked Ed.

"Like civilized men," said Alder. "The local priest or Cleric
purifies water and food with their restoration magic each morning. Farmers who live far away from them just boil it, like
Kes said."

"Oh," Ed said. He was expecting something a bit...flashier.
"What about Lotia?"

Lavy shrugged and said, "We rely on herbs and concoctions to make sure our food is edible, or at least, that's how we do it in the countryside. I've never set a foot inside a Lotian city."

"Why not?" Ed asked.

The Witch examined the faces of Ed and the rest with a distrustful half-scowl, but before long, she shrugged and said, "I was born in a dungeon. Lord Heines' domain."

"I heard about him," said Alder. "Dungeon Lady Vaine's older brother, wasn't he? A real monster, that Heines. It was good to hear about his execution, or at least I think it was. My mother was relieved when news spread about his capture at the hands of Sir Harun's Silver Company."

"I remember that fight," Lavy said, her gaze fixated on the firelight.

"How did you survive?" Alder went on. "You must've been my age when he was around, right? He sacrificed children to build his dungeons, and you lived in one..."

Ed almost choked on his rabbit, but he managed to hide his surprise and instead, focused his attention on the Witch.

She appeared reluctant to speak further, but at the same time, she also tried hard to fake nonchalance. Ed had seen that kind of reaction before. It was how he had acted after his experience in the morgue, when his family had found him. He had pretended that he wasn't scared—that it hadn't been that much of a deal.

"It wasn't much of a deal," said Lavy, tossing what remained of her skewer into the fire. "Lord Heines thought I was his daughter. My mother was one of his consorts, and many of them bore him children. He was anxious for an heir, since he and his sister were all that was left of his bloodline. He wanted a male, but he kept his daughters, hoping to marry us off. In the end, all his dreams amounted to nothing. The knights managed to trap him far from his portals, and that was it."

"I'm sorry," said Ed, automatically, even though he couldn't feel an ounce of sympathy for a man who had killed children.

"Ah, don't be." She flashed him a crooked grin. "Alder is right. The man was a monster; he deserved the Inquisition's attentions. And I'm *not* his daughter. My mother lied to him. My real father was one of Heines' advisors, a Wizard. He was little better than Heines, but he was kind to me, sometimes. He taught me my first *spellcasting* rank."

Ed couldn't think of anything to say to that. Lavy's life—and her attitude to it—was a reminder that Ivalis existed in a very different era than Earth.

Kes, for her part, lost some of the hardness in her eyes.

"Your parents," she said with a soft, dry voice, "were in Heines' party when the knights captured him, weren't they?"

Lavy's grin gained an edge to it. "That's war, mercenary. You must know how it goes."

"Yes," said Kes, holding the Witch's gaze. "I know war."

Lavy nodded to herself, looked away, back into the flames, and finished her story. "After Heines' capture, I escaped, along with the surviving members of Heines' minionship. We were near Heiligian borders at the time. Due to Sephar's Bane, there was no chance of us going into civilized society, so many went into the service of new Dungeon Lords. Kael found my group when he was retreating from his failed incursion in Eynsworth Valley. His Warlock, Master Chasan, needed new apprentices, and I was already trained in the basics of Witchcraft. And here I am."

Ed clenched his teeth and let out a barely contained breath.

I was an asshole, he realized. He had misjudged the Witch's reaction yesterday, when he had asked her about human sacrifice. He had done to her the exact same thing he had complained that the Light-aligned people—such as Gallio and Ioan—were doing to him: judging him without knowing him or his intentions.

Now that he knew her better, he could fathom a new interpretation of her earlier attitude. She reacted defensively to his questioning because she feared he wanted to start sacrificing people on his own.

He took a deep breath. He wished to forget about the entire thing, to bury his shame somewhere deep inside him and try not to think about it again. But if he did so, he would be always recalling that confrontation, and he would never let it go.

"Lavy, I owe you an apology," he said. "For yesterday, when I asked you about human sacrifices. I thought, since you were a Witch and a former minion of another Dungeon Lord, that you saw nothing wrong in murdering innocents, and that maybe you had done it before. Sorry I misjudged you. I was wrong."

The Witch's grin slowly evaporated and was replaced by a thoughtful frown. "That's strange. I don't think I've ever heard a Dungeon Lord apologize before, much less to me. Well, I misjudged you, too. When you mentioned the human sacrifice issue, I thought that you wanted me to teach you how to perform one. Because I'm a Witch, my powers come from entities of the Dark, but that doesn't mean I'm subservient to them. Those entities are just tools to me."

"I'm sure the Dark feels the same way about you," Kes pointed out. "And they're better at manipulation than a human woman."

Lavy made a dismissive gesture, without any anger to it. "Sure. But we all spend our lives being manipulated by someone or something. Even the Light does it. I may as well choose the terms of my employment. Gain something in return."

That was something that Ed could understand very well. He passed a distracted hand over his chest, atop his new heart, and felt it beating beatifically there, enjoying the food and the warmth as much as he had.

After a pause in the conversation that seemed like it would extend until they drifted to sleep, Kes said:

"It appears that I've stumbled my way into a strange company. A Witch that doesn't pray to the Dark, a Bard that's tied into minionship instead of roaming free, and a Dungeon Lord that swears he is no friend of the Hungry One. What's your story, Edward Wright? What are you doing in Ivalis?"

That's a good question, Ed thought. He realized he had an audience. Besides the expectant faces of his companions, a couple batblins had discreetly wandered closer to their fire and were studying him with rapt attention.

But, could he really tell them the truth? He was Kael's killer, and the reason Alder and Lavy were in such dire straits.

His first instinct was to lie to them to protect himself. But Lavy had been honest with him, and what would it make of him to respond to honesty with lies?

"You aren't going to like this," he started, looking poignantly at the Witch and the Bard. "I should have told you since the beginning. I guess I was overwhelmed. If you don't want anything to do with me after hearing this, I won't do anything to stop you if you want to cancel our pact..."

He told them all about his last few days on Earth. About Ivalis Online—he had to pause to explain to them what a videogame was—and what he had done to Kael Arpadel, last of his name. Ed told them about Ryan, about meeting Kharon and hearing his proposal. About the gamble they had made, and about the vision of Murmur, and how Ed had sworn to oppose him as much as he could. Finally, he told them about Kharon's decision to drop him in Hoia Forest to save Alder and Lavy, to grow in strength, and to find out the truth behind Ivalis Online. When he was done, the night was deep, and the fire was shining straight into his eyes, transforming his companions' faces into ineffable scowls, hidden by dancing shadows.

"And here I am," he finished, eyes downcast, not daring to meet his friends' gaze. "Now you know the truth. Your situation is my fault, as is Kael's death. I don't know about Murmur's plan for the mindbrood, if there even is one, but I'll help Burrova as much as I can. If you want to help me, I'll appreciate it, but if you don't—"

Alder extended a pleading hand at him.

"Wait, Edward," the Bard said. "One moment. I hoped your

story would answer some of my own questions about you, but I think whatever you answered has only given me more questions. I'll need time to process all this. But before I go to bed, I want you to know one thing. I don't fault you for Kael's death. You had no idea what you were doing, and you were clearly being manipulated by someone. It's just like Lavy said. At least now you know you are being manipulated, but have gotten something out of the deal."

"Dungeon Lord Kael was at war with the Light," Kes added, before Ed had a chance to reply. "He knew what he was risking, and he would have done the same to you, had he known about you. This is how life is when kingdoms go to war, and you'd do best to get used to it."

Ed nodded. His mouth was dry, and the sips of warm, recently boiled water did little to clear his throat.

"Thanks," he told Alder and Kes. "I'll keep it in mind."

He looked at Lavy, whose expression was hidden by the flames. "What about you?"

The Witch stood up without a response, her face still covered in shadows. Her voice, though, was as dry as Ed's. She said in a whisper: "It's late. I'd better go to bed."

And she left without another word. The three remaining humans kept a gloomy silence. Ed stared at the stars and at the strange moon, at the shadows that danced in the trunks of the trees, at everything but the other members of his group.

The batblins, on the other hand, yawned and commented to each other:

"That was fun story."

"Reminded me of Shaman Virp's tales, before the serpent dined him."

"Ah, good old Virp. Good old times. Hand me an insect, Klek, this batch is juicy."

By the time he went to sleep, Ed was so tired that he thought of his straw bed as the most comfortable bed he had ever laid upon. He fell asleep almost instantly, all his body aching with the exertion of fighting and escaping and working on his dungeon.

He dreamed of ever-increasing stats, of finding new, powerful spells, of dungeons whose hallways extended past the horizon.

Which is to say, he had a happy sleep. He didn't dream of evil gods, or crawling horrors from the Vast Wetlands.

A noise woke him up. The oil lamp by his bed had gone out a while ago, and he was surrounded by total darkness. Here, deep inside the ground, it could have been the middle of the day and he would've had no idea. Still, he guessed it to be a little past midnight.

The curtains of the room fluttered, and he sat up on the bed, his hands fumbling around for a weapon. He was about to sound the alarm, but then a voice whispered at him:

"Shh. It's me."

That wouldn't have been helpful at all, but he happened to recognize her voice.

"Lavy?" he whispered back, still mildly alarmed. "What's going on?"

He was as blind as a bat, but he still felt her how her weight dropped at the foot of the bed.

"What's going on? Are you for real?" she told him, annoyed. "In your world, are there many reasons why a woman would go to a man's bedroom in the middle of the night?"

Well, he thought, feeling his throat instantly go dry. *I can't think of many right now.*

"Move," she told him while her hands fumbled over the rough, hemp bedsheets. "It's freezing out here."

"Uh," Ed said, but he automatically did as asked. Soon enough, he could feel Lavy's warm body drop next to his, inside the protection of the sheets. She fought with them for a couple seconds, shivering a bit, until she seemed satisfied with their position.

Then, she turned to Ed, and he could feel her breath very close to his face. Her body scraped against his clothes, the two close enough to leave little to imagination. Her hair carried the scent of violets, rabbit fat, and smoke, and of something else that made Ed very aware of the way his blood coursed through his veins, faster and faster.

The Witch said nothing, but Ed could feel her eyes staring at him in the dark. The silence was as overwhelming as the darkness, and he was still confused by being awakened so suddenly.

"I thought you were angry at me," Ed said, finally, when the tension was too much to bear. "For what happened to—"

"I am," she whispered back. "*Furious.* You should know I loved Kael Arpadel, even if he never looked my way. While I don't hold you responsible for his death...you *were* involved. I spent a while, tonight, thinking what I should do about it. This was the best solution I could come up with."

Ed felt Lavy's hands grab a hold of him by his waist, and she pulled herself closer to him. He felt the waves of soft heat emanating from her body, doing more to warm him than the sheets could, and he felt her breasts pressed firmly against his chest. A long, slender leg slid between his own, almost in a caress, and then her thigh traveled upward, slowly, until it was caressing something else entirely. Her thigh was naked, and Ed's hands traveled quickly across the soft, warm body to confirm that, at some point before her entering the sheets, Lavy had managed to lose all her clothes, if she had worn any at all.

Ed's body responded, and the part of him that still had a hold on rational thought began to panic as his self-control slipped.

"Wait," he whispered, "wait. I don't understand. This is your *solution*? Why?"

Her thigh paused. Lavy softly pushed Ed on his back, and then she was on top of him, the thick, hemp sheets around them both, like a royal cape, and her hair falling in a cascade on Ed's face. She was still so close to him that he could feel her warm breathing on his neck and chin, and the hard points of her nipples pressed against his chest. And he could *definitely* feel her legs pinning his waist firmly under her.

"What of it?" Lavy whispered. "I can cope however I want. Your only concern, my Lord Wright, should be—"

She placed one hand on Ed's chest, for leverage, and lowered her face to his neck, where her lips traveled upward, slowly, until they reached his ear in a way that made goosebumps travel all over his skin.

"—are you the kind of man," she went on, whispering into his ear while her free hand lazily pulled open his shirt, and caressed his torso, "who is capable of rejecting a woman who throws herself in his bed, because she might be vulnerable and making rash decisions?"

That was a very, very good question. She was definitely vulnerable, mourning Kael in one hell of a way, and she was definitely taking a rash course of action. What kind of man was he? The courteous route would be to send her back to her quarters, and give her more time to think it over. While Ed thought about it, Lavy pulled away from his face, and her hand traveled farther down, past his waist, and closed her fingers around his erection, pulling it out of his trousers as she did so.

Ed's lungs were not receiving enough air anymore, and all conscious thought disappeared from his mind.

He groaned and raised a hand, searching in the dark until he found Lavy's breast. He cupped it firmly, pressing his thumb against the small, hard nipple, earning a soft moan from the Witch.

What kind of man was he? Not a damn monk.

At the last second, Lavy pushed herself up. "Wait," she breathed, "do that eye thing."

"What?"

"The fucking eye magic thing. Turn it on."

At that point, Ed was well past the point of caring, or needing, any kind of explanation. If she had asked him to summon an entire crowd of drones to cheer them on, he wouldn't have blinked. He activated his Evil Eye, and the Witch's body was illuminated by its eldritch light, which was much more effective than any oil lamp at pushing the darkness back.

Her eyes were wide with desire, and perhaps a hint of madness, and her semi-parted lips itched to be kissed. Her respiration was heavy, with her breasts and chest rising and falling in a rhythm that hypnotized the Dungeon Lord. He passed his hand across and down her breast, over her firm abdomen, and over her navel.

At the sight of Ed's Evil Eye, Lavy smiled in a way that was downright malicious, and heavy with desire.

"Ah, yes, that's it," she whispered. "Don't turn it off."

They went at it for an unknown amount of time, using the covers to stifle their grunts and moans, and lost in the sensation of each other. Covered by the eldritch light of Ed's Evil Eye, Lavy looked like a woman out of a pagan ritual, wild and forbidden.

After they were done, Ed found himself lying next to his friend's warm body, both of them as out of breath as the other. They stayed like that, drawing cold air into their lungs, without saying a word.

Finally, Ed's rationality slowly regained control over his tired body, and the first pair of timid thoughts made their way around his mind.

"So, this happened," Ed whispered hoarsely.

"Yeah," agreed Lavy, who had already recovered her breath. She sat on the bed and fumbled around in the greenish half-dark. "You know? I'll be honest with you. This was only one idea. The other involved the knife I was hiding in my boots...but I'm glad I changed my mind. I would have hated having to use it."

What could Ed say to something like that?

Lavy looked around. "Now, where in the Dark's name are my trousers?"

She found them, and fumbled around some more until she was fully dressed, although there was no power on Earth or Ivalis that could do anything about her tangled hair.

She jumped out of bed with her boots dangling from her hand, cursed at the sudden bite of the cold, and turned to Ed just as she started shivering.

"Sleep well, Lord Wright," she said, and she *patted* him on his back before disappearing away into the darkness, gone as suddenly as she had appeared.

Ed was left alone, stunned and already fading back into sleep, too tired to contemplate the consequences of their actions, too spent to care. He turned off the Evil Eye, and in the darkness and the silence it was almost like he had dreamed the whole event. He turned to sleep, already blacking out as he moved—

"Fucking finally," said Alder, his voice coming from behind the thin rock wall that separated his quarters from Ed's. "Alita's tits, I thought you were never going to let me fucking sleep."

Ed groaned, and covered his head under the heap of blankets. As he did so, he dragged a hand under the roll he used as a pillow, grabbed the handle of his own knife, and tossed it out of the bed.

He was glad he hadn't had to use it.

CHAPTER TWENTY

WHAT LURKS IN THE DARKNESS

A noise woke Nicolai from his drunken slumber.

The man passed a calloused hand across his forehead and grimaced. The tzuika's sweet flavor had left an overwhelming residue in his throat, and his brain was spinning inside his skull. He suspected he was in that obnoxious point where he was both drunk and hungover at the same time.

He spat on the ground by his side of the bed and sat groggily on the straw mattress.

Why was he awake?

Next to him, Marya turned in her sleep. He studied her while trying to gather his bearings. Certainly, age hadn't been kind to his wife. What she had done for him easily when they married, now, seven kids and many years of backbreaking labor later, barely got a rise out of his prick.

She shifted again, and his mean, old drunkard's heart softened a little. He caressed her hair, briefly, and willed her back to sleep.

He didn't need her for his prick; he had a wench at the village for that. Marya was the mother of his children, and she worked the farm as hard as he did, and that was all they needed.

Nicolai was about to lie down next to his wife when the noise returned again. A dull *thud,* clear as the stars in the sky, came from outside the house by the chicken shed.

His mind cleared, and the numbing mist of the tzuika was replaced by seething rage.

The fucking chickens!

So that damned fox was back at it again? Back to finish the work, to kill the few remaining poultry?

He got out of bed, cursing silently to himself, careful not to wake Marya or the children who slept huddled next to each other, at the foot of their bed, covered in piles of thick, woolen sheets.

If Nicolai had been a bit more awake, if he had been the kind of man who kept his composure even when angered, he would have noticed there were only seven sleeping shapes.

But he wasn't, and in his anger, he barely managed not to step on any of his kids while he hurried outside, anxious to catch the fox. He was itching to break the animal's neck with his bare hands.

Nicolai grabbed his woolen coat and put on his boots. Other than that, he rushed out of his home naked.

I'm going to fucking make a hat out of your hide, he thought with grim pleasure. At least it would help him keep his head warm while his family hungered during winter.

The wind was unruly, and freezing cold, so much so that a normal man may have risked his life going outside. But Nicolai was a farmer, as had been his father, and all his scant experience points had gone into *endurance*-related talents. His skin was as thick as a bull's, and he was protected by a layer of fat, thanks to all the tzuika.

He reached the chicken shed, careful not to make too much noise. It was as he had feared. There was no sight of the remaining chicken, even though they always rushed out to meet

Nicolai when he approached, no matter the hour, since he was the one who fed them most of the time.

A single, bloody feather was half-engulfed by the mud in front of him.

Nicolai could feel the blood rushing to his face, his throat already bulging out with a barely contained scream of rage.

Pigfucker! Dung-eater! Alita's fucking mercy, what use are the gods if they can't protect an honest man's livelihood?

He knew what he would find when he looked inside the shed. A bunch of feathers, broken bones cleaned to the core, and lines of meat, blood, and chicken shit streaked across the walls.

Another dull *thud,* this time clearly coming from the shed only a few steps in front of him. The scream of fury died in Nicolai's throat.

The pigfucker is still there, he realized.

Panting, the farmer dropped to his knees and closed his fingers around a good-sized rock. He didn't need any other weapon. His father had taught him how to throw, and his accuracy had been refined across the years. He could kill a fox or a wolf with a single strike, and at higher distances than this one.

Thus armed, he approached the shed and kicked it open, forcing the doors inward with the roar of splintering wood.

"I got you now, fucker!" he roared, but his raging scream shifted into terror when he saw the scene that was unfolding in front of him.

The chickens were dead, alright, dead and torn, their bodies mangled in bloody heaps beyond recognition. Entrails and bodily fluids were everywhere, strewn in a rough semi-circle around what Nicolai's mind could only describe as a dog-sized, black-shelled cockroach with a pink, soft back that looked like a brain, covered in red veins which pulsated softly as the creature fed.

When it heard his scream, the creature reared its head—if it could be called that. It had a pair of eyes to the sides and another in the front of the elongated snout-like skull, and two big holes under those, as a nose. The creature's front eyes were cat-like. They widened when it saw Nicolai.

The farmer, too stunned and too terrified to react, saw how the front of the creature's snout opened in four, like the peel of a banana, to reveal two pairs of prehensile mandibles and long, grime-covered teeth at the middle, with a black tongue slithering behind like a worm.

"No," mouthed Nicolai. "No. What are you?"

This *thing* had to be a creature of the Dark. What business did it have with a poor farmer's family in the middle of nowhere? What business did the Dark have in Starevos?

The creature dropped the torn chicken it was carrying in one of its two pairs of arms. It was hunched over, its powerful legs bent. They were almost thicker than the rest of its body, and ended in two paws armed with sharp, knife-like claws.

The creature's teeth parted, and to Nicolai's horror, it *spoke*. With a childlike voice.

"Dad?"

It wasn't just any childlike voice. Nicolai had seven children, but he could recognize any of them by the sound of their footsteps. A voice was easy. This creature, somehow, had stolen Little Ilena's voice.

"No!" he whispered. Could this be a nightmare? He tried to place his hands the way the priest had taught him, to make Alita's symbol like he was supposed to do, but his fat fingers were numb and his hands were shaking, as was his entire body, and the sign came fake and useless. A warm liquid streaked along his legs, raising trails of steam as it hit the soil in front of him. He looked down—he had pissed himself. And he still hadn't woken up.

"Dad!" the monster spoke again in Ilena's voice. "Dad, I'm sorry! I didn't want to eat the chicken, but I was so *hungry!* I couldn't stop myself, and my head hurt so much, and they smelled *so good.* I swear I didn't want to! But I needed them,

Daddy, I needed to eat them so I could grow up strong like you and Mommy."

"What are you?" the farmer asked again. "What, in the Light's name, are you? What have you done with my daughter?"

The monster stood partially on its hind legs and partially on its second pair of arms, with the first pair gesturing desperately at Nicolai to come closer. It took a couple steps in his direction, and the farmer instinctively stepped away, back into the open.

"Help me, Daddy, I don't know what happened to me! I was hungry, and my head hurt so much, and now I look like this...I'm not in pain anymore, but, oh, I'm so hungry!"

The shift in their position let the farmer better see the heap behind the monster. At first, he didn't recognize the body, with it being so broken and mangled, but he knew the shape of the tiny limbs, the wooden dress that Marya had knitted for her, the pink lasso tying her hair together, splattered with red blood and fragments of skull.

Ilena's head was gone, burst open like a melon, and the rest of her body was half-eaten—just one more meal for the creature that spoke with Nicolai's daughter's voice.

"Daddy, don't leave! I'm so *hungry!*"

Nicolai screamed his throat hoarse and threw his rock with all his strength. It hit the monster's snout squarely and left a bloody crack in its chitin right under its left side-eye, which partially fell out of its cavity and hung there, connected to the skull by a meaty thread.

The monster's roar deafened Nicolai's scream, drowned it in a howl of pain and confusion.

"Daddy!" the thing howled. "Why did you hurt me? Please, Daddy, don't hurt me! I need your help!"

But the farmer could see how the sullen hole the rock had left in the exoskeleton filled itself while the monster spoke. The eye snapped back in place.

Nicolai turned and ran for his life, venturing into the darkness, trying to reach the safety of his home, screaming all the while.

Behind him, coming closer and closer, he could hear his daughter screaming after him, begging him to stay with her, begging him to help her, to just *come a bit closer, Daddy, I need help*—

Something hard smashed against Nicolai's back, driving all the air out of his lungs, making him lose his balance and throwing him against the wet ground, where he rolled in a heap, trying to punch and pull at an enemy he could not see.

A flash of dark chitin reflected a ray of silver moonlight, and two arms, strong and sinewy, grabbed a hold of Nicolai's, pinning him in place while another two raked sharp claws against his chest, leaving streaks of fire and pain as they went. The creature was on top of him, using its weight to manhandle him.

"Daddy!"

Nicolai screamed and tried to wrestle out of the monster's hold, tried to fight back, but the monster was stronger than he was, even if it was smaller. Moonlight made the saliva glint like it was liquid silver wetting two pairs of prehensile mandibles.

"Daddy, I'm sorry!"

The mandibles came down, closed against Nicolai's shoulder, and tore a big chunk of meat like his body was made of mud. Nicolai's screaming died in his throat. He could hear, in the distance, the sound of his other sons yelling at him from inside the house, searching for him in the dark.

No, he thought. *Stay away. Don't open the door. Don't*—

"Daddy, oh gods, I don't want to eat you! I'm hurting you —I'm sorry!"

Its hind legs were tearing his belly apart, digging their long claws in until they reached his entrails, and then brutally pulled them out, over and over. Nicolai could feel his torn guts being sprawled across the ground, raising piles of steam, filling his nose with the smell of his own intestines.

The mandibles came down again, and part of his arm was gone.

Nicolai had never been in so much pain, never been so scared. But he could feel his body numbing, his brain rejecting the horror that was happening to him, unraveling back into his own mind.

But not fast enough.

"Forgive me!" the monster said, while one of its dark claws came down over Nicolai's eyes, and then the darkness was total. "I don't wanna!"

He could still hear it. He could still *feel* it eating him alive.

Oh, gods, make it stop. Any gods. Light, Dark, I don't care. Make it stop.

"It's just that—" the monster went on, tearing more chunks out of him.

"You are—" another bite, another chunk.

"Delicious, Daddy!"

LITTLE ILENA CAME BACK to her senses when the first rays of daylight arrived, warming her soft, exposed back.

What had happened?

The day was cold, but she was used to the night, and the sunlight made her groggy with sleep. And her belly was so full it felt like it might burst...

She looked around, her two pairs of eyes giving her an excellent view of the house, which was still covered in shadows.

"Where is everyone?"

Mom? Dad?

Her brothers?

She was lying on her usual blanket, in the spot that normally left her sandwiched between her older sisters, but they weren't there, and neither was the rest of her family. Only a bunch of broken bones, chunks of hair, and torn clothing. Streaks of blood dirtied the walls and the ceiling, and the wood was raked with long lines left by what must've been a pretty sharp set of claws.

"Is this a joke?" asked Ilena. "Because I don't like it. It's not funny."

She wasn't going to clean up her brothers' mess. She guessed that, at any time now, they would burst through the door, laughing at her.

She hoped they did so, soon. She was sad, and lonely.

She wanted to weep, to cry until she passed out. She wanted her mother to comfort her.

And she wanted to lick her paws, which still had torn, thin lines of sinew lodged between her claws.

There was a noise by the chicken shed.

Mom?

Dad?

She skittered across the wall, and headed to the door which had a small window, and fidgeted against the wooden panel with her claws—ill-fitted for the task—until she opened it.

The shed was empty, and there was only a pile of bones at the spot where she had last seen her father.

But something moved in the distance, far from the shed, across the line of the trees.

Was her hearing really that good, to hear something so far away? That was new. She could barely hear anything at all before she had hatched.

Growing up was interesting. She could feel her bones itch with the effort of increasing their size, the painful—but not in a bad way—sensation of her skin as it was being constantly pulled taut while her body shifted. Perhaps her family would come back once she was fully grown.

But first, she'd have to deal with the dark shapes hiding inside the bushes and the trunks of the trees. They didn't move from their place, but Ilena's instincts were as powerful as those of a veteran Ranger's. She knew they were sizing her scent up. Looking for her.

Those were hunters.

She sniffed at the air and was surprised when the current brought the scent of horned spiders.

I can smell them from here?

She would have to worry about that later. Spiders! Her body trembled with rage and fear.

Her parents had told her all about spiders. Very, very rarely, a cluster of them would venture out of Hoia, generally during a drought. During those times, they attacked farms and isolated groups of men and women, including travelers. They had even eaten children!

Disgusting creatures, Ilena thought, snapping her mandibles at them.

Something about their smell brought old grudges about them, grudges she didn't even know she had. Grudges from before she had been born.

Her ancestors had eaten horned spiders, she realized, after thinking about it for a moment. And the horned spiders had attacked her ancestors, killed their own clusters in their effort to make her ancestors starve.

And now the spiders were trying to do the same to her.

Disgusting, nasty creatures.

She could feel her body growing stronger. But she knew her growth was not yet enough for her to defend herself. Had they waited just a bit longer, just a week more...and *she* would be hunting *them.*

As she was now, though, she had to hide. The prospect didn't faze her. Hiding and lurking and waiting for her chance to strike at her food was ingrained in her, deep within a part of her mind that was old and wise—and oh, so hungry.

She knew what she had to do. The spiders were at their best in the forest, and they had the wind as their advantage. If the breeze had carried with it the scent of a swamp—*home,* thought that old part of her—she would have gone there. But there was no swamp here.

There was the smell of a human settlement, though, staining the air. Unmistakable. She knew what it meant.

Burrova.

The old part of her brain approved of Ilena's plan. She could hide in the village—there were plenty of places where no one would look, and the spiders would spend themselves fighting against the humans.

Ilena's own people would defend her, and she would have plenty of food to sate her hunger. To grow strong. Until she was ready to start her own family.

Mom and Dad would be so proud of her.

21

CHAPTER TWENTY-ONE

PARLEY

When Ed came out of the cave, he discovered he had slept almost past morning, and that the daylight was mixing warm drafts of air with the normal chilliness of Starevos.

He was wearing a jacket made of transmuted wool, with trousers of the same material. He suspected the fabric would fall apart before the day was over, considering the usual duration of all the non-dungeon related transmutations he had tried, but in the meantime, he was warm.

The young Dungeon Lord made his way with difficulty down the slope of the rocky hill and found the smoldering remains of the campsite below. Someone had made breakfast, probably Kes, and they had left a little for him. It was cold pottage, made with the remains of last night's rabbits, cooked and stored in a clay pot, which had probably been transmuted too.

The sight made his sore body ache with hunger. He wasn't sure which part of his body *didn't* hurt and ache, so he considered it a small miracle he managed to get out of bed at all. As it turned out, he wasn't used to running around fighting giant spiders like an action hero, and he was paying the consequences of overextending himself.

At least I can rest for a couple days, he thought, to give himself hope. *I can use drones to do all labor around here.*

Ed looked around while he devoured the pottage like it was the water of life itself. His companions weren't in sight, and he spotted only a couple batblins sitting around lazily in the damp grass, patting their insect-full bellies.

I'll have to find something for them to do, Ed thought, watching the pair doze off into deeper and deeper sleep. *I suspect that having bored batblins around is more dangerous than using horned spiders as back-scratchers.*

But first, where was everyone? Not even Klek or Drusb were around, much less Lavy or Alder.

He ate the last drops of soup and considered going back to grab a wooden spear. Then, the foliage shook and Kes emerged from it, frowning with a hard expression on her face.

Alder, Lavy and Klek followed after her, frowning too. They seemed to be angry at the mercenary, and Lavy had her knife drawn and hanging from her arm.

"What's going on?" Ed asked, jumping to his feet, which instantly made him wince in pain. He reached for his own knife, but didn't draw it.

"This *traitor,*" Lavy growled, pointing at Kes, "just tried to betray us all."

"What?" Ed asked, eyes wide.

Kes rolled her eyes at Lavy and said, "Oh, don't be so melodramatic. If I wanted to betray you, all of you would be *dead.* I was trying to *help* your dear Lord Wright."

"That's one hell of a way to twist what you did," said Alder, raising an eyebrow at her. "I mean, gods, Kes, you went to talk to a fucking Inquisitor!"

"What?" Ed said, again. But, again, they were too busy fighting to pay him any mind.

"Ex-Inquisitor," Kes sighed. "Gallio lost the Light's blessing a long time ago. He couldn't produce a *Sunwave* if his life depended on it."

"Doesn't change a thing!" Lavy said, raising her voice and gesturing dangerously with her hands, not dropping her knife to do so. Klek, who was walking near her, took a step back and away from both the mercenary and the Witch. "He can call his Inquisitor friends, and then we'll all hang! Except you, of course, because I'll be the first in line to gut you!"

"Don't point that thing at me, or I'll make you eat it—"

"*Enough!*" This time, Ed activated his Evil Eye and almost screamed his command.

To his own surprise, they listened to him, and Kes took a step away from Lavy's face, although her hand was still hovering over the handle of her sword.

"Good," Ed said, before he lost the initiative. "Now, Alder, explain from the beginning, on your end."

"Yessir," said the Bard. He spoke quickly, and to the point. "I woke up. Neither Lavy nor Kes were around. I went out looking, found Lavy coming back from a trip to the herbalist, but no sight of Kes. So, we sent the batblins to search for her around the forest, to no avail. We were about to wake you, when Klek found her coming back from Burrova's road, and when we confronted her, she admitted she had just talked to Gallio. We came back, you are here. Have I mentioned that green eye thing makes your skull visible under the right lighting? Because it kinda freaks me out."

Uh, thought Ed, *I had no idea.* He turned off the Evil Eye. There were no mirrors around, so he had never seen himself using his power. Lavy had demanded he use it last night. That probably said more about her than it did about him.

"Okay," he said. "Kes, please tell me why I shouldn't believe there is a group of Burrova's finest about to come knocking at our door with a lot of pointy sticks."

"What does 'okay' mean? Is that a kaftar word?" asked the mercenary, but without waiting for an answer, she went on. "Yes, I talked to Gallio. No, I did not betray you. We are still connected by our pact if you haven't checked."

Ed confirmed it. She was telling the truth. "Go on."

"I did so because I believe you." She shrugged. "Last night, when you told your story. Edward, every single Dungeon Lord I've heard about has been either a monster, or an enemy of the Light, or both. But I've never heard of a Dungeon Lord taken from another world. You know nothing of our customs, or our ancient history, or our culture. You are a stranger here, and whatever sick game the Dark One is playing with you, I believe you to be a victim, not the culprit."

"Dungheap," said Lavy. "If there is a victim here, that's you, Kes. You really believe Gallio can help him? Don't you remember what the Inquisition does to Dungeon Lords? The same thing they are going to do to us!"

Kes nodded. "Yes, I know. Because of Sephar's Bane. But Edward's presence changes all, don't you see? He can find out who is infected with that interpretation of the pact-making rules he used yesterday. Imagine all the good he could do! If he had been around during Sephar's time, surely he could have helped avoid the entire thing. A normal Dungeon Lord would've never agreed to help Heiliges, but Ed could have!"

"That's what you told Gallio," Ed said. He passed a hand across his forehead. It was too early for this shit.

"Yes. Like I said before, he is not an Inquisitor anymore. He is not duty-bound to purge the Dark-aligned. You have an amazing opportunity, Edward. If Burrova is in danger of a mindbrood, you can help save it. You can help save the lives of everyone in the village."

"They are in more danger of the Inquisition than of the mindbrood," said Alder, but without Lavy's animosity. "At least, for the moment. Just wanted to make that point clear."

Kes said nothing to that, perhaps conceding the point. But she still looked at Ed expectantly.

She was asking him to risk getting captured by the Inquisition, and if they went by their Earth's namesakes, they wouldn't treat prisoners well. He was risking torture, and death, all for the chance of saving the lives of some strangers that would probably never get over their fears of Dungeon Lords long enough to thank him. If he said no, he could stay by his corner of Hoia, growing in strength, hunting the mindbrood his own way, until he was ready to face any Inquisitor with strength to match theirs.

It was an easy choice to make.

"Take me to him," he told the mercenary.

Kes flashed him a radiant smile.

"I was right about you," she said, like a child who had just found out that Christmas had come early. "You aren't evil."

"I was right about him," Alder told Lavy, in a whisper. "He is insane."

Ed smiled at the Bard and shrugged. "Last night, I told you I wanted to oppose Murmur, remember? If I don't do this, if I'm not willing to work over our differences with Gallio and the Light before escalating the conflict, I would be the kind of person that I hate, and that Murmur loves."

"Or you would be the kind of person who lives to see winter," Lavy pointed out somberly.

ED'S GROUP met with Gallio's at a middle point between Burrova and the cave, a spot close to the stream that the batblins usually used to replenish their water.

Gallio was accompanied only by Vasil, both dressed in the full garb of the Burrova's guard, but their weapons were kept at their sides, and their arms were empty. Ed didn't fully relax, though, since he now lived in a world where people could command magic from their fingertips, and he didn't know Gallio's stats.

The young Dungeon Lord had only brought Kes with him, as a show of good faith, but also to keep his other friends away from harm if he was betrayed.

Even then, he wasn't defenseless. He was wearing the leather jerkin that he had worn against the spiders, his woolen jacked over it, his hunting knife hanging by a cord he used as a belt, and his Earth-made jeans and running shoes, which were in a better condition than his Ivalis clothes. And most importantly, his spells were full. He had two for the day, and in the back of his mind he was already planning how he'd use them, while Gallio approached him with his arms raised above his head.

"Edward Wright," said the Sheriff. Ed noted that the man's toned arms were barely scratched, and that he had no signs of injury from the fight with the spiders. "Yesterday, I didn't peg you for a Dungeon Lord. I didn't even know if you had survived our run-in with the spiders. You really think you can help Burrova against the mindbrood?"

Ed threw a dubious glance at Vasil. The pockmarked man was armed with a shortbow at his back, and he wasn't as calm as his boss. Ed could see pearls of sweat coming down of the guard's forehead.

"Sheriff Gallio," Ed said, "Kes told me she already filled you in on my story. Surely you don't want me to repeat it?"

Both of them stopped an arms' length away from the other and squared each other up. Ed had little doubt that, if it came to a fight, Gallio would win easily. But Ed had a few tricks up his sleeve.

In any case, he wasn't here to fight the Sheriff.

"Kes believes you," Gallio said, "and I believe her. She has been with us since Burrova's founding, and she has never once lied to me. If Lotia can create such sleeper agents that are capable of maintaining a lie for so long...Heiliges would be doomed anyway."

"So you don't care she has joined me?"

"In a pact, you say?" Gallio shook his head sadly. "I know very well that men and women may have perfectly valid reasons to pact with a Dungeon Lord. Threats, torture, bribery...surely you know all the tricks the Dark has to get you to its side."

I know a few.

"The law is the law," Gallio finished, after a pause to see if Ed had something to say. He turned to Kes. "I won't patronize you by pretending you didn't know what you were doing, or what the consequences would be."

Kes nodded curtly once. "Thank you."

Gallio returned his attention to Ed. "Is it true you can find the mindbroods' hosts?"

"In theory," Ed said, "yes. Though I've yet to find one."

And lucky me. I have no idea what I would do to that person if I did.

"The mages capable of performing the correct divination magic are very rare," Gallio said, "and they won't risk themselves by wandering around in mindbrood-infested lands. If, all this time, Dungeon Lords had this power...Heiliges is at a clear disadvantage, at least in regards to this."

"I don't know about that," said Ed, "and I don't care about your politics. I want to help people avoid having their brains sucked dry and replaced by a monster."

"A Dungeon Lord on the side of the Light," Gallio muttered to himself. He passed one leather-gloved hand across his blond hair, which was starting to go white at the sides. "If Alita still answered my prayers, I wonder what she would say about that."

"I don't know her," said Ed, "but if she's a reasonable goddess, she would at least give me the benefit of the doubt."

Gallio sighed. If all Inquisitors looked like him, they weren't a very intimidating order. He was a strong warrior, no doubt, but he wasn't scary. He was tired, and he was getting old.

"What do you think, Vasil?" Gallio asked.

"I should put an arrow in them both and be done with it,"

Vasil said, and he spat on the ground. "Nothing good will come from trusting a Dungeon Lord."

"Nice, Vasil, real nice," Kes told him. "I taught you how to use your damn bow."

"Ah, sod off, friend Kes," the guard said, and he spat again. "You should have let the spiders kill you instead of running to the Dark to save you. What is Alvedhra going to think of you?"

Gallio gestured at them to stop, and said to Ed, "What do you propose to do? Ioan thinks the spiders could be lying, since Starevos is not a mindbrood's natural habitat. Too cold for them. He believes we shouldn't summon the Inquisitors, yet, though I think that waiting any more would be stupid."

Ed nodded. "Agreed. From what Kes and Alder taught me about those monsters, you don't want to take risks with them. Here is what I offer. I go to Burrova, you gather the villagers, I pact with them and not with any parasite that is pretending to be them—or part of them. Then, right after, we cancel all pacts, and I walk away."

Gallio said nothing. Instead, he looked at Ed's shoes, frowning. In the end, he only said, "I see."

"He's telling the truth, Gallio," Kes reminded him. "I heard the wording in his pact, and nothing ate him after he tried to bend the rules, so the Objectivity avails it."

"I'm sorry, Edward," said the Sheriff, "but I haven't been entirely honest with you. I came here not because of Kes' urging, but because I had to shake my own doubts about you."

"What do you mean?" asked Ed.

"I'm now sure of it. I may not have my powers anymore, but I can still tell when people are telling the truth. It's a personal talent, bought with my own experience points. Both you and Kes are telling the truth when you say you want to help. This means, you are being used by the Dark. I'm sorry."

"I don't follow," said Ed, frowning himself. He was on high alert now, aware that things weren't going as he had hoped. Any strange movement and he would activate his *improved reflexes* and start throwing drones at people.

"If any other Dungeon Lord had come up to me with that offer, to pact with an entire village, I would have killed them on the spot, Inquisitor or not. It would be an obvious trick by a devious monster. It would mean they had planted the mindbrood themselves in the first place and are using its threat as leverage. But you...*truly* want to help."

"He's telling the truth!" Kes repeated. "Are you daft? You said so yourself!"

Ed sighed and said, "He thinks Murmur planted the mind-brood. Don't you, Gallio?"

"Not only that, the Dark One allowed your pact trick to work in the first place. Probably gave you the idea himself, without your noticing. If I allow you to 'help us,' Murmur will take advantage of the pact. I don't know how. But I know he will. I'm sorry, Edward, but like I said, you are being used."

"Gallio!" Kes exclaimed. "You are being paranoid! Is this how the Militant Church trains its pawns? Alita's mercy, why can't the Light be the one who is using Ed? Why does it have to be Murmur? The entire village could get purged because of your stubbornness!"

The Sheriff shook his head, sadly, without anger. "Sorry, old friend. I may not be an Inquisitor anymore, but I am still a man striving to do as much good as he can. And that means making the hard decisions, the ones no one else is willing to make. The ones that damn you whether you make them or not."

"Was that how you lost your powers?" asked Ed. "You made a decision no one else wanted to make?"

"Just say the word, boss," called Vasil, who at some point had unslung his bow.

Ed eyed him from the corner of his vision and tried to guess the spot where he would have to create his drone.

"Wait, Vasil," Gallio said, "be reasonable. We did not come

here to fight. Dungeon Lord, you have been dealt a terrible hand. You are a good person, but no matter what you do or try, all your efforts for the Light will end up advancing the cause of the Dark. I've seen this happen, myself, with my own eyes. If you truly care about doing good for the world...then know that the only good you are capable of is ending your own life."

Everyone fell into stunned silence after his words, and even Vasil lowered his bow, though it was Kes who spoke first:

"Surely, you don't mean that—"

"It's what I would do in his place," said Gallio.

"Are you really going to let Burrova suffer Sephar's Bane?" Her mouth was agape, and she could barely muster anything louder than a whisper.

"Of course not," Gallio went on, "but I won't—I *can't*—ally myself with a Dungeon Lord. It goes against everything I once stood for. I'm taking a third option. I'm summoning the Inquisition."

Kes cursed loudly, and Vasil turned to Gallio. The guardsman's face was pale, as if he had seen a ghost.

"They will kill everyone in Burrova," he said, "down to the women and the children!"

"The mindbrood will kill them just as surely," said Gallio through gritted teeth. "But it will also spread its poison to other villages! And what happens if an infected reaches Undercity? What then, Vasil? What if they reach a ship, what if they make the trip to Heiliges? They could spread through all of Ivalis! Surely the life of a few villagers isn't worth the life of *everyone else?*"

"You know these people," Vasil whispered. "You have lived among them from the start. They consider you one of them. Your duty is to protect them. You're the *Sheriff.*"

"My duty is to the Light," Gallio said, "even if the Light won't have me."

He took a few steps away from Ed, and told him, "There's

nothing else we can say to each other. I'll respect our truce here, but if I see you again I won't be able to protect you from the Inquisition. Not even if I wanted to."

"Go fuck yourself," Ed told him. "I'm going to save Burrova whether you want me to or not."

The Sheriff's hands hovered over the handle of his mace.

"We'll see about that. Not a step further, friend Edward."

"We are not friends," Ed told him while taking another step.

Gallio's hands closed around the mace's handle, and Ed's eyes flashed green.

And then, Kes ran to the middle of them, sword drawn, and horror painted across her expression.

"Stop, you idiots! Are you blind?" She pointed at a spot behind Vasil, farther up than the tops of the trees. "Look!"

A column of smoke, thick and black, rose above the forest in Burrova's direction.

Ed felt growing horror as he realized the implications. A fire. *The village is made of wood.*

He and the ex-Inquisitor exchanged terrified glances, both thinking the same thing.

"An attack," said Gallio. "We may be too late to stop the Bane."

Ed didn't dare to nod, although he agreed with the man. Instead, he said, "Let's go."

The four of them ran toward the smoke.

CHAPTER TWENTY-TWO

IT CAME FROM THE WETLANDS

E d's muscles complained with every running step he took, with every half-jump he made over roots and depressions in the soil, all while the cold air of Starevos rushed past his raw throat and into overworked lungs.

Nevertheless, the young man kept running, even while the other three—who were trained warriors—left him behind in their hurry to reach their village.

He knew the way to the road—he could reach it on his own. So, he gritted his teeth and tried to keep his breathing under control.

It was like he was wading through invisible honey, or under a permanent version of someone else's *improved reflexes*. Was the smoke getting thicker in the distance?

He had only been inside Burrova once. But all those people... they didn't deserve what was coming their way.

His Evil Eye flickered on and off, and he summoned a drone that disappeared from view as quickly as it arrived. Back in his camp there would be one drone less, and he had instructed them, before he left, to remain in sight of Lavy and Alder at all times so his friends would know something had gone wrong if he called a drone away.

I hope they see the smoke and figure it out themselves, he thought.

He stumbled when a root snagged his leather vest, and almost fell, but he managed to retain his balance. He kept running.

Burrova appeared soon after, and the view confirmed Ed's fears.

The walls were burning. Tongues of flame as wide and tall as the wall itself raged across a quarter of them, at least the parts that Ed could see. And some of the few buildings inside the village were burning, too.

The smoke was everywhere, painting the sky a dirty black, and Ed could smell it even that distance away, along with drafts of hot air mixed with the cold currents.

He stopped for a second, caught his breath, then kept running. The fire was spreading.

Where are the guards? Surely, they must have training in case of a fire? A water-hose rune, or something? Ed knew Ivalis Online had water-themed spells, so *where were the guards*?

His question didn't remain unanswered for long. As he came closer, as the smoke became thicker and the fire grew, he could see shapes scaling the west side of the palisade which hadn't caught fire yet.

Tiny, black shapes with many legs, like a living carpet, climbing the wood like it was a horizontal surface. They were followed by bigger creatures, the size of a wolf, covered in chitin, with a long horn on their foreheads above their many eyes and snapping mandibles.

Horned spiders. They flowed out of Hoia's edge, and the grass that separated the edge of the village was covered by the creatures, which marched like an army toward the walls.

Too far away from Ed for him to do anything but watch and try to reach the gates.

The pain in his body was forgotten. It was amazing what

adrenaline could do. The young Dungeon Lord crossed the remaining distance to Burrova's gates in a few minutes.

The gates were closed, but the bridge was lowered. He would have stopped to ponder the meaning of it, but he had no time. He reached the walls, pushed against them, confirmed they were locked from the inside, and activated his Evil Eye.

The ley lines under Burrova were brighter and more numerous than the ones at his cave, and they seemed to coalesce at the center of the village. They made summoning three drones a very easy task.

Ed called them to the spot a couple feet in front of him, past the gates, right over the main ley line. He felt them appear and saw the mist pass under the gates.

Unbar them, he commanded the drones, stepping away from the wood to let his drones work. *If you can't, then eat them.*

He heard the drones struggle briefly, and then, several loud crunches in unison. Something heavy fell to the ground, and Ed hurried to push the doors open. At first, they didn't budge, and his arms roared with the effort, but eventually he managed to crank the gates open enough for him to squeeze into the village.

The wave of heat reached him immediately. It was like stepping into the inside of a furnace. The smoke was flowing away from him, but even so, it was hard to breathe and to see what he had in front of him.

He started coughing immediately.

The amount of smoke inside Burrova was insane. He *knew* there couldn't be many fires inside, since there were only a few buildings. He had severely underestimated the amount of smoke even a moderate fire could produce.

After the smoke, the next thing he noticed was that no one was nearby. The place was deserted. There wasn't a soul in sight, although that meant little in all the smoke.

At his feet was a broken basket, the vegetables it carried spilled all across the ground. They had been stepped on, smashed every which way. There were other trinkets lying around that people had dropped in their hurry.

They tried to leave when the fire started, Ed thought. *But the gates were closed. Why couldn't they just open them from the inside?*

There was an iron bar on the ground, behind the gates. It was used to bar the door, judging by the chain around it. Ed's drones had eaten the door hinges that supported the bar, thus doing what the villagers hadn't had time to.

Because something had been chasing them. The spiders? Or the mindbrood?

Someone did this on purpose, Ed thought, standing over the iron bar. The chain was damning.

But what about the guards?

He was able to answer his own question not long after. He recognized their red sashes, covered in dust. The two figures were lying on the ground, partly hidden by the palisade. They were the same two that had received him yesterday.

Their throats were slashed with straight cuts, done from behind them. Their blood caked the ground in two brownish stains.

Ed approached them and examined the corpses. Their weapons were in their scabbards, and there was only surprise and agony on their contorted faces. He closed their eyes, feeling his stomach churn.

There's no time for puking, he decided.

It couldn't be a coincidence. The spider attack, the fire, the mindbrood, and now this. Sabotage. Someone was trying to destroy Burrova.

Gallio had been wrong. It wasn't Ed whom Murmur was using. It was someone else.

Ed drew an iron sword out of the dead guard's scabbard and held it firmly between his hands. He had a job to do.

"You three stay here," he told his drones, who were dutifully waiting for his orders. "Wait until you see Alder and Lavy, then guide them to me."

He walked into the smoke, toward the center of the village, listening for screams.

He found them, soon enough. He had been covering his nose with his woolen jacket, his new sword in his right hand, trying to keep walking in a straight line while his eyes watered.

The heat was overbearing, and the Dungeon Lord could barely think.

But the screams were there. In the distance, cropping up for a few seconds at the time, and renewing in different directions.

He moved slowly, knowing the mindbrood could be lurking anywhere. Ed barely dared to breathe too hard, and it was thanks to this he heard a different kind of noise coming from somewhere to his right. Cursing, panting, and the dull sound of metal striking against something hard.

The wind changed direction, and the smoke parted. Ed passed a hand across his face to clean it—only managing to smudge it further—and looked around. He was next to the forge, and there was a fight going on inside of it. The blacksmith's tools were strewn everywhere, and the combatants moved and charged across the building using the furniture as obstacles for their opponents.

He recognized Gallio, Vasil, and Kes, fighting side by side against a group of spider warriors. There were three of the creatures, aided by a small group of spiderlings. Kes' *cleave* was keeping the small critters at bay, but Vasil and Gallio could barely handle the three warriors by themselves, even though Gallio had managed to cave in the chitin at one of the spider's sides.

The wounded warrior retreated, hissing at Gallio as it did so, and the other two darted forward, coordinated, and their legs swooped at the two men. The Sheriff managed to dodge, but Vasil fell. Its opponent closed in, ready for the kill, while Kes and Gallio screamed a warning at the guard.

Ed charged, blade held low like a spear and his Evil Eye showering dust and ash in shades of green. As he did so, he started dropping drones everywhere, but was careful not to unsummon the ones by the gates.

The spider warrior stopped in its tracks and jumped away from Ed's charge, but at the same time, a pair of drones appeared in violet puffs above its head. One slipped and disappeared under the monster's legs, but the other managed to grab a hold of its horn and hang on for dear life. The spider, confused, stopped to shake it off, stumbled against a barrel of dirty water, spilled it everywhere, slipped, and then crashed against an iron bench. The drone disappeared during the impact.

Before the spider could regain its footing, Gallio was towering above it, and his mace came down on its head in a perfect, violent arc. There was a crunch of chitin being splintered, and blue blood sprayed everywhere.

The surviving two warriors took a look at the sudden change in the battlefield, turned tail, and ran away and out of sight.

Ed and Kes finished off the few spiderlings that stayed when their bigger sisters retreated, and then both of them reunited with Gallio and Vasil, who was nursing a long gash on his leg right under his leather greaves.

"Are you alright?" Ed asked the guard. The man gave him a sour look, spat on the ground, and nodded.

"Do you know what's going on?" Gallio asked Ed.

"I was hoping you knew," Ed said. "The guards at the gate are dead, and the door was barred. How did you enter?"

"We climbed," said Kes. "We didn't see anyone by the palisade, so we came here. There are groups of villagers running around, and we tried to gather them when these spiders attacked us."

Ed trusted the mercenary's words. They had a pact, after all.

This meant that Gallio and Vasil hadn't been the ones who had killed the guards.

Another batch of screams claimed his attention. These ones were close, coming from behind the forge.

"Let's go!" exclaimed Gallio, and he charged in the direction of the sound without looking back to see if he was being followed.

"Damn it!" Kes muttered. Her sword was dripping blue and the blade was dirty with stuck pieces of chitin and guts. "He'll get himself killed!"

"He has the right damn idea," Ed said, then rushed after him.

"Here we go again," the mercenary's voice reached him, and then she passed him, and shortly after Vasil did the same.

Ed crossed a bunch of small, tight rooms that made up the interior of the forge, past tools and sheds, and then he stopped dead in his tracks. He had reached a storage area, storing mostly farm equipment and riding chairs, but also some guardsmen weaponry and armor.

If he went out there with zero combat training and only his leather jerkin as a defense, he would run out of luck sooner or later. He *had* to spare a few seconds to better equip himself.

He dashed toward the leather armor, which was close to him anyway, and hurried to fit himself with the greaves, a helm with a nasal guard, and the braces. He used two drones to help him tighten the straps and save himself precious seconds. He was done in under a minute.

Sword in hand, Ed ran out of the forge. The other three humans were in the middle of a side street with a mud-covered road and were pointing their weapons at a nearby group of four spider warriors.

No. Ed squinted and took a better look. The middle spider was bigger than the others—it was almost as tall as he was, and larger. It was one of the two princesses. And the group she was leading wasn't moving from their spot because they were cutting off the escape of a terrified family that was cornered by their side of the forge building.

"Stay away from them!" Gallio yelled at the spiders, pointing at them with his mace. "Don't you dare hurt them, or I'll crush you all!"

"Foolish human!" the spider princess told him. "The smell of the mindbrood permeates this village! We chased it all the way here! If it feeds on enough people, it will soon grow enough to start laying eggs! Then we will *all* die!"

"I said—" Gallio walked toward them like a man strolling through the park, while Vasil nocked an arrow to his bow and aimed it at the princess "—stay away from them."

While the Sheriff spoke, his left hand ruffled through a small bag tied by a string to his belt. Ed didn't miss the polished stone that Gallio discreetly got out.

The Dungeon Lord realized what was about to happen, and turned his head to Kes.

"Go get them!" he told her, gesturing at the family. He and the mercenary began to run as Gallio raised his hand, stone at the front, and the spider warriors jumped toward the family.

Oh, shit.

The fireball crossed the air, whistling as it went, and detonated right in the middle of the monsters' group. There was a flash of white, a deafening noise, and a wave of force caught Ed by the shoulders and smashed him against the ground while driving all the air out of his lungs.

Ed groaned, and tried to get up. His head was spinning, and he stumbled face-first into a mouthful of dirt. He tried again, succeeded, took a lungful of ash-laden air, and then blinked hard to clear his vision.

There was no sight of Kes, the spiders, or the family. The *fireball* rune had created a huge cloud of dust which covered everything in front of him. Behind him, Vasil was struggling to stand up, his bow broken under his body.

Gallio had fared better, and was approaching Ed nonchalantly, but as he got closer, the Dungeon Lord could see the cold rage reflected in the Sheriff's blue eyes.

"Kes?" Gallio asked him.

"She was faster than me," Ed said. "She's inside the cloud."

"Let's help her. I don't think I killed the princess."

But before they could reach the cloud of dust, a blood-curdling scream roared behind them. It was Vasil.

Both Sheriff and the Dungeon Lord turned at the same time, and found out that *something* had landed atop Vasil's chest, and its prehensile mandibles were open right in front of the guard's face. The man struggled without success to free himself, pinned to the ground by two pairs of long, thin arms and a set of powerful hind legs, which ended in claws as sharp as daggers. It was smaller than a man, but it was heavy, and had a mix of insect-like articulations with the powerful muscles of a chimpanzee.

To Ed, who had grown up with Earth's movies and literature, the creature looked like something taken out of a Lovecraft's love affair with H.R. Giger. And that was where comparisons ended. There were no special effects on Earth that could imitate the way the monster's two pairs of eyes furiously turned in all directions, the appearance of an entire body covered in plaques of exoskeleton as thick as a suit of armor, or the way saliva flowed out of its mouth and oozed onto Vasil's face.

"Help me!" Vasil screamed.

"Help me!" the monster screamed, in a perfect imitation of a little girl. "They're trying to kill me!"

"It can talk!" said Ed, too stunned to even react.

"Sephar's Bane!" said Gallio, and he rushed to produce a new rune from his bag. Too slow. Too late.

"Don't attack me!" pleaded the monster. Its claws were digging deep holes into Vasil's arms and shoulders, but it didn't seem to be aware of this. It was looking straight at Gallio. "You have to help me! I woke up like this, and I'm killing so many people, and I don't know why! Oh, gods, I can't stop!"

Before Ed or Gallio could do anything about it, the mandibles closed around Vasil's head, engulfing it completely. The monster made a guttural noise and shook its long-snouted head like a dog's, its neck bulging with strength. There was a sickening, tearing noise, and as the monster's head rose, the body of the guard fell limp to the floor, its entire head missing, a spray of blood painting the ground a dark brown and sending curls of smoke up in the air.

Ed felt a scream of terror die in his throat. The creature was looking him in the eye, and it was slowly *chewing,* its mouth full, a trail of blood and gore dripping out of its snout.

He could hear the *crunch* that Vasil's skull made inside the monster's engorged mouth.

At that moment, Gallio roared and raised the *fireball* rune. The creature moved so fast it was a blur of brown-and-black motion, charging straight at them—

This time, the explosion happened so close to Ed that he didn't realize when the darkness overtook him.

THE WORLD WAS BURNING pain and hard surfaces. There was something hard and edged cutting his arm, painting a clear line of fiery sensation in his mind.

Ed spat out a mouthful of dirt, gagged, fought for air, breathed in as much dirt as oxygen, coughed again until he feared he was about to asphyxiate, managed to regain his composure, and opened his eyes.

He was alive, and for the looks of it, all his limbs remained were they should have been. He spat dirt again, and it came out mixed with saliva and blood. He had bitten his lip at some point.

"Fucking Gallio," he muttered.

If Ed's ribs weren't broken, they *would* be bruised tomorrow. He felt like a train had passed over his torso.

Slowly, memory of his last seconds of consciousness came back to him. The mindbrood.

Ed reached down and grabbed his sword, which had been under his body when he fell. It was a small miracle he had managed to only cut his arm a bit instead of skewering himself. A thin trail of blood traveled down his arm and under his leather bracers, flowing from a wound by his bicep. It wasn't deep, but just a few inches lower and he would've severed the artery in his arm.

He raised the sword in front of him and took a measure of his surroundings.

The mindbrood was gone, and so was Gallio. There was a small, crater-like protrusion in the ground at the spot where the Sheriff's *fireball* had hit, just a few feet away from Ed. Hell, perhaps the Sheriff had tried to get rid of two enemies for the price of one.

Ed was alone, except for the lifeless body of Vasil, crumpled in a heap by the forge. It looked inhuman, unrecognizable. It was hard to think that, just a few seconds ago, it had been a human being. Ed looked at it, grimaced, and turned away.

If Gallio and the mindbrood were gone, he had to find them, and finish this.

He made his way to Burrova's center, in the direction he had last seen Kes. He was sure he would need reinforcements.

CHAPTER TWENTY-THREE

HAIL, SPIDER QUEEN!

I n the distance, he could see the governor's house burning.
Flames engulfed the entire structure, rising as much as half
its length again like red arms that tried to grab the sky.

The column of black smoke was thick enough to hide the
palisade of the northern section of Burrova, and the rain of ashes
made Ed's eyes water with every step. Every now and then, a tiny
ember smacked against his skin, gave him a jolt, and made
him wince.

His arms were getting tired of lugging the sword around. It
was heavier than it looked. No one had ever told him about the
weight. It was never an issue in the movies.

He gritted his teeth and forced himself to ignore the pain in
his forearms. He didn't need finesse to use the sword as a baseball
bat. Still, he dragged the tip of the sword through the ground as
he walked, to conserve energy.

Every now and again, he heard screams, or watched spider
warriors crawling through burning wreckage, never close enough
to him to start a fight. They were hunting, too. Looking for the
mindbrood, just as he was.

So he followed them, from a distance, through thick smoke

and clouds of dust, deeper and deeper into Burrova, until he reached the market. Ed snuck his way through to a broken stall and used it as a hiding place before any spider could see him and from there, he took a good look at the situation.

He found people.

They were covered in web, at least two dozen of them, with more being hauled in by whatever spider warriors remained in Amphiris' entire cluster. Not many. Ed suspected the Queen was betting it all, her entire family, on this brutal attack.

The Queen herself was there, directing her cluster personally. When Ed saw her, he ducked under his stall, just in case her vision was better than her daughters'.

He had to concede it to her, it was a sound strategy. Attack early, with overwhelming force, while her enemy was young and weak, instead of waiting around while it grew in strength.

If only she had chosen a battlefield other than Burrova.

He had little doubt what destiny would befall the captured villagers. Few of them moved, and whatever skin was visible beneath the web was yellowish and sick from the venom. Ed managed to recognize the governor's figure—he was the fattest—and the wide shoulders of Heorghe, the blacksmith.

The others were farmers and merchants, and trade workers, mostly unfamiliar faces, but all innocent. They would get eaten alive by the spiders so Amphiris could replenish her cluster's numbers.

There's no way I can fight them head on, Ed thought. He lacked strength. He lacked enough power. It was almost ironic. He had traveled all this way from Earth because he desired the power to make a difference, he had sold his heart for it, and now he was here and could do nothing but watch...

No, screw that, he thought. It was true that he couldn't go around throwing fireballs at will, but he *had* power. It was time he started using it.

He dropped his sword next to him and knelt while grabbing

handfuls of dirt. The ground was hard, compacted by years of constant walking above it. But his drones could eat rock without issue. Under that kind of bite, the soft ground of the village would part like hot butter.

He turned on his Evil Eye. The ley lines converged over the burning wreckage of the governor's house. The fire would be no issue. Underground cared nothing for that fire.

He summoned five drones to his side, careful not to expose them to the spiders' line-of-sight. The purple-and-pink robes looked out of place in the rain of ash, but the drones' expressions matched his. They were grim and determined.

"I want to build a dungeon," he told them, pointing at the burning house. "With a dungeon Seat right under there. So start digging."

AMPHIRIS GAZED upon the work of her cluster approvingly. The losses had been terrible, and it would take her years to restore her cluster to its normal size, but the mindbrood had nowhere to go, and thanks to her, it had no food and no victims to lay its eggs into.

It had been a good thing they had found the creature as soon as they did, while it was a newborn. Any longer and it would've proven too much for a single cluster to handle, if the legends about the Bane's rate of growth were to be believed.

As it was now, her daughter, princess Laurel, had sighted the mindbrood at the northwest, being chased by Burrova's protector, the Sheriff. Laurel had taken half of Amphiris' remaining warriors and was in hot pursuit of both. Soon, nothing would threaten Amphiris' cluster again.

Not entirely true, she reminded herself. The Queen's job was never done. Other clusters would seize upon her children's weakened state and would force her to lose a lot of territory. Perhaps she would have to relocate her nest, even. It was a cruel state of affairs, since Amphiris was also protecting the other clusters from the Bane, but such was Nature.

The Queen reached the center of the market and clacked her mandibles in approval at her hard-working warriors. About half of Burrova's population had been captured already, with the other half still running near the north gates, which were as barred as the Southern ones. Amphiris had no idea who had locked the gates, but she was not one to question her good fortune.

Instead, she made eye contact with the fat King of the human cluster. She could feel her mouth water in response to the man's fear. Rulers always tasted the best. Authority recognized authority, and it was a treat like no other to dine on a defeated King.

She would gain so many experience points after she was done feeding—perhaps she wouldn't have to worry about losing territory after all.

A noise took the King's attention away from her, which irritated the Queen. Spider hearing wasn't as good as the humans, so she had to look the King's way to see what the fuss was about.

His house had collapsed into itself, disappearing from view and letting only the giant tongues of fire be visible from its hole in the ground.

"You humans like to dig deep," she told the man. He could not answer, since his mouth was covered by web.

That was a necessary precaution. Some humans could cast magic if they were allowed to speak and although Amphiris' scouts had found no mages among Burrova's population—except for the Rangers, who could use magic-like talents—she hadn't made herself Queen by being careless.

The King mumbled something unintelligible her way, and shook his head vigorously. The Queen had no patience for pleading. At best, listening to her food complain and beg gave her headaches.

"Over there," she told the King, pointing a sticky leg at the northwest corner, "see those spiderlings? Those are my scouts. They come to tell me that my warriors have found another big group of your cluster and are capturing them as we speak. I know this because of the way the entire group ebbs and flows. They move like this when they're happy, and they're happy because they know they'll be rewarded. I'll let most of them live, for I must replenish the losses your guards gave the cluster before we killed them."

She reveled in the man's despair, but a part of her didn't share the mirth. The two Rangers could've swayed the course of the invasion; the Queen knew it. She had seen the devastation those *explosive arrows* could bring to a warrior.

Granted, the female had been consumed by the poison yesterday and was probably dead. But where was the other one?

She wasn't one to question good luck, but it was indeed suspicious. She decided she would set her spiderlings on lookout duty, making sure there was no one hiding among the wreckage of the marketplace. Caution made for an old ruler. It was a lesson that this human King should have learned, before this happened.

Perhaps they wouldn't have allowed the Bane to penetrate their midst.

In the distance, a part of the northern palisade was finally engulfed by the flames when the wind shifted. Instead of burning in place like a good wall, it immediately collapsed, causing such a ruckus that even the spiders heard it. Many stopped working to see the structure collapse. The Queen could feel the ground under her feet tremble, which was unexpected given the distance, but who really understood how those fickle human structures worked? Not her.

Meanwhile, her cluster was admiring the flames as they consumed the wall. They may have been hard workers, and loyal, but they could be so short sighted...

"Don't just stand there!" Amphiris exclaimed, using the natural spider-language instead of the humans' Common. "Warriors, go guard that exit before any infected villager has a chance to leave!"

The ground trembled again. To be exact, it was trembling constantly, a series of tremors whose vibrations made her mandibles click in concern, her ancestral instinct recalling earthquakes that previous Queens had faced. But these tremors were small, of little concern, and she assumed they were related to the palisade, which was falling by itself now, as if the northern side had triggered a chain reaction.

Good, she judged. *Good riddance.* The palisade had been built out of a lot of trees the humans had taken from her territory. Those trees had made for good cover, and excellent hunting spots.

Her warriors were well trained. Instead of letting the tremors slow them, they hurried to drop their new prisoners at the pile, then rushed to meet with their already running brethren. Amphiris was left with only five warriors and most of the spiderlings, which was good enough to protect her from whatever remained of Burrova's defenders. And her favored daughter, Laurel, would return soon enough with more warriors.

Amphiris was left with little to do but watch her progeny set to their assigned tasks. The Queen was more used to this than to fighting, and all this activity had made her very, very hungry.

It's no big deal if I have dinner early, she thought. *Just half a snack, before my victory feast.*

Perhaps she could keep the King alive if she ate carefully, so he could see how her cluster devoured his, later tonight. In her experience, humans could survive having part of their extremities eaten for a reasonably long time.

Another tremor, this time stronger, and this one sounded like a rockfall. She stopped dead in her tracks, and for a second thought it was indeed an earthquake. But it passed, just like the others had. Just another wall that had collapsed.

Yes, all this activity had made her very hungry indeed.

Her mouth watered, and she clicked her mandibles in satisfaction.

"We are going to have so much fun together, you and I," she told the King without looking at him.

But when she started to turn in the King's direction, she discovered that the man wasn't where she had left him. In fact, few of the humans were. There was only a hole in the ground, almost big enough to fit her whole. It had appeared out of nowhere, and if she had been just a few hundred feet closer to the entrance, it would've opened under her.

As she watched, her many eyes detected a small contingent of tiny creatures in purple-and-pink robes, coming in and out of the hole, carrying the webbed humans with them into the underground right in front of Amphiris' stunned progeny. There were already less than a dozen humans left, and the few among them who were conscious were looking at the imps with a mixture of terror and hope.

It was that look which transformed the Queen's surprise into unadulterated hatred.

They were messing with her *food!*

"Who?!" Amphiris roared, fury surging through her veins. "Who dares?!"

Silence was her answer, silence and an obscene gesture from one of the imps.

But Amphiris' ancient instincts recognized this magic. She remembered the metal spires and siege towers breaking through soil and bedrock, entire castles coming to life in a matter of seconds, tunnels appearing in the middle of a nest and spitting out hordes of monstrous regiments, carrying with them slavery and devastation for her kind.

This was how the old Dungeon Lords fought, bringing war and death to their enemies instead of sitting placidly in their lairs, waiting for bands of adventurers to come kill them.

Amphiris recalled the young man with the Mantle's smell,

how he had run away from her and her daughters. Was he the one behind this?

"What are you looking at?" she asked her warriors. "Kill the humans, capture that tunnel!"

Her voice pushed her spiders back into action. The five warriors hissed and roared and charged at the imps with horns ready to impale and mandibles ready to bite and tear.

The imps saw this and started moving faster, trying desperately to outrun the charging spiders. They would be too slow…

Two of the warriors disappeared from view when holes burst open in front of their path, craters just big enough to engulf them whole and no more. A third warrior managed to jump over another hole, stopped, looked over her shoulder, and then charged again. The ground all around her simply collapsed this time, like the soil underneath it had disappeared all of a sudden. The spider plummeted, screaming in terror, and had half her legs trapped in rocks and upturned ground. Three of her legs were broken, and dirt covered her eyes and mandibles.

Amphiris realized it wasn't just a collapse, but an improvised ramp, and started running toward her fallen warrior, but she wasn't as fast as her spiders. A man in leather armor ran out of the opening, an iron sword in hand and flaming green eyes visible through the cloud of dust that surrounded the scene.

Before the Queen could reach them, the man drove his sword straight through the warrior's mouth, almost to the hilt, with the tip of the weapon coming out of the spider's head covered in brain matter and blue blood.

The warrior thrashed in agony and almost sent the man flying through the air, but he managed to hang on to the sword's hilt. Mandibles snapped closed just an inch above his wrists, and as the spider died, she slumped forward, almost burying him under her. The man jumped back, looked over his shoulder at the approaching Amphiris, hurried to set his sword free, and ran back into the tunnel just as the furious spider Queen reached her dead daughter.

"Come back, coward!" she demanded, but the man was gone. She tried to follow the ramp, but it was too small for her. She remembered the man was a Dungeon Lord, and she changed her mind about meeting him on his turf.

"Go get him," she called, instead, to her two remaining warriors, who had changed course when they had seen their Queen join the fight and were just reuniting with her. "He has little experience points, go and overwhelm him!"

The warriors looked at the ramp, then at their Queen, and hesitated. Amphiris hated to admit it, but they were right in doubting. She wouldn't enter herself.

She gestured with one long, powerful leg at a contingent of spiderlings, "You, lead the charge! Whoever bites him and lives gets to grow old!"

The spiderlings lacked the warriors' risk recognition, and they happily ran through clouds of dust until they reached the ramp. Amphiris calculated their numbers to be at least three hundred.

Nothing happened. The ramp made a sharp turn downward, and she could not get a good look.

Minutes went by while the Queen and her two warriors waited. The dust slowly settled back. The imps had disappeared back into their hole, leaving at least six humans behind, including the broad-shouldered blacksmith and his daughters.

"They got him," Amphiris declared. "Deparia, bring me his corpse. Don't dare hesitate again, or you will become food for your sisters."

"As you command, my Queen," the warrior told her. She gave the other warrior a last look of despair and disappeared under the ramp.

After she was out of sight, the earth rumbled and the entrance collapsed with a muffled growl of displaced rocks.

Amphiris jumped away, by instinct, and saved herself when the collapse grew in intensity and became a deep hole that swallowed whole her last remaining warrior so fast that the creature didn't have time to scream.

"No!" Amphiris roared. She dared risk a glance down the crater, and discovered that her daughter had been impaled against sharp wooden spears that had been waiting for her at the bottom.

He can build traps!

But how? Where was he getting materials?

Desperate, Amphiris examined the battlefield, while moving in a zig-zag pattern, trying to remain a step ahead of the tremors that shook the earth.

The King's nest! The house that had collapsed!

If she didn't stop this now, he would gain control of the entire village. And perhaps of the mindbrood...

The tremors reached close to her, and she changed directions at the last second. The Dungeon Lord had invested a lot of energy in saving all the humans he could. So, she ran at the six that remained, at full speed, her powerful legs easily carrying her over crater and holes that opened her way as she did so, never big enough for her to fall down them.

Her mouth watered at the sight of the trembling blacksmith, who was aware of her approaching shape, but could do nothing about it.

Come out, little Lord, she thought. *Come out and join my feast!*

Another hole, barely big enough to fit a warrior. But big enough for her front right leg to fall down its length, and for her momentum to carry her forward before she could stop herself.

There was a sickening crunch, and Amphiris roared in pain as her leg broke away from her body in a spray of blood; then her weight came crashing down just a few feet away from the blacksmith.

The Queen screamed in agony and fear and tried to upright herself. She had dirt in her eyes, and one of them had burst when her head had smashed against a jagged rock. Her hearing was off, but she could smell the Mantle approaching her. The Dungeon Lord.

One of her functioning eyes saw his figure standing in front of her, his face a mask of severity marred by sweat and effort.

His sword was covered in blue blood, and he had the tip pointed at her.

Amphiris tried to stand, to impale him with her horn, but the man jumped back, and a shower of tiny imps fell out of nowhere and over her head. She could feel tiny hands grabbing at her eyes. One of them *bit her eye*—

"Arghhhhh!" She rolled over in a frenzy, sending all the imps flying away and destroying them. Her legs flailed about, and she fought to regain her balance, to recover. Strings of web shot everywhere, trying to hit an enemy she couldn't see—

The sword flashed in and out of view, and her remaining front leg exploded in pain at her joint and showered her with another spray of blood. The Queen's roar was cut short when the sword cut another leg, and then another.

He was maiming her. Methodically, extremity by extremity, dancing around her flanks while she could do nothing but wail, hit after hit, never stopping long enough for her to try and fight back.

"Noooo!" she screamed. "Stop! Stop! Mercy, Dungeon Lord, mercy!"

The attacks stopped.

How many legs had she lost already? Half of them? More?

If he didn't kill her, the other Queens would. A maimed Queen rarely had time for her extremities to grow back. Such was Nature's world.

So, she invoked her last resort.

"Mercy, my Lord, I am defeated!" she begged again. "I'll put myself in your service in exchange for my life! I'll put my entire cluster at your service!"

Silence. But she wasn't losing any more legs.

Her two remaining eyes saw the blurry figure of the Dungeon Lord standing in front of her, sword in hand.

"Last time, you offered me a pact," she reminded him, without daring to answer his question. "I have reconsidered the offer."

"I told you we would meet again," said the Dungeon Lord, in a soft voice. "You were going to eat them all, weren't you?"

"I can help you!" she told him. "I know Hoia's secrets better than the Rangers ever will, and they can be *yours* if you let me live. I know the mindbrood better than any human, I can help you capture it, kill it or harness it if you desire. I can make you more powerful; I can provide you with hundreds of expendable warriors!"

Was he even listening to her? She managed to shift her body around, to follow his gaze. The last of the blacksmith's family was disappearing down the big crater. Once the girl was gone, he gave the Queen his full attention.

"That offer has expired, Amphiris," he told her. "Goodbye."

The Queen *roared* like she had never roared, and managed to jerk her maimed body upward, her mandibles looking for a human neck with all her might and power put behind the bite.

There he was! Her last-ditch effort had caught him by surprise. He missed his footing, fought for balance, all with her mandibles coming closer and closer to his neck.

Amphiris could almost taste his sweet blood—

And then, too fast to be possible, he began to squat while driving his weight forward, sword gripped like a spear, tip aimed straight at her face, her bite missing his hairline by millimeters.

How?

Too fast! He should have died there! The tip of the sword reached her mouth just as the answer came to her mind.

I forgot, she thought as the iron pierced her, *that's his only combat talent.* Improved reflexes, *isn't it? I should have remembered. I should have—*

There was only pain.

ED HAD EXPECTED that Amphiris would die after a hit like that. The Queen *was* dying, just not as fast as he would have liked.

"Aurrgghhh!" The spider thrashed and convulsed and spewed envenomed saliva and blood everywhere, her mandibles and her horn swinging about, as deadly now as they had been before, fumes of vapor flowing from the ground where the blue goo splotched.

Ed's blade had reached her brain, he was almost sure of it, but still the Queen refused to die. Seeing her like this was more sickening than the very act of killing her.

He stepped back, away from her pointy ends, but forced himself to not look away. After all, he had done this. It was his responsibility to see it through the end. He sighed, then let his body relax. The effort of using his *improved reflexes* had almost knocked him out, and it was the first time he had used them today. It was clear he wasn't yet recovered from yesterday's efforts, and now he felt like his body was made out of slush and trembling muscles.

"Aurgghhhhh!" Amphiris went on. More blood splashes, more vapor, more thrashing.

Part of him was sickened by what he had done, since the creature was clearly intelligent and articulate, even if she liked to eat humans. The other part just wanted the Queen to stop screaming incoherently and die already.

"You have to end her," a woman's voice whispered somewhere behind him. "Otherwise, it will be days before she finds peace."

Surprised, Ed jolted and turned back with a jump. The speaker was a spider. A princess, to be exact, and she had another five warriors with her.

"Oh, shit," he whispered. He was unarmed, and his drones hadn't prepared new tunnels to keep the fight going. He glanced at Amphiris, who still had his sword pierced through her. If he could reach it, he could activate his *eldritch edge* and perhaps drive the spiders back—

"I wish to parlay," the spider interrupted his thoughts. The warriors next to her hadn't moved, and instead retreated a couple steps, as if to give the two of them ground to talk.

"You do?" Ed asked, surprised.

"My name is Laurel, princess of Amphiris' cluster," the princess went on, as if chatting over tea and cookies. "I saw the fight from afar, but it was already over by the time we reached you both. You see, we were carrying more prisoners for the feast, but now I wish to set them free as a show of goodwill."

She gestured at two warriors and sent them on their way to four sacks of human-sized webbing not far away from them. Ed watched them go, not sure if he was stepping into a trap, or if Laurel's intentions were sincere.

"Auuurghhhh!" Amphiris screamed behind him.

"Ah, shut up, Mother," the princess told the dying Queen. "Die with some dignity."

The Queen didn't listen to her daughter's advice.

Ed was definitely sick now.

"What do you want?" he asked the princess.

"An alliance, of course," she said. "Isn't it obvious? With our Queen gone, the cluster won't be able to survive the winter, and the other clusters will take our land and burn our nests. We need a new Queen, and we also need a powerful ally to protect us while our numbers replenish."

"You are men-eaters," Ed told her.

"Indeed," said Laurel, "but men aren't the only meat we can eat. If our feeding habits displease you, we'll change them."

"Will you?" asked Ed. He wasn't expecting the spider's cooperation.

"Of course, my Lord. Whoever refuses to stop will be killed and devoured. As the new Queen, I'll be within my right to do so."

Ah, so that's why you're anxious to deal with me. You want your mother's throne.

"Auuuuuurghh!" said Amphiris.

"And if I don't accept?" Ed asked.

"Then most likely we'll both die fighting each other, and the mindbrood will escape our grasp, eat your kind, lay its eggs in the survivors' brains, and leave them to spread the Bane to other nests like Burrova."

I figured as much, he thought. Still, the idea of allying with the spiders pleased him as much as a spiderling bite to the crotch.

On the other hand...wouldn't the spiders be better under his command than roaming free, preying on innocent people? Perhaps he would be able to use them to do some good.

Look at me, he almost laughed aloud, *already having to convince myself I'm not going Dark.*

He looked Laurel square in her many eyes, and nodded an agreement.

"I extend to you a pact," he told her, and the familiar mist spread out of his chest and fingertips while his Evil Eye blazed green, showering the spider in eldritch shapes and shadows.

The creature retreated at the sight of him, with her remaining warriors doing the same.

"You look like the undead," Laurel muttered. "Such a sight will drive fear into the hearts of my enemies."

"My terms are as follows," Ed went on. "You will tell me the truth. You will obey my commands, as long as they are reasonable. And you won't prey on innocent humans—or any intelligent life, for that matter. In exchange, you and yours will be protected to the best of my ability, and I won't lie to you or harm you."

"I accept," said Laurel, and the mist touched her, connecting her with the Dungeon Lord and making her his minion. It soon did the same to her warriors, who accepted it as soon as they were able to. "Congratulations, Dungeon Lord, the cluster will follow you. You have increased your power on this day."

"Congratulations, Queen Laurel." Ed smiled fiercely, and he was aware that this, too, was part of the Lordship's ancient traditions. "May our friendship be long and prosperous."

They weren't two different creatures bound by necessity, then, but two rulers who had allied themselves to become more powerful, together, than they had been as enemies. For the faintest of instants, Ed saw Laurel as she saw herself. A beautiful and terrible Queen, whose rule had just started.

Who knew what she saw when she looked at him?

Then, the moment passed. The Evil Eye turned itself off, and Ed was back to feeling tired and sickened.

"Now that that's done," Ed said, "we go hunting for the mindbrood."

Last time he had seen it, it had been with Gallio. Ed found himself wishing that the Sheriff had had better luck than he had at finding it.

"I can spare two warriors," said Laurel, "my Lord Wraith. The other three I need as bodyguards. My sister is still out there, and she may not agree with my coronation."

"Why not come with me?" Ed asked, and added, "And what do you mean, 'Lord Wraith'?"

"That's the undead you most remind me of," the spider said, then chuckled dryly. "I have to stay here, my Lord, because I must claim my mother's ancient memories for myself, if I want to be a Queen. I'm afraid I'll be of little use until I do so. Instinct, you see, is a ruler even more powerful than you are."

Ed raised an eyebrow, and then realized that Laurel was eying her mother with hunger reflected in her eyes. A shiver went down Ed's spine, and it wasn't from the cold.

Are all creatures in Ivalis obsessed with consuming each other?

He almost smacked himself. Of course they were. Earth was no different.

"You do you," he muttered, and then, louder, "Can I trust you to protect the villagers while I'm gone?"

"You have my promise I won't take even a small bite," the new Queen said. "Even if we weren't bound by pact, I'll have more than my share of meat in a moment."

Ed shook his head, took a deep breath, and went to retrieve his sword from Amphiris' still-convulsing body.

CHAPTER TWENTY-FOUR

RENEW YOUR VOWS

G allio had seen Burrova grow since he had arrived in the first caravan. What to many Inquisitors would mean a life sentence in exile, he had transformed into a chance to begin anew—to start a life far away from Dungeon Lords and their machinations, away from the intrigues of the Heiligian court, and away from the terrible responsibilities the Church expected him to shoulder.

He had *created* this village, in a way, and for a time he had been content. Perhaps the gods could be merciful, after all. Perhaps the Light had finally forgotten about him.

Ah, how did that saying go?

Never wonder if that's the hardest Fate can hit you, he thought, while Burrova burned around him.

He raised a hand in front of his face to protect his eyes from the hot ashes and the smoke, and walked crouched in the shadow of the burning wreckage of what had once been a seamstress shop. Her name was Marya, which was common enough for Starevos. But Gallio had known this Marya personally, a middle-aged lady whose husband had died during the first caravan to Starevos.

Was she still alive? Had she managed to escape from the Bane, and from the spiders? Would she be able to escape from *him*, if he accepted the duty the Light demanded of him?

Not fucking likely.

It seemed that Edward Wright's presence had doomed his little village. The day he appeared, asking for adventuring work, was the day that the fate of Burrova had been sealed.

He scanned the shadows of the seamstress' shop, looking for movement. The mindbrood had escaped him after a long chase, and the idea of the lurking creature getting near the people under his protection made him sick.

There was movement in the area behind the shop. Too small to be humans, too numerous to be the Bane. But they were coming his way, trying their best not to be detected. Too bad for them, he had bought the *alert* talent when he was but a boy.

Gallio gritted his teeth, readied his mace, and hugged the corner between the shop and the alley, exposing his back to the embers of the fire.

The first warrior appeared close to him, unaware of the ambush. Gallio roared and brought his mace down with all his strength, a movement he had practiced over and over again at the academy until it had become second nature.

The spider's many eyes widened in surprise, and then the mace reached its head. The horn broke in a thousand shards, and the chitin beneath it crunched, and blood and goo sprayed out like a small fountain.

The spider screamed, tried to jump back, but its legs failed it and it collapsed, its body already shaking in its death throes before it knew what had happened.

The remaining warrior was faster than its companion. It jerked to the right, ducked under Gallio's sweep, made a feint with its horn that forced the Sheriff to step back, and then shot a string of web his way.

He tried to jump away, but the liquid substance hit his leg and glued him to the ground, and his movement catapulted him against the hard ground and almost broke his knee.

"No!" Gallio screamed. That hit should never have landed. When had he become so slow and clumsy?

"Stop!" the spider said, while it hissed at him. "Stop! We are not your enemies anymore. A pact has been made."

"What are you talking about?" Gallio demanded. Behind the warrior, a small stream of spiderlings surged beneath its legs and surrounded the Sheriff.

"Queen Laurel and the Wraith," the warrior said, "have become allies. The Wraith killed Queen Amphiris in singular combat, and now we serve him. The humans are safe. You are free to join us in the hunt for the mindbrood."

Gallio's blood curled. He didn't even hear the spider's last phrase.

The Wraith! It hadn't taken Edward long to learn how to play the Dungeon Lords' game. How fast would Murmur's corruption work on him? First, a spider cluster. Then, a kaftar cackle. Then mercenaries, Warlocks, naga...

Dungeon Lords and spiders and mindbroods, all of them being strung along by the Dark, all of them playing with the lives of his people while they made their alliances and their schemes.

And Gallio could do nothing but watch.

"Are you part of the Wraith's allies?" the warrior said. "If you are, join us. The Bane must be caught."

"I'll never join you." Gallio spat at the ground, and tugged at his leg, trying to free it. No avail.

He was too old, too weak. He couldn't do it. Not by himself.

"Then you'll be a prisoner. The Wraith will know what to do with you." The warrior turned to leave while the spiderlings advanced, closing on the Sheriff.

Dungeon Lords, the Bane, and spiders. His people in the middle of it all. And the Light? Where was it?

If all the Light has is me, then I will have to be enough.

The man managed to kneel, his fists digging long trails of dirt. He was muttering to himself.

"—not merciful," he said, as the critters closed in. "That's what I know, now. You are not merciful, Alita. So don't grant me mercy. *That,* I don't expect from you any longer. Not mercy, not respite, not forgiveness. Return me my power! And I will never leave your side again...I'll be your faithful servant until the day of my death, that I offer to you! Pact with me, goddess, and I'll make the Light's will be done!"

And the goddess answered. The smoke around him parted, like an invisible giant had blown it away. A rush of heat and power shot straight through his heart and spread all over his body.

A familiar sensation, one that he had felt years before, when he was young and hopeful. The goddess was not merciful, but she was practical, and she never let go of a useful tool.

Gallio would be her tool. The power reached his eyes, and they glowed bright, white, absolute. His mace shone with golden carvings, drawn in fiery lines of molten silver.

The spiderlings stopped in their tracks when the Inquisitor stood, and the web that held him burned away like it was nothing.

The spider warrior turned back.

"What?" it asked, as the burning white gaze of the Inquisitor shone upon him and sentenced the spider to death.

"This is the only mercy the Light knows," Gallio explained. "And it is called...*Sunwave!*"

The explosion of white light engulfed them all.

ED STUMBLED, and closed his eyes. He barely managed to remain on his feet, but he had to use his sword as a stick for balance.

What the hell?

His heart felt like something hot and cruel had pierced it. The brightness! Had that been an explosion?

He had never seen anything like it. A semi-circle of pure white light engulfing half a block.

The explosion disappeared as suddenly as it had come, but it left an afterimage. The Dungeon Lord blinked several times and cursed loudly.

"Are you hurt, Lord Wraith?" asked one of his two spider warriors.

"That light," he told his spiders, "was a spell, right?"

"We have never seen it before," the spider said, "but we are only two winters old. Perhaps you should ask our Queen? Her memory goes far."

Ed shook his head. No time to backtrack. He had to find the Bane. Besides, he could bet what the explosion had been.

Gallio.

It made sense. A former Inquisitor, with Light-aligned magic. It seemed the man had renewed his vows.

With any luck, he had killed the Bane. Ed had learned not to blindly trust luck, though.

"Let's go," he said, pointing in the direction of the explosion. "Perhaps our enemy is there."

They ran as one, the spiders easily keeping up with his tired legs. They passed by the ruins of the scant buildings of Burrova while the palisade burned around it all.

At least the fire hadn't managed to spread further. A stroke of luck, but also Ed's doing. His drones were hard at work bringing down the unburnt parts of the wall and any surviving buildings nearby. He hoped he could deprive the blaze of its fuel. If the flames spread to the forest, it could be disastrous.

But it will be even worse if the mindbrood gets away.

There were more villages like Burrova, and a port that could spread the infection to the whole of Ivalis.

"Lord Wraith, look," one of his spiders called next to him. "Over there."

Ed looked at the direction pointed to by a long, hairy leg, and saw a semi-circle of spiderlings and three warriors surrounding a pair of women who had their backs against the half-collapsed wall of a tannery.

The people were armed, and for the moment they were keeping the creatures at bay. The smoke parted, and Ed got a better look at the humans.

"Everyone, stop!" he said, as he recognized Kes and Lavy. The Witch had her hand raised, no doubt readying to cast a spell.

"Edward!" Lavy exclaimed when she saw him approach. "Look out, next to you!"

"No, don't move!" Ed ordered, sensing the mercenary and the Witch were about to turn his spiders into mincemeat. "These are my spiders!"

They didn't belong to the group Laurel had with her, so he had to hope these warriors had heard the news about the change in management.

"What?" said Kes, looking away from the warriors in front of her and to Ed.

To prove his point, he pointed at the spider warriors that surrounded his companions, and said:

"Step back. *Now.*"

"They killed half of my sisters," the warrior at the front told him, her mandibles hissing angrily. "The big one even killed Princess Calomis."

"And you invaded her village. Let's call it even," he told the warrior, "because the Bane won't be as understanding."

Reluctantly, the spiders broke their semi-circle and allowed Kes and Lavy to step away from them. They reunited with Ed.

"What's going on?" Lavy asked him. "The spiders are obeying you, now?"

"I killed their Queen," Ed explained, "and the new one is more reasonable."

"Dungheap! And here I thought we were the ones heading to rescue you," Lavy said.

"You killed Amphiris? How?" asked Kes.

"Huh...well, I founded a Dungeon underneath Burrova," he said, unsure of the mercenary's reaction. "And used tunnels to trap her."

The mercenary's eyes widened in surprise. She looked around like expecting to see the dungeon carvings in the tannery ruins.

"Well, the Inquisition can't kill us any harder," she muttered, then shrugged.

"That's the spirit," Ed said. "Now, what about you two?"

"I killed the Princess after Gallio's fireball, but lost track of you two," Kes said. "Instead, I found Lavy, who was looking for you with Alder and your batblin friend."

"Where are they?" Ed asked.

"We left them with Ioan," said Lavy, "and sent them to the marketplace to rescue the villagers. Since I still have my two spells left, I went with Kes to look for you. Now that Amphiris is dead, I guess there's one battle left. Looks like we may win the day, after all."

Ed barely heard a word after Lavy mentioned Ioan. A part of his mind that had been nagging at him since he entered the village came back to the front of his mind.

The two soldiers with their throats slashed. The gates barred.

Amphiris and her daughters strolling through the grass, accusing Ed and the adventurers of carrying the Bane's smell about them.

The Dungeon Lord paled, like he had seen a ghost.

Oh, shit.

"Edward?" Lavy asked.

The man turned to Kes, so quickly the mercenary jumped a step back in surprise.

"Kes!" he said. "Has Ioan been acting strange at all, lately?"

"Why do you ask?"

"Has he left town? A trip south, perhaps?"

"Not at all," she said, raising an eyebrow at him. "On the contrary. He regularly goes north, to Constantina, to get us provisions. He went on such a trip shortly before you and I met."

Ed scratched his chin, and thought hard. He knew so little about Ivalis...but Constantina, he had heard a bit about the city, before.

A nasty place, almost lawless, filled with cutthroats and thieves. And, perhaps, with smugglers?

Who knew what a man could find in such a place? An egg, perhaps?

But, why?

There was no time to figure it out.

"Follow me," he told the entire group, spiders and humans alike. "We go back to the market!"

Without looking to see if he was followed, he set on his way. A second later, Kes and Lavy reunited with him.

"What are you doing?" Kes urged him. "The mindbrood is not there! It'll avoid concentrations of people until it's strong enough to face us—it's basic predator behavior!"

"I think Ioan brought it here," Ed said.

"The Ranger?" asked Lavy. "Why do you think that?"

He shared with them his suspicions. The dead guards, Amphiris smelling the Bane in the forest and mistaking Ed for the guilty party, and Ioan's absence from the battle until now.

Who else was left to suspect? Vasil was dead, Kes had a pact with Ed, Alvedhra was clinging to life, and Gallio was fighting the mindbrood just like everyone else. Only Ioan remained unaccounted for.

It wasn't much, and it was very flimsy as an accusation. Why would the Ranger do such a thing? Where had he found a mindbrood egg?

When Kes pointed this all out, Ed shook his head.

"There's just one other thing."

"What?"

"He knows I'm a Dungeon Lord," he said. When his companions failed to understand the implications, he added, "and he knows you are my minions, right? He was in the forest, he saw the same thing as Gallio. Why was he so quick to ally with you before I caught up with you two? Because an innocent person, like Gallio, would've assumed I—the closest Dungeon Lord around— was behind the mindbrood's appearance without any other evidence, and would've been distrustful of my minions."

The mercenary paled, just as Ed had, and cursed under her breath.

"We have to hurry!" she said. "If he's infected and gets away... he has straight access to Undercity!"

And the port. Ed nodded, shook his head to clear his face of sweat, and urged his legs forward to match the mercenary's brutal speed.

As it turned out, there was no need to hurry.

When they arrived at the marketplace, Ioan was already waiting for them, his hunting knife against Alder's neck. The Bard looked at Ed with pleading eyes, but he didn't move. At Ioan's feet lay the broken corpses of the two bodyguards of Laurel, although there was no sign of the Queen herself.

"We meet again, Dungeon Lord," the Ranger said, and he smiled at Ed with a rabid glint in his dark eyes. "You've kept me waiting."

CHAPTER TWENTY-FIVE

LORD WRAITH

W hile he stared at the knife in front of his friend's neck, Ed was in little mood for talking.

"Let him go," he told the Ranger.

"That would defeat the point of taking a hostage," the man said.

Ed ignored him, then commanded the drones by his Seat underground to start digging a tunnel under the Ranger's feet. While he did so, his Evil Eye flashed for half a second, although he tried to avoid it.

"I wouldn't do that," Ioan said. "I saw your fight with Amphiris. If the ground does so much as to shake slightly, your Bard here is going to have two smiles instead of one."

There was no room for doubt in his expression. Ioan meant business.

Ed stopped his drones, but he managed to sneak a good look at the Ranger's stats:

- Ioan, Human Ranger. Exp: 900. Unused: 0. Brawn: 14, Agility: 15, Spirit: 11, Endurance: 16, Mind: 13, Charm: 8. Skills: Melee: Improved III,

Sharpshooting: Advanced I, Knowledge(Starevos):
Improved III, Survival: Advanced II. Talents:
Explosive Arrows, Precise Shot, Multi-Shot, Minor
Healing, Advanced Reflexes, Greater Endurance,
Starevos' Son...

He's a fucking killing machine, Ed thought with dismay. If it
came to a fight between the two of them, he had little doubt the
Ranger would come out on top.

"Ioan!" Kes stepped in his direction before a warning gesture
from the Ranger made her stop. "What do you think you're
doing?"

"What does it look like?" said Ioan. "I'm heroically facing, by
myself, the evil Dungeon Lord that brought Sephar's Bane to
Starevos!"

"That's *not* what happened, and you know it."

Ed glanced at Kes' sword arm. If the mercenary lost her
temper, Alder wouldn't be walking out of this.

Is there any way we can repair a slashed neck in time?

Kes lacked healing magic or skills, and Lavy's magic was
combat-related.

How far could he abuse the transmutation rules? As far as his
powers were concerned, they were standing in his dungeon, so he
could order the drones to create a medical wing—

Not fast enough, he thought, then discarded the idea. *I'd have
no idea what to do.*

"Drop your weapons, Edward," Ioan told him, while ignoring
Kes. "Come closer, but remember, if you flash your Evil Eye even
for a second—"

"Yeah, I got it the first time," Ed said. He let his sword fall to
the ground and did the same with his knife.

"Don't do it," Lavy muttered. "He'll kill you as soon as you are
in range. Stay where you are and we are in a stalemate."

"Not exactly," said Ioan. "Stay where you are, and I'll kill your

Bard, and then I'll use my bow to kill you. Haven't you seen what my *explosive arrows* can do to a body?"

He's lost it!

"You can't expect to get us all," said Kes.

"So, who'll be first? I'll kill at least two, and that includes your Dungeon Lord...unless he's willing to sacrifice all his minions to kill me. Will you do that, Edward? That's what the Lords of old would do, without hesitation."

Ed looked the Ranger in the eye while he walked toward him. He stopped a few feet away from him, far away enough from Ioan's knife to activate his reflexes if needed.

"That's what I thought," Ioan said.

"Let him go."

"Come closer, and we'll see."

Ed's gaze darted away from Ioan for a brief instant, anxious to find anything around that could break the stalemate in the Dungeon Lord's favor. Where was Laurel? Amphiris' body was lying there, uneaten. Perhaps Ioan had killed her...

Movement. By the smoldering ruins of the governor's house. Ed hid his reaction and returned his attention to Ioan.

"At least tell me something," Ed said. "Why do it? I get why you want to blame me, but I don't get why would you bring the Bane here in the first place."

"He's working for Lotia!" Alder exclaimed. The Bard's knees trembled, and a pearl of sweat dropped down his forehead and onto his lips. He clearly did not expect to survive the next few seconds. "Run, Ed! You must warn Heiliges!"

Ed bent his knees, ready to jump at Ioan if his knife hand did so much as tremble...but instead, the Ranger laughed.

"Ah! Once again, the word of a Bard proves useless. Lotia! What would I want with Lotia? Murderous cultists playing at nobility, the lot! No, they are only useful for one thing, and that thing is to be conquered by Heiliges."

"Is that what you want?" Ed told him. "War with Heiliges?

The Inquisition's going to come here, you'll tell them a Dungeon Lord released a mindbrood, and that you killed me. You tell them I am Lotian, and somehow they believe you. Then, if I understand how they work, the Inquisitors kill you and all survivors. Then Heiliges goes to war with Lotia, which is something they don't need any encouragement to do. Doesn't sound like you are getting anything out of this."

"A fast learner, eh? Perhaps I am truly doing Ivalis a favor by killing you here. Who knows what you would have become otherwise?" Ioan's tone was mocking. "Well, Dungeon Lord, you're starting to understand our world, but there's still much to learn. Doing all this gets me three things."

He nudged Alder forward, and the Bard almost lost his balance. Ioan forced him to remain still, and slowly, he made his way to Ed.

"First," he said, his voice rising above Alder's complaints, "by killing the Dungeon Lord who brought us Sephar's Bane, I'll become a hero."

"The mindbrood is still out there," Ed told him. "You are forgetting that part."

"I'll deal with it, easily. Everything is accounted for, friend Edward. After the egg hatched, I made sure the worm infected a little farmer girl. You know why? It makes the hatched brood smaller. Weaker. Less food while it's in the *womb*, you see. And the brood is young, inexperienced, easy to trap. It won't be able to lay eggs for a couple days more, time enough for me to kill it."

More steps. Ed calculated that he was now in range of the knife, if the Ranger lunged at him. He would strike soon. But first, he would kill Alder.

"Second, by dying by the hands of the Inquisition, I'll become a martyr to the people. The hero who saved thousands of lives, killed by the Heiligians? Oh, that will give the Bards something to sing about!"

A third step. Ed tensed all the muscles in his body. He could feel the adrenaline being pumped into his veins, his mind going into overdrive, time slowing down even without his *improved reflexes*. The next couple seconds would define who lived and who died.

"And third—" Ioan's smile was manic, and his knife hand trembled slightly. The blade nicked Alder's neck, and a line of blood flowed down his skin. The Bard whimpered and closed his eyes "—while the stupid Lotians and Heiligians go kill themselves, Starevos will finally regain its independence!"

He said so with the aplomb of someone who knows himself a hero, and it almost floored Ed as his mind refused to parse the fact that, even in a different world, a man had become a mass murderer because of his personal politics.

There was no time for that knowledge to take root. The Ranger's arm tensed. Ed's Evil Eye flared, and he opened his mouth, ready to release a spell—

And a shrieking batblin jumped out of one of Ed's tunnels, carrying a wooden spear longer than he was. Ioan turned to the batblin's charge, but Alder's body got in the way, slowing him down.

Before anyone could react, the wooden point of the spear pierced the Ranger's side an inch above his right hip. Ioan screamed, and his arms jerked instinctively down, forcing the spear out of his body. In doing so, he dropped his knife, and Alder ran away from him with a long, jagged cut in his neck's skin, but no deeper. The Bard stumbled and fell on his face.

The batblin pushed the spear an inch deeper into the Ranger's side, using every ounce of his strength.

"Klek!" Ed exclaimed—

The batblin flashed him a fierce smile and said, "Everyone always forgets about me."

"—look out!"

The Ranger's kick caught the batblin square in his soft belly, hitting him so hard that Klek was lifted inches off the ground and launched away, coming down hard against the rocks and rolling away several feet until he came to a stop, sprawled out and unmoving.

"Fucking *pest!*" Ioan said, tearing the spear out and tossing it away while blood flowed down his leather armor and stained his trousers. He looked at Ed and unslung his bow from his back. "This ends now."

"Now, Laurel!" Ed screamed.

The web came from behind one of the destroyed stands, a gooey string thicker than a man's arm. It *almost* hit the Ranger.

Ioan saw it coming, and moved faster than Ed thought possible. He ducked under the shot, so fast that he was a blur, and jumped away from it like a dancer, all of that in less than a blink. As he did so, he loaded two arrows to his bow.

Kes and Lavy rushed at the Ranger, and a crow made of arcane energy flew into view like a projectile, going straight at the Ranger's face.

In one fluid movement, Ioan swatted the crow away using his bow, and then opened fire on Kes and Ed, one arrow for each.

Ed barely had time to summon a drone in one arrow's path. The other one passed him by so fast he felt the breeze as it went. It hit something behind him.

"No!" The Dungeon Lord turned back, and saw the arrow broken at Kes' feet, her sword raised in front of her like a barrier. The blade had a long scratch across its middle, and the mercenary seemed as surprised to be still alive as everyone else.

Ioan cursed all the gods whose names Ed recognized, and then more. Still moving monstrously fast, he loaded three arrows and tensed his bow.

"Can you create three of those fucks at once?" Ioan spat, glaring at Ed.

No, I can't, the Dungeon Lord thought. *Not fast enough, at least.*

Laurel rushed away from her hiding place, shooting strands of web at the Ranger. They were smaller shots than her first one, and slower, so Ioan dodged them easily, but it bought Ed some time.

The fight was getting out of control, and fast. They could overwhelm the Ranger, but he was faster than all of them, and the range on his bow made him deadly.

Worse, something was *eating* Ed's drones, the ones he had working underground, trying to open a new tunnel under the Ranger's feet, which was a doomed plan anyway, since the Ranger wasn't giving him enough time to dig.

If Laurel was hiding by the stalls, what did I see moving next to the house?

His eyes widened in realization. Maybe, just *maybe...*

He improvised a new plan.

The first step was not dying within the next second.

He activated his *improved reflexes* just as Ioan loosed the three arrows toward him. Ed vaguely saw in slow-motion how the Ranger loaded yet another arrow while his first shot was midway through the air.

Even with his extra speed, the arrows were too fast for him. He fell face-first to the floor and saw the arrows ripple through the air. He caught the middle one with a sacrificial drone as he fell, and twisted his body away from the second arrow's path. The third one passed a hair-breadth above his head.

Time resumed just as Ed hit the ground. His body shot out waves of heat from the effort of using his talent, and all the muscles in his body felt taut to the point of tearing.

Ioan wasn't faring much better. His version of *improved reflexes* was more powerful, but much more taxing, and his face was red with effort, veins bulging inside his neck and through his arms, which were trembling furiously, like he was fighting exhaustion.

His next shot missed. Ioan resumed moving normally, and began to load yet another arrow.

Ed found Lavy, made eye contact, and told her, "Get him near that hole in the ground."

It was his last hope. As a Dungeon Lord, he could *feel* the blueprint of his dungeon at all times if he were near it. The hole he was looking at was connected to the main tunnel, the one his drones had created to reach the governor's house so they could build his Seat under all that handy wood.

The same tunnel where something was eating all his drones.

"Enough!" roared Ioan. "Enough! You all die here. Not a step farther, Kes! You can't block an *explosive arrow!*"

His arrow was empowered by the red stream of rending magic that Ed had seen in the forest. The Ranger aimed his bow at him.

"*Drop it,*" Ed said. His veins vibrated as his power spent itself. Deep inside his brain, there was a struggle against Ioan's will, briefly, at the speed of thought.

"You think you can give orders from your position? Oh, by the gods, I'm truly going to enjoy seeing your body break." The Ranger laughed, and then released his fingers from his bowstring.

The bow sprang, but the only thing that it shot was air.

"What?" Ioan looked down at his feet where his Explosive Arrow lay. He looked up at Ed with rage and fear freezing the muscles of his face. "Control magic?"

"Just a *minor order,*" Ed told him. "Nothing special."

The Dungeon Lord had hoped that the arrow would explode after it fell. He had kept his spell hidden from Ioan with the idea that the Ranger would kill himself with his own ability. Apparently, Objectivity had some friendly fire protection built in, at least for Ioan.

It was time for plan B.

"Now, Lavy!"

"*Witch spray!*"

Three fiery spheres projected themselves through the air in Ioan's direction. The Ranger's speed shot up once more, and he jumped back much faster than the orbs could react. The magic followed him, but he drew his scimitars in a flash of metal and cut down the spell midair with ease.

Ioan's smile grew frantic. Blood was streaming down his nose and into his mouth, staining his teeth red.

Kes' charge reached him, then, and her longsword and his curved blade clashed so hard Ed was sure both of them would break. They did. There was a noise like glass being crushed, and both weapons bent down their middle like they were made out of butter and not metal.

Ioan screamed incoherently, and he let go of his now useless sword. His arm hung by his side, paralyzed.

Kes, on the other hand, had been expecting the impact. She let go of her bent sword and kicked Ioan square in the chest, all her weight behind it, hard enough to send the man stumbling backward.

Ed saw Ioan's stunned expression, the trickle of bloodied saliva flowing down his chin, his arms flailing about. Then he stumbled into the tunnel's hole and disappeared without so much as a noise.

The Dungeon Lord exhaled loudly. His lungs felt like they were about to burst from the effort. He swore right there that the next thing he would do, if he survived the day, would be to get into shape.

He stood up, dusted himself off, helped Alder back to his feet, then hurried to see if Klek was still alive.

"What's down there? Some sort of trap?" Lavy asked him while he moved.

"I hope so!"

Ed reached the batblin's body. Klek was breathing, and when Ed turned him belly-up, Klek's eyes opened weakly. His bat-like nose was broken, and his lips were bloodied, but he smiled weakly at the Dungeon Lord.

"I earned so much experience for that."

"Are you okay?" Ed asked. He knew the batblin could be

bleeding internally. He also knew he lacked the knowledge, or the tools, to do anything about it.

The batblin shrugged. Then, his smile vanished, and he said, "I can hear it coming up. Careful, Lord Edward."

Ed, who lacked the batblin's *echolocation*, heard it just seconds later. Claws raking against rock and soil.

"Get ready!" Ed yelled as he rushed for the spot where he had left his sword. "Don't get near it!"

"What?!" Kes screamed. Then she heard it too.

And then they all saw it.

The mindbrood erupted out of the hole like a cannonball, its exoskeleton covered in viscera and blood, its claws glinting in the midday sun. It landed just a few feet away from Kes, who jumped away by sheer instinct.

The Bane carried something bloodied, square, and meaty in its first pair of arms. It left the thing fall to the floor, and only then Edward did recognize it. Ioan's torso, his torn leather armor, and his mauled head so broken it was almost unrecognizable. Almost. His remaining eye stared at Ed, accusingly.

"I heard you!" the Bane shrieked at the mauled corpse, and drove a claw through the head, piercing it like a melon. "I HEARD YOU! You did this to me!"

The monster stabbed the head again, and again. Even Kes had to look away. The mindbrood didn't stop screaming at it.

"I ate my parents! BECAUSE OF YOU! You turned me into this! You did it! You did it! *You!*"

Lavy reached Ed and put a hand on his shoulder to get his attention. The Witch was pale, and dirt-infused tears were flowing down her face. "It's brutal, Edward. She's suffering...she doesn't realize what she is. She was too young to understand."

Ed tried to answer, but there was a knot in his throat. Words failed him.

It was Laurel, the spider Queen, the natural enemy of the Bane, who put into words what they were all thinking.

"We have to end its suffering."

At that, the mindbrood stopped its attack on the corpse and looked at them. There were pieces of skull lodged in its jaws. Somewhere behind Ed, Alder retched.

"You are adventurers," the monster told them with the voice of a little girl. "You have magic, don't you? Fix me! Please! Please, I don't want to be like this anymore! Make it stop!"

"Gods have mercy," Kes whispered. Her face had the complexion of wax about to melt, and her breathing was short and fast. "Oh, gods, it's just a little girl..."

Not anymore, thought Ed, who felt like the horror was now a part of him, that he would never stop shaking, even if he survived the day. He glanced at the mindbrood's back, at the exposed brain-tissue. *No, she's not human anymore. But she doesn't know it.*

"Hurry!" the monster bellowed, and begged, and her arms gestured as if groveling. The result was grotesque, sickening. "I am hungry again. I'm so hungry, all the time, even after I just ate, I can't stop it. I don't want to be a grown up anymore!"

Ed forced his fear and his disgust down, away from him. If he let himself be paralyzed, if he let the mindbrood get away, he would be condemning whatever remained of that girl's mind to a lifetime of horror.

He willed his heart to beat steadier. His hands to stop shaking. The Evil Eye flared and he raised his sword.

"Don't you worry," he told the mindbrood. He walked toward it. "I'll fix you. Don't be scared."

"What are you doing?" the Bane asked him. It eyed the sword with mistrust, and its body tensed, ready to jump. "Stay away! I *will* hurt you!"

Maybe it would, easily. Ed couldn't see its stats—they were protected by the same magic that had hidden Kharon's.

"*Eldritch edge,*" he said, and his sword was enveloped in dark green flames. There was emptiness in the intangible part of his body that controlled his magic. That had been his last spell of the day, so he needed to make it count.

"What's that?" asked the brood.

"Magic," Ed said. Even keeping his voice steady was a tremendous effort.

"I want to eat you," it told him. "The urge is...so strong..."

"Careful, Ed," said Kes, but Ed gestured at her to stay away. If anyone else approached the Bane, he had little doubt it *would* attack, or run away and hide.

"Can you resist it?" Ed asked the Bane. How much was left of that girl? Doubt gnawed him. Laurel was a giant spider, and she had become his minion. Perhaps this little creature could—

"Yes!" the Bane roared, spitting pieces of skull in all directions. "I can! But *I don't want to!*"

Its hind legs propelled it at terrible speed in Ed's direction, claws at the ready, bloody fangs bared.

"*Now!*" Ed exclaimed, lowering his flaming sword, ready to hold his ground.

A drone's terrified head appeared over the Bane. The drone clung to the monster's back with one hand and all its tiny strength. The other hand was raised above its head, fingers closed around Ioan's magic-infused arrow.

The Bane stopped in its tracks, digging its many pairs of claws into the ground and showering slivers of rock everywhere. It roared, and raised its long arms to grab at the drone—

The drone pushed the arrow into the brain-tissue of the monster's back.

The explosion followed instantly. It was loud, and bright, strong enough to unsummon the drone and make the Bane's back erupt in a cloud of torn tissue, blood, and exoskeleton.

Ed was already rushing at the creature before it had time to fall.

The mindbrood howled in pain, blood flowing like a river out of its snout. Ed saw himself reflected in the creature's soulless eyes.

No, that was not a little girl. But that was no excuse to prolong its suffering.

He ducked away from the mindbrood's weak slash, held his sword in front of his chest with both hands, and jumped at the creature's head.

"Die!"

The unholy sword hit the snout's side, left a long gash, slid into the creature's open maw, and Ed's weight pushed the blade into the terrible head all the way down to the hilt.

The Dungeon Lord fell hard, rolled away from the thrashing monster, jumped to his feet, and watched the flames of his blade spread around the mindbrood's head. The brood's exoskeleton crackled and darkened like burnt plastic under the *eldritch fire*.

Please be dead, please be dead, if he had to listen to that voice dying in agony, he was sure he would go mad.

Instead, the mindbrood raised a hand to the hilt protruding out of its mouth, tugged at it blindly while the heat cooked its eyes, and collapsed to the ground, dead.

Ed exhaled, and turned his gaze up. The fire was dying across Burrova, Hoia wasn't burning, and the giant clouds of dark smoke atop the village were being dispersed by the wind of Starevos. For the first time since he had arrived in Ivalis, Ed welcomed the cold breeze as it flowed around his body.

It was done.

THE GREEN FLAMES cast a multitude of shadows as they spread all over the body and slowly devoured it. The smell was sickening.

Ed turned away from the visage, holding his breath as best as he could. His friends were already rushing at him, including Klek, who was clutching at his bruised belly, and Laurel, who was unhurt and feeling quite smug.

The spider Queen was the first to greet him, and then she left to resume her...ritual devouring of her dead mother.

Best not to think about it too much, Ed thought.

"Are you alive?" Alder asked him. The Bard was clinging to the cut in his neck with both hands, like he was still unsure the knife had missed his jugular. "I thought it had disemboweled you!"

Kes gave him a look, nodded, and went to make sure the Bane was really dead. Ed heard her work behind him, but he decided that was not an image he needed in his head, and didn't look back.

"It was a close call," he told the Bard.

"You idiot," Lavy said, "Kes could have handled it—there was no need to risk your life like that!"

"It would have run from Kes," he told her with a tired smile, "like it did from Gallio. It thought I was easy prey, that's why I could kill it."

"You could kill it because it didn't realize there was a drone clinging to its back," the Witch said. Apparently, Lavy wasn't the kind of woman who would cry and rush to hug and kiss the hero after battle. "How did that happen?"

"I ordered the drone to jump straight to the brain tissue," Ed said. "In my world, people know the brain has no nerves...no feeling, that is. I had hoped the brood worked the same, and took the risk."

"Alita's fucking tits," Alder muttered, staring at Ed, his eyes wide.

"What he said," said Lavy. Then she smiled at him. Even through the layer of dirt, ash, blood, and grime, she was quite the attractive young woman. "I can't believe we are still alive."

"Yes," Ed agreed, and flashed her a grin, "we are alive. We won the day."

"Not only that," Klek smiled, still clearly in pain, "we have a new dungeon, and more troops. And I just passed Drusb's experience points."

The batblin looked so pleased with himself it was hard not to laugh. But Kes' voice sounded behind Ed and drove his elation away.

"It's not over, yet. We still have to deal with *him*."

The Dungeon Lord followed Kes' gaze, and cursed himself for forgetting—

Gallio, the reborn Inquisitor, was standing in the middle of the market's main street, covered in blue blood. His eyes shone with a white light as if on fire. His gaze was fixed upon Ed, who could almost feel the heat exuding out of it, like a furnace.

CHAPTER TWENTY-SIX

THE INQUISITOR

W ithout a word, the Inquisitor walked slowly toward Ed's group.

"We don't have to fight," Ed told him as he approached, "the Bane is dead."

"I'll be the judge of that," said Gallio.

He stood in front of the burning corpse, looking at it with disgust, the way a person might look at meat gone bad. Kes and Ed remained where they stood, but Alder and Lavy, who knew of the Inquisition's reputation, kept their distance.

After a while, he walked away from the corpse and examined the battlefield. He found Ioan's remains, and nudged them with his boot. He seemed to recognize the Ranger's cowl, because he turned to Ed and said:

"What's Ioan doing here?"

"He started all this. No idea how he got the brood's egg, but he wanted to blame Lotia for it—make Heiliges go to war with them. To make Starevos independent, and himself a martyr."

"That's some story," Gallio said calmly. "How do I know you're not making this up?"

Ed shrugged. He kept the man's gaze, and both of them just stood there, glaring at each other.

"Where are the villagers?" he asked.

"Alive," Ed said, "and I'll release them as soon as possible. Amphiris is dead, and the spiders are under my command. They won't harm Burrova again."

"On that, we agree." Gallio's burning gaze set on Laurel, who was calmly munching on her mother and ignoring the Inquisitor.

Ed clenched his teeth. He and his friends were in no position for another round of combat, but Gallio didn't seem to be faring much better. He was covered in bites and scratches all over, his red blood mixed with that of the spiders, though the venom didn't seem to be having much effect on him.

"They were chasing the Bane, just as much as we were," Ed said. "Yes, they destroyed the village. But the people are alive, and thanks to the spiders no one is infected. I don't have to pact with anyone to confirm it. Look at the body! It's too young to lay eggs."

"The spiders were going to eat my people."

"And you were going to kill them," Ed reminded him. "Maybe you still are. What are the Inquisitions' rules?"

Gallio's burning eyes disappeared and were replaced by a tired, pale blue glance at Ed.

"They'll kill everyone. The risk is too great."

"And you will just let them?" asked Kes, scowling at him. "Was that how you earned your powers again, by swearing to be the Inquisition's dog?"

Gallio shook his head. "I swore allegiance to the Light. It was my fault this happened in the first place. I wasn't strong enough. Now I am. I'll serve Alita's wishes as long as I am alive. I'll do whatever she asks of me. So something like this never happens again."

"You sicken me," Kes told him. "A god who keeps slaves is as bad as the Dark, and you offered yourself to her willingly."

"Kes, don't make him angry!" Alder exclaimed from afar.

The Inquisitor was about to answer Kes, when Ed interrupted him:

"What does Alita ask of you, now?"

That was the only question that mattered, after all.

Gallio didn't need much time to think through his answer, "That I do my duty."

Kes' hand hovered over her knife, but Ed gestured at her to wait.

"I see," he told Gallio, with a smile. "Well then, you should get to it."

Gallio nodded, and exhaled. He appeared as tired as Ed and his friends. The lines of his face added decades to his age.

"What will you do with them?" he asked Ed. "With my people."

"I'll release them as soon as they've recovered," he said. "I'll drop them off in the neighboring villages and have them pretend they weren't in Burrova during the attack. Not everyone was here today, right? Not all the farmers come daily to the market."

Gallio nodded. "It could work, if they keep their mouths shut. But the Inquisition might purge the surrounding villages, just in case."

"Well," said Ed, "that depends on what you tell them."

Gallio raised an eyebrow at him. "What do you have in mind?"

"How about this? There was this young Dungeon Lord who got manipulated by the Dark. He released a mindbrood, but you and the heroic Rangers of Burrova managed to defeat the monster before the Lord's plan was ready. Ioan gave his life in the process of stopping him, and Alvedhra barely survived a fight with the Lord's spider minions."

The Sheriff's smile was genuine. "Yes, that may work. But where does that leave you?"

"Exactly where I was going to be," Ed said. "They think I'm the villain. I don't mind. I don't like their methods, and I wouldn't be their ally even if they asked. Meanwhile, I investigate Ioan's plans. He couldn't have worked alone, unless Undercity breeds mindbrood eggs and sells them. If there are people with those eggs out there, everyone's in danger. I intend to go to Undercity and find them. Make them answer for their crimes."

"What if I just share all of that with the Inquisition?"

"Well, they failed to stop Ioan's group in the first place. Are they subtle enough to uncover a conspiracy while ensuring *not a single egg* escapes? Or will they just set the entire city ablaze and purge Starevos, all while the real culprits evade them?"

Gallio nodded and passed a gloved hand through his ash-laden hair. "Sounds like the Inquisition, yes."

"Well, I'm a Dungeon Lord," said Ed, extending his arms and offering Gallio his best, most charming smile. "If I'm not subtle enough, someone will come and kill me. Who else is better suited for the job?"

"If I ever suspect you, even a tiny bit, I will end you. And I'll tell the Inquisition everything."

"I expect nothing less."

"I may kill you anyway, Edward. If Alita's will sends me your way, her will be done."

"You do you."

Both men nodded, and then Gallio did something unexpected. He extended his open palm at Ed. Ed stared at it for half a second, then accepted the handshake.

Apparently, this was too much for Alder.

"Everyone, stop for a minute!" the Bard demanded.

When Gallio and Ed turned to him, Alder lost a bit of steam, but he kept going. "I don't understand! Gallio, you were talking about 'oh, I must do my duty!' and then Ed was all, 'ah, let's spin a careful half-lie to the Inquisition!' and now you are shaking hands! What, in all the gods' names, is going on?"

Ed laughed, long and hard. All the hidden tension left his body while he did so. It wasn't a happy laugh, more like the kind provoked by a mixture of strong emotions and adrenaline finally spending itself. His hands trembled as he laughed.

"See, Alder, turns out I am not the only one who likes to bend the rules."

"That," the Bard told him, "doesn't explain anything at all."

Gallio sighed, and said, "When I lost my powers, all those years ago, the Inquisition expelled me. That's part of the rules. An Inquisitor without powers is just a warrior. I was sent to Starevos as a sort of exile. Here, I became a Sheriff. My duty as a Sheriff is to protect the people of Burrova. Alita asks that I fulfill my duty, so I am. By protecting Burrova from the Inquisition. From myself."

The man took in the stunned looks of Kes, Lavy, and Alder, and shook his head. "Of course, as soon as I go meet the Church, I'll be sworn into the ranks again, and that loophole will cease to apply. If I ever see any of you again, it will be as enemies."

"Come whenever you want," Klek challenged him. "Klek— the Ranger Slayer—will be ready for you!"

The Sheriff barked a laugh. A happy one, but marred by cynicism. "You should be, critter. If your Lord hasn't taken his own life by then, I'll be glad to do it for him and save him from himself."

Ed's smile vanished. He and Gallio exchanged glances, and the Dungeon Lord could tell the Inquisitor was serious.

"We'll see," Ed whispered.

"Indeed," Gallio whispered back. His eyes glinted under the sun with only a tiny hint of the power they contained.

The Sheriff sighed, and walked away in the direction of the western gate, which was still smoking. "When I return, you all better be gone. I'll check up on Alvedhra. With any luck, the herbalist's hut missed all the action. Is there any message I should give her?"

He nodded at Kes, who grimaced like she had been stung by an arrow. The mercenary said nothing, but hurried to keep the man's pace and spoke to him for several minutes, after which she returned to Ed's side, eyes downcast.

"She could come with us," Ed offered.

The mercenary shook her head. "Trust me, Ed, it's better this way. Our life expectancy isn't the best. We may have won the day, but there will be more battles. It will only get harder for you as your name gains fame. There could come the day when Inquisitors and mindbroods are the least of your troubles."

"That seems hard to believe," he said, with a smile without any humor behind it.

Alder, Lavy, and Klek reunited with them, and together they watched the man slowly walk out of sight.

Before he was gone, Gallio looked over his shoulder, briefly, and said, "The spiders call you Lord Wraith, Edward. Did you know that? *Lord Wraith*. I think you should find out what a wraith is, the first chance you get. It will be quite enlightening."

With that, he left. Ed felt a sense of relief. They had come very close to killing each other, this time.

The Dungeon Lord was sure it wasn't the last time they would meet. He felt it in his bones, that his story and Gallio's were deeply intermingled, and that it was just beginning.

CHAPTER TWENTY-SEVEN

AFTERMATH

The batblin cloud was hard at work freeing the villagers from their web bindings, while the drones and spiders carried the last of them to the safety of Ed's hidden cave in Hoia.

The Dungeon Lord looked around with tired satisfaction. The place was brimming with activity in a way he had never expected. Everyone was working together. Alder and Kes were out to meet with the herbalist, who was working overtime to make anti-venom potions for the elderly, the young, and those few who had reacted badly to the paralyzing agent.

Klek caught Ed's glance and gave him a thumbs up. The batblin had earned almost as much experience as Ed had, and it seemed the rest of the batblins finally respected him, at least a bit. He was directing the cloud's efforts, standing atop a rock and looming over them. Close to him was Laurel, directing her spiders from a giant web she had created at the corner of the chamber.

Speaking of experience points, Ed would have to think long and hard about what to do with his. A bit more than a hundred points, and well earned. According to Lavy, he ought to have earned an easy thousand for killing Amphiris and the mind-brood, but a large part of his victories had been due to good luck.

He didn't intend to rely on luck forever. He was already, according to the way the Objectivity rated him, a very, very different person than he had been before coming to Ivalis.

He was okay with that. It was an interesting world. And seeing his dungeons, and his people, steadily grow in front of him filled him with a sense of accomplishment stronger than earning any amount of experience points.

All his life he had been yearning for a feeling such as this. It was intoxicating.

But the rewards of the day still made his mouth water.

- You have gained **108** experience. Your unused experience is **109** and your total experience is **315**.
- Your attributes have increased. Spirit +2. Charm and Mind +1.
- Your skills have increased. Athletics +1. Untrained Combat and Dungeon Engineering +5. You learned Leadership +5.
- There are new talent advancement options for you...

Lavy's voice interrupted his musings.

"Edward, could you come here for a second? We need to talk."

Ed shrugged and deactivated his Evil Eye. The Witch was sitting by the main tunnel's entrance, watching the sunset. In just a few hours, it would be too cold to remain outside, but in the meantime, Ed sat beside her.

"We never talked about last night," Lavy said, avoiding eye contact.

Ed could sense the direction the conversation was about to take, so he steeled himself. It could be a challenge just as deadly as the day's battles.

"Yeah, I figured we ought to discuss it sooner or later," he said.

"Look," Lavy started, and then visibly strained to find the right words.

Ed decided to help her.

"We should remain friends, don't you think?"

Lavy's eyes widened in surprise, and then her face flushed with relief. "How did you know?"

"Like I said, I'm not new at this," Ed laughed. "It's okay. There's no need to make it awkward."

The Witch gazed down, and fidgeted with her fingernails like a child. Then, she nodded to herself, and said, "Thanks, Ed. But I think I owe you an explanation."

"You really don't—"

"It's not like you aren't attractive, I'd say you're alright—"

"Thanks, I guess."

"There was nothing wrong with your performance," she went on.

"Uh, why would you mention—" Ed said, panicking a bit, but the Witch kept going:

"It's just...I was dealing with a lot. I still am—obviously—not over Kael. And I'm not sure I've fully processed the knowledge that you were involved in his death. It's hard to believe, you know? Even coming from you. You seem so...new to Ivalis, so unaware of our old rivalries and hatreds. To be honest, it's refreshing. I don't know what will happen to whatever it is that we are building, but I admit, I'm very curious to see where it takes us. But I just...can't see you *that* way, you know?"

"Well, I appreciate the honesty, Lavy. Thanks," Ed said. And it was true. He preferred the Witch as a friend. He would never admit it to her, but she had seriously freaked him the fuck out. It had been kind of sexy last night, but he knew that would get old very, very fast. He had not forgotten that she was into the Evil Eye making his skull glow in the dark.

Lavy flashed him another smile, the pure image of innocence. "I always saw Dungeon Lords as these distant, delicious tyrants who murdered their way into power. You are many things, but you aren't a murderous tyrant I think. Maybe that's good...I don't have that many friends, you know, since most of them are dead."

She stopped and searched for the right words again.

"What I am trying to say is," she went on, "I hope you and Alder live. Even if you don't...I promise you, I'll become a powerful Witch and will raise your spirits as my undead servants, so we can still go on adventures together."

"Oh, boy..." Ed gulped nervously and patted the woman on the back. After a moment, he added, "You know, Lavy? That's the nicest thing a girl has ever said to me."

They watched the sunset together, in happy silence.

EPILOGUE

L ater that night, Ed dropped into his straw bed like a sack of rocks. He had thought he was tired in Burrova, but it was nothing compared to his current state. He planned to rest for a week. Perhaps he would hibernate during winter, like a bear.

The villagers were a piece of work. They were terrified of the spiders, and Ed didn't blame them, given what the creatures had done to them. But this also made it very difficult to deal with Burrova's population, and the fact that no one trusted a Dungeon Lord made it even harder.

In the end, he had had to create a hall just for them, and guard the door with his batblins. The villagers were *kinda* prisoners, at least until Ed could explain to them it was in *their* best interest not to go running to the Inquisition to tell them what had happened.

He had no idea what he would do if some refused to hear him.

I'll have to be very fucking persuasive, he thought, while watching the flicker of the flame inside his oil lamp. It was almost hypnotic.

His eyes began to close on their own. It was funny. Back on Earth, he had never been able to fall asleep this easily.

Something in the air awakened him. The scent of formaldehyde.

The Dungeon Lord stared at his oil lamp and realized the flame had frozen in place. The orange tongue appeared cold, and it emitted no heat.

Ed stood up and left his quarters.

A tall man in a black suit, Earth-made, was waiting for him with a satisfied smile that was just a tad too long. His face lacked any other features.

"Kharon," Ed greeted him. His well-deserved rest would have to wait. "I was wondering when you would appear."

"I should have come sooner," the man agreed, "but I didn't expect you to accomplish your task so quickly."

"What can I say? I'm liking it here."

"The Dark is very glad to hear that. Contrary to popular belief, we enjoy when everyone is satisfied with our pacts."

Ed raised an eyebrow at that. "Isn't Murmur angry? I ruined his plans. I killed that Bane of his."

Kharon scratched his chin with his long, black fingernails, and widened his eyes in exaggerated confusion.

"You think Murmur brought Sephar's Bane to Burrova? Why would he do something like that, and then summon you here? The first thing you did was try to kill the Bane, and you ended up succeeding. Against all odds, yes, but succeed you did."

"No idea. I was hoping you'd tell me. I admit, I'm confused. Ioan wanted Heiliges to go to war with Lotia, and everyone's sure Lotia would lose a direct confrontation with them. Isn't Murmur allied with Lotia?"

"Indeed," said Kharon. "They're his best source of sacrifices. That's why he had to make sure they were well protected."

Ed suddenly wasn't feeling as smug. No, he didn't like this conversation anymore.

"You're saying...Murmur wanted me to kill the Bane all along?"

The realization struck him like a punch to the face, and Kharon's happy grin confirmed it.

"Isn't it fantastic?" the boatman said. "Murmur made sure that everyone won in the end. Alita's agent found his faith again, you got to be the hero you've always wanted to be, and his faithful flock are safe to keep the sacrifices flowing his way."

Ed passed a hand over his hair and backed against the chamber's walls.

"But I almost died," he told the boatman. "Why would he risk it, sending me? If he really wanted to avoid war, he could've summoned someone more powerful."

Kharon shrugged. "I didn't lie to you last time we met, Edward. The Dark is really in good need of new servants. There's something out there killing us, calling themselves Heroes, but holding no allegiance to the Light. Murmur still hopes you'll find them, and deal with them when you're ready. In the meantime... well, he found somewhere you could grow stronger, and while you were here, he found something you would be happy to help him out with. And you did."

The boatman sighed, and added:

"Don't go around thinking you're *too* special, Edward. That's some personal advice. Murmur's reach is spread wide, and he pays attention to many things. He recently made a dozen gambits with people like you, with similar intentions, all across Ivalis. He has done this for thousands of years. Not all of them pan out. Almost all of them die. It's only the ones that survive who become legends..."

Ed's glance was smoldering, and he didn't need his Evil Eye to make his feelings clear.

"Oh, don't be like this. You did a good deed, Edward, even if you helped Murmur. Are the lives of all these villagers worth so little to you? And war is a terrible thing, don't you agree? It should be avoided, if at all possible."

"Fuck you, I don't need you to validate my actions."

Kharon laughed. "See? You are recovering already! Earthlings are so resilient! Or I wonder if that's just the way *you* are, Edward? Few people would've acclimated themselves to a world transplant as fast as you have. A little too eager to leave Earth behind, in my humble opinion. I can almost see the path your thoughts are taking. Let me guess, you'll still go to Undercity, won't you?"

That much was true. Just because Murmur wasn't behind the Bane was no excuse to allow the *real* culprits to run around, unstopped.

It didn't matter if the Dark thought Ed was being manipulated. As far as he was concerned, as long as he remained true to his morals and his own ideals, the schemes of laughing gods were irrelevant. Let them think they won the day.

Ed and his friends had saved many lives. They had done *good.* Let the Dark and the Light sort themselves out.

Edward Wright knew where he stood. He knew who he *was.*

"I'm glad you're taking this in stride," said Kharon. He gestured at the wall next to him, and a portal materialized instantly. Ed could see, behind it, the black labyrinth that was the dimension where the Dark lived. "It's much more enjoyable to deal with people who have a sense of sportsmanship. Good luck in your endeavors, Dungeon Lord. Here's a reward for you, by the way. A hero deserves a prize when they finish the quest, don't you agree?"

The boatman pointed at him and Ed's mind sizzled with arcane knowledge. He was aware he had just learned a new spell, one powerful enough that it needed a rank more in *spellcasting* before he could use it.

"This spell is called *Murmur's reach,*" Kharon explained. "It's not one you can learn on your own. Murmur only gives it to the worthy. You may use it, or never think about it again—whatever you want. Today, you have proven very worthy, indeed."

With that, the boatman crossed the portal. He grinned smugly at Ed one last time, and started to gesture at the portal to close.

"One more thing, Kharon," Ed said. "We'll meet again. You can bet your life on it."

There was something in the Dungeon Lord's grin that made Kharon falter. When the portal closed, a second later, the boatman wasn't smiling anymore.

But Ed was.

EDWARD WRIGHT

Species: Human
   Total Exp: 315
   Unused Exp: 109
   Claims: Lordship.

Attributes
   Brawn: 9
   Agility: 10
   Endurance: 9
   Mind: 12
   Spirit: 14 (+1 Dungeon Lord mantle)=15
   Charm: 12 (+1 Dungeon Lord mantle)=13

Skills

Athletics: Basic (VI) - The owner has trained his body to perform continuous physical activity without penalties to their Endurance. For a while.

-Basic ranks allows them to realize mild energy-consuming tasks (non-combat) such as running or swimming without tiring. Unlocks stamina-related talents.

Untrained Combat: Basic (VII) - Temporal skill, can become trained or be improved to open the brawling branch.

Dungeon Engineering: Basic (VIII) - This skill represents the user's knowledge of magical constructs pertaining to dungeoncraft. As it improves, it opens new rooms and traps, as well as adds to the Dungeon Lord Mantle capacity of storing the user's own blueprints.

Combat Casting: Basic (IV) - Pertains to the speed and efficiency of spells cast during combat or life-threatening situations.

-Basic status allows the caster to use spells every 20 seconds - 1 second per extra rank. The caster must say their names aloud and perform the appropriate hand gestures.

Leadership: Basic (V) - Reflects the owner's capacity for inspiring and managing his troops and minions. For a Dungeon Lord, improving this skill adds to the bonus he and his minions receive, if partnered with the right talent.

Talents

Evil Eye - Allows the Dungeon Lord to see the Objectivity of any creature or item. If the target of his gaze possesses a strong Spirit (or related Attribute or Skill) they may hide their information if the Lord's own Spirit is not strong enough.

Energy Drain: Active. Very Low.

Dungeon Lord Mantle - The mantle is the heart of the Dungeon Lord and represents the dark pact made in exchange for power.

-It allows the Dungeon Lord access to the Dungeon Lord status and powers, as defined by the Dungeon Screen.

-It allows the Dungeon Lord to create and control dungeons, as per the limitations of his Dungeon Screen.

Energy Drain: None.

Improved Reflexes - Allows the owner to experience increased reaction time for a small burst of time.

Resist Sickness: Basic - Allows its owner to resist disease and sickness.

-Basic status allows the owner to resist non-magical sickness as if they had Endurance of 15 and were in optimal conditions (clean, well-fed, rested).

Spellcasting - Represents the owner's magical ability.

-Basic status allows the caster to use and learn all basic related spells of their domain. Extra ranks improve each individual spell's characteristics, such as range or damage.

-Allowed spells: 1 basic per day + 1 basic spell due to Dungeon Lordship

Energy Drain: Active. Varies per Spell.

Spell List

Minor Order - Command. The caster forces a target creature to follow a simple order, as long as said order is not immediately against the creature's moral code or presents a threat to its life.

Eldritch Edge - Enchantment. The caster adds a magical flame to the edge of a weapon. This flame makes the weapon magical for the duration, allowing it to bypass weak magical defenses and mundane ones.

Murmur's Reach - ?

AFTERWORD

Thank you for reading Dungeon Lord. I hope you had as much fun reading it as I had writing it.

Please, consider leaving a review about your experience with Dungeon Lord. A couple sentences are enough to let the book better reach other readers who will enjoy it.

Ed, Lavi, Alder, and Res' adventures will continue in the next installment of the Wraith Haunt's series. I hope to see you there. Ed will travel to Undercity and must square off against the organization that smuggled the mindbrood egg, all while dealing with the assassin and thieves guild, the local Inquisition detachment, and an undead infestation. This time, Ed's skills will be tested to the limit, and if he wishes to survive, he'll need a Dungeon unlike anything he has built before.

If you'd like to contact me, you can do so at author@hugohuesca.com

Until next time!

-Hugo

KEEP IN TOUCH!

If you want to find out about Dungeon Lord's next installments before anyone else, you can do so here:

www.subscribepage.com/dungeonlord

There's also a couple pages in Facebook where I'm known to hang out. These following are dedicated to the LitRPG and GameLit genres, which are about fantasy and science fiction that mix a game-like element to the story. They're growing genres with a lot of cool, experimental fiction being written every day. If you enjoy RPGs, check them out, maybe you'll find something you like.

www.facebook.com/groups/litrpgsociety
www.facebook.com/groups/gamelit
www.facebook.com/groups/gamelitsociety

If you're looking for a community wholly dedicated around videogame-related fiction, check out

www.facebook.com/groups/litrpggroup

It's the biggest one around, and there you'll usually find authors and readers living in harmony.

ALSO BY HUGO HUESCA

RUNE UNIVERSE

Space Opera, Videogames, and Cyberpunk meet for this action-packed thriller.

There are infinite worlds in Rune Universe, but only one of them holds the key to Cole's salvation.

The Complete Rune Universe Trilogy is available now.

EDGE OF CONQUEST

A thriller set in the background of a space war between the Earth and its former colonies in deep space as they struggle for independence.

Joseph Clarke is a former soldier fallen in disgrace. He has sworn never to fight again, but when the rebellion comes knocking at his door, he must break that promise.

For a woman forgotten by history has been found alive, hidden in a remote planet, away from the grasp of the Tal-Kader conglomerate, the corrupt corporation that governs the Edge with an iron fist.

As the flames of war threaten to engulf the Edge, Clarke must team up with a genetically-enhanced assassin to beat Tal-Kader's fleet in a race to the planet where the woman is hiding. But Clarke's actions could bring the Edge to a conflict much greater than a mere civil war — it could mean a war against Earth.

Edge of Conquest is available now.

11757329R00194

Printed in Great Britain
by Amazon